HISTORY'S PAGES
THE KNOCKNASHEE STORY - BOOK 3

JEAN GRAINGER

Copyright © 2025 by Gold Harp Media

All rights reserved.

No part of this book may be reproduced in any form or by any electronic or mechanical means, including information storage and retrieval systems, without written permission from the author, except for the use of brief quotations in a book review.

To my grandparents, who lived through the war and never wasted anything.

I was born in London in England in 1934. I went through, as a child, the horrors of World War II, through a time when food was rationed and we learned to be very careful, and we never had more to eat than what we needed to eat. There was no waste. Everything was used.

— JANE GOODALL - PRIMATOLOGIST AND
ANTHROPOLOGIST

CHAPTER 1

KNOCKNASHEE, CO KERRY, IRELAND

AUGUST 1940

'Now then, *a stórín*,' Grace Fitzgerald cooed softly as she laid Odile into her pram, a sturdy contraption of wood and leather that Dymphna's late husband, Tommy, had made for their two small children out of an old drawer and bicycle wheels.

Paudie and Kate O'Connell were eight and six now, and the pram had been in their turf shed for the last few years, but Declan McKenna, her fellow teacher, had cleaned off the rust, and Pádraig O Sé, the cobbler, had donated a fresh piece of leather for the rain cover where the old one got cracked with the bad frost last winter, and Dymphna had made new cushions.

'We're going for a nice sunny walk to meet your Aintín Tilly off the bus,' Grace continued as she tucked the bag of bottles and napkins and clean folded baby clothes into the foot of the pram. 'And she'll take you back to the farm, where your Mamó Mary will be delighted to have you home again.'

Grace's best friend, Tilly, had gone to see her sister, Marion, in Dublin, and Mary O'Hare's rheumatism was very bad at the moment, so Grace had been minding the baby for a few nights. Having the company of another human being in the house, even one as small as Odile, had been lovely. Since Dymphna O'Connell left to be housekeeper to the priests, the place could seem very empty during the day. And even Agnes, bitter as she had been, was another person in the house at night, but now there was nobody. She wasn't nervous – Charlie and Declan McKenna were just across the road, and her neighbours all were close by – but it did feel lonely at times.

She sighed. 'I'm going to be lost without you, Odile.'

Odile gurgled, smiled gummily up at her and waved her tiny fists. Her blue eyes had turned to brown, and her fair hair was darkening too. At four months old, the sturdy Parisian baby was thriving in Knocknashee and showed no signs that being dragged halfway across Europe in a leather bag and landed in the southwest of Ireland had taken the slightest toll on her.

Grace laughed. 'I know, *a stór*, life is good and I shouldn't complain.'

Straightening up from fixing the baby's blankets, she caught her own reflection in the hallstand mirror. The summer sun had lightly tanned her skin and added threads of gold to her flame-red curls, which tumbled below her shoulders now that Agnes wasn't here to say she was 'making a show of herself' by letting it hang loose. And her new dress of emerald-green cotton was the exact colour of her eyes.

She'd made it herself. Peggy Donnelly at the draper's had slipped her six yards of the material with a wink and a nod, well outside the rationing restrictions, so she'd been able to cut the skirt long enough to hide her right leg, which was shrunken by polio. Everyone said the dress looked very smart on her.

She'd first worn it when she turned twenty in June, at a little party for her birthday that her friends gave her. Dymphna O'Connell had brought a lemon cake, which she'd saved up her sugar ration to ice, and Tilly arrived with a whole honeycomb in a wooden box and a cream lamb's wool cardigan knitted by her mother. Father Iggy presented her with a pretty silver cross on a delicate chain, Charlie McKenna brought her a rose bush for her front garden, and Declan gave her a book about the Aztecs and told her she looked lovely in green.

After that she'd only worn the dress for Sunday Mass, taking it off the moment she was home. But lately she'd had a thought. She wasn't likely to be going anywhere fancy, well, ever, so she might as well wear it on other days also and get the good of it.

She had new shoes as well. Dr Hugh Warrington, her polio consultant in Cork, had sent her a calliper he'd ordered from England, and it was lighter and less cumbersome than the last one he'd found her, so she'd asked Pádraig O Sé to make her a different pair of shoes to go with it, of soft blue leather instead of stiff ugly black. The right shoe still had to be built up and had holes in the heel into which to slot the steel, but they were comfortable and looked quite nice.

She left the house, pushing the pram down the stone path. The light sea breeze off the ocean was lovely and warm, and fragrant with the scent of the sweet peas clustered over the fence and the rose bush Charlie had planted in the corner. The bush covered the patch where Agnes had burnt their parents' things, leaving a scorch mark on the wall.

Through the gate from her garden into the schoolyard, she could see Patrick O'Flynn, a lanky, freckled twelve-year-old with ears that stuck out like a toby jug, sitting on the steps of the schoolhouse; he was earning a few pennies by watching his father's six skinny mountain sheep as they ate down the grass and weeds, getting the place ready for when school started again. Ned the pony kept the grass short in the field behind, but the playground was better cropped right down. Mountain sheep were the best for that, though they needed watching like hawks; they were right divils for leaping walls.

Eileen, Patrick's mother, had stopped Grace after devotions last Sunday night to thank her for giving him the job and letting the sheep have the grass in the yard. With eleven children and only three small rocky fields, everything was scarce in the O'Flynn house. The two oldest girls had gone into service as soon as they turned fifteen, one with Dr Ryan and another with an old lady in Dingle; their oldest boy was apprenticed to a fisherman and often came home with a few mackerel or a salmon; and their second son, Fiachra, was the junior postman. But that still left six young ones under ten, and Patrick who was twelve.

As Grace walked slowly down the cobbled street, Charlie McKenna came out of the thatched post office, ready for his second postal round of the day after sorting out the letters with Nancy O'Flaherty, the postmistress.

'Nothing for the O'Hares, Charlie?' she asked. 'Save you the spin out – I'm meeting Tilly off the bus?'

'No, Gracie, still nothing.' Charlie looked sympathetic; he knew that Tilly and Mary O'Hare were anxiously waiting to hear word of their brother and son, Alfie, who was in Paris, fighting the German powers of occupation of that city. Or at least they hoped he was, and not already captured by the Germans or something awful like that. Charlie added comfortingly, 'There's no postal service to speak of out of the occupied places these days, so he probably can't get word out.'

'I'm sure you're right, Charlie,' she agreed, praying that was true.

'I'd say the letters from America are disrupted as well,' he added, now leaning over the pram and delighting Odile by shaking the little wicker rattle Declan had made, with the dried berries inside. 'Though Peggy Donnelly heard from her brother in Boston today, so it's hard to tell which ones will make it across or not.'

The postman said this last part very kindly, but Grace felt a stab of sadness. She had been hoping the reason she'd not got a letter from Richard Lewis, only a telegram to say he'd got home safely, was because of the battle in the North Atlantic, so it was hard to hear there were others getting through. She understood why Charlie had let her know; it was better to be prepared if Peggy mentioned it. But it still hurt.

She'd almost collapsed with shock when Richard arrived out of the blue in Knocknashee a few weeks ago with his friend Jacob Nunez, handed Odile to her and Tilly, then left again three hours later to get his ship back to the United States. His telegram had arrived a week afterwards, saying he would write soon, so she'd waited and waited, but nothing ever came.

She'd repeatedly gone over those few hours in her head, when he'd sat in her house and then walked with her to the beach to see the spot where she'd thrown the bottle containing her first letter into the sea. It had been like a dream, it was all so strange, and sometimes she was sure she'd imagined the whole thing. He was even better looking in real life than in his photos, and he'd said the same to her – that she was more beautiful than her photo. But everything had been so fast, so rushed, it was impossible to know if he seriously liked the look of her or was just being nice.

Probably just being nice, given her bandy leg and the way she wasn't quite five feet tall while he was a six-foot athletic young man. She could picture him now, running long-legged across the beach towards the bus, where Jacob Nunez waited impatiently for him to board the bus.

Her last sight of him, the sun in his blond hair.

And now he was back in America and might as well be the man on the moon in terms of how far he was from her. Not just geographically but in every way. He was like a bright star that shone, and she'd got to sit in his glow for a while, but then he was gone.

'So I'll see you later, Grace,' said Charlie, taking his bike from where it leant against the post office wall and slinging his leg over the crossbar. He was thoroughly recovered from the shingles now. 'Will you come over for a bite with myself and Declan later, before the two of ye look over the new books that arrived for the teaching course? I have a couple of rabbits I snared earlier and carrots and potatoes from the garden.'

'I will, Charlie, sounds lovely.' She smiled. 'And I'll bring over one of the Madeira cakes Dymphna brought up to me earlier.'

She and Charlie's son, Declan, who was a year older than Grace and taught the senior children in the two-room school where Grace was headmistress, were starting a correspondence course in September, with a tutor called Miss Harris who was based in the Drumcondra Teacher Training College in Dublin. It wasn't unusual in rural schools for teachers not to be officially certified, but Grace felt it was important to read up on the theory as well as learn from experience, and it would mean Declan could earn a better wage as a qualified teacher. At the moment he was being paid as an assistant teacher and would never be able to afford a wife and family – though he always claimed not to be interested in any of the girls who chased after him, swooning over his brooding dark looks.

As the postman cycled away, Grace limped on through the village square, leaning on the handle of the pram. A few of her pupils were using sticks to knock conkers, as they were called, out of the big horse chestnut tree, then stripping off their prickly green coats and making holes in the burnished nuts with a nail and a hammer to thread them with string. They would then do battle with the conkers, whacking them off each other while trying to crack the opponent's. Knuckles got a right walloping in that game, and she'd been scared to play it as a child, but Tilly had had a twelvie, which meant a conker that had smashed twelve of her opponents' offerings. Nothing scared Tilly.

As soon as the Angelus bell rang out from the church, they would be called home for their tea, but until then the children were making sure to enjoy the last week of the summer holidays.

Two little girls from the infant class, May O'Shaughnessy and Dearbhile Deasy, were sitting at the side of the road plaiting daisy chains to wear as necklaces. Another group had made squares on the ground with twigs and were playing hopscotch, while a swarm of boys raced up and down the cobbles after Patrick O'Flynn's football. Patrick had got that ball for his tenth birthday and had passed it down to his younger brothers. It was a treasure for the whole village, where a real leather ball was a rare sight.

'Hello, Miss Fitz! Hello, Odile!' chorused several of the boys and girls when they spotted her coming with the pram, rushing across to coo over the baby. Mikey O'Shea, eight years old himself now, leant over the pram, swinging his conker on a string, grinning as Odile tried to grab at it.

'Is that a tooth coming through?' Áine Walsh gasped, pointing at the bud beginning to poke through Odile's lower gum.

'It is, Áine, and isn't she being good about it?' said Grace. 'She's not complained once.' And it was true. Odile was such a funny, sunny little thing most of the time, though she had a fiery temper too. When she was hungry and didn't get her bottle soon enough, she could be heard two parishes away.

Patrick's younger sister, Máire, stroked the baby's round cheek with her finger. '*Is leanbh álainn thú,* Odile,' she said. Odile gurgled in agreement, and all the children laughed.

'Sure, listen to her,' said Mikey. 'She'll be talking in no time.'

'She will,' agreed Grace.

Though she wished there was someone in the village who could speak French as well as Irish to Odile. The O'Hares had let everyone believe Odile was Alfie's daughter. Nobody questioned it, because Alfie was so unpredictable and wild – nothing about him could shock anyone, not even him marrying a Frenchwoman called Constance and sending their newborn baby home to be minded while they stayed in Paris to fight the Germans. Sergeant Keane, a decent man, had called up to the farm and said technically the baby should have some paperwork or something. But he said he understood about the Emergency, and that if Mary O'Hare, who knew all about herbs and had cured his wife of a terrible cough, said her son was the baby's father, then that was good enough for him.

But Odile's real father was a Parisian Jew called Paul Dreyfus, who was married to Constance's sister, Bernadette. And when the French couple came to find their baby after the war, which would take some explaining in itself, it would be hard on them if their child spoke only Irish, and maybe a bit of English if she'd got as far as going to school… though surely the war wouldn't go on for another five years?

She walked on, but when she got to the bus stop outside the undertaker's, it was deserted. She had arrived with time to spare, and Bobby the Bus was usually at least half an hour late anyway, so she pushed the pram on down the street past the shops so Odile wouldn't get bored. The baby didn't like to be still.

Bríd Butler came to the door of her sweetshop as Grace passed. She also exclaimed over the new tooth and insisted on giving Odile a tiny spoonful of strawberry ice cream, making the infant coo with delight.

'Mrs Butler, you'll spoil her. She's too young for sugar,' protested Grace mildly.

'Ara, Miss Fitz, a little bit of ice cream is good for the teething. And sure isn't it full of real strawberries and cream? As healthy a treat as you can get. And thank God we have local milk and fruit here – it means I can get past the rationing for lots of the ingredients.'

All the businesses and shops were suffering with the shortages, though at least in the rural areas, there were fresh vegetables, meat, fish and milk to be had.

'Will Mr de Valera keep us out of the war, do you think?' Grace asked. Looking at Odile and thinking about the baby's parents in France, sometimes she had doubts that staying neutral was the thing to do.

Biddy O'Donoghue joined in the conversation from the door of her grocer's shop. 'Well, with petrol and everything else rationed and tax gone to seven shillings in the pound, we're in it after a fashion anyway. But the English are scared stiff the Germans will do a deal with the republicans and we'll have Germans here and England will be facing them on two sides.'

'It's awful, isn't it?' asked Grace. 'I keep thinking about those girls in Campile in Wexford last Monday.'

'Twouldn't do you good, so it wouldn't.' Biddy shook her head. 'They thought first that 'twas because the creamery there was supplying butter to British soldiers, but now they're saying it was just that the Germans were running out of fuel and needed to drop the bombs to get home, without a thought who might be under them, even though we're a neutral nation, much to the vexation of that other óinseach...'

Grace didn't need clarification that the 'other óinseach' was

Winston Churchill. In Biddy's book, there wasn't a hell hot enough for the British prime minister.

Bríd had glanced up anxiously at the clear blue sky as Biddy spoke, and Grace looked up too. Could a German bomber fly over them and drop a bomb, either on purpose or by accident? It had happened in Wexford, so maybe.

'More lies from London. The Germans wouldn't do that. It's so close to Wales there, the pilot might have thought he was over Pembroke,' said Pádraig O Sé, joining in the conversation as he made his way to his cobbler's shop. He was one of those who considered England's enemies to be his friends and didn't like to think the Germans would deliberately drop a bomb on Ireland.

He'd been especially outraged when the *Irish Times* tried to tell men how to join the British Army in a way that sought to outfox the government censor. An anonymous contributor wrote that he'd been told there was a nudist colony in Belfast, at 72 Clifton Street, and men were queuing up to become members. Upon arriving there, he described stripping down completely, and 'then we, nudists, filed out and along the coconut matting to the stairs. At the top, five doctors set to work to test our fitness for His Majesty's forces!' Of course 72 Clifton Street was a British Army recruitment office, and the newspaper was rapped sharply on the knuckles for publishing the address under the pretence of telling a funny story.

All of the Irish newspapers were subject to the government's say-so on what could be printed these days. The country was divided between those who were on the British side and those like Pádraig who saw 'England's difficulty as Ireland's opportunity', so T.J. Coyne, the Controller of Censorship, insisted that all coverage stay clear of the controversy, which meant the press had become very sparse on detail and circumspect on opinion about what was happening.

Grace had learnt a lot more about the progress of the war from Richard's previous letters and the clippings he sent her when he was reporting for the *Capital* from Paris, before the Germans invaded. It was another reason she wished he would write; he had a real knack for telling the story of the conflict through the eyes of those actually living it, making you feel like you were there.

'Hello, Grace!'

It was Declan, his voice snapping her out of her reverie as she walked on. He was coming uphill towards her from the direction of the strand, and he had a pretty girl on his arm – Bridie Keohane, Nancy O'Flaherty's niece, who was usually so light on her feet she could dance like a butterfly but at the moment was limping badly and leaning on Declan.

'Hello, Declan, hello, Bridie. Goodness, what's happened to you? Did you hurt your foot?'

'I did, and it's fierce sore, Grace,' said the girl in her sugary voice.

'I was down for a swim,' said Declan, 'and Bridie appeared on the strand just as I was getting out of the water. Then she slipped and twisted her ankle on the rocks, so I'm helping her home.' His indigo-blue eyes creased in a warm smile as he stopped in front of Grace, his damp dark hair curling slightly over his pale, lightly freckled forehead.

'I don't know what I'd have done if you weren't there,' simpered Bridie, gazing up adoringly at him. Bridie had set her cap at Declan and made no bones about it, finding all kinds of reasons to hang around him, flirting outrageously; it didn't at all surprise Grace that Bridie had managed to find herself on the beach just as he was coming out of the water.

Not that Bridie was the only one. All the local girls had their eye on Declan. He was a fine catch, especially now that his pale face had lost the brooding darkness that had hung over him when he first came home from the reform school in Letterfrack. These days he was relaxed, serene and calm, with a sardonic and quirky sense of humour.

'Where are you off to with the little boss?' He tickled the baby and made her giggle, while Bridie pouted and fidgeted and seemed to forget which ankle was sore.

'Just as far as the church. We'll light a candle and then back up the hill to meet Tilly off the bus. Odile will only get restless if I don't keep moving.'

She walked on with a wave and a smile, leaving him to the mercies of the lovelorn Bridie, who clearly planned to have him bring her all the way to her father's farm on the far side of the village. John Keohane had a fine few acres that would all be coming to Bridie as the only child, and maybe she was hoping the sight of so much land would melt Declan McKenna's heart towards her and encourage him to propose.

And why wouldn't he marry her? Grace asked herself as she walked on past the parochial house. Bridie was very pretty, and she would have money, even if Tilly did say the girl was 'too sweet to be wholesome'. But Tilly was an unusual person and believed in straight talking; she was not the sort of girl to flutter her eyelashes at anyone.

Outside the church Father Iggy was standing in the sunshine with his hands behind his back, the afternoon light twinkling off his bottle-top spectacles. When he saw Grace, he came over.

'Hello, Father Iggy,' she said, happy to see him.

'Well, 'tis yourself, Grace, and young Miss Odile. She's growing every time I see her, God bless her.'

'Indeed she is. She's a sweet little thing, though, so long as she gets her own way.'

'Ah sure, that's women for you.' The priest winked to show he was joking as he dangled his rosary beads in front of Odile.

'Oh, we won't listen to that talk, will we, Odile? And women running every house in the parish?' She smiled at the priest as she shielded her eyes from the bright sunlight. 'We were going to light a candle. We're waiting for Tilly off the bus.'

'Righto, in with ye so, and say a prayer for me while you're there. God knows I need it.' He put his rosary beads back in the pocket of his soutane. Grace knew he kept a few toffees in there too and wondered if Odile would still be here when she was old enough to get one. The children would crowd around him as he walked down the street in hopes of a treat.

She and the baby went inside, and Grace lit the candle, whispering prayers for her parents, for her sister Agnes and then she said a special prayer for Odile's parents, Paul and Bernadette.

When they emerged into the sunshine once more, Father Iggy was still outside. 'I'll join you in the walk if you ladies don't mind?'

'We'd enjoy it, but if it's a message you need doing, I'm happy to save you the trip?'

'I need the exercise, Grace,' said the chubby little priest, patting his waistline. 'I'm a bit too round again now that Dymphna is our housekeeper. She keeps on baking these wonderful cakes, God bless her. Sure only last week Pádraig O Sé said to me, "'Twould be quicker to climb over you than walk around you these days, Father." I can't understand how Father Donnchadh manages to stay so thin.'

Father Donnchadh Lehane was the new curate. He was nice and tried to help out where he could, but he lived on his nerves and was very timid. Father Iggy had confided in Grace that the curate was an only child who was much cosseted by his mother, and he'd got a terrible shock when she died and his very religious father sent him off to the seminary at ten years old.

'But I think Father Lehane has a bit more colour in his face these days, Father Iggy?'

'Ah, he does. Dymphna has been wonderful for him in other ways than food. She understands grief and talks to him a lot about his mother, and she tells him how sad her children were when her Tommy died. Talking of which, I'm thinking of having a little ceremony and wondered what you might think about it?'

Grace smiled. 'I'm no expert on religious matters, Father.'

'But you have a warm heart and a good head on your shoulders, which I sometimes think is every bit as good,' Father Iggy reassured her. They were true friends, Grace and the priest, and it was a big part of the reason the town went along so harmoniously now.

When Canon Rafferty was the parish priest and Agnes Fitzgerald ran the school, Knocknashee had lived in terror, with the children being beaten daily and terrorised parishioners being denounced in the canon's snaky, whispery voice from the pulpit every Sunday. Now that Agnes was dead and the bishop had moved the canon to a parish in Tipperary, and Father Iggy was in charge of the school board and Grace was headmistress, it was as if the pall of fear had been lifted off the village. Even the bad-tempered Pádraig O Sé was in a better mood these days.

'So what were you thinking, Father?'

'Well, I've a notion to bless the *cillín* and say a requiem Mass for the repose of all the souls buried there. I know a lot of them are not known to the people of the parish, but some are, and in particular I was thinking of Dymphna and her children. I know God has taken Tommy to himself. Our Lord understands the terrible pain he was in when he died, but I think it would help Dymphna a bit if I blessed his grave here on this earth.'

Grace felt a huge rush of affection for the brave little priest. He was so different from the apologetic curate he'd been when he arrived, bullied and put down by Canon Rafferty; he was a more confident man now in lots of ways. But he'd never become arrogant, never lost that personal, caring touch he'd always had, and it showed in how he wanted to help Dymphna heal her broken heart.

When Tommy O'Connell walked into the sea, leaving a note saying how sorry he was, the canon had refused Dymphna's husband a funeral, saying those who took their own lives died in a state of mortal sin and therefore could not be laid to rest in consecrated ground. So Tommy was buried by his neighbours in the *cillín*, the unofficial graveyard that had served for centuries as the final resting place for unbaptised infants, new mothers who died before being churched, beggars, strangers and anyone the Church deemed unworthy of a Catholic burial.

'I think that's a wonderful idea, Father,' she said, feeling tears prick her eyes. Dymphna was slowly recovering now from her awful loss, but for a long time she had looked so careworn and tired; grief, financial worries, the shame that some people – including her own mother in Dingle – had made her feel about the way Tommy died had all taken their toll.

Father Iggy nodded, satisfied. 'Sure I don't know if it's strictly Church protocol, but I can't imagine the bishop would mind, as long as we don't make a big thing of it.' He chuckled. 'And sometimes 'tis easier to ask for forgiveness than permission if you know what I mean.'

'I know exactly, and it's a good, kind thing for you to do, Father. Like you said, I'm sure God has Tommy at his right hand already, but it will be a great comfort for Dymphna.'

As they strolled past the draper's shop, Grace noticed Peggy leaning on her counter, absorbed in reading a letter. She looked up with a smile. 'Hello, Miss Fitz! Hello, Father! Isn't it a lovely day? My brother in Boston has written to me. He went down to Florida for his holidays. Do you know there are alligators in America? Grace, that dress is lovely on you!'

'All thanks to you finding me the material, Peggy.' Grace smiled, feeling another pang about Richard's lack of correspondence but able to hide it, thanks to Charlie forewarning her.

'Sure it was in the back room for years. It was either you or the moths,' lied Peggy, with an airy wave.

'It's getting away!'

The swarm of small boys who had been playing around the square earlier was rushing towards them; someone had kicked the football too hard, and it was bouncing down the cobbled street towards Grace and the priest. Quick as a flash, Father Iggy trapped the ball with his right foot and, with a cry of triumph, took off. His soutane was blowing in the wind as he raced towards the square, dribbling the ball in front of him, holding up his black robes, pursued by whooping children, their young clear laughter ringing out around the village.

It was so good that Father Iggy was the head of the school board now instead of Canon Rafferty. When the canon used to come to check her pupils' catechism, they would sit in terrified silence, afraid to move a muscle in case they got beaten. But when Father Iggy came in, which he did almost every day to do lessons with anyone who needed extra help, all the children clamoured to tell him what they'd been learning. He even taught a bit when he had time, his personal passion being history.

He'd had the older ones enthralled last term when he told them that his uncle was Monsignor Michael Cullen, who was secretary to the archbishop of Dublin at the time of the Easter Rising and there when Count Plunkett had come to tell the archbishop that he'd been to see the pope in Rome, to inform him the Irish were going to rebel against their English occupiers. Benedict XV had asked if there was any other way, but the count had told him there wasn't. The children hung on every word as Father Iggy explained how his uncle went up to deliver the count's message to the archbishop. He was ill in bed, only seeing his doctor, so the Monsignor had no choice but go down to the GPO where the rebellion had begun and hear the confessions of the Irish heroes of the revolution who wanted to die as good Catholics.

Sweet, kind Father Iggy was loved by the children before he told that story, but afterwards he took on hero status, to be so closely connected to such powerful princes of the Church and State.

Grace was still smiling as the Dingle bus passed her, Bobby the Bus being nearly on time for once. There must have been no funeral wakes being held in any of the houses he passed on the way for him to stop at to 'pay his respects' and finagle his usual glass of whiskey.

CHAPTER 2

*B*efore Grace could push the pram the last few yards uphill to the bus stop, Tilly had already jumped down, as lithe and athletic as ever, her haversack slung across her back. Grace envied her friend her agility, feeling very slow and cumbersome by comparison.

'Hello, Aintín Grace, hello, Odile, *a chroí*,' cried Tilly as she strode towards them. She was dressed even more unusually than normal, with a beautiful wine-coloured fedora on her head and a black velvet jacket over her men's trousers and shirt. Her dark wavy hair had grown a little and was now at her jawline, and it shone like the conkers the children knocked out of the big horse chestnut tree.

'Well? How was Dublin?' Grace asked.

Tilly swept Odile up out of the pram and held her towards the sky as the baby squealed and kicked excitedly. 'Ara, grand altogether. They're sweet kids, but why anyone would want so many, I'll never know. Odile's quite enough work for me! Anyway, do you see this beautiful hat I'm wearing – wait till I tell you! An amazing thing happened on the train from Dublin to Dingle…'

'Do you want to come over to my place for a cuppa and a slice of Madeira cake while you tell me?' suggested Grace as Tilly paused to tuck the giggling baby back into her pram. 'Dymphna made some for the priests and brought a spare one up to me. She was giving out that she'd had to use lard and not butter because of the rationing, but you wouldn't know – you have to try it.'

'No, I'll come for it tomorrow. I'd better get home to Mam – she made me promise not to dally when I got back but bring Odile straight up to the farm. It makes me laugh how that child has Mam wrapped around her little finger. She dotes on her. I don't know what we'll do when her parents turn up.'

'I don't know what I'll do either,' said Grace wistfully. She really loved Odile and was delighted that Tilly had decided they were both the little baby's aunties. Though if Alfie did marry Constance, then Tilly really would be Odile's auntie while Grace would still be just an honorary one. It was hard to have no family of her own.

Well, she had her brother, Maurice, who was a priest in the Philippines, but she'd kind of given up on him. She'd been only a baby when he was last in Knocknashee, and all she'd heard from him during her life was his twice yearly Mass card saying he was praying for her, and what was the point of that when he didn't even know her.

She'd sent him a long telegram after Agnes died, asking him to write, but all that had come in the post was another Mass card.

'Ara, we'll jump off that bridge when we come to it, and by the looks of things, nobody will be going anywhere for the foreseeable if Herr Hitler gets his way,' said Tilly, in her usual careless way. 'Will you walk with me as far as the turn up by the cemetery? Or is your leg tired after pushing the pram around? I can take Odile from here if you're wrecked?'

'No, it's grand. I'll come that far with you, and I'll push the pram if you don't mind – it actually helps to lean on the handle. And I want to hear the story of what happened on the train.'

But the story had to wait, because Father Iggy joined them again on the walk back down the hill, puffing and out of breath and wanting to know about Dublin, and Tilly had to tell him all about Marion's six stepchildren, and the baby girl of her own she'd had last Easter, and the new baby she was already expecting that was going to be called Alfie if it was a boy.

The Angelus bell rang out over the town and the bay, and they bowed their heads for a moment in prayer.

Father Iggy made the sign of the cross. 'Well, goodbye then, and see ye at Mass tomorrow,' he said cheerfully, then trotted off, rubbing his hands in expectation of a delicious dinner of three pork chops with apple sauce, followed by blackberry tart. It was a far cry from the days when Kit Gallagher fed him and Father Lehane on half a mackerel each and no dessert.

'So, Tilly, finally, what was this amazing thing that happened on the train?' Grace asked as they walked on.

'Well...' Her best friend's eyes sparkled. 'I was just sitting there reading that latest book by Radclyffe Hall, *The Unlit Lamp*, the one Jacob gave me from Sarah – he'd put his photograph of Alfie and Constance inside it, remember?'

'Of course I do.' Tilly and her mother had been delighted by the sight of the handsome Alfie sporting a week's worth of stubble, with his arm around his girlfriend, who had a wide, charming face, dark eyes and a small, pert mouth. The picture was framed now and sitting on the mantelpiece up at the farm.

'Well, this woman on the train saw me reading it and –'

'How're ya, Tilly?'

Tomás Kinneally, who had the farm beside the O'Hares', had been drawing seaweed from the shore with a donkey and cart as fertiliser for his land, but he had stopped at the turn to the cemetery and waited for them, staring at Tilly unashamedly as she and Grace approached with the pram. The silly little man was short and bald, but he had half a notion of Tilly, even though he was deluded if he thought she'd look sideways at him.

'Grand, Tomás. That's a fine haul you got there.' Tilly nodded at the piles of seaweed.

'I could spread a bit in your top field if you want?' he offered, eager as a puppy.

'If you've it going spare, I'd be delighted,' she said carelessly.

Tilly worked the farm singlehandedly and accepted help from her neighbours, and she in turn helped them; it was how it was done around here. But Grace was still surprised when she accepted Tomás's offer – the foolish farmer might read something into it. Sure enough he continued to hang around, favouring her with his goofy smile, which made him look even worse because it showed his two missing front teeth.

'Well, goodbye, Tomás,' Grace said firmly. 'I'm just having a chat with my friend Tilly here.'

'I can wait…'

'*Slán abhaile*, Tomás, we'll be ages yet.'

'Well, *slán*, Miss Fitz, Tilly.' The little man's shoulders slumped as he went reluctantly on his way, leading his old grey donkey up the stony lane. His and the O'Hare farms were beyond the cemetery, on the side of the rocky hill that gave Knocknashee its name, the hill of the fairies.

'You shouldn't encourage him,' she admonished Tilly as he passed out of sight.

'I'm not!' Tilly grinned.

'Well, letting him spread seaweed on your fields is…'

'A new form of flirting? God, Grace, you need a social life, girl.' Tilly gave her a friendly shove. 'What Bridie Keohane does with Declan, now *that's* flirting. I think you need to put poor Declan out of his misery. You know he'd drop Bridie like a hot spud if you gave him the slightest encouragement.'

She laughed. 'Oh, stop that, Tilly.'

Her best friend teased her all the time about being some kind of femme fatale and Declan being mad about her, but it was only old *rawmeis*. She and Declan were friends, nothing more. He'd had a whole trip to New York and back to say any different, and he never had.

'Now, go on and tell me, what happened with this woman?'

'So…' Tilly looked like she was going to burst with excitement. 'She started talking to me about the book – she knew it, and she'd read *The Well of Loneliness* as well – and asked me where I got it when it was banned, which I didn't even know it was, and I explained about Sarah Lewis. And then she introduced herself. Her name is Eloise, she's Swiss. She moved to Dublin at the start of the war and teaches German and French and Italian, because apparently the Swiss speak all three, imagine. And she's an amateur photographer as well – that's why she was on her way to Dingle, to take pictures of the coastline because she heard it was beautiful.'

'She sounds very interesting,' said Grace, thinking she'd never seen Tilly's eyes shine in quite that way before.

'Oh, Grace, she's not just interesting, she's so… She's not like anyone I've ever met. She was wearing trousers, and she admired my jacket – I bought it in Dublin. And this is her hat. She gave it to me as a present because she said it went with the jacket – wasn't that so generous of her? And it looked much better on her than it does on me. She's beautiful, tall, taller than me, and slim, with short wavy blond hair and the most amazing blue eyes. She grew up in the Alps, so misses the mountains. Her family were farmers, so she was really interested in our farm. And Grace, you won't believe this, but she wants to visit me. She has to go back to Dublin after Dingle, but she said she'd come back down here as soon as she can.'

'Well, that will give everyone something to talk about!' The arrival of a tall, multilingual Swiss woman would surely be a source of fascination to the people of the town. Richard and Jacob had only been here for three hours, and the place was still whispering about it. 'And if she does visit, maybe you could get her talking a few words of French to Odile?'

Tilly nodded eagerly. 'Good idea. And she will come, I'm sure she will, and I did warn her about everyone staring at her, but she didn't bat an eye. She said she's from the same kind of place, small and rural – people there are as curious about strangers as they are here. We talked about it for a long time, coming from places like this. We always think foreign places will be so much more…I don't know… advanced or something, but it's just the same. Now' – Tilly took the pram from Grace and pointed it up the hill – 'the sheep need tending and the spuds won't dig themselves, so me and my little apprentice here better get going. Are you sure you'll be all right walking home, Grace? I can bring the horse and trap back down to you, if you want to wait?'

'Not a bit of it. I'll see you tomorrow.'

'You will, and we'll have more time. God knows what state the place above will be in while I've been gone.' Tilly picked up the baby out of the pram again and waved her tiny hand, saying in a high voice, '*Slán*, Aintín Grace!'

Grace waved back. '*Slán*, Odile! *Slán*, Aintín Tilly!'

'*Slán*, Grace.' Her best friend settled the baby down again and raised her own hand in farewell as she pushed the sturdy pram up the steep rocky road.

As Grace went slowly home, she noticed that even after all the walking she'd been doing, she wasn't limping too badly. Not as badly as Bridie Keohane, anyway – that was, when the girl could decide which ankle she had twisted. And it wasn't just the new calliper. Her leg had been so much better since Declan had built her that little bath house with a tank and combustion chamber to heat up the water so that she could have warm baths to ease the pain from her polio. The contraption had been turf-fuelled at first but now ran on gas, and recently the local hotel had him install four of them for the guests, and a hotel in Dingle was interested now. Between his work at the school and making hot-water tanks and now Bridie, Grace hoped Declan would have enough time for the teacher training course once they got started.

She was really looking forward to having dinner with him and his father this evening, then unwrapping the big parcel of books that had arrived yesterday morning, tied up in brown paper and string, that they'd kept until today to open because she was busy minding Odile.

She thought the two of them studying together would be nice, and she hoped Declan would too. It was always more enjoyable to do that sort of thing with company.

CHAPTER 3

ST SIMONS ISLAND, GEORGIA, USA

THREE WEEKS EARLIER

Dear Grace,

I'm sorry it's taken so long to write; it's been a crazy time here. I have so much to say, so much to ask you, that I almost don't know where to begin. Sometimes I think us meeting in Knocknashee like that was a dream. Was I really there? Did that actually happen?

I want to say that you are even more beautiful than I imagined...

With a groan of frustration, Richard balled up the sheet of notepaper and fired it into the wastebasket near the foot of the wicker sofa in the conservatory.

This was not how it was with him and Grace, stuck for words, trying to find a way of saying what he meant. Usually he spoke openly, freely, from the heart. But the basket on the floor beside him full of crumpled paper told another story. He reached for the open bottle of beer on the table at his elbow and tilted it to his mouth.

What did he want? That was easy. He wanted to tell her how she was the most wonderful girl he'd ever known, how meeting her in person in Knocknashee a month ago was the best thing to ever happen to him. He desperately wanted to say that he loved her.

So just do it, he chided. *You call yourself a writer, so write down what you feel.* But instead he stumbled and stuttered over the words and tore up each effort in exasperation.

When he had first laid eyes on her, it had been like electricity. He was almost certain she had felt the same.

But what if he was wrong? On the beach he'd asked her about her time in New York with Declan McKenna, and her gorgeous face had lit up and she'd said in her soft voice, 'It was amazing.' Amazing. That word was burnt into his memory. Did she mean the city or the man? If it was the man...

No, don't risk it, better to remain friends, to be there for her always, not force her into a decision that can come to no good either way.

If he told her he loved her and she said she loved him too, she would have to abandon everything she knew to be with him – her home, her friends, her teaching career, everything she valued – for a life of danger. Because he couldn't give up his job as a war reporter. He and Jacob were heading to England as soon as Lucille, who ran the office at the *Capital*, could find them tickets.

And on the other side of it, if she didn't feel the same way about him but was in love with Declan, how could they keep writing to each other? Everything would change. They would never be able to be easy and open and honest with each other again.

With a heavy sigh, he put the beer down and pulled the notepad towards him once more, resting it on his thigh as he reclined on the conservatory sofa.

Dear Grace,

It was lovely to meet you in Knocknashee. I will treasure the memory always.

How is Odile? I'm sure she's thriving under the expert care of Tilly and her mama. How the poor kid survived my and Jacob's poor ministrations, I'll never know, but somehow she did.

I haven't received any communication from the Dreyfuses or from Alfie. Please let me know if you hear anything. And write anyway, even if you don't.

As I telegrammed, Jacob and I got home safe, despite a couple of U-boat warnings.

The ship was hugely overcrowded with us Americans, cots placed up on deck, five and six people in two-bed cabins, people squashed in everywhere and almost everyone just grateful for the ticket home. One lady, a fur-clad, bejewelled old matron, demanded a better cabin and refused point-blank to share. She was given short shrift by the stewards, and three other girls were put in with her. Jacob and I had no cabin at all, but we took cots on the deck, and while it was cold at night, it was fine; we just muddled through.

Kirky, our editor at the Capital, was glad to see us—well, as glad as he is about anything—and he actually gave us a backhanded compliment about the articles and pictures we sent back. He said they connected well to the common American, so "we weren't as dumb as we looked" even though "you, Lewis, in your fancy clothes, clearly have no idea how the common man lives." And I thought I was dressed in ordinary clothes! Jacob says it's because I snuck off to spend the night in the St. Regis so I could get them ironed, while he insisted on sleeping with the bedbugs in some god-awful boarding house.

One thing we did agree on—we have asked Kirky to send us back, this time to England. We've suggested an illustrated weekly column about people trying to live their ordinary lives in wartime—schools, food, transport, hospitals, government, we'd cover everything. He knows from when we were in France that we have a knack for getting people to open up to us, and he knows readers like it, so in the end, it wasn't too hard a sell and eventually he agreed. Of course, he called us "dumb, foolhardy kids" and accused us of "tryin' to be heroes," among other things, but I think he's a little bit proud of us too.

Now deciding we want to go and actually getting there are two entirely different things. It's not easy, but Lucille, the scary woman in the office who sorts out everything, is working on it, so now we have to just wait. Germany has blockaded Britain completely, so getting in or out is very difficult. But Lucille knows the British ambassador and thinks she can persuade him to help us find a way. She says that anything that encourages American inter-

vention, like sympathetic reporting from the front lines, goes down well with the limeys.

Meanwhile I've been doing a piece on hurricanes—it's the season for them here. We had a pretty bad one just recently, fourteen-foot waves, millions of dollars of damage all the way from Florida up the coast to the Carolinas. Charleston and Savannah got the worst of it. I've been talking to the people whose property was damaged or destroyed, and they say they're sure the hurricanes are getting worse, though why that would be, I don't know.

But as interesting as hurricanes are, local reporting is not enough for me anymore. I feel like I got a chance at life in Europe, and it's whet my appetite.

Things are sure heating up over here on the subject of the war. A general of ours, Pershing, came on the radio to encourage people to support aid going to Britain. He said democracy and freedom were under threat worldwide, that Hitler and Mussolini had overthrown liberty, and that if America was to send help to Britain, as she stood alone, it was the best way of keeping the war on that side of the Atlantic. But then on the same day, Lindbergh, the famous aviator, spoke at a rally against getting involved, claiming we need to strengthen our military so nobody can invade us, and if we stay out of foreigners' business, nobody will have any need to come after us.

He's singing from the same hymn sheet as Ambassador Joseph Kennedy, who is always saying Britain doesn't have hope, which plays right into the isolationists' hands. I hear that Randolph Churchill, Winston Churchill's son, said, "I thought my daffodils were yellow until I met Joe Kennedy." Apparently Kennedy is very ambitious politically, but I can't see how he can recover from this, unless he sends his own sons to war or something.

Jacob hates people like Lindbergh and Kennedy. He almost got us blacklisted by Gideon Clarendon last week, the editor of the Savannah Morning News, and he'd commissioned a picture spread about the annual regatta of the Savannah Yacht Club. While we were there, Jacob said something along the lines of he thought the whole thing was stupid and self-indulgent and people should open their damned eyes and see what's going on in the world instead of dressing up like peacocks and swigging champagne. Well, the recipient of this speech was the commodore's wife, and she almost combusted in indignation. So you see, if we can't get him back to Europe, he'll have to find a different profession, 'cause he sure is burning bridges over here.

I thought Sarah would be mad at him, but she wasn't. He's made her much more radical these days. She cares deeply about politics and far less about money. She has learned to drive—not very well, admittedly—and has taken a course in first aid. Like Jacob and me, having been over there and having seen the war with her own eyes, she says she can't just sit here in America doing nothing, she has plans of her own, she's itching to do something meaningful. Though I'm not sure she knows what exactly—she doesn't say...

He stopped and looked up in surprise at the roar of a car whose gears were being ground mercilessly. It accelerated up the solitary road to the house and skidded to a halt outside. Moments later someone's feet rattled up the front steps and around the side of the wooden wraparound porch, and Sarah stormed in through the double glass doors of the conservatory.

He could tell she was fuming as she threw herself into the wicker armchair near the foot of the couch and reached for the remains of his beer. Her brown eyes were dangerously bright, her mop of dark curls hanging unkempt to her jaw, her red long-sleeved dress rumpled from the long drive.

'What's up?' he asked mildly.

She exhaled through her nose and shook her head. 'Our mother is such a pill, Richard. Truly, how did we draw such a short straw? I swear I can't stand her, I can't.'

Richard waited patiently to find out what their mother had done now. Only Caroline Lewis possessed the skill to get under Sarah's skin like this. She'd hurt Richard too, deeply, but she didn't make him want to throttle her the way she did his sister. It was as if their mother knew the exact buttons to push to have Sarah explode, and then she would condescendingly demand that Sarah control herself.

'I was summoned there for lunch – you know how she does – and she launched right in. How irresponsible and childish we were running off to France, how you and I were raised in the lap of luxury and given every educational and financial and social advantage, and then for us to throw it all back in her face, so spoiled and ungrateful, you know, the usual.'

Richard did know. Their mother was like a broken record since they'd come back from Europe. She was mortified in front of her high-society friends that her children had lowered themselves to work for a Yankee newspaper and gone travelling around Europe with Jacob Nunez. She made no secret of the fact that she was appalled by their choice of companion. If she knew Sarah and Jacob were together, she'd blow a fuse.

She was still furious at Sarah for breaking her engagement to that chinless wonder Algernon Smythe, and at Richard for letting the beautiful heiress Miranda Logan slip through his fingers. The two most eligible young socialites in Savannah were married to each other now, and Caroline Lewis was always harping on about their 'perfect' marriage. Richard would never betray his ex-girlfriend by telling his mother this, but Miranda was already so bored with Algy, she had taken a lover to keep herself amused – a Costa Rican man who never talked about yachts.

Sarah lived in the family home when she wasn't with Richard in St Simons and so she was obliged to put up with their parents, but he often wondered why he continued to go back there whenever he was summoned for Sunday dinner. Maybe it was because of how his father had secretly followed him out of the house that day, after Richard had announced he was going to France, and had shaken his hand and wished him luck – all out of the hearing of his wife. Not that Arthur Lewis had shown him any open affection since; he just sat there eating moodily while their mother harped on.

'There's no point in reacting, Sarah. You know what Mother is like. She's trying to goad you.'

'No, this is different.' Having drained his beer, she leapt up and strode to the drinks cart, where she made herself an enormous gin and tonic. 'You?' she offered, waggling the Waterford Crystal glass at him, clinking with ice cubes.

He shook his head. 'How?'

Sarah took a wedge of lime from the bowl Esme had set out earlier beside the crystal decanters and glasses and took a long sip of her cocktail. 'She started saying awful things about Jews. You should have heard her – she'd make a good Nazi. She said how Jewish bankers were trying to drag us into this war for their own profit, and they wanted to impose socialism on everyone, and no wonder everyone hated them.'

'Really? That's a bit strong, even for her.' Richard could now see why Sarah was so upset. After all they'd heard for themselves in Paris about the way the Jews were being treated, it must have been very hard for her to hear this from her own mother.

'I mean, how can bankers be socialists? She doesn't even make *sense*.' Sarah fumed as she added more neat gin to her half-empty glass. 'Imagine what Jacob would think if he knew my mother was capable of coming out with stuff like that. I had to get out of there. You're sure you don't want one of these?'

'I think I probably do, after that. So you stood up and left? Good for you.' He usually deplored his sister's penchant for the dramatic, but in this case, he thought it fully justified.

Sarah fixed his drink, her back to him as she delivered the next bombshell. 'Yes, but not before I told her that Jacob and I are a couple.'

'You did *what?*' He sat bolt upright. 'A couple in what way?'

'I told her that we are in love. I'm sick of lying about it.' She handed him the drink and threw herself back into the wicker armchair with a triumphant smile.

'Oh, God… You didn't… But what did you say exactly?' He prayed she hadn't admitted to sleeping with Jacob. She'd never even admitted it to him, though it was obvious.

'The truth! That we were living as man and wife in Europe, and I love him, and that if she can't accept it, then that's unfortunate but it won't be changing.'

'Oh, God…' Their parents would be horrified to think their daughter was sleeping with anyone, let alone a Jew. No doubt this would be brought down on his head now too. There was nothing they could do to Richard – he had already been cut off by them financially following his refusal to follow his father into the bank – but he'd always felt a bit guilty about turning a blind eye to what Sarah was up to. It wasn't fair, but the rules for men and those for women when it came to sex outside of marriage were completely different. 'What did they say?'

'Mother went all quiet and her eyes went cold like an alligator in the swamps, and then she ordered me out of her house and told me never to set foot in it again, so basically I've been disinherited, disowned and banished.'

His heart sank. Sarah might be more serious about life these days, but she still had no idea what it was like to live without access to money. She had been raised a princess, in a gilded cage of privilege. In Paris she'd been strong and resilient and able to rough it, but that had been a one-off adventure, not a way of life.

'Did Mother really say she was cutting you off? In those words? What did Father say?'

'Nothing. Didn't need to.'

He thought rapidly. 'Maybe they'll come around if you got engaged at least.'

'Don't you get it?' Her eyes flashed furiously. 'I don't want to lie any more, and I don't want their money. I don't want *anything* from our parents, ever again.' In her temper she kicked off her handmade leather sandals so that they skittered across the floor, landing in two different corners of the conservatory. Tomorrow morning, Esme, the housekeeper who had minded them since birth, would pick the shoes up and leave them in Sarah's room, and Sarah wouldn't even notice that there were people around her paid to keep her life smooth and easy and clean.

He said, half to himself, 'Well, at least they can't touch your share in this house or your trust fund from Grandma.'

'Exactly. And you're managing just fine on your trust fund, aren't you?'

'Yes, though...' He winced and sipped at his drink.

His sister might have forgotten, but the sum in his and Nathan's trust funds from their grandmother was four times that in hers. As a privileged society girl, the assumption was that she would marry well and have no need to buy herself anything other than a few lunches out or trips to the theatre with friends. Plus both he and Nathan worked – and what could Sarah do?

'I know what you're thinking,' she said sharply, 'and I know it's a lot less, but I won't be crawling to you for a handout. I can earn my own money. I know you and Jacob are just itching to get back to Europe, and when you go, I'm going with you. I can afford the ticket from my fund, and I'm going to ask your editor to pay my expenses as a translator.'

He was taken aback. 'You want the *Capital* to pay your expenses?'

She bridled. 'And why not? Just because I'm a girl, is everything I do supposed to be for free? No, Richard, when we're in New York, I plan to meet your editor and I'm going to tell him face to face how much I contributed to your and Jacob's work because I can speak French and German and Italian.'

Richard winced at the idea of Sarah confronting the hard-bitten editor, who already thought Richard was too much of a 'posh boy'. What would he make of the entitled, demanding Sarah Lewis? 'I don't know, Sarah. Kirky's a tough nut to crack. He's a very cynical man...'

Sarah scoffed and tossed her dark curls. 'The point is, your "Kirky" is a man. No man is a tough nut to crack, not for me. And men aren't cynical around women – they're always trying to impress us on some level. Speaking of which...' She looked down into the wastebasket between her chair and the foot of the sofa, poked in her hand and stirred the crumpled papers. 'Dear Grace, Dear Grace...' she read, then tutted at him. 'So you still haven't gotten up the courage to tell that Irish girl you like her? Because I know you do. Jacob said you went all starry-eyed when you met her – he thought it was hilarious.'

Ruefully, Richard shook his head. 'Well, I'm not going to lie, I did like her, yes. But no, I think it's better to leave it. That McKenna fellow she went to New York with is much better suited for her.'

Her eyes flashed again. 'How do you know, for God's sake? And how dare you make that decision for her? Just write and tell her and let her make her own mind up between the two of you.'

'It's not that simple.' He already regretted talking to her about it.

Sarah was not like him. She charged into every situation all guns blazing and asked questions later.

'It *is*, though. Stop second-guessing her, stop taking her choices away. Tell her the truth. She'll either accept you or reject you, but whichever way, you'll know and you can get on with your life. And so can she.' She stood then and came over to him, placing her hand on his shoulder, speaking more gently. 'If this war is teaching us anything, it's that nobody is guaranteed a future, so if you love her, just be brave. You never know – it might just pay off.'

He sighed. 'I don't know.'

'It's good to be honest. You'll feel better. Now that it's all out in the open about Jacob with Mother and Father, I finally can breathe. By the way, I refuse to stay at the hovel' – it was what she called the apartment Jacob shared with a bunch of misfits – 'so I'm going to call him now to come here to live with me. Is that OK?'

'Of course it is, yes.' But his heart sank. If their parents turned up and Jacob was staying here…

'And then I'm going to find Esme and tell her he's moving in. And don't worry, I'll pretend to her he's staying in Nathan's room as usual, because while I don't care what our parents think, I do love Esme and I don't want to scandalise the poor woman. Now write your letter, and for God's sake, mail it right away. And use the public mailbox on the boardwalk so you can't change your mind and fish it out again.'

She dropped a kiss on his head and was gone, and moments later he could hear her on the phone in the hall, and after that greeting Esme in the kitchen.

Picking up his fountain pen, Richard began again.

Dear Grace,

I've written this and rewritten it around fifty times, so this time I'm just going to say what I feel and hope you don't run screaming.

Meeting you was wonderful. I loved it. You are everything I've dreamed and more, and I curse that bus for pulling me away so soon after I arrived in magical Knocknashee. I wish I'd had the guts to tell you that I love you and that meeting you in person was the best thing that ever happened to me.

I don't know how close you and Declan are—maybe you're only good friends. Or maybe I have no right to say these things, but I have to. I love you, Grace. I've never felt about anyone in my whole life the way I do about you, and if you'd have me, I'd move heaven and earth for us to be together.

If you don't want that, I'll accept it and never mention it again, but please don't cut off our friendship. Just write back something cheerful, like you never got this letter at all.

Yours with all my love,
Richard

He folded the letter and stuffed it clumsily into an envelope – he was all fingers and thumbs – smoothed it, addressed it, stuck stamps to it and went out the double glass doors onto the wraparound porch, then down the front steps into the garden. At the gate he walked straight past their family mailbox, the one where you could put the flag up to indicate outgoing mail and where he could easily take the letter out again before the collection tomorrow – something he'd done several times already. Instead, this time he took his brave, foolhardy sister's advice and walked down the boardwalk that overlooked the Atlantic Ocean to where there was a public mailbox. Refusing to allow himself time to ruminate and hesitate, he threw the letter in, his heart pounding.

There. It was gone. She would get it, and his fate was in the lap of the gods.

* * *

LATER THAT EVENING he sat in the large comfortable den, where the wingback chairs were upholstered in light-blue silk that their mother had had shipped from France especially to complement the pale-green art-deco scroll sofa. 'Eau de Nil' she'd called it and he and Sarah had sniggered at her trying to sound French. On the floor, covering the walnut floorboards, was a Chinese silk rug in blues and aquas. This house, like their family home in Savannah, had been decorated with no expense spared.

Sitting in one of the armchairs, one socked foot tucked up beneath him, he tried to read a book, but nothing could keep his attention. The letter in the mailbox wouldn't be collected until tomorrow. In his mind it pulsated and glowed like a coal.

In the car that pulled up outside the house, its headlights sweeping past the curtains of the den, he assumed was Jacob. Like Sarah, the photographer had learnt how to drive on returning from Europe, because he never again wanted to do a bus journey like the four-day trip they had taken across Ireland to Knocknashee. He'd bought himself a very rusty second-hand Ford, nothing like Sarah's natty green two-seater, but he still had to keep it hidden down a side street from his roommates, who considered all property to be theft.

Above his head Richard could hear his sister's footsteps coming to the top of the stairs, and he decided to stay where he was, not to get in the way of their reunion. The person crossed the hall to the door of the den and opened it. Richard looked up in surprise to see his father standing there, the perfect Southern gentleman, in his cream linen suit, with a pocket watch and white fedora. For all that he was as rich as Croesus, Arthur Lewis had the common touch and could speak to a farmer in battered overalls as easily as a head of state. It belied his sharp mind the way he peppered his speech with Southern colloquialisms, and though she would never reprimand her husband, Richard remembered how he and his siblings would suppress a smile as their mother winced when their father said 'goshdurnit' or addressed them collectively as 'y'all'.

'Ah, Father, hello. I...I wasn't expecting you.'

His first thought was to reach for his shoes, embarrassed for his father to catch him lounging in his socks. His second thought was *Why is he here? Has he come to order Sarah home? This is going to be awful, and what if Jacob turns up in the middle of the fight?*

'Will you have a beer, Father?' he asked calmly.

'Thank you, Richard, I will.' Arthur Lewis took a seat on the art deco sofa.

Richard rang the bell and Esme appeared. 'Esme, can you get my father a beer please? And one for myself.'

'Right away, Mr Richard.'

'Thank you, Esme.'

'Thank you, Esme,' Arthur Lewis added warmly. He was always courteous when he addressed the help. His mother wasn't rude to them – that would be uncouth – but she was cold.

While the housekeeper fetched the beers, the two of them sat in awkward silence; the clock on the wall ticking loudly was the only sound. He and his father were not chatty at the best of times, but this felt excruciating. Upstairs all was silent. It seemed his sister had disappeared back into her bedroom and was keeping out of sight.

A minute later the housekeeper returned with a tray of glasses, ice and two bottles of beer already cold from the refrigerator, which she set down on the table between them before leaving the room.

Richard leant forward, stretching out his hand to the tray, glad of something to do. 'Shall I pour a glass for you, Father?'

'Not at all.' To Richard's astonishment, Arthur Lewis – a stickler for manners and doing things the right way – took one of the cold beers and swigged a mouthful straight from the neck. Setting the bottle back on the tray with a bang, he wiped his moustache with his silk handkerchief and asked, 'Well, Richard, can you call your sister now?'

Oh, God. 'Well, sir, I, er…'

'There's no reason to pretend she's not in this house. I saw her at the top of the stairs when I came in. Just call up to her, and let's get this over with.'

With a sinking heart, Richard stood up and crossed the room where he opened the door into the hall. Sarah was hovering at the top of the stairs, listening. Silently he beckoned to her. She scowled and looked nervous, and seemed about to retreat again, but then got up her courage, stuck out her chin and descended as proud as a painting he'd seen of Mary, Queen of Scots, on her way to execution.

As he turned to walk in front of her into the den, she swept past him. 'You wanted to see me?' she snapped at their father, with no trace of deference or respect.

Richard touched her arm from behind, murmuring softly, 'Sarah…'

She shook him off. 'There's no need to stay, Richard. I don't need my little brother to stick up for me or tell me how to speak to my own father.'

Arthur Lewis was on his feet. 'That's true, Sarah, but I still want to see both of you, if you don't mind, please. Richard, will you stay?'

'Ah, yes, sir, of course.' Was it his imagination, or was something different in his father's demeanour? Did he seem less forbidding somehow?

If so, Sarah hadn't noticed; she was as belligerent as ever. 'If this is to ask me to apologise to Mother, then you've had a wasted journey. The things she said were unforgivable –'

'I agree. I'm here on my own behalf, not your mother's.'

She stopped mid-flow, taken aback. Then jumped straight back on her high horse. 'Daddy, I know Jacob isn't what you had in mind for me, and Mother said the most appalling things, but I won't give him up.'

'Did I ask you to, Sarah?' He was using his mild, reasonable manner, the iron fist in the velvet glove that had gotten him so far in the cutthroat world of private banking.

'No, but I assume it's why you're here,' she retorted, but Richard could hear a softer note in her voice. Out of their parents, she liked their father better; they were the most similar, both extremely clever but also pig-headed and authoritative in the way they spoke.

'Shall we sit down?' Arthur Lewis indicated the wingback chairs. Sarah took one and Richard the other, while he resumed his seat on the sofa opposite.

'I know you're both wondering why I'm here…' He stopped, swallowed, cleared his throat, reached for the bottle on the tray and took another swig of beer. 'And no doubt you'd rather I wasn't.'

Sarah met Richard's gaze with raised eyebrows.

Richard, equally puzzled, had a thought – was their father nervous? Surely not. Arthur Lewis was normally as emotional as a clam; nervousness was just not part of his make-up. Sometimes Richard wondered what he felt about this man. He hadn't been a tactile or loving parent, he was always working, and besides, he was too well dressed to risk getting dirty playing games with his children when they were little. But he was reasonable and generous, they'd wanted for nothing, and he had never once beaten them or even raised his voice. Now that Richard thought about it, he'd never done much to interact with them either way, negatively or positively.

Noting that neither of them had contradicted his last statement, Richard's father allowed a small smile to play around his lips under his bushy moustache. 'So,' he went on, 'I'll get straight to the point. A lot of our boys, and maybe even our girls, are going to get caught up in this European business in the coming months, and maybe even years. Roosevelt is going to let us be dragged in one way or another.'

The siblings let their father speak, falling into the old habit of being passive listeners as he pontificated about the political situation, even though they were the ones who had been on the front line.

'And I fear you two are stuck in it already.'

Again a statement, not a question, so they stayed silent.

'And I just wanted to say' – he inhaled and fixed first Richard and then Sarah with a searching gaze – 'that I am very proud of you both. Your mother is upset. She thinks you are in danger, or were, and will soon be again, and that comes out as…well…madder than a wet hen.' He gave a little chuckle. 'But I think you are both brave young people, and I'm proud of you.'

Richard felt a rush of warmth for his father, the little boy in him so glad to be praised, and opened his mouth to say something. But the other man held up his hand.

'Not yet, Richard, I'm talking.' But he said it with another small smile, like he knew well what he was like. 'What I want to say is, I'm a self-made man, I didn't inherit anything.' He waved his hand around the opulent room to suggest his origins were humbler than this, that it was his wife's taste in this room. Arthur Lewis's background was not a topic ever discussed. Caroline Lewis came from old money and preferred to let it be thought her husband was the same. The Lewis grandparents were dead long before Arthur moved to Savannah, so there was nobody to refute the impression – except possibly Uncle

Harold, but he was *persona non grata* now that he lived with a married Catholic woman on Tybee Island.

'I arrived at Harvard, not broke but not far off it, I won a scholarship and because I was smart and I could hold my own in social situations, and I worked my way up as fast as I could, met your mother and married well.' He glanced again around the house, which their mother laughably called a summer cottage when it was in fact a very substantial home. 'Your grandmother on your mother's side left her wealth to you children, because I insisted on making my own money. Your mother trusted me. I built my way up to running my own bank. And though Caroline would like you to follow in my footsteps, Richard, and I would too, I admire you for taking a stand and doing what *you* want to do. You've both got more guts than you can hang on a fence. Sarah, you could never be stuck with that limp rag Algernon Smythe, and I'm glad you refused him.'

'You are? Really?' Sarah was incredulous.

'Yes really. Look, what I know about journalism doesn't amount to much more than a hill of beans, but I know grit when I see it, and you two have it in spades.'

'Thanks, Father, that means a lot.' Richard finally got a word in edgewise, but his voice was choked and came out almost inaudible.

'It means a lot to me as well,' said Sarah, more clearly, her cheeks pink with pleasure. 'I'm glad you see I've been working, Father, and not just being a parasite like I would be if I'd married Algernon Smythe or kept relying on you for money.'

'Sweetheart, you would never be a parasite, it's not in your nature.' Their father stroked his moustache solemnly as he regarded her. 'And I just want to say that your mother might well be talking about cutting you off and all of that – she's sure got her tail up now – but I won't be, and contrary to what she might think, I'm still wearing the pants in this family.'

'I don't need your money, Daddy. I'm going to get the *Capital* to pay my expenses this time around –'

He cut her off with another wave of his hand. 'You are my daughter, Sarah. Both of you are my children. And I am sure you will earn your own money doing whatever it is you do, but my resources, my connections and my support are always available, so never land yourselves in trouble or misery for lack of funds. My wallet is open to you both, always.'

'Oh, Daddy...' She stood and walked to him then, and he pulled her down beside him on the sofa and put his arm around her.

'I know you're fixing to get back there, so you two watch out for each other now, you hear me? And don't go doing anything downright stupid. There's no point to being all hat and no cattle, as they say in Texas. Just you watch yourselves over there, and that Jacob Nunez guy too.'

She moved out of his embrace to stare at him in amazement, and he placed both his hands on her shoulders, studying her face.

'I do understand about love, Sarah, believe it or not. When I first saw your mother, I knew she was the one for me, even though she was so far above me on the social scale, it felt impossible. I decided she would be mine, and I charmed her until she agreed, and I still feel the same way after all these years. If this man Jacob Nunez has wooed and won you, despite your differences and the snobbery of Savannah high society, if he truly is your choice, then he's got to be some man, because it's not every man who would have the courage to take you on.'

There were tears in her eyes. 'He is a good man, Daddy, I promise, and he wants to marry me. We're waiting until he can go into his uncle's business after the war.'

'I trust you to do what's best, sweetheart.' But he looked mightily relieved.

Richard wasn't sure he trusted Sarah to do what was best. He wasn't convinced of Jacob's attitude regarding the jewellery business, or of Sarah's attitude about marriage, but they'd cross that bridge when they came to it.

'Thank you, Daddy,' she said softly.

'So you both take good care, you hear me? I do not want to get a telegram saying some German put a bullet in my child, am I clear?'

'Clear.' She snuggled against him.

And then for the first time that Richard could ever remember, his father opened his arms to him as well, beckoning him over for a hug. Richard went to him, sat on his other side, and for a long few minutes, Arthur Lewis, the unemotional banker, embraced his son as well as his daughter.

CHAPTER 4

KNOCKNASHEE, CO KERRY

SEPTEMBER 1940

The third week in school was over, but Grace was still at work; she had stayed behind to pin up all the wet paintings on a line strung across the classroom. She taught the four- to eight-year-olds while Declan managed the older children, and they'd just had their usual Friday afternoon art lesson.

It saddened her to see how many of the pictures were of planes flying across the mountains and ocean, dropping bombs, when usually it was donkeys and lambs and dolphins that got painted. Even though Ireland was a neutral country and there was so little in the papers about the war, even the smallest children were picking up on the fear and worry caused by what Ireland called 'the Emergency'.

In the senior classroom, which was divided from Grace's only by a thin partition, she could hear a gruff voice talking angrily. One of the fathers, a local fisherman and a brute, had come into the school to have a go at Declan about something.

She listened as she balled up the sheets of newspaper she'd used to cover the desks and stuffed them into the stove to be burnt. If the man got out of hand, she would go in and put a stop to it with her authority as headmistress, and even call Sergeant Keane if necessary, but Declan was so much more confident these days, so she didn't want to interfere unless she had to.

The fisherman's problem seemed to be the practical classes that Declan gave all his pupils on Friday afternoons, where he taught the boys as well as the girls how to wash clothes and make a loaf of soda bread and darn a sock and fix a seam. He'd learnt all these things in the Letterfrack reformatory, where he'd spent his childhood, and he saw no reason boys shouldn't be instructed to care for themselves the way a girl was taught. His father, Charlie, had had to fend for himself after his wife, Maggie, died, and it had been hard for him to learn everything from scratch. And some of the bachelor farmers around the town, like Tomás Kinneally, lived in squalor, the poor men not knowing how to look after themselves.

The children loved Mr McKenna and all the practical things he taught them, but right now Oscar Kerrigan was busy telling Declan in no uncertain terms that no son of his was going to be sewing like a woman.

There was a pause in the diatribe while the bullying fisherman caught his breath, in which Declan calmly asked him if he could mend fishing nets. To Grace's amusement, Oscar spluttered and said that of course he could but that it wasn't the same thing at all.

'If you say so, Mr Kerrigan, but it's joining two things together with a needle and thread or gut, so I don't see how it's that different. But suit yourself. If you don't want your son to make the best nets in the business, so tight that not one fish can escape, that's up to you.'

A silence fell in the room, and then a door banged and Mr Kerrigan went stomping and huffing down the corridor past the junior classroom and out the front, which he closed behind him with another bang.

A moment later Declan popped his head into Grace's room. 'I'm off now. Bridie sent her mother down to me asking for a book to read – she's bored at home with her foot up on the stool.'

Grace smiled to herself. It appeared the mother had joined the daughter's campaign to win Declan's hand in marriage. 'That's nice. What book will you bring her?'

'I thought maybe *The Death of the Heart* by Elizabeth Bowen. What do you think?'

'I think it's a great choice,' said Grace, who had read that book last year and thought it might be fitting. It was a story of a young naive Irish girl who goes to London with her head full of romantic notions but who finds the reality of adult life far more complex and difficult than she'd imagined. If anyone had romantic notions, it was Bridie. 'And well done seeing off Mr Kerrigan. You put a stop to his gallop.'

'Ara, 'twas funny seeing him trying to weigh the advantages of having his son sew like a woman. I know for a fact his nets are full of holes, he does it so badly. Don't forget we have a study night tonight. Dad has a fine stew made with a few lamb chops.'

'Ah, Declan, you should both come to me for once. I owe your father far too many meals.'

'Yerra, 'tis no bother to him. He loves cooking for you and having the two of us studying afterwards at the kitchen table together.' He smiled. 'He says it's company for him.'

'Well, I'm glad of the company myself,' she admitted.

She was getting used to being alone in the house beside the school, but she still didn't like it. Downstairs in the kitchen and sitting room, she'd done her best to make everything cosy, lots of ornaments and rugs and pictures. But upstairs everything apart from her own room seemed too quiet and sad. There was Maurice's tidy bedroom, empty but for the bed, where he hadn't slept since Grace was a baby. Then the spare room that had once contained all of her parents' things, until Agnes, in a fit of rage, burnt the lot, including their loving letters. There was the big front bedroom that had belonged to Eddie and Kathleen Fitzgerald, and which Agnes had taken over until her stroke – that room too was silent and full of ghosts. The place needed voices and children and a family. It was sad to think she would probably be rattling around in it alone until she died an old maid.

After Declan left she stayed behind in the school to sweep the floor and make sure no crumbs or bits of food were left around from the children's lunches. Janie O'Shea would usually do this, but she was off with chicken pox. They'd had an infestation of mice last October when the cold weather came – she'd had to borrow Nancy's black and white cat to put the run on them – and she was determined not to have a repeat invasion this year.

'Grace, here you are. I went to the house first, but I saw the gate open and thought you might be here.'

Grace looked up with a smile to see Father Iggy in his black soutane. 'How are you, Father, are you well?' She'd missed him today; usually he came in for a couple of hours in the afternoon to teach any children who needed extra help with their reading and writing.

Father Iggy was such an asset to Knocknashee National School. Between the priest and Janie O'Shea, who was fifteen now and received a small wage as school monitor, Grace really felt like she was getting a handle on the huge numbers of children who had enrolled. Eighty-nine this year, up seven from last year. Ever since she'd taken over as headmistress from Agnes, there were whole families of youngsters turning up she'd barely heard of before, from remote little farms up in the mountains.

'I'm... Well, to be honest, I'm not the best, Grace.'

She felt a stab of worry; he looked white and strange, not himself at all. 'What is it, Father? Has something bad happened?'

'I... No, no...nothing bad. Just...well, Bishop Reynolds thinks... I mean...' He took the duster from her desk and began to clean the blackboard.

'You don't have to do that,' she said, thinking with amusement about what Agnes would say if she could see the parish priest wiping the board, but also wondering what on earth was going on.

'I might as well make myself useful while we're talking.' He started placing the children's little chairs up on the desks.

'Father Iggy, please tell me what's the matter? And what is it that the bishop thinks?'

'Bishop Reynolds thinks… Well…hmm. He thinks…well, that it's time for me to move on to a different parish.'

'Oh, Father Iggy, no.' Tears came into her eyes; this was terrible news. She sank down into her chair behind her desk as he swallowed, clearly upset by the news, though he couldn't say it outright of course; it was not for him to criticise the bishop or question the Church.

'So that's it, Grace.' He straightened a crooked painting of the bay done by a pupil. 'I'm sad about leaving Knocknashee, I'm not ashamed to say it, but we clergy are not masters of our own destiny. I must go where I'm sent. But I wanted you to hear it from me.' He tried to smile, but she saw the pain there. He didn't want to go, she could tell, but priests had to be obedient. Even admitting he was sad was more than he should say.

'And where are they sending you?' she asked.

'To Cork…'

'Oh! Well, Cork is nice. Which parish?' It was a long way off, but it cheered her to think she'd be able to see him when she went to visit the Warringtons, as she did maybe twice a year.

'Blackpool Parish, on the north side of the city. The bishop feels they could use more help, what with being such a big parish, so that's where I'm headed.'

'Oh, Father Iggy…' She didn't trust herself to go on. This decent, kind and gentle man was being sent into the poor, tough area of Cork city from the gentle, rural parish of Knocknashee, where he was minded by Dymphna O'Connell and loved by all. It was going to be a big change for him and didn't seem fair.

'Ah now, Grace, 'twill be all right. I'm looking forward to the challenge, and I must go where the bishop thinks I can do the most good.'

'And when will you go?' she asked miserably. 'Do we at least get to keep you for Christmas?'

'No, the bishop wants me gone as soon as possible. This Sunday will be my last Mass said in Knocknashee – I'll use it to say goodbye –

and by the following Sunday, I'll be concelebrating with the four other priests in Blackpool.'

'Oh, Father…' She was shaken. Even when the canon got moved on, rumour had it for having his hand in the collection plate, there had been a time lag of months while everything was sorted out.

'Ah well, I'm sure it's for the best. And Father Lehane will hold the fort once I'm gone. He's a nice man.'

'He is, but we'll miss you so much, Father Iggy, all of us. And the children in the school, well, I don't know what I'll tell them. They really are so fond of you, with your great stories for them and all the things you tell them about.' She hated the thought of the little faces of the boys and girls when they heard their lovely Father Iggy was to be taken from them.

'I'll miss you all, too.' The priest looked ruefully around the classroom at the forty-five paintings pegged up on the washing line and the shelves that were stocked with books.

There was quite a big library now in both rooms, because as chair of the school board, Father Iggy was always thinking of what to buy to improve the children's learning. Because of him they'd always had enough art supplies, and a big globe as well as a large colourful map of the world and another of Ireland to replace the one torn down by the brutal Francis Sheehan, the teacher the canon brought in after Agnes sacked Grace.

Her mind was still in a whirl. 'I just don't understand, Father. Everything was going so well…'

The little priest walked up and down a few paces, his hands clasped behind his back, and seemed in two minds about whether to tell her something. 'Well, it's my own fault. But Grace – and you must never tell Dymphna this – the thing is, Bishop Reynolds was very cross about me blessing the *cillín*. He found out somehow – I think someone complained. Sure I suppose I should have petitioned him first really, but I genuinely didn't think he'd mind.'

She was horrified. This was awful. Who had betrayed Father Iggy? Had Father Lehane disapproved and said something? But the curate was far too nice to do anything to hurt Father Iggy, and besides, he was very fond of Dymphna and she of him; he was just the sort of lost soul she liked to rescue.

At least Dymphna's job as housekeeper was safe, because Father Lehane would definitely keep her on when he became the parish priest instead of Father Iggy. 'I wonder who Father Lehane's curate will be?' she said, half to herself. She hoped he would be a nice man, and maybe a bit less shy than the current curate.

'Ah...' Father Iggy, who had begun to pace again, threw her a nervous look. 'Well...'

Her heart sank. Why did he look so upset? 'Is it someone...' She wanted to say 'awful' but didn't, because Father Iggy never said a bad word about anyone, not even about Kit Gallagher when she was starving him and Father Lehane half to death, and especially not about fellow members of the clergy. It simply wasn't acceptable for a priest to criticise other clerics.

'Father Lehane is staying on as curate.'

'Oh? But you said he was going to...'

'Hold the fort, I know, but just until my replacement comes in.'

'I see.' She felt disappointed for Father Lehane, but he was very young and new, she supposed, maybe too raw for the bishop to promote. 'Then who is going to be the next parish priest? Do we know?'

'We do, Grace. It's Canon Rafferty.'

She felt the colour drain from her face and ice water churn in her stomach. Her heart thumped in her chest, a prickle of sweat on her back. This couldn't be happening, surely not. It was too much to bear, losing Father Iggy, universally adored, and to have the dreadful canon back, universally loathed.

'And it's definitely to be the canon returning, is it?' Her voice sounded weak.

She felt terrible that her biggest concern had suddenly become not the loss of her friend Father Iggy but the imminent arrival of Canon Rafferty back to Knocknashee.

He hung his head. 'That's what the bishop said, and I've no reason to doubt it.'

Grace had never told Father Iggy the things Agnes had revealed to her about Canon Rafferty when she was dying. Up until then, Grace had thought the worst thing the canon had done was to knowingly collude with Agnes to misuse Grace's wages. But he was so much more wicked than that.

It seemed Agnes had fallen in love with Canon Rafferty when she was just a girl, and though Grace would never know if their relationship went beyond infatuation on Agnes's part and encouragement of that on his, he had used his position of power to manipulate her sister into dreadful wrongdoing. Agnes hadn't just stolen Grace's savings to wine and dine the man she idolised; she had helped him spirit Charlie McKenna's newborn daughter, Siobhán, away to America and sell her to a childless couple there for three thousand pounds – money that went straight into Canon Rafferty's pocket.

But these weren't things she could tell another priest.

'I was sure he was gone to Tipperary for good.'

'Well, no,' said Father Iggy, squirming with the awkwardness of having to defend the bishop's decision. 'It was only a temporary posting, it would seem. The bishop has communicated to me that the canon was only needed in Tipperary for a short time while the Monsignor there recovered from illness, but thanks be to God, the man was restored to full health and so the canon is able to come back now that there's a vacancy here.'

'But Father, what am I going to do?' she burst out, unable to help herself. 'If he's the head of the school board instead of you, what will happen to us, all the progress we've made, the books, the art?' She felt like adding that the poor children were terrified of the canon, and with good reason, but again she held back out of respect for the difficult position the priest was in, having to defend the Church.

'The school will be fine, Grace. Sure you're in a great position to continue, lots of experience.'

'There's no point in pretending, Father. I know we are good friends, you and I, but I don't get on so well with the canon.'

'Well, I'm sure Canon Rafferty will see the great work you've been doing here, and what a marvellous teacher Declan is becoming, and

Janie as well now, and he will be very pleased to see how you and Declan are working towards your qualifications, which will make your jobs even more secure...' His voice trailed off, because of course he wasn't sure of any such thing.

Grace just sat there in silence, trying to take it all in. How was she going to cope? She'd faced the canon down once, and won; she'd forced him to make her headmistress of the school so she could sack the dreadful Francis Sheehan. But that was when poor Agnes was still alive, as a potential witness to the way he'd stolen Grace's money... and Agnes was now dead.

Father Noel Dempsey in New York knew about the canon selling babies, but the canon had accused Father Dempsey of being the culprit, and now the innocent priest was essentially incarcerated in a retirement home in New York, playing endless games of chess against himself.

Father Iggy tried to smile at her. 'Please don't worry. You really are a wonderful teacher, and I hope you know that. Canon Rafferty will see it too. Especially in these worrying times, when everything is scarce and parents are worried, you make school a bright place where they can just be children, full of joy and wonder.'

'Thank you, Father,' she said dully, knowing the canon hated nothing so much as joy and wonder, in children or adults. 'And you'd have made a fine teacher yourself, but your vocation led you to a higher calling. And that's as it should be,' she added quickly, in case he thought she was suggesting he would make a better teacher than priest.

'Thank you, Grace. I've loved it here, and teaching the children what bit I did was a great honour for me.' He smiled sadly. 'Now I'd best get on, lots to do.'

Standing at the school door, she watched him walk away down the street towards the church, his head bowed and feet shuffling slowly, and then she went into her own house with an equally heavy heart.

* * *

THE WORST THING was having to tell Declan and Charlie about Canon Rafferty.

Charlie had made such a lovely dinner of lamb stew and potatoes, onions and carrots – it was delicious – but Grace had to force it down, she felt so sick at the thought of breaking the awful news.

Only last March Declan had threatened to go to Tipperary and drag the truth out of Canon Rafferty about where his little sister, Siobhán, had been taken when the canon decided Declan's newly widowed father was unfit to rear his own children. Declan was terrified that his sister was out in the world somewhere, maybe suffering the same kinds of abuse he'd had to endure growing up in the terrifying orphanage of Letterfrack.

Before he could carry out his threat, though, Richard had gone to New York and tracked Siobhán McKenna down. She was fifteen-year-old Lily Maheady now, of Rockaway Beach, New York, with an Irish-American father and an Italian-American mother. Declan and Grace had visited, under the pretence of Declan being a distant cousin of the father. And he saw with his own eyes that the girl had loving, caring parents and a happy, carefree life, and that had taken away a lot of his pain and rage.

Even better, Lily's mother, Sylvia Maheady – perhaps guessing the unspoken truth – had written to Charlie, who had been unable to go to America because he'd come down with shingles, sending him photos of Lily and her little sister, Ivy.

Charlie had gazed at Siobhán's photo for the longest time when it first arrived, unable to speak – apparently she looked so like her mother, it was uncanny – and now the photographs were on display in frames on the dresser. It was as happy an outcome as it could have been.

But despite Declan being relieved about Siobhán, Grace knew there was still a vulnerable part of him that he kept tucked away, the hurt boy who spent so long in Letterfrack, not knowing why his father didn't come for him...and hating and fearing Canon Rafferty for ruining his childhood.

She still hadn't said anything by the time Declan cleared the plates away and cut three slices of apple tart and Charlie made the tea. But when they were all sitting around the table again, she finally brought herself to tell them what Father Iggy had told her.

'Rafferty is coming back here, to Knocknashee?' Charlie went quite white.

Declan stared at her in horror. 'That snake is going to be walking the streets of this town again, putting the heart crossways in everyone?'

'He is. I'm dreading it too, and I just know he's going to make the children's lives miserable, coming into the school and beating them if they don't recite their catechism perfectly,' she said.

'We won't let him,' said Declan firmly.

'I wish it was that simple. He'll be chairman of the board of management and can sack us any time. He can easily argue that we're not even qualified teachers, and we won't have a leg to stand on.'

'I could tell him I know he sold my baby sister for three thousand pounds,' said Declan darkly.

'No, we can't do that, Declan, we can't have any investigation into Siobhán's situation,' said Charlie quickly. 'She doesn't know she's adopted. If we make a thing of it now, she might get to find out somehow. It wouldn't be right. The Maheadys are good parents. They don't deserve to have their lives turned *trine chéile* because we have a grudge against that terrible man.'

'Then what can we do?' Declan sighed deeply as he ran his fingers through his dark hair.

'We'll just all stand together, all of us, as a town – you, me, Grace and everyone. We won't let him scare and divide us like he did before – we have the measure of him now. And he won't have Agnes Fitzgerald as the headmistress backing him up and doing his dirty work for him. God rest her soul,' Charlie added hastily, remembering Agnes had been Grace's sister. 'And sure Father Lehane will still be curate, and Dymphna will be the housekeeper, so that will help. She won't treat him like a god like Kit Gallagher did.'

'Mm...' Declan looked doubtful, and Grace knew he was thinking the same thing she was – that the idea of either Father Lehane or the soft-hearted widow having the courage to stand up to the canon about anything was probably wishful thinking. But Charlie was right; there were plenty in the town who had the measure of the canon now, and maybe he'd realise that and stay out of people's way?

* * *

THE NIGHT WAS NOT FULLY DARK when she got home. She thought she would fill her bath and soak for a while. Her leg was aching badly, as it sometimes did after an art class; there was a lot of walking around and bending over the children's desks, then the clearing up afterwards.

She rested in the hot water and allowed her mind to wander as the heat worked its magic.

She'd done two hours of study with Declan. It was even more imperative that they be qualified as soon as possible now that the canon was back, and working together was wonderful. She enjoyed the funny way Declan saw things, and his quick mind and the simple way he explained things that she didn't understand, like a complicated maths equation, and the respectful way he listened when she knew something better than he did, about geography or history.

They'd talked some more about how to deal with the canon and decided to see first if his move to Tipperary had put manners on him at all. He might be afraid of a repeat move if he overstepped any marks.

Still, she should have a word with Janie O'Shea. The canon didn't love Janie either, because one of the reasons Grace sacked his protegee Francis Sheehan was because he pushed little Janie against the wall before slapping the boy who defended her across the face.

At fifteen, Janie was only just old enough to be a school monitor, which was a tenuous position, but she could perhaps study in the evenings as well to become a teaching assistant, then later a fully qualified teacher herself.

Yes, she should talk to Janie, just advise her to stay out of the canon's way as much as possible; she'd do that on Sunday when she saw her at Mass. Father Iggy's last Mass…so impossible to believe. He was such a good friend, she hated to lose him. At least they could write, and when she visited the Warringtons, she could visit him, but it wouldn't be the same as meeting him in school or in the street. And she wasn't the only one who would feel his loss keenly. Everyone loved his Masses. His sermons were often funny, and he spoke of love, friendship and compassion, of how Jesus was a friend to those others shunned and how nobody was without fault, so there should be less judgement and condemnation and more understanding and kindness. The opposite of that other spiteful wretch, who loved to decree from on high how they were all rotten with sin and must repent constantly. People left Father Iggy's Mass with a smile on their face and a renewed energy to spread goodwill, whereas people left the canon's Masses feeling spiritually battered.

The future looked bleak on several fronts. The war was raging; Hitler was proving to be a formidable enemy. And she'd just read how the government in the South of France, which was, according to Charlie, just a puppet government for the Germans, had decided to lock up anyone they deemed a threat to the state, communists being their main target. She thought often of Odile's parents and Alfie and Constance and said a prayer they were safe.

Her mind wandered on again, down the highways and byways of her life. Still no letter from Richard. Was there something she'd said or done when he was in Knocknashee that had bored him or put him off their friendship?

He'd acted delighted with it all, and even with her, but his life was so big, so full of important things. He was a war correspondent, and it didn't get more serious than that. Probably he'd been sent off on another mission already and the last thing he had time for was to write to the headmistress of a two-room school in a tiny town with one cobbled street, perched on the edge of Ireland between the mountains and the sea.

Or maybe he had written. Charlie had said the post was patchy. Though she'd not heard of any ship going down or anything like that.

Not that the Irish newspapers were reporting anything, so that didn't mean much.

The water had cooled, and she reached for the hot water with her toe to get the sensation of more heat on her leg…but the water ran cold. The gas had run out. She hoped it wasn't an omen of her future in Knocknashee, all that had been so pleasant turning cold.

CHAPTER 5

SEPTEMBER 1940 THE SS ODEON - NEW YORK TO LISBON

Lucille had managed to get Richard and Jacob travel documents and tickets to sail aboard the *SS Odeon* to Lisbon, the only free port left on the European continent. Because of the German blockade around Britain, sailing directly there wasn't an option. As a favour to them, she'd also procured the same documents for Sarah, once Richard had sworn that she was his sister and working as his translator, not a girlfriend he was trying to sneak in. That she was in fact Jacob's girlfriend was another omission. Lucille didn't need to know that.

The two of them decided to make a brief stopover in Detroit on the way to New York to see Nathan and Rebecca and the girls – the unspoken reason being in case something awful happened and they never got to see their older brother and his family again.

Nathan hugged both of them tightly when they left. Like their father, he was normally more inclined to shake hands, but the fact they were going into danger broke through his defences.

'Take care, you guys, and come home safe. Don't take any dumb risks...'

As they set off for the train station, Nathan and his wife and daughters stood waving to them from the top step, and Richard waved back out of the rear window of the cab. 'Nathan's a lucky man, such lovely children,' he said, as the little family group dwindled out of sight.

'I'd say he envies us, though,' said Sarah, leaning back in the corner of her seat.

'You think?' He was surprised. He'd always perceived his older brother as completely self-assured and content in his way of life.

'Of course he does. Who wouldn't? Off on our adventures, doing as we please, answerable to no one...'

He laughed. 'Kirky might say different.'

'Don't worry about Kirky, he's putty in my hands. But seriously, Richard, would you want to be settled down with children at this moment in history? Laden with responsibility, a wife like Rebecca to be kept in fancy clothes, daughters who need piano lessons, everything pulling at you, stopping you from spreading your wings? While you and me, we're off to the other side of the Atlantic, and not just witnessing history but writing about it for a newspaper, and maybe influencing public opinion in a way that might save the world.'

He looked out of the window at the large expensive houses, each accommodating a well-off professional family. 'You're right, I suppose.'

'Of course I am,' she said, as pedantic as their father. 'And that's the price of marriage. You settle down, you have children. The journey is over. I love Jacob, but I'm glad he thinks like me, that especially while this war carries on, there are more important things than diapers and dentist visits.'

Richard was reminded of Paul and Bernadette Dreyfus, entrusting their baby to his and Jacob's care while they stayed to fight. He wondered how they were and hoped they were safe. Alfie and Constance too. Now that was real bravery – to be in the thick of the war, not just reporting on it.

Still thinking of family, his mind went to Grace, as it so often did. She still hadn't written back to him. He woke up in a cold sweat some nights, convinced his letter had horrified her. He was glad he'd sent it, though. Sarah had been right. Just getting his feelings for her off his chest had allowed him to breathe. He'd spoken the truth, and now it was up to Grace, for better or worse. Each day he waited was torture, however, and now he was leaving, and if she did write, the letter would arrive in St Simons when he was on the way to Lisbon. Esme would forward anything that arrived, but with everything so precarious in the world right now, he wasn't confident he'd even get it.

That was if she replied at all. She might not. Or maybe she would write back to say she loved him. Maybe she wouldn't. Maybe she would but add that she wasn't ready to give up everything she knew, that the price of their being together was him coming to live in Knocknashee, settling down, having children.

How would he feel about that? It would be so strange, so alien, like walking into a different world. Could he live there? Could he learn Irish? What would he work at? He could hardly become a fisherman or a farmer, which is what most people there seemed to do. Could he write for an Irish newspaper? But Knocknashee was so far from everywhere – he supposed he'd have to live in Dublin or at least Cork if he was to do that?

He sighed and pushed away the thought. There was no point in him worrying about it; it was all in the hands of the gods. If Grace loved him, she loved him, and they would work it out.

If she didn't... He shut that thought down.

Meanwhile there was the war.

* * *

JACOB WAS ALREADY in New York, visiting with his uncle for the same reason they'd stopped off to see Nathan and his family, and Sarah and Richard checked into a respectable hotel. Nothing like the St Regis on Fifth Avenue – Jacob would have a canary if he saw that place – but clean and decent.

His sister had made an appointment to see Kirky the following morning and flatly refused to have Richard or Jacob along. Kirky had agreed in theory to her going to Europe with them, pending meeting her. 'If I want to present myself as a capable human being, I can't have my little brother and my boyfriend being all patronising about what a great little woman I am,' she said firmly. 'I'm doing this my way or no way at all.' More shades of their father.

While she was at the offices of the *Capital*, Richard popped down the road to visit Mrs McHale, who the last time he was in New York seeing Kirky had spent all day helping him track down Father Noel Dempsey in the parishes directory.

The Irishwoman greeted him with delight and wanted to know how he'd got on, had he found the priest, was the priest the one he was looking for, and if he was, did Richard get what he wanted from him, because there was surely more to the story than he'd let on at the time.

Richard was reminded of a book he'd read a few years ago, *The Murder at the Vicarage* by an English novelist named Agatha Christie; it starred an old lady of similar age to Mrs McHale, who had an equally inquiring – some might say nosy – mind and the same relentless style of questioning. Miss Marple was her name, and he smiled at the similarity. Mrs McHale looked like a sweet old grandma, but underneath she was sharp as a tack.

After Mrs McHale plied him with coffee and cake in the sitting room, he gave in and explained about the babies who were sold for three thousand pounds apiece, until one of the adoptive parents complained to the bishop about the exorbitant price and the finger got pointed at Father Dempsey, who was innocent.

Mrs McHale's eyes widened; she was horrified but also intrigued. 'This woman Agnes Fitzgerald was selling babies, and it got blamed on that poor priest?'

'Agnes Fitzgerald only sold one. The others were brought over and sold by a woman named Kit Gallagher.'

'Oh dear, oh dear.' She poured herself a third cup of tea from the enormous teapot, shaking her head. 'How could women do such evil things? I pray it worked out well for the little mites at least...'

'Well, I suppose the real villain of the piece was a priest named Canon Rafferty. He was the one who blamed Father Dempsey for taking money for the baby that was complained about to the bishop.'

'*Canon Rafferty?*' Mrs McHale's voice dripped with distaste, and her lips pursed into a thin line of contempt.

He stared at her in shock. 'You *know* him?'

'I do, Mr Lewis.' She nodded. 'I've never met him, but I've heard tell of him, and that's quite enough for me to believe what you're saying. I spent all my childhood holidays in Dingle, remember, and still have relatives there –'

'Of course. I remember you said.'

'– and they told me the priest in Knocknashee was, well… Hmm. This is not right. So, Mr Lewis, if you don't mind, I'm going to look into this. That poor Father Dempsey should not be taking the blame for that other awful man. He was only trying to do the right thing and is being punished for it. I can't believe the poor bishop fell for it. He's such a dote, but he's easily fooled. You know how these clergymen are.' She dropped her voice to a conspiratorial whisper. 'The best in the world and what have you, but not exactly able for real life, if you know what I mean? Another coffee, Mr Lewis?'

* * *

'So Kirky agreed to put you on the payroll,' Richard said to his sister as they made their way across the almost empty deck to the stern, where Jacob leant over the railings, taking photos of the Manhattan skyline.

The *Odeon* had pulled away with no flag waving or cheers, just silently forging its way out into the potentially treacherous seas. With only thirty passengers on board, they'd been allocated a cabin each, and it was such a different experience from the journey they'd had back in June, when they'd been crammed in like sardines.

'Is that disapproval I hear, little brother?' Sarah arched an eyebrow in reply. 'Of a little woman like myself demanding a real wage, like a man?'

'Not at all. It's just Kirky can be a tough nut to crack.'

'Well, I can be very persuasive. I told him he needed me to keep you two out of trouble and to stop Jacob in particular from storming the Reichstag. Men always assume girls are more risk averse, that we'll be sensible and refuse to let our men do rash things, so he went for it.'

'I can't believe he could sit in a room with you face to face and believe you'd be the cautious one.' He grinned.

She punched him lightly on the arm. 'I'm more sensible than either of you and twice as smart. And he only offered about half of what you two are getting, so don't worry, I'm not suddenly being treated as your equal or anything.'

'But you are my equal,' he said seriously.

'I am?'

'Yes, you are.' He put his hand on her shoulder as they walked, surprised to see a sensitivity there that he wasn't used to in his normally confident older sister. 'And make sure you ask me for money if you need it, don't go short.'

'I don't think I will. Daddy lodged a hundred dollars into my account,' she said, less prickly now.

He gave her shoulder a squeeze, pleased with their father for supporting her. 'Good to hear. I told him I'd send a telegram once we dock.'

'Sure.'

Neither of them mentioned their mother.

They reached the railing and stood a few feet away from Jacob, keeping out of the way of his work. He snapped the Statue of Liberty as it got smaller and smaller and the wide white wake stretched behind them, screaming gulls circling overhead.

'It's so strange to be going back when everyone else is trying to get home to the States, don't you think?' she asked as she scanned the scene behind them.

Richard considered her question. 'It is, and it's daunting, but I'm excited too. I know it's not going to be a party, but something about being right where the action is, seeing it for myself, is exhilarating. I don't want to sit this one out.'

'And will you try to get over to Ireland again?' When he said nothing, she looked at him sympathetically. 'Still no word? Well, you never know, maybe her answer got lost or the boat sank or something.'

He shrugged. 'Maybe. I'm still glad I wrote to her, though.'

'Will you write again, even if you hear nothing back?'

'I will. I asked her to just carry on writing as if I'd never mentioned my feelings if she isn't interested, and I think she will. One of the reasons I was so conflicted about writing the truth was I didn't want to jeopardise our friendship. I sure hope, even if she's not interested in me romantically, that she feels the friendship is worth saving. Besides, I have to tell her about Miss Marple.'

'Miss Marple?' her brow furrowed in thought. 'You mean from Agatha Christie?'

He laughed. 'I meant to say Mrs McHale, though she is like Miss Marple. She's planning to dig up some dirt on Canon Rafferty. She's furious about the other guy, Father Noel Dempsey, having to take the blame.' On the long journey north, he'd filled Sarah in on the whole story. 'If Grace ever runs into the canon again, some damaging information might come in handy for her.'

She touched his arm approvingly. 'You're a good man, little brother. You put your heart on the line, and even though you've heard nothing back, you're still not going to abandon her as a friend.'

'Of course not. To me, her friendship is the most important thing, and that's what I told her.'

Despite his words, couldn't help but feel a pang of envy as Sarah stepped away from him and put her hand on Jacob's shoulder. The photographer put his arm around her waist, the two of them leaning against each other, gazing towards the horizon as the ship forged powerfully through the waves. His sister had both a friend and lover in Jacob.

He wished he could have the same.

* * *

A FEW HOURS into the voyage, they were all called to a meeting in the dining room, where the captain explained that boat drills would be frequent and were to be taken extremely seriously, as the threat of attack was imminent. The ship sailed under full lights with the letters USA painted port and starboard, and the stars and stripes waved fore and aft. This, he said, he hoped would be enough, as U-boats would have been warned not to interfere with American ships for fear of provoking a military response from Washington, but that was just a hope, not a certainty. Hitler was not known for sticking to the rules.

'If the siren is heard, go immediately to your muster station. Take nothing but the bare essentials. You should already be dressed warmly. Sleep fully dressed – I don't want to see anyone shivering on deck at 3 a.m. in pyjamas. Be prepared to go to the lifeboats immediately if you are instructed to do so. I need no histrionics, nor do I want anyone deciding it's just a drill and rolling over in bed. I have full authority on this ship, and I will ensure that my orders are followed to the letter of the law. Am I making myself clear?'

The thirty passengers all nodded nervously.

That night the siren awoke him with a start. After the captain's warning, he had slept in his clothes, so all he had to do was take his passport and his papers, stuff them into a pouch he had around his neck under his undershirt, shirt and sweater and, meeting Jacob and Sarah in the corridor, make his way with them to the muster station. He wished he could take his Underwood portable typewriter, but the captain had been adamant – nothing but yourself and the bare essentials. He didn't think the man would see a typewriter as an essential unfortunately.

There they were instructed to put on life jackets and get into the lifeboats. An hour later, once the captain was confident everyone knew what to do, they were allowed to return to bed. Several times on the voyage it happened, and each time it turned out to be a drill, but no one complained; it was always a relief to find out it hadn't been real.

The purser, Andy Pawlowski, was a funny guy from Queens, New York, with the broadest New York accent Richard had ever heard. As they trudged to the deck for yet another drill, shivering in the salty sea-sprayed breeze, he would shout, 'This will only take loooong if ya make it take loooong!'

Sarah loved to mimic him and insisted on actively following him around just to hear him speak, and Richard interviewed him, thinking his might be a good story, how he and his fellow crewmen got an extra buck a day in their pay for doing this route, and that while the trip back to the States from Europe was murder – too many people, not enough crew – they got a break on the trip over. This was Andy's third trip to Lisbon.

He was a Yankees fan, sure they were headed for a win in the World Series, and ribbed Richard about his team, the Detroit Tigers, so they had an easy rapport.

'You guys know you're gonna have to wait for a while in Lisbon, right?' he asked as he leant over the rail with his cigarette, flicking ash to the stiff starboard breeze as Richard scribbled in shorthand in his reporter's notebook and Jacob clicked away with his camera.

'We were told to go to the US consulate?' Jacob looked out from behind his lens. 'And we'd get a berth to England?'

'Yeah, you gotta do that, but that city is the only free port in Europe, ain't hardly elbow room there, refugees from all over, everyone tryin' to get out. People book their passage before they get the papers, before they leave home, some of 'em, so a lot of the people we got booked on won't never show, so we take whoever we can, based on priority. The consul there ain't got time to wipe his ass, poor schmuck, what a crummy job he got...'

He smiled and apologised to Sarah for his crude language; she was stretched out in a deck chair nearby, listening.

She laughed. 'I'm not as sensitive as I look.'

'Well, yeah, the guy is battin' people off all day every day. You can't get a visa without a ticket, but havin' a ticket don't mean nothin' if you don't get the stamp sayin' you can go. Desperate people, Jews a lot of them, they'll go anywhere – South America, the States, Dutch East

Indies, England, wherever they can get to. It's a mess, let me tell ya, so I'd settle in for a wait if I was you.'

When they docked in Lisbon a week later, after what was thankfully an uneventful crossing, the purser shook their hands. 'Good luck, you guys. You're gonna need it.'

* * *

THE CAPTAIN ORDERED the gangplank be removed immediately after the handful of passengers were off the ship. Long lines were waiting on the quay, people ready to take their places aboard, hundreds and hundreds of them, it seemed, and the captain was afraid of being rushed by desperate people.

Andy was right; Lisbon was teeming with people of every nationality. Several languages could be heard, and there were men in uniform everywhere, some Allied, some Germans. Intermixed with them were so many women and children. Richard wondered where the locals were. It was a beautiful hilly city with cobbled streets, and the white stone buildings seemed to glisten in the autumn sunshine. The ocean sparkled, and if it were not for the almost palpable panic and despair in the air and the huge overcrowding, it would have been an idyllic place to stay. Maybe when this war was over, he'd take Grace here, he thought.

They went to the consul as instructed and handed in their credentials and, after an hour's wait in a packed corridor, were ushered into an office.

'Welcome to insanity.' The man who summoned them spoke with a Chicago accent, pronouncing 'insanity' like *inseaanity*. He was in his thirties, tall and thin, and looked exhausted. His shirt needed to be washed, and he had a week's worth of stubble on his hollow cheeks.

'I'm Donald West, an assistant to the consul. I know you've got clearance to get to England, and we will do our best, but as you can see' – he gestured to the hordes outside – 'the embassies decide who goes where. Germany, Italy, Britain and us all have airline offices here, but you need to get the go-ahead from the embassy first. So what I can do is register you now, and if you try this *pension*, it's what they call a boarding house, you might get a room, or two if you're lucky.' He passed them a piece of paper with a name and address on it, adding, 'We'll let you know when we can get you out.'

'How long will it be, do you think?' Jacob asked.

The man shrugged, 'A week, a month, who knows? We'll let you know. It's based on priority so…'

'Aren't journalists priority?' Richard didn't want to be pushy, clearly everyone here was dog-tired but if they didn't get to London, half the point of being here was gone.

'Sure they are…but so is everyone else, y'know what I mean? I'll send it through to the British – they want American newspapermen.' He glanced at Sarah. 'I don't know if they'll have room for a girl, though.'

'I work for the newspaper as well,' snapped Sarah.

'Sure you do.' He shrugged, too tired to be polite. 'So over there at the embassy, they might bump you up the list, who knows? It's not up to me, but I'll make sure they see it. That's the best I can do.'

He gathered their paperwork, handing it back. 'Don't worry, there's plenty of food and drink here, and with US dollars, you can get whatever you want. Welcome to Lisbon.'

Like Andy Pawlowski, the ship's purser, he pronounced it *Liz-ben*.

Then the meeting was over and they found themselves out on the street.

CHAPTER 6

KNOCKNASHEE, CO KERRY

Grace spent three weeks trying and failing to find a supply of bottled gas. The rationing was terrible. Coal and timber were also impossible to get, the turf was all anyone had now to burn, and they had to be sparing even with that. It was unseasonably cold, winter seemed to have come overnight. The house was cold all the time except in the kitchen, but what she missed most were her warm baths for managing the ache in her leg.

After she realised she was never going to be able to find gas, she asked Declan for help, and he said maybe he could find a way to run the system efficiently on turf without having to burn too much of it.

He spent all Saturday morning and most of the afternoon building a tightly sealed fireproof box with a funnel that didn't let a single bit of heat go anywhere but into the copper tank, which he insulated in a triple layer of sheep's wool, making it so bulky that it took up half the bathhouse; he had to move the bathtub further into the corner.

By the time he'd finished, his clothes were covered in oil and turf dust and he said he'd not come back into the house for fear he'd dirty the place, that he'd stay outside and wash himself down with water from the barrel of rainwater outside the back door.

While she was waiting for Declan to come in, she put the kettle on the turf-fired range for a cup of tea – the gas stove was also out of gas of course – and went to fetch a towel for him as well as an old green pullover of his that he'd left there when he was cutting the hedges between her house and the school; that way he wouldn't have to put his dirty shirt back on again.

When she stepped outside to give him the towel and jumper, he was leaning over the barrel, stripped to the waist, sluicing his torso and hands and arms and slicking back his dark hair with the rainwater, long enough when wet to plaster the nape of his neck. Grace found herself thinking his hair would have a bounce in it when it dried. She always used the same soft water to wash her own hair, as her mother had done before her, letting it dry naturally in the sunlight, and it made soft, shiny curls.

He looked over at her with a slight smile, then took the towel from her, rubbed the water out of his hair and began drying his arms and chest, which were toned and muscular. When he'd finished he handed it back to her and she gave him the old green knitted jumper, which he pulled on, one arm at a time, his dark-blue eyes never leaving hers.

Suddenly shy, she wondered why she was just standing there, watching him dress, but then he must be used to girls gawping at him, like Bridie Keohane following him to the beach to watch him swim.

'How is Bridie?' she asked, willing herself not to blush and act girlish around him. 'Is her foot any better?'

'I think her foot is just fine when she needs it to be,' he said, a touch of amusement in his voice.

'That's…good. She's a nice girl, isn't she?'

'She is. But not as nice as one particular girl, and I'm afraid I've had to explain to her that my heart is elsewhere.'

'Oh, poor Bridie, she must be very disappointed. Is it Sally O'Sullivan you prefer?' asked Grace lightly.

'It is not.'

'Then who?'

She asked the question teasingly, but instead of making a joke in return, he said nothing. In the silence as they stood looking at each other, she became aware that the wireless, another thing he had fixed for her, was playing a soft song in the kitchen, 'The Nearness of You' by the Glenn Miller Orchestra.

It isn't your sweet conversation
That brings this sensation, oh no.
It's just the nearness of you...

It was one she loved. When it came on the radio, she would often imagine someone holding her in his arms and dancing to it, and in her imagination, she would have two good legs and the man would be tall and handsome and...

'Will you dance Grace?' Declan asked, as if he'd read her mind.

She laughed with surprise. 'Oh no, I can't dance.' She indicated her leg, but he shrugged.

'Sure Tilly told me in Dingle you danced with the owner of Cullen's Celtic Cabaret himself, and he told you to never stop dancing. Have you danced since?'

Her eyes pricked with sudden happy tears at the memory of dancing with Peter Cullen. He'd been so kind to her and danced very slowly, and she'd thought at the time it was the best night of her life, that there'd never be a better one, ever, however long she lived. 'Not really. No. Not like that.'

'Well, if you can dance with Peter Cullen, you can dance with me.' He held out his arms, and somehow she just nodded and walked into them.

When you're in my arms and I feel you so close to me,
All my wildest dreams come true...

The song washed over them as they swayed in time, and he danced as slowly as Peter Cullen had, holding her, like she was really dancing, properly. She had to rest her cheek against the soft wool of his jumper. She could hear his heart beating steadily and felt the strength of his arms around her.

I need no soft lights to enchant me,
If you'll only grant me the right

To hold you ever so tight
And to feel in the night the nearness of you...

As the song stopped, she stepped back, but he reached down and tilted up her chin with one hand so their eyes met. A small smile lifted the corners of his mouth. 'Do you know now who I think is the nicest of all the girls, Grace?'

'Well, I...' She was beginning to wonder if she did know, but how could that be true? All the most beautiful girls for miles around fancied Declan McKenna and chased after him, lovely girls, tall and slender and light on their feet.

'It's you, Grace,' he said, so quietly she could barely hear him. 'It's only ever been you for me. You know that, I suppose?' His voice was husky with emotion.

'I didn't,' she said simply, quite bewildered. 'I really didn't.'

He ran his hand over her copper curls. 'You are so beautiful, but you have no idea, and that's what makes you even more special.'

'But I'm not...' It was such a kind thing for him to say, but all she could hear in her mind was Agnes's loud, harsh voice telling her no man would ever want to look at her, let alone marry her.

That funny, crazy, red-headed young policeman Brendan McGinty in New York had claimed he wanted to marry her after a week, but he was just a charming messer and he'd known she had to go back to Ireland; she still thought if she'd gone mad and said yes, he'd have changed his mind and run a mile. Declan was different. He was quiet and serious, and though he had a quirky sense of humour, he never said things he didn't mean.

'You are special,' he said softly, 'and more than that, you're special to me, Grace. And maybe I shouldn't have said this – I've been afraid to. And maybe I'm an awful eejit to think someone like you would look sideways at a fella like me, but I love you, so much that sometimes I think I'll drive myself mad from it all. So I was hoping, praying really, I suppose, that you might consider...'

Her head was spinning. Tilly had always joked he was in love with her. She hadn't believed it, but now...

'I know we're young,' he said softly, 'and I don't want to rush you into anything, so I won't. I just want to know, is there any chance for me at all or should I just forget about the whole thing?'

He drew back and looked at her, and she felt a wave of affection for him. He was such a warm person, and he'd always been so kind to her. What a fool she'd be to turn him down flat, to say he had no chance. Where would she ever find someone so handsome, so good, who loved her, who would always be there for her, who wouldn't just drop everything to go haring off into the distance when something more interesting called.

An image came into her head of Richard Lewis racing away across Knocknashee strand towards the bus, the sun in his blond hair…

'I will think about it, Declan, I really will. I will consider you, and I'm glad you asked.' The words sounded a little formal, even to her own ears, but his almost navy-blue eyes widened in pleasure and surprise.

'Really?'

She smiled. 'Really.'

'Can I kiss you, Grace?'

'Oh… I suppose.' She was hesitant as this seemed fast, but she was also curious and hopeful. Earlier this year it had been impossible to imagine that any man would ever want to kiss her. Agnes had always ruled out the idea of any man 'taking her on', as she put it. But then Brendan McGinty had rowed her out to the middle of the boating lake in Central Park and told her the polio didn't matter to him if she wanted to marry him. He'd kissed her gently on the lips, and it had been nice if rather surprising. She only had fond thoughts of the big muscle-bound New Yorker who called himself Irish, though nobody in his family had set foot in this country for generations.

'You suppose?' He looked a question at her, with a twinkle of fun in his eyes.

She laughed. 'Well, all right then. I mean, yes.' And she allowed him to pull her close. He dipped his head – he was a lot taller than she was – and she could see at this close distance his long curling lashes and the sprinkle of freckles across the bridge of his nose. He kissed her softly, lingeringly.

The memory of another kiss came into her mind. Richard Lewis, before he sprinted away across Trá na n-Aingeal, the angel's beach, had dropped a very brief kiss upon her mouth. But it was not like this. His kiss had been light, regretful, a kiss of farewell, but this was the kiss of a man who wanted her in his life forever, who would never leave her.

There was a rush of feet and a baby's bubbling laugh, and then Tilly burst in through the gate that led from the field behind the school, a bag over her shoulder and carrying Odile in her arms. Declan went back to towelling his damp hair.

'Hi, Declan, hi, Grace! We came up on the horse, didn't we, Odile? To see Aintín Grace and Uncail Declan…'

'Come here to me, *a stór*,' said Grace, taking Odile and burying her face in the child's darkening curls to cover her confusion. 'How lovely to see you.'

'I'll go then,' murmured Declan, gathering up his tools, his pale face softly flushed and a gleam in his dark-blue eyes as he glanced at Grace.

'*Slán*, Uncail Declan! Grace, guess who's coming to Knocknashee for definite?' Tilly was bubbling over with delight, her dark-grey eyes lit up with pleasure. She was dressed bizarrely as usual, in a man's pullover with red sleeves and a dark blue and mustard striped body and a pair of trousers held up with bailer twine, but everyone looked a bit bedraggled these days. The pullover was probably one she knit from ripping out another old jumper or blanket and tying the wool pieces together.

'Is it Alfie?' Grace's gaze trailed after Declan's departing figure, tall and narrow in his green jumper, with his dark hair drying into waves from the soft rainwater.

Tilly laughed. 'No, better than Alfie. Sorry, I don't mean that. Of course I shouldn't say better than my own brother, but still… Guess again!'

'Someone belonging to Odile?' She felt a pang of sadness, and then immediately guilty for it – of course she should be relieved if Odile's family were alive and coming to claim their precious daughter.

'No, not them either. It's Eloise! She's going to try and get here in the next couple of weeks, she says, sooner if she can. You know what the transport is like...'

The trains from Dublin to Dingle, and then the local buses, had become much less frequent in recent weeks due to fuel rationing, and everyone had to make do, in that as in everything else, travelling not when they wanted but when a seat was available.

'I mean, I'll be amazed if she gets here any sooner, but she wrote she's excited to see me and intends to move mountains. Oh, Grace, you're going to love her!' In her enthusiasm, Tilly clenched her fists with excitement, and Odile imitated her, squawking and bouncing vigorously up and down in Grace's arms until Grace was afraid she might drop her.

'That's wonderful news, Til. I'm happy for you. And Odile seems as excited as you are.' Odile let out a screech and waved her little arm in the direction of a branch on Grace's mother's cherry blossom tree, where a robin had landed.

'It's probably stupid, I know, and I only met her on the train but... Sorry, here, I'll go put the kettle on. I have some spuds and onions here for you, and turnips and cabbage.' She swung the cloth bag off her shoulder as they went together into the house, then dumped it on the kitchen table.

'Well, I won't starve with you around, Tilly, that's for sure.' Grace smiled as she took the cushions off the rocking chair and put them on the floor, propping Odile against them, while Tilly moved the kettle onto the hot part of the range. 'I'll get peeling those potatoes in a minute and make a shepherd's pie for dinner, though there'll be more carrots than lamb, but still. And I've some rhubarb in the larder – I'm so glad of all the work Dymphna did putting it in jars last spring – so I'll make a crumble for dessert if you want to stay. It will be too much for one.'

'No thanks, Grace. I need to get back to the farm and start trying to clean out Alfie's bedroom for Eloise – it's an absolute state. Mam and myself have just dumped everything we couldn't find a home for in there since he left. The whole place needs a clean really, but I haven't time. Why don't you invite Declan and Charlie?'

'Mm…' Grace moved away, busying herself warming the teapot and getting down mugs. When she turned around again, Tilly was looking at her askance.

'What are you blushing for, Grace? And come to think of it, why was Declan McKenna looking furtive earlier when I came in on top of you?'

'Tilly, he was not, of course he wasn't. He was just hot from working on the bath house. He's converted the boiler so it can burn turf…' Grace tried to sound nonchalant as she set the tea things on the table and sat down, but Tilly's eyes were dancing with devilment.

'Grace Fitzgerald, you are the world's worst liar. Tell me everything, this minute.'

Grace sighed. 'Like I said, Declan was trying to get the boiler working again. We can't get gas, so he was changing the –'

'For God's sake, Grace, stop blathering about the bloody boiler. Tell me what actually happened.'

'That's what happened! He fixed the boiler, and he was covered in oil and dust, and he washed in the rainwater, so I brought him a towel to dry himself and I gave him an old jumper he'd left here because his shirt was filthy.'

Tilly laughed and clapped her hands, and Odile imitated her, chortling and patting her soft little palms together. 'Go on, Grace, he was half naked and –'

'He was *not* half naked,' protested Grace crossly, her cheeks burning now. 'He put the jumper on straight away.'

'Well, something happened, didn't it? Tell me, or I won't let you alone at all, day and night. Haven't I told you everything about Eloise?'

'It's hardly the same,' said Grace, pouring the tea.

Tilly looked at her askance. 'And why is it not the same?'

'Because Eloise is a *friend*.'

Tilly grinned and pounced. 'I see. So you're saying, Declan is… something different from a friend?'

'I didn't say he wasn't a friend. We work together and we see each other every day, like we've always done.'

'But something happened that made him *more* than a friend? *Different* from a friend? Come on, Grace, spit it out and stop acting so coy. I'm going to get it out of you one way or another. What happened after he put his jumper on?'

She was usually good at keeping a steady face – years of teaching and dealing with Agnes had helped – but Tilly knew her so well that resisting her interrogation was probably futile. Definitely futile, in fact.

'All right, well then, a song came on the wireless. It's this one I really like, you know, it's called…um…'The Nearness of You'. It's the Glenn Miller Orchestra, and…'

'And?' Tilly demanded in frustration.

'And then he asked me to dance, like I'd done with Peter Cullen, so I did… And then…' Now her face was really burning; she felt so silly and naive.

'Then?' pressed Tilly, as Odile made *oohing* noises.

'Well, he asked…said that he liked me, and asked was there any chance for him at all or should he just forget about the whole thing, and…'

'And you said? God, Grace, it's like pulling teeth.'

'Well, I said I'd consider it. And then he asked if he could kiss me and I said yes, and it was nice.'

Tilly burst out laughing again. 'Nice? Is that all? Nice?'

'All right, it was very nice, lovely, great. I don't know the words to describe it, but it was good.'

'So when can I expect to walk you down the aisle?'

Grace chuckled at the thought of Tilly giving her away. 'Now don't go getting all excited about that. I only said I'd consider him. We're not getting engaged or anything like that. It's just a nice thing between us – we're not telling everyone.'

'I'd say Declan's already making plans. He must be over the moon.' Tilly was grinning hugely, and Odile clapped and cooed.

'Of course he isn't. He wouldn't!'

'Well, he'll have to tell Charlie anyway. He can hardly keep it from him any more than you can keep it from me.' Tilly stopped grinning then and looked serious. 'I suppose you'd better tell Richard.'

An odd little shadow crossed Grace's heart. 'Do you think? I was waiting for him to write back to me first?'

'But this changes things, Grace.'

'Changes things how?'

'Ah, come on, you know very well how. When he came to Knocknashee, I saw the way you looked at each other, and I know you say nothing happened when you went to the beach…'

'It didn't. We just talked, and then he had to rush off. And he said he'd write, but he hasn't, and there's other letters coming from America. Sure Lily sent a postcard to Declan the other day, "from his American cousin".'

'Did she? That's lovely. I don't know, though. I still think you should write to him even if he hasn't written to you. Don't you think you should, just to let him know? You owe him that, surely?'

'God bless all here,' Charlie called as he let himself in the front door. Grace never locked it. Unlike the days when Agnes ruled and nobody dared pop round, her house was an open house for her friends now and she loved that it was.

'I've come for a hammer Declan left here. He sent me for it rather than come over himself. He said he was in the middle of something…' Charlie headed for the door into the yard.

'Grace was just about to come over to invite you to dinner tonight,' Tilly shouted after him, with a naughty wink at Grace.

'Well, that would be lovely, thank you, Gracie. The few scraggy bits of mutton left in Carroll's weren't exactly appetising, but I was resigned to getting them on my way home for our tea, so you're saving us from that fate,' the postman smiled as he came back in with the hammer and went out through the front door again.

Grace glared at Tilly, who giggled madly.

'Well, I had to say it.' She chuckled again as Odile broke out into peals of laughter as well. 'Declan's gone too shy to come here and you've gone too shy to go there – someone has to give you two a helping hand!'

CHAPTER 7

Dear Richard...
She was at the kitchen table. The sitting room was out of bounds now because fuel was so scarce. She could only afford to light the range and not any of the fires in the house.

Charlie and Declan had come to dinner as Tilly had arranged; they weren't long gone home. They'd had shepherd's pie and rhubarb crumble and chatted about Lily's postcard. Everything felt so normal, it was like nothing had been said between her and Declan only a few hours ago. But as she saw them out, Declan pulled her aside and whispered with a grin, 'Da is quizzing me all day, he says I look shifty. I think he guesses.'

She'd smiled up at him and squeezed his hand.

'To be honest, Tilly got most of it out of me earlier. She knew something had gone on because we were both blushing.'

She wondered what Charlie would think if Declan told him. She hoped he'd be pleased. He had become such a father figure in her life, and now if she and Declan did end up getting married, they would be related. She found the idea of joining the McKennas appealed to her.

I realise you must be so busy, so I thought I would write to you instead of waiting for you to write to me. I'm sending this to you at the Capital *in New*

York because I don't know where you are and I assume they do. But wherever it is, I hope you're safe. I pray for you every day.

Life here is all go as usual. It's hard to believe it is, I know, Knocknashee being such a little place, but for us it is a hive of activity.

Tilly has a friend coming to see her, a Swiss woman called Eloise. She met her on the train from Dublin. She seems delighted with her. I hope Eloise is as miraculously wonderful as she's being made out to be. The way Tilly is going on about her, I will be disappointed if she's anything short of an angel.

Odile is so sweet now – I wish you could see her. She can roll over and sit up with cushions and has two bottom teeth. She imitates Tilly in everything. If Tilly laughs, she laughs, and if Tilly gets overexcited, she bounces around as well. We are praying every day that Alfie and his girlfriend, Constance, are alive and well, and also Paul and Bernadette Dreyfus. I can't imagine how life is for them now. The press here is very vague about it all, and we've had no letter from him. People here remember what living under a hostile regime is like, so they have sympathy for the countries Hitler has invaded.

I have very sad news, I'm afraid. Father Iggy has gone, banished to the streets of Cork city. Everyone misses him so much; he was so kind. Father Lehane is running the show at the moment. He's so shy, we can hardly hear his sermons – he tends to mumble – and he's afraid to come into the school, but at least he is a nice man. That's not the worst of it, though. It seems Canon Rafferty is coming back, the hellfire sermons and him denouncing everyone from the pulpit. Living in terror of putting a toe astray is not something we are looking forward to.

It will be especially difficult for Charlie to have to put up with him, now that he knows the true story of what happened to his baby daughter, though thanks to you, Richard, he knows his precious girl is safe and sound and well loved. Lily sent a postcard the other day of the beach she lives near, and Ivy, her little sister, signed it as well. It's pinned now to the dresser in Charlie's kitchen, next to the framed photos of the girls.

I'm praying Canon Rafferty will give me a wide berth, though he'll be chairman of the school. It's a worry now that Agnes is dead. I did have something on him while she lived, but now the only one to corroborate his wrongdoing is dead. So it's my word against his and I don't think I'd stand much of a chance going up against him. Hopefully he'll think I have enough evidence *about him living high on the hog on my wages and won't want to risk annoying me in case I go to the bishop. Before he left he was very smarmy towards me, though to be honest, smarmy is even worse than him looking at me with those cold gimlet eyes. He's like a snake either way with his whispery voice. When I think of how he manipulated my sister, it makes me shudder.*

The weather is brightening up here. It was terribly cold last week and I was fearful we were getting an early winter, but as she does, Mother Nature changed her mind again and it seems an Indian summer is happening, which is something to be cheerful about even if the news about the war isn't. Lizzie tells me what she reads in the English papers in the ladies' reading room in Cork, and even they are censored now, with some articles cut out of them. Richard, you are the best source of information for me; I don't know what I'd do without you. I loved your articles from Paris. So please, even if you're too busy to write, keep sending me your clippings in the post, even if it's just about what is going on in America.

There was a piece in a British newspaper about the persecution of Catholics in Germany, which was shocking. Nuns in Nazi prisons, priests in concentration camps, Catholic leaders shot, even cardinals being harassed. It's barbaric. Not that it happening to Catholics is worse than the Jews, of course not, but the Jews are outnumbered two hundred to one, where Catholics make up almost half the population. How can any sane government antagonise so many of its citizens and expect to be popular? I suppose it's just a case that the hellish forces are unleashed now and there's no stopping them. Once they have got rid of the Jews, those hooligans will need another group to torment.

Grace paused and meditatively bit the top of her fountain pen, the one the Warringtons had given her as a present. She should tell Richard about Declan. Why was she finding it so hard? It wasn't the news of the century, just that they were 'doing a line' – that was what it was called in Knocknashee. They weren't getting married...even though that was where it would probably lead. You didn't try out lots of different people as potential partners in Knocknashee – you just knew someone all your life, decided they were the best one for you, did a line, got engaged, then booked the church.

The fact that she'd already been kissed by Brendan McGinty and then Richard Lewis (though of course the second one wasn't a real kiss) would be a terrible scandal if it was known to the town, especially as she was a teacher and had to be very respectable.

Smiling, she dipped her pen in the lilac ink and went back to the sheet of cream paper.

I only have one other piece of news, and I know you'll be happy for me. Declan McKenna – do you remember him? – has asked me to consider him, and I said I would. We're not engaged, and we're not going to make a big show of ourselves around the town or anything, but he is going to tell his father tonight and I've already told Tilly, who said I should write to you, as I always tell you everything.

Yours,

Grace

As soon as she'd signed her name, she folded the sheet into an envelope, addressed it *Richard Lewis, c/o The Capital, New York, United States*, stuck on several stamps out of the book she kept in a tin box on the dresser, put on her coat and headed out to the post office.

Standing looking at the green iron postbox, she hesitated with the letter in her hand as the moon rose yellow over the thatched roofs of the town and threw her shadow against the post office wall.

A full minute later, with the strange feeling that she was closing a door in her life, she pushed the letter through the slit. The night was so quiet, she heard it fall inside with a soft thump.

* * *

THE FOLLOWING MORNING, snuggled up warm under her blankets, Grace went over yesterday in her mind, from the moment she'd danced in the yard with Declan to the final act when she'd paused a moment before posting the letter to Richard.

Had there been a part of her waiting for the American boy to write back to her first, saying what he thought about meeting her in Knocknashee? Maybe...

But why? Even if he had written back something soft and sentimental, it could never work. Their worlds were different in every way, and the idea of being in love with Richard Lewis was like thinking she could be in love with Clark Gable or Buster Keaton.

She'd been right to post that letter. She had closed a door, but it was a door into a fantasy world, a land over the rainbow. And by closing it, she'd opened another one. A door into a real-life future. Declan was here, and he was good and handsome and clever and kind. He was from her place, he understood her, he loved her – she was sure of that – and he was one of her people.

Would their future unfold the way these things always unfolded in Knocknashee? Probably it would, and there was nothing wrong with that.

Imagine, if they got married, they would be Mr and Mrs McKenna, and they'd run the school here together just as her parents had done. The apple wouldn't have fallen far from the tree, but it rarely did in Knocknashee. And if she and Declan were as happy as Eddie and Kathy Fitzgerald, they would be doing all right.

Her mind drifted to dreams of her wedding day. She'd ask Dr Warrington to give her away. She'd have to convince Tilly to be maid of honour, and force her into a dress for once.

And then would there be babies? One? Two? Six? Lizzie Warrington had explained to her one day that there was no reason she wouldn't be able to have children; the polio had no impact on that. She'd blushed when she heard it, and it seemed such an irrelevant piece of information, considering she never thought she would marry. But now, would it be possible? Would she hold a little baby of her own in her arms? She'd been lonely for so long, first when Mammy and Daddy drowned, then all those years in the hospital, and then coming home to live a cold, empty life with her sister. The idea of this house being a home to children, a home for a family, her and Declan's family, was one that warmed her heart in a way she'd never imagined possible.

Her pleasant reverie was interrupted by a pebble hitting the window. She got out of bed, pulled her soft crimson dressing gown around her, pushed her feet into her tartan slippers and limped to the window. There was Declan in the front garden, smiling up at her, clean-shaven and shielding his eyes from the low autumn sun. She opened the window, and the air was soft and warm, a total turnaround from last week.

'I thought we might walk to Mass together?' he called up to her.

'I'd better get dressed so,' she replied.

'It might be an idea, right enough. Father Lehane is very shy.' He jerked his head in the direction of the church, where the first bell was ringing to call the faithful.

'I'll let you in, one minute.' She closed the window, made sure her dressing gown was properly buttoned and tied and went down to open the big front door.

'Good morning,' he said gently as he stepped into the hall, closing the door behind him. 'I woke up worried that yesterday was a dream. It wasn't, was it?'

The vulnerability in his face melted her heart. There was a slight nick on his cheek, a dot of blood there, and a tiny speck of shaving soap in his ear. Without thinking, she reached up and wiped his ear.

'No, it was real, and I was just lying there being a lazybones, fantasising about our future, imagining this house with a family in it...' She blushed then. It was ridiculously forward to be discussing such things, she realised. They'd kissed once and that was all. She was being like a schoolgirl trying out her married name on the back of an envelope. 'I'm sorry, I'm getting way ahead of myself.'

He put his hands on her shoulders to stop her turning away and looked down into her eyes. 'You're not. The faster we get to the future, the better, as far as I'm concerned. I'm scared stiff you'll realise I'm not much of a catch before I can persuade you to the altar.'

'Don't be daft. You are a fine man, and every girl in the place has eyes for you. 'Tis I who is not exactly the best prize, so if anyone –'

'You are perfect, Grace Fitzgerald, absolutely perfect. And Da was delighted when I told him we're doing a line. He says you've always been like a daughter to him anyway, and he will be proud to have that made official.'

'Now you're the one getting ahead of yourself, Declan McKenna,' she teased. 'Who said anything about official?'

'Well, I can but hope.' He grinned at her, but then a shadow crossed his face and he became serious. 'There is one thing I'm afraid will get in the way of all this.'

'What is it?' she asked, suddenly anxious herself. 'Is it...' Was he afraid of seeing her leg? She was always careful to cover it up with long skirts; even the dressing gown she was wearing reached the floor. 'Is it my leg?'

He smiled, giving her shoulders a fond little shake. 'Don't talk nonsense, Grace. There's not a bit of you I would change. No, it's...' He removed his hands and plunged them into the pockets of his grey flannel trousers, vulnerable again.

'Tell me what's worrying you,' she said quietly, looking up at him.

'Richard Lewis.' He said the name as if doing so caused him pain.

She held his gaze and said steadily, 'What about him, Declan?'

'I...I just thought he might be...'

'Might be what?' She needed him to say it.

'The one you were waiting for, I don't know. You write each other these big long letters, and then when he turned up here... And he's, well, rich and worldly and American and everything I'm not. I'd been all set to tell you how I felt, but then he arrived and I just couldn't. I thought you wouldn't want me if he was an option...'

She didn't answer for a moment, remembering herself standing in the cobbled street last night, hesitating, the letter to Richard in her hand.

Then she said firmly, 'Firstly, Declan McKenna, you know perfectly well that you are the best catch around here for miles, and don't pretend you don't. And yes, Richard and I are good friends, and we have very open and real conversations in our letters, but we have never even for one second strayed into the world of romance. It's not like that. He's – I don't know how to describe it – like not of my world, and it's lovely to dip into his and him to mine, but it was never going to be a real thing, not like what you and I have. And that's why I wrote to him last night about you and me and posted the letter that will go off tomorrow morning.'

'You wrote to him about us?' Declan's dark eyebrows raised in surprise.

'Yes, because he's a real friend and I know he'll be nothing but happy for me. So there's your answer, Mr McKenna. You have nothing to worry about when it comes to Richard Lewis.'

Relief flooded his pale, narrow face, and she could see the tension leave his slender body. 'So you don't love him?'

'I love him as a friend, and I want him to be happy, but I don't love him like I love you,' she answered honestly. And it was true. She did love Declan in a different way – more real, solid, comforting. 'Now let you put the kettle on for a quick cuppa before we go while I go back upstairs and get dressed for Mass. But once the people here figure out you and I are together, you'd better not be seen coming in and out of this house without your father or Tilly or someone else here with us. We've enough to deal with without causing scandal.'

The bells pealed once more as she went into her bedroom, shut the door, got changed into her emerald-green dress, tied up her red curls with a matching green ribbon, pulled on her new blue shoes and fixed her calliper.

As she looked at herself in the mirror, her neat but curvy figure, the steel slotted into her shoe, she breathed a sigh of relief that Declan really did seem to want her, polio and all. She wasn't a fantasy he had built up in his mind, he'd known her since they were children, he loved her the way she was, and she would never have to worry about the likes of Bridie Keohane…or Miranda Logan.

She was making the right decision.

* * *

OUTSIDE THE CHURCH Charlie kissed her cheek and whispered how happy he was about herself and Declan. But inside, as poor Father Lehane stammered and stuttered his way inaudibly through the Mass, she couldn't help noticing Bridie Keohane sending her daggers, along with her mother. Sally O'Sullivan looked cross as well, and some of the other girls.

Declan seemed oblivious to the angry flutter. In the end she had to nudge him sharply and whisper to him to focus on the sermon instead of turning his head to smile at her and finding every opportunity, under the pretext of sharing the prayer book, to touch her hand.

He'd told Bridie his heart was elsewhere, and now he was making it all too clear where that 'elsewhere' was. She didn't feel ready yet to face down the offended damsels of the parish, all of them raging that the most eligible bachelor in Knocknashee was doing a line with little Grace Fitzgerald with the twisted leg.

CHAPTER 8

Richard's letter arrived the next Thursday, and it took her a moment to realise it was from him because the stamps were English and not American.

The handwriting was unmistakeable, though, and Charlie must have recognised it too, because he looked worried as he handed it to her. She suspected he saw Richard as someone with the power to break his son's heart.

She thanked him brightly, like she hadn't noticed anything was amiss, and carried the letter back to the kitchen to read over her toast and marmalade. Not that she felt like eating now.

In fact she felt quite hot and sick.

What if Richard Lewis had written to say he had fallen in love with her when he saw her? What then? He'd said she was more beautiful than her photo that day on the beach…

Without checking the postage date, she ripped it open, her heart beating fast.

It was dated three weeks ago.

And it included a couple of newspaper cuttings from the *Capital*.

17 Meadowfield Gardens
Elephant and Castle

London SE17
October 12, 1940
Dear Grace,

Well, it's finally happened. I'm in London, England, and the bombs are raining down, sirens night after night. It's amazing to see the fighter planes going at each other in the sky and burning debris falling all around.

Don't worry, Jacob and Sarah and I shelter in the local underground train station while it's happening, but every morning we emerge rubbing our eyes to the sight of more destruction. It makes me laugh sometimes to think how relieved we were when we finally got the call to say we'd been approved for transportation to England from Lisbon; we really had no idea it would be out of the frying pan into the fire.

See, the first place we sailed for from America, was Lisbon, Portugal, which I now call Leeze-bone, like a local.

The city was chaos, nothing short of it, with crowds arriving every day from all over Europe, every language, every color, every creed, just showing up thinking they are safe now at last, but of course they're not. This is only the beginning of the next part of the story. There are nowhere near enough places on ships out for the people that are coming, and the scramble for visas and tickets is a constant daily activity.

It sure does focus the mind on the human cost of all of this. The newspapers report the words and actions of Hitler, Churchill, and all the rest, but the regular people, who have no say whatsoever, they're the ones who bear the brunt.

Sarah is a great asset. Can you believe she persuaded Kirky to put her on the payroll? An achievement in itself! And her language skills were invaluable with the French refugees and German Jews; we spent all our days in Lisbon talking to them. Seeing old people and little kids, carrying all they own, willing to take a ticket to anywhere, anywhere at all that isn't here, was heartbreaking.

I've enclosed a couple of articles. One is about two French sisters, how the older one carried the little one in a suitcase when she was escaping on the train. The other is the story of the family of people from Danzig who tried to hold out against the Nazis. They told us how they felt when they realized that their so-called allies weren't coming to help, how there was no way they could win against the might of the tanks, how the Polish army had horses and the Germans were in tanks.

Before coming here I guess I had no beef with the Germans. I didn't even know any Germans. Jacob told me a lot, and it seemed unbelievable, but now, seeing the effects on real people who are blameless, well, it's hard not to feel something akin to hatred for them.

We finally got the call and were told we'd be leaving for England by clipper the next day. So with huge relief we packed up our things. We were told to ditch our suitcases as they are too hard to stow, and we had to put everything into a pillowcase—easier to stuff into a small space.

So we showed up and boarded the flying boat. It was more luxurious inside than I'd anticipated, carpeted, with comfortable seats, and it had four motors, bigger than the Pan American Baby Clippers. It took fourteen of us to England over ten hours. They supplied blankets to keep us warm, so it was comfortable if still terrifying.

Eventually, thankful to be alive, we landed. The flying boat makes a terrific noise on landing—it sounded like something ripping—and then we were down, surrounded by other boats of all descriptions, all covered in camouflage.

A motorboat was sent to take us to dry land, and it struck me that as soon as we were on terra firma, we really were in a country in the thick of war. People everywhere here are in uniform, the windows all taped to avoid flying debris in the event of a hit, people on bicycles going every direction.

We were brought into a reception office and given a cup of hot tea. I know I'm going to have to get used to it. At home only old people or sick people drink tea hot, but maybe my palate will adapt. Right now I'm not a fan, but after the long, cold trip, any hot liquid was welcome.

We were questioned and had to fill out about ten different forms, but the man in charge was genial and surprisingly cheerful for a guy in his situation. In fact—and I know the Irish have had reason to think very badly of the English—everyone here is courteous, friendly, and generally upbeat. Considering the devastation the Luftwaffe have inflicted on them, the deaths, the injuries, the destruction, it's remarkable. It's like they refuse to be downhearted.

Whatever Hitler intended, to break the spirit of Britain by bombing their cities to dust, just hasn't worked. If anything it has united them in their belief that they will prevail.

Once we were processed, we were taken to the railway station and sent on our way to London. The train journey was considerably less comfortable than the flying boat—we had to stand because it was so packed. It was still light when we started out, and it was fascinating to see the barrage balloons, pulled down into farmland and woods, ready to be floated again when night fell. Every field was dug with trenches, and some had white poles sticking up, I don't know why. But it really feels like every field, every tiny little bit of land, and every person on it is determined to repel Hitler's forces should they invade.

As we neared the built-up areas, we could see each house had a bomb shelter in the yard, a uniformly constructed thing, and many grew vegetables in the dirt on top. Nothing going to waste here. Then as dusk fell, the train's blackouts were pulled down, with only a square cut in each one the size of two stamps to peer out of and see where we were, not that we could tell because all the stations have the names and any identifying signage removed. If you were new here, you'd have to rely on someone knowing which station the train was at.

At one stage an old man got on. He was once well dressed, you could see, but his coat was torn and his shoes needed to be fixed, and when the conductor came around, he had the wrong ticket. I'm not sure exactly what the issue was, but he had to get off the train. I tried to offer him some money to buy whatever kind of ticket he was supposed to have, but he just shook his head, thanked me, and shuffled off.

Jacob, Sarah, and I took turns resting on a ledge about two inches wide. We were stiff and sore from standing. Still, nobody here complains, no matter how hard the deprivations, and we were determined to follow suit.

There was a man on the other side of Sarah who was an expert on the rhythm of tracks, and he explained to us how you could tell, even when you couldn't see out, whether you were above or below ground, in a tunnel or going over a bridge. We found him fascinating.

A lady next to me had some sandwiches and offered us one. I felt terrible taking some of her meager lunch, but I was so hungry, I did take one and split it with the other two. It was nothing like what we'd call a sandwich—*thin coarse bread, with a scrape of margarine and some pinkish meat cut so thin it was almost see-through—but to me it was like a juicy steak.*

The lady told me her son was in the navy, her only child, and that he looked like me. Her husband and brother had died on the Somme, so she was alone now. She was fifty-one, she said, though she looked older, and drove an ambulance.

The women here have endured two wars in their lifetimes, losing their husbands and fathers and brothers in the first one and now expected to send their sons to this one, and I felt such a range of emotions, wondering if it was right to ask American mothers to do the same.

The train was so packed with soldiers, all fully battle ready with pack and rifle, and in the way that the British work, all the privates and Non-Commissioned Officerss were in third class while the officers were in first.

I squeezed my way up and down the train at one stage, just to get a sense of it, and what struck me was the packed third class was full of chatter and fun while the officers in first seemed sour and silent.

I thought we were in London long before we were. The city and suburbs seemed to go on for miles. We were stopped and shunted into a siding more times than I can remember, troops or munitions getting priority, I guess.

But finally we arrived, and we went to the United Press office where a bunch of American newspapermen hang out. One gave us an address to go to for lodging the next day but directed us to the Savoy for that night. It was hard to navigate around in the pitch-black. Cars and even buses have only pinpricks of light allowed, so it's hard to see traffic. We nearly lost Sarah under a huge bus that was going so slowly we couldn't hear or see it, but Jacob yanked her back in time.

The Savoy had cardboard over all the windows and doors, but we managed to find it and were admitted once we said who we were. Grace, I wish you could have seen it. The lobby was buzzing, waiters carrying drinks, a jazz band playing in the bar, people eating, and most dressed in their pajamas! Many spent the nights in the hotel's own bomb shelter, so they dined, had a few drinks, and went below then to sleep.

We were exhausted, so we just had some food sent to our rooms and ate, and I fell into the deepest sleep I think I ever had. Hitler himself could have been standing over me, Grace, and I think I would have barely opened an eye to look at him.

The next day, refreshed and our bellies full, we set about getting our credentials in order. Boy, do those guys love forms. We had to fill out so many at the police station to get a ration book, a press pass, a National Registration card. We had our photos taken, and I must have signed my name fifty times. But eventually we were bona fide newspapermen, and we had passes to access areas that civilians were restricted from entering. I felt like such a grown-up, Grace, not a kid playing at being a journalist.

Being in Paris before the Nazis invaded was amazing, but it felt like regular life there. But this, this is different. This is war, and I'd be lying if I didn't admit to feeling excited and scared out of my mind at the same time. As we left the police station, we spoke to an Air Raid Protection warden who told us to avoid going a particular way because a German ace had crash-landed on the roof of a building, so we had to go around a longer way. The way he said it, like there was a minor road accident, struck me. They were used to this—it had been going on since September—and it really proved to me that humans can get acclimated to anything. Even this terror.

London looks nothing like it did last June when we passed through. Huge chunks of buildings are gone, piles of rubble everywhere, buildings obscured by sandbags, and everyone in khaki. But as I said, they are a tough people.

My new address, a boarding house of sorts, is on the top of this letter, so you can reach me there if you want to write. A guy from the Chicago Tribune *tipped us off about it. It's packed with people. Because of the bombing, everyone is having to "bunk up," as they say here. We are three of fifteen boarders. Most of them come and go to sleep, and we interact very little.*

At least the house is sufficiently downmarket to impress Jacob, though Sarah gets very annoyed with him for refusing to let her spend our father's money on decent rooms in a hotel.

They are dining at the Savoy tonight—she absolutely insisted. Father sent her some money recently, which was good of him. She had something of a run-in with our mother before we left Savannah; it was to do with Jacob. Mother strongly disapproves of their relationship, which is hardly surprising from her point of view. Anyway, to our amazement, our father turned up in

St. Simons and insisted that whatever Mother said, he hadn't cut us off, so to just ask if we needed anything.

I'm wondering about asking him for the money for a car over here; it would make life a million times easier. I had considered asking Kirky, but I didn't want my ears chewed off; even from this distance, I wouldn't poke that bear. But at the same time, I do want to make my own way.

I'm now sitting at the desk in their room, which even has a gas stove and a kettle to make coffee (what they call coffee—it's not like any coffee I've ever tasted, but it's amazing what you'll get used to). Actually technically this is my room. We have a very stern landlady named Mrs. Price, and Jacob and I are supposed to be sharing while Sarah has a little room of her own. In reality they have the larger room and I have the tiny storage closet.

Grace, I'd love to hear from you and get all the news of Knocknashee and find out how Odile is doing. How old is she now? Is she sitting or crawling or doing anything interesting yet? As you can tell, I know nothing about babies. I might swing out that way again in a few months if I'm still in England, but I'll have to get my bearings here for a while and try to not look like a dumb Yank without a clue about anything.

Yours,

Richard

PS I've heard nothing from Alfie O'Hare or his girlfriend, or the Dreyfuses. Have you? Let me know if you do. There are a few French refugees in London, but it's hard to tell who is on what side, so even if I run across someone with Parisian connections, I'd be nervous about asking if they knew Alfie—I wouldn't want to give him away to an enemy.

All I know for sure is that wherever they are, Paul and Bernadette are feeling very relieved that Odile is safe and well and being cared for.

PPS I was waiting to see if anything came of this before writing to you. Nothing has, but I'll tell you anyway. While I was in New York waiting for the boat, I dropped in on Mrs McHale—remember me telling you about her? She helped me find Father Dempsey, and she wrangled the whole story out of me (don't worry, I didn't mention Lily's name or any details about her), but it turns out she knows Canon Rafferty by reputation and she's going to do a Miss Marple and exonerate Father Dempsey, though to be honest, I don't see how after all these years; the trail must have gone very cold. I can't imagine

Kit Gallagher will betray the canon, not the way you've described her, and the only other person who might have betrayed him was your late sister. And she might not even have known about the other babies, or the baby that led to the complaint to the bishop.

* * *

GRACE'S HANDS shook as she put down the letter. It was hard to know how she was feeling.

Disappointed?

No, she felt grateful.

She was doing a line with Declan McKenna now, so she could hardly go on writing to Richard if he decided he was in love with her too – it would be like a betrayal. So it was just as well he had written like he'd always done, bright and newsy, inquiring after Alfie and including that intriguing postscript about Mrs McHale, with nothing to suggest his feelings for Grace were anything more than friendship.

It was for the best. This way she could keep him in her life.

But please, God, let him be safe...

The picture he'd painted of war in London differed greatly from what was being reported in the papers in Ireland. He said the local train station was safe to shelter in, but it all sounded so dangerous. Supposing a random bomb fell during the day while he was out and about and not in the shelter, like it had in Wexford?

It did feel strange to her, the way he spoke of the heroism and bravery of the English people, as if he liked them. They were the same people who burnt and raped and murdered here in living memory, led by Churchill.

Some Irish people did join up to the British Army – the *Irish Times* was encouraging it – and a lot of upper-class people in Dublin still had the vestiges of loyalty to British rule, but for the poor of rural Ireland, wearing a British uniform and swearing allegiance to the king was something they could never countenance.

Well, almost never.

Maura O'Donoghue had caused a scandal last Monday by having a big bust-up with her mother in the shop in front of everyone and the following morning was nowhere to be found. The rumour was that she'd hitched a lift to Dingle and on to Cork, where she took the train to the north with plans to enlist in the British Army as a nurse or something.

Grace wondered if Richard could understand why that had so upset her parents, embarrassed them really, especially Biddy O'Donoghue, who could barely say the name Winston Churchill without spitting. She, like many others, had never forgiven the British leader for sending the dreaded Black and Tans to Ireland during the War of Independence.

Charlie told her a story only last week of how one of the brothers of Neilus Collins – she forgot which one; they all looked the same, old and gnarly and afraid of a bar of soap – had been engaged to a girl from out Ballyferriter way. Her brother was a Volunteer, and the Black and Tans came to the house looking for him one night. He wasn't there, but that didn't stop the Tans burning the cottage and knocking the man of the house unconscious with a rifle butt, and then they raped the girls, his sisters. That was in 1921, only twenty years ago, and people had long memories around here.

She went back to the letter, wondering why it had taken him so long to write it after his visit to Knocknashee. There was no mention of an earlier letter that might have got lost. He wasn't asking her why she hadn't written back. So this must be the first letter he had sent since he'd seen her face to face in June.

Had he simply been too busy with his life, or had he been unsure what to say to her after that strange, brief meeting of their two different worlds?

That day in Knocknashee, as soon as he stepped off the bus with Odile in his arms, it was like the prince out of a fairy tale had walked out of a book to say hello. And he'd behaved like a prince, so polite, so gentle, so kind. That tiny kiss he had dropped upon her mouth before he ran for the bus… She'd been tempted not to wash her face ever again. And for almost a month afterwards, she'd secretly dreamed he might feel the same way about her, that she was some sort of princess.

She laughed at herself now, shaking her head. What a ridiculous, childish dream. With her limp and her calliper, she was hardly anyone's idea of a princess, and she wouldn't be going to the ball any time soon.

It was Declan McKenna who had made her feel like the most beautiful girl in the world, slowly dancing her around the back yard to the sound of the Glenn Miller Orchestra on the wireless, playing 'The Nearness of You'.

Putting the letter aside, she read through the two clippings he had sent her and was soon absorbed in the words of Richard Lewis, the war reporter. It was such powerful writing, and Jacob Nunez's photographs absolutely captured the haunted, defeated yet somehow determined faces of the refugees. The end result was an amazing piece of journalism.

With a rush of pride in her friend, she got out her lilac ink and notepaper from the dresser. Her last letter must still be on its way, so she didn't need to repeat herself; she would just answer this one.

Dear Richard,

Thank you for your lovely long letter. I always get a thrill when I feel the fatness of the envelope, knowing it's going to be a long one. I rely on you for my information about the war, because honestly here, I now realise, only what they want us to know gets through because of the government censor. Please send me more clippings – keep them coming. I put them in a scrapbook, and when I read over them, I have to almost pinch myself that these wonderful pieces were written by my good friend Richard Lewis.

As I read your articles, it always strikes me how you have this unusual way of getting people to speak honestly to you. I know this from first-hand experience. There's something about you that makes people trust you, confide in you. It's not a common gift, Richard, but you have it in spades, as we say over here. I think it's because you don't judge, you just listen.

It's good to hear that Sarah is such an asset. I can't imagine being able to speak so many languages, but it's wonderful that with her help you can listen to the true stories of people who fled Hitler. They're so heartbreaking and poignant, but also it's so important that they are heard.

Please do take care of yourself over there and write as often as you can to let me know you're alive and well, and Sarah and Jacob as well. We still have no word of Alfie here; I hope you can find out something in London. His mother is afraid for him, I know, though she's very brave about it. Alfie always was a bit wild, so she's had a lifetime of worrying about him. Tilly says she knows he can survive anything, but I know she's worried for him too – it's just not like her to say it. We are praying for him every day, as is Marion in Dublin. It's all we can do.

I'm so happy your father wishes you well, and I'm sure your mother will come round about Jacob when she sees Sarah is happy. That's the most important thing surely. I'd give anything to have my mother and father back, so cherish your parents, Richard, no matter what, because when they're gone, they're gone.

Yours truly,

Grace

PS That's so interesting about Mrs McHale. I can just picture her as Miss Marple – I do love Agatha Christie. I wonder if she will be able to find anything out? The canon hasn't appeared yet, so I'm hoping Father Iggy got it wrong, or the bishop has changed his mind again. Father Lehane is doing just fine, even if we can't hear his sermons. He's good at visiting the sick and the old, and I think he's getting a bit braver. He actually looked me in the face the other day without blushing.

She stopped and sat tapping the pen against her teeth. She wondered if she should mention about Declan again but decided not. She didn't want to make a big thing of it, like she thought it would matter to him when so many more important things were happening in his life. Instead she just added another postscript.

PPS I know this is short, but I wrote to you care of the *Capital* only five days ago, and obviously you can't have got it yet, so this is just an addendum really.

CHAPTER 9

The young pupils of Knocknashee National School sat reading their books in rows of contented silence.

Most days Grace read to the children aloud, but each Thursday afternoon, for an hour before the end of school, she would let them select any book they liked from the school library and read quietly to themselves. There were no questions to be answered on the piece, no pressure. All they had to do if selected was stand up and talk about the book and give their impressions of it.

Behind her, as she corrected homework, she could hear Declan through the partition, gently and slowly explaining to the older children how to divide 3487 by 26. His endless patience and lack of frustration at repetition were what made him a wonderful teacher. He never raised his voice, and the children lowered their volume accordingly.

She remembered her father used to always say, 'There's no point in roaring at children. They'll always be able to roar louder and for longer, and that only leads to pandemonium, so silence is your friend in the classroom.'

It was ten minutes to home time, and she rang the small bell on her desk. Her pupils, many reluctantly, closed the books and returned them to the shelf before coming back to their seats.

'Now, who wants to tell me about what they read today?'

A forest of little hands shot up; they were so eager for her good opinion.

'Thomas O'Shea.' She nodded to a skinny, bright-eyed, black-haired child.

Thomas was turning out every bit as bright as his older brother, Mikey.

It was amazing how the scared little boy that Agnes had been about to beat before Grace stopped her had turned out so well. There had never been anything wrong with Mikey but a tendency to liveliness. It was only that Canon Rafferty hated him 'trick-acting' at Mass and had always encouraged Mistress Fitzgerald to take the leather to him.

Young Thomas was reading a book of Irish mythology at the moment, the story of the Brown Bull of Cooley, and of Queen Meadhbh, Ailill, and the warriors of Conchobar, king of the Ulaid. He was as lively as Mikey, and he got increasingly animated as he told the story, especially when he got to the part where 'the warriors of Ulster were under a *geis* not to kill, so Cú Chulainn held off the whole Connaught army by himself.'

In his excitement, he leapt around the room, waving a pretend sword, while the other children looked on in fascination. His best friend was Paudie O'Connell, another real bright spark and they encouraged each other. Grace laughed; the way her pupils learnt about things and re-enacted them through play always delighted her. The book was of course in Irish, and while they did read in English as well, the English books never elicited the kind of animated response books in their native language did.

'What is all this trick-acting, Mistress Fitzgerald?'

Like small birds when a hawk swoops over the woods and fields, every child in the place froze and went silent. Thomas O'Shea skittered back into his chair, and even the infants who were too young to be in school when the canon left could hear the menace in that whispery voice.

Grace knew she should get up at once to greet him, but instead she remained seated, staring in shock at the apparition in the doorway, in his long black soutane, his three-pointed biretta on his head. The canon was exceptionally pale for someone who'd lived by the sea for so long, but he didn't enjoy the outdoors so that probably explained it. He'd not changed a bit. Still the shiny pale skin, the thin whispering voice, the long fingers.

Somehow, with Father Lehane doing the Mass Sunday after Sunday, she'd been lulled into a false sense of security, a feeling that Father Iggy had been wrong about the canon returning. But here he was at last, his white hair even sparser and his scant eyebrows hanging down in long wisps over his rheumy eyes. He had a missal clutched under his left arm, and he stared at the cowering children in contempt.

'Good afternoon, Mistress Fitzgerald,' he said in his whispery voice.

She hated being called that. Mistress Fitzgerald had been Agnes, the dreaded headmistress who beat the children. Grace was Miss Fitz and liked it that way. It showed her pupils weren't scared of her.

She forced a smile. 'Good afternoon, Canon Rafferty.'

'You need to keep better order, Mistress Fitzgerald.' As he moved toward her across the classroom, he drew out every 's' like the hiss of a snake. 'Like your sister did, before her sickness, the poor misfortunate woman...'

Grace felt such a rush of rage, it made her want to punch him in his smug reptilian face. How dare he talk about Agnes being unfortunate when he hadn't once come to visit her after her stroke? Poor besotted Agnes, who had done so many wicked things out of love for this disgusting man.

But she maintained a cool dignity as she rose to her feet. 'You're very welcome back to Knocknashee, Canon Rafferty.'

There was no avoiding it. With Agnes gone as witness to his despicable crimes, she had to show him the deference he thought he deserved. The parish priest was always the head of the school board, and so this odious man could dismiss her any time he wanted. Her livelihood, and maybe Declan's as well, depended on her staying in his good graces.

He touched the desk very briefly with long white fingers. 'Mistress Fitzgerald, I'll assume you are doing your Christian duty in keeping these children mindful of their souls –'

Just then the bell for end of school rang in the corridor. Grace offered a prayer of thanks for Janie O'Shea's punctuality and clapped her hands. 'Now, off you go, children. Take advantage of the fine weather. Out you go now.'

As they stood to troop out into the sunshine, the canon raised his hand. 'Sit down,' he ordered, his voice like the crack of a whip, louder than usual.

The children looked to their beloved Miss Fitz, unsure of who to obey, and she had to think quickly. 'Take your seats for one more minute, everyone.' She smiled as if this was on purpose, not an example of the canon trying to undermine her.

There was the clatter and scrape of chairs as the children nervously resumed their seats and sat there wide-eyed, wondering what was going to happen next.

'Now, Mistress Fitzgerald...' The canon picked up the wooden pointer from Grace's desk, the long, heavy one she used to indicate things on the blackboard or pick out countries from the maps on the wall, and weighed it in his hand. 'I think I will hear the children say their catechism.'

Her heart sank. Since Father Iggy had gone, no one had tested the little ones weekly on their catechism. Father Lehane was too shy to come into the school, and she preferred teaching them art and music and having them read stories. How stupid of her not to prepare for this moment by focussing more on their prayers.

'Let's start with this young trick actor.' He brandished the pointer menacingly at Thomas O'Shea.

The poor child went white and cringed, but Grace smiled encouragingly at him from behind the canon's back. With a nod the lad got to his feet and, with a deep breath, summoned Cú Chulainn from his toes.

'Who made you?' the canon fired at him, his mean small eyes daring the boy to get it wrong.

'God made me,' said Thomas, his hand balled in fists by his side.

'Why did God make you?'

'God made me to know Him, love Him and serve Him in this world, and to be happy with Him forever in the next.'

With a huff and a scowl, the canon snapped at the clever boy to sit down, then stood rapid-firing catechism questions to the other older pupils.

'To whose image and likeness did God make you?'

'God made me to His own image and likeness.'

'Is this likeness to God in your body or in your soul?'

'This likeness to God is in my soul.'

To Grace's relief, the other children seemed to have been infected by Thomas's bravery and answered loudly and correctly.

Losing patience, the canon pulled a much harder question out of the air. 'Define transubstantiation,' he snapped at eight-year-old Maureen Canty.

Grace braced herself, but to her amazement, Maureen rose to the occasion, though the poor child was clearly terrified.

'It is the ch-ch-change of the substance of b-b-b-bread and wine into the substance of Christ's body and blood by a validly ordained priest during the consecration at Mass, so that only the appearances of bread and wine remain.'

It poured out as a meaningless torrent of sound. Grace was sure Maureen didn't understand a word of what she was saying, but she knew it. She must have remembered it from the baby infants class. Grace had always thought some of the imagery and terminology of Catholic doctrine were a little too graphic for little ones, crowns of thorns and whippings, not to mention fires of hell, but Agnes and the canon thought differently.

No acknowledgement from Canon Rafferty, no smile or word of praise.

'Explain the difference between temptation and sin!' He pounced on Gobnait Molloy, and Grace's heart sank. Gobnait was a good girl, the late miracle child of a couple who had long given up the idea of being parents, and she was much adored, her dark-brown pigtails lovingly tied up every morning and her clothes always immaculate. She was a very obliging child, but she forgot everything when she was nervous.

As the poor girl got slowly to her feet, on the brink of tears, a joyous shouting filtered in from the schoolyard. Some boys from Declan's class, released into the autumn sunshine, were kicking a ball from one to the other. The canon drifted to the window, his hands clasped behind his back as he gazed out, scowling, trying to see who was making the most noise. 'More in their line to be on their knees praying for redemption,' he muttered under his breath.

Grace saw her chance. She stepped forward and held her own small brown catechism in front of Martha's eyes, open to the page of the question. Martha glanced at it and nodded gratefully.

'Well, girl, I asked you a question?' The canon turned from the window just as Grace got back to her own chair.

'Temptation is a strong inclination or suggestion to sin, which may come from the devil, from something outside us or from our tendency toward evil as a result of Adam's fall. Sin is knowingly and willingly breaking the law of God, not merely the inclination to commit evil,' the girl rattled off.

'Indeed, indeed.'

Bored and irritable, he moved on to younger victims, the four- and five-year-olds who weren't yet in school when he was the priest in Knocknashee. With them there were lots of mistakes, and each time one of the babies didn't know the answer, the priest shot Grace a triumphant glance. He reduced them all to frightened tears by telling them their immortal souls were in grave peril and that he would expect a significant improvement when he returned or he would have no option but to 'reassess how things were being done', this last bit said with a gimlet-eyed glare at Grace while tapping the heavy pointer on his open palm.

Mentally Grace abandoned several of her favourite lessons, like art and music and storytelling. She knew she didn't dare risk the infants making such a poor showing the next time, and it took a lot of hours a week to get something as long and complicated as the catechism into such young brains, even when they weren't scared stiff of getting things wrong.

It was nearly half an hour after school was due out now, and she couldn't hear anything from the room behind her. Janie O'Shea would normally stay to tidy both classrooms and make sure everything was in order for the morning, but Grace couldn't hear the sound of sweeping, so the fifteen-year-old school monitor had clearly decided it was best to keep out of Canon Rafferty's way as well and had left with Declan.

At last the priest snapped, 'Class dismissed,' and her pupils filed out very quietly with bowed heads, not at all the happy, bouncy children they had been that morning. Normally she would stand at the door saying goodbye to each one individually – she made a point of doing that every day, greeting them as they entered and left the school – but today she stayed standing behind her chair, knowing this wasn't over.

As the last child left, the priest took a turn of the classroom, still holding the pointer and the missal, frowning at the maps and the globe and the shelves of books and cupboard of powder paints, the children's paintings pinned to the walls, the collection of tin whistles stored in their wicker basket on top of the school piano. All evidence of irreligious learning. In Agnes's day, the only picture in the school had been of the Shroud of Turin.

'Well now, Mistress Fitzgerald,' he said, finally coming to a halt in front of her desk. 'I see you have your feet well under the table here.'

'I do enjoy my job, Canon Rafferty,' she said in a neutral voice, though her heart was pounding.

'I'm glad to hear it.' He replaced the pointer on her desk, and when he looked at her, she was surprised to see him attempt a smile – a cold, greasy, smarmy affair that didn't reach his eyes. 'Now, I have a question for you, Mistress Fitzgerald. How is Father

Fitzgerald these days? Is he still abroad in the missions, in the Philippines?'

She was completely taken aback by this reference to her brother. 'Yes, I think so.'

'Does he not communicate with you?' His little black eyes narrowed.

'He sends me a Mass card twice a year, Canon Rafferty, so I know he's praying for me, and that is enough for me.' She was embarrassed having to admit that her brother never wrote to her properly, but the canon seemed pleased and satisfied by her answer.

'And what more would you require than to be prayed for by your own brother, a priest.' He nodded. 'He would have no call to talk to you about worldly things.'

'Of course, Father. It's all I could wish for.'

'And you, of course, pray for him?'

'I do, Father.' She wondered where this was going. The canon had never mentioned Maurice to her before.

'We need to all pray for his safety. Japan is a growing power in the Far East. But the Philippines are under the thumb of America, are they not?'

Grace glanced towards the map of the Pacific on the wall, surprised at the canon showing an interest in politics. 'I believe they are, Canon Rafferty.'

'Then as long as America has the sense not to come into this war, your brother is perfectly safe. Nonetheless, it is a hard life on the missions, and life is uncertain in the current climate. So I am intending to raise money from the people of this parish so Father Maurice can do good for the less well-off while the Emergency continues. We will have a monthly collection, and the Church will make it a cheque, and I will post it to your brother.'

'I'm sure he would appreciate that, Father,' she replied cautiously, but then couldn't help adding, 'If you think the parish can afford it?' She hated the idea of Maurice being used to squeeze even more money out of her neighbours, who were poor enough as it was, especially with everything that was going on.

'I hope you don't *object* to the idea, Miss Fitzgerald.' His voice sharpened. 'I don't think the bishop would be very happy if you were to *object*.'

'It's not that I object, Canon Rafferty, it's just, well, everyone in Knocknashee is so poor themselves, with the rationing and the tariffs and the Emergency and everything…'

'It is easier for a camel to go through the eye of a needle than for a rich man to enter into the kingdom of God. Matthew 19:24,' quoted the canon sententiously.

'I know it, Father.' She clenched her hands by her sides. It was infuriating to be preached to about the danger of wealth by this lover of fine wines and rich dinners and fancy hotels. She was sure his expensive car was parked outside the parochial house as they spoke, and she wondered how shy, nervous Father Lehane was coping with this monster turning up. And poor Dymphna…

Though Dymphna's sweet cakes were even better than Kit Gallagher's, so maybe the canon wouldn't be too harsh on her.

'Unlike Father Ignatius O'Riordan,' continued the priest, pronouncing Father Iggy's name with an especially long malevolent hiss, 'I intend to remind my parishioners that their immortal souls are more important to them than a few spare pennies to be wasted on cake and toffee. Don't you agree with me, Mistress Fitzgerald?'

'Yes, Father.' She knew she must keep smiling, she mustn't get sacked; she had to protect the children in her care.

'And on the matter of immortal souls, I wish to have a word with you about your own behaviour…'

He placed his knuckles on the desk and leant forward, showing his yellowing teeth – there was a strong, sweet scent on his breath; he'd clearly been at Dymphna's cakes, followed by a drop of brandy – and Grace tried not to flinch as she braced herself for whatever might come next. You never knew when the canon was going to accuse you of the most outlandish things. She'd never forget that awful Sunday, after Agnes threw her out of their house and Charlie had taken her in, when Canon Rafferty had preached a homily about single women living under the same roof as men to whom they were not related, causing scandal and bringing shame.

'I hope you agree with me, Mistress Fitzgerald, about the importance in your position of setting a good example for the children?'

'I do, Father.' Surely there was nothing she could be accused of?

'So I have to say, I was very surprised to find out from Mrs Keohane about yourself and Declan McKenna. It is not suitable for young children to be taught by a man and a woman who choose to meet in secret rather than enter into the sanctity of marriage.'

'That's not true!' Grace burst out, unable to stay meek any longer in the face of such an insult.

The gimlet eyes gleamed with triumph. 'Not true, Mistress Fitzgerald? When Mrs Keohane tells me you were seen coming out of your house together with this man *before* the hour of Mass on a Sunday morning? I cannot tolerate such goings-on when as chair of the school board, I am responsible for children's souls. Teachers who engage in...in such *activities* cannot be allowed to continue in their jobs.'

The door of the classroom opened suddenly, and Declan McKenna stood there, looking pale and dark, drawn up to his full height. 'Is everything all right, Miss Fitz? Canon.' He acknowledged the priest, barely civil.

Grace felt a rush of gratitude towards him. So he hadn't gone home and left her alone to deal with this horrible monster. At the same time, she didn't want to drag him into this; he was sure to get angry and upset and endanger himself. 'Hello, Mr McKenna. Yes, everything is fine. It's just that I and Canon Rafferty were having a chat. How is the long division coming along?'

'Getting there, I think. Some of them have it, more not yet, but we'll all get there in the end.'

'That's good to know. You don't need to wait, Mr McKenna. I will lock up the school myself when the canon and I are finished.'

But Canon Rafferty had no idea of letting Declan go. 'Long division, Mr McKenna?' he asked as he swivelled slowly to face him. 'So very good of you to help out in the school, very good. And you are working as a teacher of mathematics though you are not qualified?'

'I am an assistant teacher, but I will be qualified very soon, Canon Rafferty. I have passed a number of tests already and will be taking my exams next May, in hardly more than six months' time.'

It was remarkable how calm Declan was being. He'd changed so much from the eighteen-year-old boy who had arrived back in Knocknashee beaten and cowed from his twelve years in Letterfrack. Back then he'd been unable to look anyone in the face. He'd kept his head down and let his hair fall over his eyes, and the sight of a priest made him tremble in fear. But now he regarded Canon Rafferty with a smile – although not one Grace recognised.

'Grace,' he went on, coming towards her, 'have you told the canon the happy news? I'm sure he will be delighted to be among the first to congratulate us on our engagement.'

'Oh, er, no, I...' Her voice dried up. She wasn't quite sure what to say. Her heart raced, and she felt her cheeks go pink. 'I mean, not yet...'

'Engagement, Mistress Fitzgerald?' The canon swung his head from side to side on his long, scrawny neck, glancing suspiciously from one to the other of them. 'You didn't mention an engagement?' He looked pointedly at her hand. 'You're not wearing a ring, Mistress Fitzgerald?'

'But Canon, I only proposed to Grace last weekend. It was a complete surprise to her, but to my delight, she accepted me, and since then we are only waiting for a chance to go on the bus to pick the ring in Tralee – it goes so infrequently these days because of the fuel shortages. Grace, I spoke to Bobby Spillane this morning and he'll be going on Saturday.'

'That's wonderful,' she said weakly. Her head was spinning. Declan must have overheard the canon threatening her about seeing him 'in secret'. The last time the canon had insulted her from the pulpit, it had taken all his father's persuasion to stop Declan from confronting the priest, and he was clearly determined to never let such a public humiliation happen to her again.

Canon Rafferty had a face of thunder. He'd clearly been expecting a heated denial from Declan as well as Grace and had been looking forward to throwing them both to the mercy of the town gossips. He glowered as Declan put his arm around Grace's shoulders.

'Very well. If this is the truth, I will do you the honour of blessing your marriage in my church, because as I have often had cause to say, a young *healthy*' – he emphasised 'healthy', with a scathing glance at Grace's leg – 'a young *healthy* woman should be married and produce children. It is what she is put on earth to do. So on the day I marry you to your husband, Mistress Fitzgerald, I will say a special prayer that your ill health will not preclude you from your duty to the Lord.' And he glided in his long black robes towards the door, slamming it behind him.

Grace sank into her chair, deeply shaken, and buried her face in her hands. They waited to speak until they saw him walk across the schoolyard and out the gate onto the street.

'Oh God, Declan, he's awful, even worse than I remember.' Her heart was pounding and she felt sick. It was all so horrible, the catechism and then his threat about exposing her and Declan for immoral behaviour, and then to be reminded of her disability and have it implied she couldn't have children because of it.

Declan managed to stay calm, but his voice was cold. 'How *dare* he insult you like that. I'm not letting him pray over us at our wedding. I'd love to tear that stupid hat off his head and shove it down his throat.'

She shook her head, her face still in her hands. 'Don't, Declan. You know how powerful he is, and besides, any wedding is a long way off yet, and please God that long streak of misery will be long gone by then.'

She looked at him when he didn't answer. He stood there awkwardly, and a silence hung between them in the still classroom air.

He was the first to break it, his voice uncertain. 'I wasn't trying to force your hand there. I just could see where he was going. But will we go to the jeweller's in Tralee and get an engagement ring?'

She thought about it. 'I suppose we had better now. I mean, we've told the canon. But any ring will be fine – it doesn't have to be an expensive one from Tralee…'

'It's just, well, in Tralee I know the whole stock by heart. I've hung around there so much, thinking should I just go in and buy one and present it to you. There's some fine ones, and I have the money saved from all the boilers I put into the hotels, but I wasn't sure what ring you'd want, so I would really like it if you would come with me and choose one?'

'You were getting ready to do this? It wasn't just a show for the canon?' She was amazed and flattered that he'd been planning this when she'd had no idea.

'I was, and I thought we could have our lunch out in the hotel and make a day of it?' he asked nervously.

She wanted to hug him. The vulnerability that lurked beneath his competent and stoic exterior always melted her heart. 'All right, we'll do that so.' She nodded. 'And I'll make you spend all your money on me, and then you'll regret it.'

His blue eyes darkened with worry. 'I regret nothing about you, Grace, nothing at all. I never imagined in all those long lonely nights in Letterfrack that I could ever feel this happy, but I am and you're the reason. I don't want to make you do anything you don't want to do, Grace. If this is too quick, just say it. It was just when I heard him threatening your job…'

Her heart melted some more. He was so unsure of her. 'You're not making me do anything, Declan. I'm happy to wear your ring. I know it's not the same, but I was convinced that nobody would ever want me, that I'd die an old maid, alone. So this is such a happy surprise for both of us, we should make the most of it.'

'So we're officially engaged?'

She grinned. 'Well, I don't know about that. Most *proper* engagements start with a proposal and an acceptance,' she teased, 'and not just announced out of the blue as a way of outsmarting Canon Rafferty.'

At that he came around the desk to her side, went down on one knee and took her hand. 'Will you marry me, Grace?' he asked simply, gazing up at her with his dark-blue eyes.

Her heart turned over at the love in his face. He was so gorgeous, so kind, so everything, and she loved him back, she really did.

Just for a moment, though, she fought a slight panic. Once she said yes to him properly, not with a laugh or a comment about not rushing things but properly, then it was official; they weren't just doing a line. In Knocknashee engagements always led to the altar. There was really no going back.

Yet she'd always known that doing a line was going to lead to an engagement – and why would she want to go back? She wouldn't, of course not. She was just nervous because of the speed of things.

'I will, Declan,' she answered, as simply as he had asked the question.

Unshed tears pooled on his lower lashes. 'Is this real, Grace? Are you saying you'll marry me?'

She smiled and nodded. 'It would be an honour.'

He stood and drew her to her feet, then slowly pressed his lips to hers. Without even intending to, she allowed her arms to reach up and go around his neck, drawing his kiss deeper. He pulled her closer, his arms around her waist, and on and on they kissed. Her mouth opened to his and her thoughts swam in her mind, incoherent and nebulous, her whole body focussed only on this kiss, this place, this man.

'You're all I think about, day and night, do you know that?' he whispered against her mouth. 'Your face, your hair…everything about you…'

Pulling away from him, Grace moved towards the classroom door.

'Grace, I'm sorry. I'm getting carried away, I know.' He gazed after her anxiously, clearly worried his passion had frightened her.

'I want to get carried away with you, Declan.'

'Really?' His forehead was creased in doubt.

Reaching the door, she looked up and down the corridor, then returned and led him by the hand back through his own classroom, then into the small office where she kept the school supplies and the filing cabinet. The room couldn't be seen from the windows and had a bolt on the door, which she slid closed.

'I know girls aren't supposed to encourage boys, and we are certainly not supposed to respond to you but...' She gently pulled his head down to hers.

'Oh, Grace...' He smiled and closed his eyes, then slid his arms around her waist and drew her to him even more tightly than before. Then his lips were on hers, but this kiss was different to the others. This was urgent and powerful...

The sound of the door opening into the junior room on the other side of the partition startled them both and they sprang apart. There followed the cheerful sound of Janie O'Shea whistling as she stacked the children's chairs on the desks and started sweeping, then cleaned the blackboard.

As Grace smoothed her dress and hair, giggling, Declan leant his head back against a pile of atlases and groaned softly. 'I can't wait to get an engagement ring on your finger, Miss Fitz. But most of all, I can't wait to get you up the aisle.'

CHAPTER 10

LONDON, ENGLAND, OCTOBER 1940

Richard strode up the street to their boarding house in Elephant and Castle, an area named after an ancient pub that had been knocked down and burnt down and rebuilt more times than London Bridge.

It had struck him as one of the weirdest pub names he had come across in England, up there with the Dog and Duck and the Frog and Lettuce, and he'd been saying as much to Jacob a few days ago when one of their fellow lodgers, a bespectacled woman named Miss Juniper, who was on her way past them down the stairs, paused to inform them it had originally been called the Infanta of Castile, in homage to the wife of Edward the First, a Spanish princess, but to London ears, the Spanish title sounded like Elephant and Castle.

Miss Juniper was always a fountain of knowledge. She seemed to know everything about everything, though nobody knew what she did for a living. If asked, she'd say vaguely that she worked in administration, but Jacob was certain she was involved in something that the British called 'hush-hush', the secret service or something.

'By the way, Mr Lewis,' she'd added, 'my mother's cousin is American and she reads your articles, and when Mother told her I was living in the same house as you and your friend here, the photographer, well, she was very impressed and said to tell you to keep up the good work.'

'Your mother's cousin reads the *Capital*?' Richard still found it incredible that people read his features and sometimes mentioned them to him.

'No, the *Boston Globe*, that's the only one she reads.'

He and Jacob stared after her as she left the house. 'Well, well, our articles are being syndicated,' said the photographer, after a long, astonished pause. 'So that's why Kirky gave us a pay raise, and Sarah too, not out of the goodness of his heart. I was a bit surprised. Typical of him not to tell us why – wouldn't want us getting big heads, would he?'

As Richard reached the front door of Number 17, the postman was coming down the street, whistling.

'Anything for me or Sarah Lewis or Jacob Nunez?' he paused to ask.

"Ang on, 'ang on...' The grey-haired mailman rummaged in his bag. He was a cheery Cockney who was always telling jokes. They were real shaggy dog stories, but Richard felt an affection for the old guy, long past the age where he should have retired, doing his bit to deliver the mail and keep spirits up. 'Did you hear about the man who went into the public records office to change his name?'

'No?' Richard stood, waiting patiently.

'Well, the clerk says, "Sir, with the war on, we've got more important things to do."

'"Oh, but it's very important I change it," the man says. "Please, I'm begging you. I can't go on with this name, not now."

'"Go on then, what's your name?" asks the clerk with a sigh.

'"Adolf Stinkbum," the man replies.

'"And what do you want to change it to?" asks the clerk, feeling sorry for the poor bloke. And the man replies, "Maurice Stinkbum."'

He honked at his own joke, and Richard found himself joining in.

It wasn't that funny, but there was something so endearing about the old man and his silly stories.

'Now, here you go, sir – three for you today, nothing else.'

Standing on the steps of Number 17, Richard checked the envelopes. The first was his pay slip from the *Capital* – Lucille wired his wages directly to a bank account in London so he could access his money here.

The second was from Miranda, of all people; he could tell from her writing. She must have gotten the address from Sarah, who was still friendly with her.

The third had Irish stamps and was addressed in that familiar hand, in lilac ink.

Finally.

Heart pounding, he checked the date on the postmark. It had been sent some time after the first letter he had mailed to her, the one where he declared his love. Every time he remembered what he'd written, he felt a wave of nerves and panic.

If you'd have me, I'd move heaven and earth for us to be together. If you don't want that, I'll accept it and never mention it again, but please don't cut off our friendship. Just write back something cheerful, like you never got this letter at all.

So now, at last, here was her answer.

He rubbed the envelope between finger and thumb, checking its thickness. It was thin. Not good. Rejection letters were always thin; he knew that from when he'd first started trying to get into journalism. He felt slightly sick and very cold, despite his good coat, bought from Macy's in New York last Easter, and his soft grey fedora that the British called a trilby, pulled down over his forehead.

Open it, Richard. Get it over with.

But not here in the street. After letting himself into the house, he ran up the rickety stairs and into the tiny room he'd been allocated by his sister and Jacob. There was only room in here for a narrow bed, a flyblown mirror on the wall and a metal wastebasket he had turned upside down to use as a bedside table. All his clothes and other belongings were in his suitcase under the bed.

He threw his pay slip into an envelope he kept under the bed beside the suitcase – it was where he stored all his paperwork and everything he wasn't sure what to do with – then sat on the bed and looked at his other two letters, unsure which to open first.

Of course he *knew* which one he wanted to open first. He had been waiting for a letter from Grace for months.

But he was afraid to read it.

So he opened the one from Miranda.

Dear Richard…

His ex-girlfriend's handwriting was rather sloppy, with lots of smudges.

I've just come back from some horrible regatta—of course, where else would I be—listening to my husband going on as always about ropes or brasses or something that I have no idea about and couldn't care less about…

Richard couldn't help smiling. He could just picture Miranda making that attentive face, the one where she was miles away in her head while looking at whatever idiot was holding forth as if he were the cleverest man in the world. He didn't know how they did it, but all Southern girls seemed to be taught this trick.

Poor Algy is such a dreary old bore. He genuinely only has one topic of conversation. I swear I'll go crazy listening to him talk about boats all the time. Today they were all spouting some gibberish about the Auld Mug, the prize won by the winner of the America's Cup or something. Who cares? Just some other yacht-loving jackass. Oh, Richard, I feel like I've made the most awful mistake…

Richard winced; he felt awkward even reading this. He did feel sorry for his ex-girlfriend. She was a clever, fun-loving girl, and Algernon was most definitely not fun. But she'd settled for him because she wanted the money and the status and the huge house. And this was the price, he guessed. There was certainly no way she could have tolerated hacking around Europe with Richard like Sarah was doing with Jacob. She might not think it, but she'd made the right decision.

I'm afraid I'm a few sheets to the wind as I write this. (Oh God, I'm picking up Algy's awful habit of turning every single thing into a seafaring metaphor!) I've had too many glasses of champagne, and now I think I'll refill my glass...

Her handwriting got harder to read in the next paragraph. He deciphered something about having gotten rid of her Costa Rican lover, who had started wanting her to leave her husband, and then a scrawl saying *I still love you, Richard Lewis*, after which the letter finished abruptly, with her signature and a row of XOs, which girls all seemed to put on letters these days to indicate kisses and hugs.

He ripped it into pieces; it was the gentlemanly thing to do. Judging by her drunken handwriting, his former girlfriend wouldn't even remember having sent it, and he had no desire to ever remind her. Last time they'd met, she'd expressed regret that things didn't work out between them. He felt no such thing. He liked her a lot, and she was clever and beautiful, but he knew now that she had never been the one for him, even if he hadn't realised it at the time.

There was only one girl who had occupied his thoughts ever since he'd laid eyes on her in the flesh last June. Maybe he'd loved her before that, though it would be ridiculous to think he'd fallen in love with someone he'd never met.

He couldn't put off opening her letter any longer. This was the moment of truth. He had written to her about how he felt. And here, at last, was her reply. He took off his shoes and coat, kicking the shoes under the bed and laying his coat across it. He propped up his pillows and stretched out.

Butterflies in the pit of his stomach, he ripped the envelope open.

Dear Richard,

Thank you for your lovely long letter. I always get a thrill when I feel the fatness of the envelope, knowing it's going to be a long one...

He read about she relied on him for news of the war, and how she kept all his articles in a scrapbook. That made him smile. He was flattered that she thought people confided in him, they did he supposed. She said they'd had no word of Alfie and she mentioned Mrs McHale.

Resting his head back against the wall behind him, with its peeling wallpaper, Richard allowed himself to breathe again. This letter was clearly a response to his second letter, the one sent from England. So that was it. She wasn't going to mention his declaration. No response was a response. He should just be grateful she'd not cut him off. Or maybe it never arrived?

She seemed very friendly and warm, not awkward at all. She said she loved his letters, she relied on him, she seemed to admire him. The most likely thing was that the first letter got lost. Plenty of mail was going missing these days, with the war being fought in the North Atlantic. If his hadn't arrived by now, chances were it was at the bottom of the ocean. Despite his request for her to never mention it if she didn't feel the same way as he did, he knew Grace and she wouldn't just say nothing. He was sure of it.

Which meant he hadn't exposed his heart to her after all.

It was disappointing in a way, but also a relief. As good as it had felt to get his feelings off his chest, it had been terrifying waiting for her response and fearing the worst. Now it looked like he had a second chance to keep her as a friend.

And he still had time to declare his love if it ever seemed like the right thing to do. He could take a holiday, in the new year maybe, and get back to Knocknashee, see her face to face again. And this time, instead of just rushing off after giving her the lightest of kisses, the sort of kiss you'd give a friend, he would linger, and he would see…

He went back to the letter with a lighter heart and reread the first postscript, which had puzzled him. What did she mean about the canon not having appeared yet? There was obviously something about it in the letter she'd sent to America. Surely Canon Rafferty wasn't coming back to Knocknashee? That would be a disaster. He wondered if Mrs McHale had gotten anywhere with her detective work yet. It sounded like Grace might need his help with this.

It felt warm, comforting, to think about coming to her aid.

Maybe this was how his relationship with Grace was intended to be. Soulmates, supporting and helping each other from afar.

CHAPTER 11

KNOCKNASHEE, CO KERRY

'That awful yoke of a priest, I had to give him short shrift this afternoon.' Tilly looked quite triumphant as she set a huge basket of vegetables on Grace's kitchen table. She then lifted Odile out of the same basket, brushed some loose dirt off her clothes and sat by the range, bouncing the giggling baby on her knee. Her wine-coloured hat sat at a rakish angle.

'Why? What happened?' Grace glanced up in alarm from where she was sitting, sewing a gilt button back onto a burgandy velvet dress. Lizzie had made it from a pattern. She'd said the fabric was donated, but Grace just knew she'd used up all her and probably Hugh's coupons to buy it. She'd sent it with a 'congratulations on your engagement' card. The Warringtons knew Declan and were thrilled for her. She would ask Hugh to give her away, she thought. She'd never worn red, but Lizzie assured her it would be beautiful with her colouring, and she had to admit it did suit her. She planned to wear the dress to Tralee tomorrow when she and Declan went to get her engagement ring.

'Oh, don't worry, nothing I couldn't handle.'

'Tilly, please don't underestimate that man. He's more dangerous than you realise.'

'He's not. He's just a cowardly, pathetic snake.'

'But what was he up to, coming to the farm?' Grace worried her best friend didn't take the canon seriously enough. He'd been openly hostile to her before he left for Tipperary, but she didn't care because her farm continued to thrive. Everyone still bought her eggs and honey and cabbages because they were so good, and her potatoes were legendary, like balls of flour; Biddy O'Donoghue always sold out within an hour of them landing. Seaweed fertiliser apparently was the trick.

'The usual. Sticking his nose into our business, asking to see Odile's paperwork or something. Mam is a bit scared of him, but I'm not. I said to him, "She's a tiny baby, for God's sake! What do you think? She's a spy? An enemy agent come to gurgle the secrets we don't know out of us?" That shut him up. He oozed around the kitchen for a bit before he could think of the next thing to say, which was to ask if we were sure Odile was related to us? Mam was nearly in tears at that, and I asked him how could he say such a thing when she was the dead spit of Alfie's wife, and I pointed to the photo of Alfie with Constance in Paris, where they have their arms around each other and look so happy and lovely. Well, he went over to look so closely at the photo, I could tell he was trying to see if Constance had a ring on her finger, though you can't tell by looking. And do you know what he said then?'

'No...' But Grace had a nasty feeling she could guess.

'He asked if Alfie and Constance were married in the eyes of God. Can you believe that?' Tilly's voice rose in genuine indignation. 'How dare he suggest Odile might be illegitimate! I told him he had a right cheek, suggesting my brother wouldn't marry the mother of his child!'

Grace suppressed a smile. Tilly's anger was sort of funny, considering the last any of them knew, Alfie wasn't married to Constance. And anyway, Odile wasn't even their child – she was Constance's niece, which explained the likeness. The canon might be a vile, horrible man, but in this case, his creepy ability to sniff out other people's secrets wasn't far off the mark.

'And then,' Tilly said, even more outraged, 'he said to get married in the Catholic Church, Alfie would have had to write to this parish for a letter of freedom, and there was no record of that.'

Grace had a cold, sick feeling in her stomach. This was not good. 'What did you say to him, Tilly?' She hoped her friend hadn't got too argumentative.

Tilly grinned. 'I said my brother didn't need any letter from the Catholic Church to get married in a registrar's office, and when that nasty snake tried to argue that meant they weren't properly wed because the Catholic Church wouldn't recognise it, I said, well, tell that to the French Republic, which always supported Irish freedom from the English.'

'Oh, Tilly.' Grace sighed, fearful for her friend. 'Please do be careful. You don't want the canon trying to take Odile off you. It wouldn't be the first time.'

Tilly wrapped her arms tightly around the baby on her lap, as if the priest might appear any minute to drag her away. 'Ara now, Grace, he wouldn't, he couldn't...'

'He's done it before, Tilly, and you know that. So I'm telling you, be careful. Did he say anything else?'

'Not really, just more of the usual, like I should marry that Tomás Kinneally fellow next door, and how a woman's place is in the home, and I should leave the man's work to the man and clean the house because the place is filthy and not fit for a child...'

'And did you promise to clean it?'

Tilly laughed. 'No, I did not. I said this was a farmhouse, and it's never going to look like the parochial house, all gleaming and spotless because the likes of Dymphna O'Connell are cleaning up after him all the time, and that's true, isn't it?'

'Mm...' Grace wasn't sure how to be honest without offending her friend. Between Tilly tramping in the mud and sheep droppings from the fields and Mrs O'Hare unable to reach the dresser with her bad back or bend down to clean the floor because of her knees, there was always a thick film of dirt and dust on everything in the O'Hare farmhouse, which her best friend had obviously got used to. She wouldn't put it past Canon Rafferty to send in the dreaded 'cruelty men', as everyone called the inspectors from the National Society for Prevention of Cruelty to Children; they often accused poor and working-class parents of neglect and took their children away to be reared by the nuns or in the industrial schools.

Tilly and her mother were not poor. They weren't wealthy either, but they managed fine due to Tilly's hard work and entrepreneurial spirit. They were good, loving people who adored Odile, but Grace could see that it might not look like an ideal situation. An inspector could be quite capable of classing people like Tilly, with her man's clothes and out in the fields all the time carrying the baby around in a basket, and Mary, who was crippled with the rheumatism and also a Bean Feasa and a *seanachai*, as 'degenerate, incapable and abnormal' and not fit to rear a child.

'Grace, why are you looking at me like that? The place is not that bad?' said Tilly as she teased a clump of dried mud from Odile's dark hair. 'You have to say if it is. I mean, Eloise is going to be coming to stay soon. I don't want her thinking I live in a pigsty. She's from Switzerland, and they're mad clean over there – Alfie told me. He came through there on his way from Spain to Paris. I gave Alfie's bedroom a wipe down, but it's hard to stop the cobwebs coming back. I couldn't give a hoot about things like spiders normally, but do you think she'll be OK with that?'

Before Grace could think of how to put her worries about Tilly's cleaning skills and Mary O'Hare's ability to run after a toddler once Odile started moving, there was a rattle of feet down the hall and Dymphna burst into the kitchen, tears running down her face, six-year-old Kate looking woebegone at her heels.

'Dymphna, what's the matter?' Grace got to her feet as quickly as she could with the calliper, putting aside the red dress and pulling out a chair for the widow, guiding her to sit down.

'The canon says he doesn't want me working for him any more,' sobbed Dymphna as she sank onto the wooden chair.

'Oh God, what happened?' Tilly looked pale and guilty. 'Was it me? I was only just saying to that long streak of misery how he wouldn't be able to manage without you. I hope I didn't set him off...'

The widow shook her head as she gulped and mopped her eyes. 'No, it wasn't you, Tilly, it was me. He was saying such horrible things about Tommy, and how Father Iggy should never have blessed the *cillín*, and that's why the poor man got sent to Cork. I never knew – Father Iggy never said. He was doing me such a kindness, and I ruined his life because the bishop got to hear of it...'

'It was hardly you who told the bishop,' objected Tilly, rocking Odile as the baby began to whimper in sympathy with Kate, who was crying as well now. 'So don't blame yourself for that.'

'I as good as did – I told my mother,' sobbed Dymphna. 'And I shouldn't have, but she was being so cruel about Tommy's death and I wanted her to know that the Church had welcomed Tommy at last. Maybe it was the sin of pride. And it seems she went and found Canon Rafferty in Tipperary – they go way back – and 'twas him told Bishop Reynolds, and you should have seen the smug look on him. He said my mother was a good holy woman and I should follow in her footsteps. And then I couldn't help myself, I couldn't hold my tongue even for the sake of keeping my children fed – I told him my mother was no Christian woman, she was cruel and spiteful and so was he, that Father Iggy was twice the priest he was and...' The poor, meek woman dissolved into fresh floods of terrified tears. 'I can't believe I said those things to him. What'll he do to me?'

Grace and Tilly sat looking at her in amazement and wonder. The gentle, long-suffering widow had never said boo to a goose in her life, so it was hard to imagine her standing up to the canon that way. Though it was no surprise he'd thrown her out if she had; he hated people he couldn't bully into submission. And now how was the poor woman going to pay the rent on the tiny thatched two-roomed cottage she rented off Tom O'Donoghue and feed her two small children?

Grace had paid Dymphna before for looking after Agnes and kept her on for a while after Agnes died, finding her a few hours as the school cleaner, until Nancy O'Flaherty got her the position in the parochial house. But now Janie O'Shea was getting paid for the school cleaning work and there was no money to spare anywhere; wages had gone down and prices gone up with the Emergency, and jobs were very hard to come by.

Dymphna couldn't be left to starve, though. 'There's plenty of work here in this house for you, Dymphna, while you get on your feet,' said Grace, trying to calculate how much she could spare out of her own salary, which had been cut back.

'There is not, Grace. There wasn't any work to do after Agnes died, not after I'd finished making fresh curtains and everything, and even they didn't need doing, not really,' said Dymphna, sobbing again. 'And I won't take money off you for nothing. I'll find something, somewhere…'

'Dymphna, if it suits, you could come up and do our place,' said Tilly, with a glance at Grace. 'I'm expecting a visitor, and I'd like to have Alfie's room ready for her. I have a feeling Grace doesn't think it should be full of spiders, though what harm they do apart from getting rid of the flies, I don't know.'

'I'd be happy to, Tilly.' Dymphna gulped, wiped her eyes and smiled slightly. 'I'll come up one of the days now that I'm free and give the place a going over for you, no trouble at all. There'll be no charge – you've been so kind to me.'

'Sure I've done nothing,' Tilly protested. 'And it's not just the cleaning that needs doing, so I'm told…' She smiled ruefully at Grace. 'You would be a great help with Odile. Poor Mam is so bad with her knees, and caring for a baby is difficult to manage with the farming. She's not quite crawling yet, but she can roll and needs someone watching her all the time. She nearly ended up in a ditch full of brambles last week. You know, why don't we make it a daily thing, nine to six, five shillings a week? I could produce more vegetables and keep a few more sheep if I had more time.'

Grace felt a huge rush of affection for her friend. It was true she and her mother could probably use the help, and hopefully it would keep the canon at bay, so it was a very good idea to have Dymphna take over the running of the house and the childcare, but five shillings was a very generous offer. An experienced cook in a big upper-middle-class house in the city wouldn't get more than a pound a week at the most.

'Ah, Tilly, will you stop. There's no need for that much money.' Dymphna was wide-eyed at such generosity.

Tilly laughed. 'You haven't spent a day at our place or you wouldn't be saying that. You'll have your work cut out for you, you can be sure of it. This little madam is a right taskmaster.' She gave Odile a cuddle, and the baby giggled. 'So we really do need some help, and of course you can bring Kate and Paudie with you in the holidays, and they won't go hungry. I'll keep you in turnips and cabbage and everything you need if you'll just cook me my tea in the evening to save Mam the difficulty.'

'Well, I'd love to, if you're sure.' The relief was written all over Dymphna's face.

'I am.' Tilly smiled, stretching out her strong sun-browned hand to shake the widow's thin, pale fingers. 'And let you start tomorrow, because I don't know when my friend is coming. Any time soon was last I heard.'

'I will, Tilly. The first thing I'll do is I'll get Alfie's room all scrubbed and ready for her, floors and ceiling and walls and everything. I'll wash all the sheets, and I have a nice clean blue patchwork quilt I'll bring up, if that suits?'

'That sounds perfect, Dymphna, and maybe it will help if I seal up the window in there against the spiders?'

'It might, Tilly. I'd say it won't matter if it won't open. It's coming into the winter now, and there will be a wicked wind rattling through it with the height you're on, so if it's closed permanently, at least your visitor won't freeze to death in the night.'

It was lovely to see the widow look so relieved and already

throwing herself into her new role. It would be a million miles better than working for Canon Rafferty anyway. Dymphna loved Odile already and was a very motherly soul as well as a wonderful housekeeper and cook. Now she stretched out her arms for the child. Tilly passed her over, and Odile cooed and crowed, pushed her hands up to pat Dymphna's face and gurgled with delight.

'Can I play with her?' Six-year-old Kate also loved the baby.

'You can. Why don't we put her blanket on the floor and you can both get down there. It's warm enough in here, I think?' Tilly rooted in the basket for Odile's big woollen blanket that Mary O'Hare had knitted for her.

Dymphna took the blanket, discreetly brushed all the dirt off it, then laid it out and placed Odile on her back, making the baby laugh as she tickled her tummy. Kate took down the box of toys Grace kept on the shelf for when children were visiting, a dolly and a ball and two jigsaw puzzles, and placed it on the floor.

'She's too small for jigsaws, Katie, but she might like to see the dolly?' Dymphna said gently.

'Will you have a cup of tea, now that's all settled?' Grace stood up again and headed to the range. 'Oh, and I have some of those buns you brought up to me on Friday evening, Dymphna.'

'Oh, that's another thing. If you can make us a few of those buns every week, I'd be your best friend.' Tilly winked at Dymphna.

'See how fickle she is, Dymphna?' teased Grace. 'I get dumped as best friend over a bun. You wouldn't want to be relying too heavily on Miss O'Hare now, would you?'

'Oh, I wouldn't get between you two now.' Dymphna chuckled. ''Tis a very foolish person would do that.'

'Maybe so, but I'm thinking this Swiss woman who's coming will run me close as a rival.' Grace chuckled as she got down the tin of tasty buns.

Tilly laughed. 'That will never happen!' But she was blushing all the same. Her best friend was clearly mad about this unknown woman, and Grace couldn't help feeling a tiny bit hurt. Ever since they were little children, she and Tilly had been as thick as thieves, and it felt a bit strange, having someone else in the mix.

Of course, she shouldn't complain. She had other friends herself, including Richard. And now she had Declan, who as her husband would become the centre of her world. So she shouldn't begrudge Tilly new relationships of her own. She just hoped this Eloise was worthy of her.

CHAPTER 12

LONDON, ENGLAND

NOVEMBER 1940

Sitting in the Petit Club Français, an elegant Georgian building in St James's Square and a wartime watering hole for French exiles and their friends, Richard listened closely as General de Gaulle addressed the gathered press in broken English with the help of his official interpreter. Normally Richard and Jacob didn't bother with staged news conferences where no questions were taken, but Kirky had wanted his view on this one because de Gaulle was making a name for himself.

Jacob and the other foreign photographers stood on the sides of the room, snapping away, their flashes illuminating the salon, which had beautiful hand-painted wallpaper. On rows of gilded chairs sat newspapermen from all over the world. Richard recognised most of the faces now. They were all here to report back to their countries from valiant London, which stood alone facing an occupied continent, and today they were taking down every word from the self-styled leader of the Free French, which they would report as if it were gospel and not just whistling in the dark.

The general was an arrogant man who had appointed himself the saviour of France when hardly anyone in that country even knew his name. He was immensely tall, six foot five in his smart uniform and polished boots, his brush moustache yellow with constant chain-smoking. Soon after he'd escaped to England last June, he had made a broadcast on BBC Radio, calling all French officers, soldiers, engineers and others who were now on British soil or would be in the future to join with him and build an army to fight the Nazis.

Today, as far as Richard could understand him, was more of the same – how France would never be defeated, how it would stand strong against the Germans, that it was not over, that the allies of France, Britain and America would prove more than a match for the German war machine, that all French people needed to do was to be strong, to join him in London with or without weapons, and when the time was right, they would march triumphantly back to reclaim the French Republic.

The general's condemnation of the conservative and deeply antisemitic Vichy government, led by Marshal Pétain, was as scathing as ever. Pétain, a hero of the Great War, claimed his government was truly French, independent and self-governing, and not the puppet Nazi government the foreign press presented it as, but de Gaulle had nothing but contempt for his old and far more famous comrade.

Real news from France was sketchy at best, but Richard had written a number of well-received articles for the *Capital* based on a series of interviews with the French refugees arriving daily in England. Most of them agreed with de Gaulle, that Pétain was an enthusiastic collaborator with the Germans. The German line, of course, was that if the French simply cooperated, then they had nothing to fear from their invaders – which nobody beyond Berlin believed.

It was true, however, that the brutality shown to the Poles in the east was not evident in the way the Germans were treating the French for now; the Germans seemed to at least consider the French their racial equal, unlike the misfortunate Poles Hitler was mowing down mercilessly. But Richard feared if the French thought Hitler regarded them as anything other than beaten, they were very much mistaken.

The varying degrees of enthusiasm for Pétain or de Gaulle seemed to be caused by infighting between the French fascists, the socialists and the communists, and Richard suspected this was precisely the way the Germans wanted it to be.

Almost all of the Vichy government sources seemed to him to be labouring under a huge misapprehension, that somehow France's capitulation and defeat and subsequent acceptance of German occupation was going to create a new European order that would make France a powerful nation once more, either against or side by side with Germany.

As he sat scribbling in shorthand his views about what the general was saying this evening, Richard wondered if de Gaulle had read any of his American articles. He doubted the general would be thrilled with his description of the situation if he had, but it was how he saw it, and Kirky was happy with him so far.

The general had moved on to speaking about America and was adamant, like Churchill, that Richard's country needed to be in the war. The tide was turning that way back in the States, but the extent to which America would be involved was still a matter of grave contention, and Richard found that understandable. Supplying military hardware, food and supplies was one thing, but American boots on European soil was something quite different – particularly with France so divided. America was still punch-drunk from the Great Depression, and the bitter memories of the so-called war to end all wars was still in the public consciousness. Europeans, and the British in particular, seemed to have a selective memory where American history was concerned. The Boston Tea Party wasn't for nothing. George Washington had led America out of bondage to a British king who saw the colony as nothing more than a source of revenue and a resource to be plundered. The United States of America's Founding Fathers freed his countrymen and women from British tyranny, so thinking they would be enthusiastic to fight once more with the old enemy was a big assumption.

When Grace explained to him why Ireland was neutral, that because Ireland was forcibly and brutally subjugated by Britain for eight centuries and had only gained her freedom by force of arms in the last twenty years, he understood. Because in a way, though it was back in the eighteenth century, America was the same. They too had gotten out of the clutches of the British, at considerable cost, but no British person he'd met seemed to understand that, or even consider that America would not relish rushing to the aid of a country that had once been such a bitter enemy. Despite that, he had no doubt that America would come to Britain's aid. But when the people here accused Americans of not understanding history, what they meant was *their* history. He would argue that the English could use a few American history lessons too.

Focussing once more on the general as he went on and on, Richard knew this chronic disunity in France was also why he had been reluctant to ask any of the French people he had interviewed whether they knew anything about four particular members of the French resistance – you didn't know who to trust. The fate of Alfie O'Hare, Paul or Bernadette Dreyfus, or Constance, Bernadette's sister and Alfie's girlfriend, could be put at risk even by one conversation within the earshot of the wrong person. Nobody was under any illusion that London wasn't awash with Nazi spies.

Sarah, who could eavesdrop on French conversations, had been trawling the known communist bars around Stepney and Deptford, hoping to hear French communists speaking together, but she'd had no luck. Most of what she picked up, she told Richard, was Londoners' deep working-class unrest at the seeming injustice of the Blitz. Middle-class houses with gardens could add an Anderson shelter, but those who lived in the East End, rows of back-to-back terraced houses with no yards, were left with very few options, and they were feeling it the most. Some factories had underground shelters, and there was the Tube of course, but it was nowhere near enough.

The boarding house where he and Jacob and Sarah were living had no shelter, and they'd spent a lot of nights in the Tube station nearby, but at least they weren't living in the East End, which was taking the brunt of the bombardment because of the docks and factories.

Sometimes the air raids came five or six times a night, from sunset to sunrise. The Germans took off in France a few minutes before darkness fell and arrived over London a few minutes after dark; you could set your watch by them. Every single night, for long weary hours, the drone of the Luftwaffe, the scream of dropping bombs, the pounding of guns... And all around the clenched teeth and ragged nerves of the people as they waited for the explosions, all the time wondering, how near is it? Is it timed? Did it fall but not detonate yet? Would they see the morning?

In the Tube station, the conditions were cramped and the air smelled foul, but there was an upside – he was able to spend hours talking to ordinary people. There were enough reporters recording every word out of Churchill's mouth – and de Gaulle's – so for the most part, he and Jacob preferred to focus on real-life stories. They were getting quite a name for themselves back in America, Kirky told them.

Richard had spent time with mothers who had to send their little ones to the country for fear of the bombs, while they worked long hours in munitions factories. Jacob had photographed dances, the wild abandon of people who might not live to see the next day. They reported on what was available to buy in the shops, how rationing really impacted people, what it felt like for kids going to school with their gas masks. They went to see a soccer match, a local derby, played on a field that looked like it had been trampled by a herd of elephants – but that didn't deter the fans or the players. He wrote of bread and marg, and a horrendous meat-like substance called Spam that was made in the USA and gaining popularity here because it was cheap. Jacob wouldn't eat it being Jewish and nobody in the Lewis household would ever have encountered such a thing, but the Brits seemed to love it. Jacob sent photographs of people drying tea leaves to reuse them over and over until they barely darkened the water.

They filed photographs of how all the colour had been removed from chocolate wrappers because it was a waste of ink, so if children ever got a treat, and that was rare, it was just wrapped in white paper with little marking. Richard even included some recipes in his copy, like pigs in blankets or potato-peel pie. Americans lapped it up because they had a fascination, and a degree of dread too, at how they would fare in the same circumstances.

The one constant he wrote about was the complete and utter refusal of the people to be cowed. They were angry certainly, exhausted and worried of course – it showed in their faces – but defeated never. Churchill was doing a great job in that regard. Richard had yet to meet a British person who was in any doubt whatsoever that they would win the war.

He'd reported with amusement how at the movies, when the air-raid siren went off and the instruction on screen was for everyone to go to the nearest shelter, people didn't move, they just sat there and waited for the all-clear. They were not easily rattled, that was for sure.

A cheeky waitress in a Lyons' Corner House had asked him what he was writing one day, and he told her. She said when he was writing about it, he should call the last war German War 1, this one German War 2 and 'keep going until we run out of numbers.'

As his mind wandered, bored of de Gaulle's pomposity, a scuffle from the back of the room caught his attention. Someone was heckling the general in loud French.

Moments later a small, slight man was manhandled out of the meeting by de Gaulle's aides amid a lot of shouting. Richard's French was still poor – he used Sarah to interpret for him when he was doing his interviews with French refugees – but he had been getting his sister to teach him in the evenings, and he caught the general gist of what was said. It seemed the heckler was a communist and thought that de Gaulle was sitting pretty here in England, making nice speeches, while his fellow countrymen and women were risking their lives every day by doing the dirty work of resisting the Nazi occupation.

More interested in this opinion than in de Gaulle's self-aggrandisement, Richard stuck his notebook into his bag and followed the commotion outside into the street, where the man had been unceremoniously dumped on the pavement and lay sprawled on his back.

As de Gaulle's men re-entered the press conference, Richard crossed to where he lay spreadeagled on his back, and offered the Frenchman a hand up. 'Can I buy you a beer?' he asked, in very bad French.

'*Non, merci,*' said the small man dourly as he dusted down his threadbare jacket and retrieved his cap, placing it on his head and walking away. Richard followed him, suddenly convinced this might be a chance to make a connection to Alfie and his friends in the resistance.

'*Connaissez-vous* Paul *et* Bernadette Dreyfus?' he asked quietly as he caught up with the man. The Jewish communist and his wife had been in Paris a lot longer than Alfie, so he reckoned that was a good place to start.

The man stopped and turned to look up at him. There was a livid scar running from below his ear to under his shirt, and his green eyes glittered with mistrust. 'No? Why?'

'Do you not know them from the French Communist Party?' It was Richard's turn to be suspicious now. If this man was a member of the party in Paris, surely he knew the Dreyfuses? Maybe he was a spy…

'What's it to you?' the man asked bluntly.

Richard took out his press pass, showing him to be a journalist and American. The man glanced at it but didn't scrutinise it. It had opened many doors for Richard since he'd gotten here; everyone was anxious for the Americans to see the war from their point of view.

'I work for the *Capital* in New York, but I was in Paris before it fell. I knew the Dreyfuses, and Alfie O'Hare and Constance – we used to drink in the Papillon Rouge with Amelie Boucher.' Richard hoped he'd given the man enough to trust him. Something told him he knew exactly who Richard was asking about.

He noticed a slight change in the man's demeanour. He was in.

'I don't know the comrades in Paris. I was in Poitiers, then Vichy.' He extracted a battered pack of Gitanes from his jacket pocket, struck a match and began to smoke. 'I only went to Paris recently, because something needs to be done and Vichy is not where it will happen. They're too busy writing their own commendations for when France is a dominant world force again. Deluded, the whole lot of them. Including that old fool Pétain and that yellow windbag de Gaulle.'

He stalked off in the direction of Russell Square, but Richard stopped him again. 'You're sure you never heard of the Irishman Alfie O'Hare?'

'An Irishman?' The man turned to look at him, his expression neutral.

'Yes, he's the boyfriend of Bernadette's sister, Constance, and he asked me to bring Paul and Bernadette's baby to his family in Ireland, to keep her safe.'

The Frenchman stared at him; he appeared to be processing this information. Then he gestured with his fingers to see the press pass again and asked, 'Are you Richard Lewis?'

Richard handed him the pass but was taken aback. 'That's right. How did you know?'

The man smiled and clapped Richard on the shoulder, all trace of suspicion gone. '*Alors*, let's get that beer, or what passes for beer here. I've been sent to find you, *mon ami*, so this is a lucky coincidence.'

'So as you know my name, may I know yours?' Richard asked as they fell into step beside each other.

'Didier Georges, but everyone calls me Didi.'

'Did Alfie send you to find me?'

Didi nodded. '*Oui*, the idiot got himself arrested the same time as I did. We were both guests of SS man Helmut Knochen.'

'Alfie was arrested by Knochen?' Richard felt a sick chill; he had heard of the head of Parisian security.

Didi pointed proudly to the scar on his neck. 'A little going-away gift from when we escaped… Managed to climb out of a window with each other's help, dodge the guard at the front and run like the wind down Avenue Foch. The scar is from climbing through a broken window. Alfie got away, an *évasion chanceuse*.'

'It really was,' he said, agreeing it was a lucky escape. He knew about Alfie's reputation, of somehow being able to survive anything.

'He's a good man, thinks like me. We need to join forces with people who can actually do something, not just talk about it – Jews, socialists, communists, patriots, religious people, even that fool de Gaulle, I don't care. But we need to unite everyone who wants to repel the German rats from our country, together now, and no more infighting. This is what they want, us at each other's throats so we can't turn on the filthy Boche.'

'You're right,' agreed Richard. This would make a good article, though of course Didier would have to remain anonymous.

'Of course I'm right. De Gaulle wants to do things the old military way, from the comfort of London, with marching armies, but that's not going to work, not now. We need subterfuge, spies. We need to disrupt the German war machine in France, make the conducting of the occupation impossible for them, weaken them so that when the armies do come, and they have to come, the Boche will be in disarray.'

They turned onto another street, and Richard was relieved to see a pub on the next corner called one of those weird English names, the Fiddler and Moon. It was half past nine, and he'd begun to worry they would miss last orders. Pubs in London were busiest around 6 p.m., when men leaving work came in for what they called a glass and a half, which he'd learnt meant a pint and a whiskey chaser, but they shut at ten on the dot.

But Didier shook his head and insisted on walking on, fast and surprisingly knowledgeable, through the maze of streets between Russell Square and Kings Cross for another twenty minutes.

Finally he stopped at another bar called the Union Tavern. The place was empty except for two women at the bar, which was an unusual sight – women didn't go to pubs much, Richard had noticed. They looked the two men up and down as they approached the counter and blushed when Richard smiled at them.

The barman came over and nodded at the Frenchman, who turned his back and slid into a seat in a dark corner, almost out of view of the bar. The barman then asked Richard what he wanted. He ordered two pints of beer and brought them over to Didier, sitting next to him. Raising their glasses together, they stiffened their shoulders, took a sip of the warm, flat ale, winced simultaneously, then laughed.

English beer was truly disgusting; they were clearly united on that. Beer was meant to be light, cold and refreshing, not soupy, room temperature and dark, but it was all they could get so they had to put up with it.

'Do you have any cigarettes?' Didi asked when he'd stopped laughing.

Richard didn't smoke, but he always kept a few packets of Wix in his bag, the closest British imitation of American cigarettes, because he found people always wanted them and would talk more easily if they were puffing on one. He took out two boxes and gave them to Didi, who accepted them gratefully, putting both boxes in his jacket but smoking another of his own foul-smelling Gitanes.

'Do you come in here often?' Richard asked. 'The barman seems to know you.'

The Frenchman grinned and made a zipping motion across his mouth. '"Loose lips sink ships,"' he said, quoting one of the slogans of the day, then took a drag on his cigarette.

'OK, but tell me this – what do you know about Alfie?' The Frenchman's green eyes were open and honest, but he still wanted to check Didi wasn't just pretending to be a comrade of Tilly's brother.

Didi shrugged; he wasn't offended by being questioned. 'Irish, father dead. Has one sister in Dublin, another at home in the west with the mother – she looks after the family farm. He was with the International Brigades in Spain. He's with Constance, the sister of Bernadette Dreyfus. Has a scar on his chest where he ran into the business end of a bayonet in the Basque country. Check my credentials with whoever you want – I am who I say I am.'

Richard believed him. 'And he's still alive?'

Didi shrugged again. 'He was last time I saw him, ten days ago. I decided to get out of Paris for a bit. Now that the Gestapo have had a good look at me, it's time for a change of image. But he decided to stay with his girlfriend, so...' He took another draught of the beer, wincing again.

'And you don't know anything about Paul and Bernadette Dreyfus?'

A shadow crossed Didi's face. 'I do, I just wasn't sure of you earlier. Alfie told me to tell you if I ever found you. I was going to telegram to your newspaper and try to reach you that way. Paul was lifted, sent to Aincourt, in Seine-et-Oise. Most of the communists were sent there. He was shot dead for allegedly trying to escape.'

Richard felt his stomach turn over. He remembered the cheerful man, saw him in his mind's eye, gently rocking his infant daughter while Bernadette served *boeuf bourguignon*, the beef stew of onions, mushrooms and red wine, cooked for a whole day. He and Bernadette loved Odile so much, and now that little girl would never know her father.

'And Bernadette?' He dreaded the answer.

'Alfie had no idea. She wasn't with Paul when he was arrested. As to where she is now, it's impossible to say. She wasn't at any of the usual places afterwards – Constance looked everywhere and put it out among our people. She may well have been lifted, sent east, or she might – and it's not very likely – have escaped. If she has managed that, she will lay low. It's impossible to know who to trust, so best trust nobody.'

'What are the chances she is still alive?' Richard asked, realising how foolish the question sounded.

Didi just shrugged. 'Like I say, impossible to know. Not good, I would say. Neither Alfie nor his fiancée has heard from her since, but that doesn't mean anything. Nobody in our line of work stays anywhere very long, and we keep strict silence on information. Different strands of the network have specific tasks. There is no crossover for security reasons.'

Richard contemplated his glass. The relief of hearing about Alfie was overshadowed now. 'Will you ever go back?'

'I will, once I've grown my hair and beard and dyed it, just to change my appearance a bit. But I'll make contact with the British here first, tell them everything I know about the Nazi swine, then I'll have them drop me somewhere else in the country. Paris is too dangerous for me now.'

'If you see Alfie ever again, please tell him that Odile is fine, she's being well looked after in Ireland by his sister and mother, and that she's safe. And if you could tell him his family and friends are worried for him and praying for him every day.'

'Prayers?' The communist laughed. 'We are going to need more than prayers, *mon ami*. If I run into him, I'll tell him, but I can't promise anything.'

The barman rang the bell for closing, and Didi stood up, draining his pint. 'Now I must go. *Bon chance, camarade.*' He shook Richard's hand. 'And do all you can with your fountain pen to bring your country over here, *le plut tôt possible s'il vous plait*, eh? *A la prochaine.*'

Until the next time, Didi had said in French. But as he departed through the door of the pub, Richard wondered if there would indeed be a next time that he would cross paths with Didier Georges.

'On yer own, love?' asked one of the women from the bar, sitting down beside him in the Frenchman's place.

She was pretty, nicely dressed, and for a moment he wanted to say *Yes, I am alone. Very alone.* The shock of hearing about Paul Dreyfus and his sadness for Odile made him long for simple human comfort, the feel of someone's arms around him, a kiss, a touch. Everyone was the same, he thought, looking for animal comfort in these times. Flings and affairs were happening everywhere he looked. The other tenants at 17 Meadowfield Gardens were always sneaking girls in, dodging the watchful eye of Mrs Price, who he was beginning to suspect was not so watchful after all, despite her stern demeanour. And why not take comfort where you could, when you might die at any moment?

But he wasn't that kind of man, and besides, his mind was full of Paul Dreyfus and Odile and Knocknashee, and he couldn't stop thinking about how upset Grace would be when she heard.

The young woman looked at him hopefully, watched by the other from the bar, who might be her sister, they looked so alike. 'Want to join us at the bar, buy us a drink?'

He smiled at her and downed the rest of his tepid beer. 'Thanks, but I'm with someone,' he said politely as he stood to leave.

* * *

HE AND SARAH and Jacob stayed up until the small hours, drinking bottles of decent American beer that Sarah had managed to wrangle from the generous Texan businessman upstairs.

They spoke about the friends they'd made in Paris, and the death of Paul Dreyfus. How many more tragedies like this would happen before America came into the war? It made their work seem so much more urgent.

He also told them that Didier seemed to have a special relationship with the Union Tavern, that he'd insisted on going there and the barman seemed to know him. Jacob and Sarah made a note; if it was a pub where French communists hung out, the conversation there might be interesting.

That night the air-raid sirens stayed silent and the three of them were able to stay in their own beds for once, instead of on a Tube platform.

Even so, Richard couldn't sleep.

He sat up reading a book by Charles Dickens, *Oliver Twist*, set in London a hundred years ago, when aircraft and bombs had not yet been invented. He thought about Grace and worried about baby Odile. And in the end, as the first fingers of sunlight poked up over the old, resilient city, he got out of bed, dressed in the tiny gap between his bed and the wall and was waiting outside the post office before it opened.

Once it did, he sent a telegram to Knocknashee.

NEWS FROM FRANCE. AO'H & C ALIVE. BD MISSING. PD KILLED BY NAZIS. R.

Later that day he followed it up with a short letter. He decided to stick to using initials instead of names. As Didier had said, 'Loose lips sink ships.'

Dear Grace,

You will have received by now my telegram about PD, and that there's a baby girl who will never know her father. It is a tragic story, but at least she is safe and loved and looked after by her aunt, and I'm sure he knows that, wherever he is, and is looking down on her.

I found out about PD's fate from a Frenchman I won't name in case my letters to you are being read. If so, hello to you, whoever you are. This man met A less than two weeks before when they were escaping from the Gestapo. The Frenchman was injured, but of course A got away without a scratch before he disappeared again. Incidentally the Frenchman referred to C as A's fiancée, so that's interesting. Maybe the war has made A realise how important love is, in this brief time we have to live.

It was A who told my French friend how PD died. He was arrested, detained in Aincourt, in Seine-et-Oise, and shot for allegedly trying to escape. It is a tragedy. He was such a lovely man. Where BD is now is impossible to guess, but people work on a need-to-know basis, so I think even though she is missing, we can hope for the best.

Write soon,

Richard

CHAPTER 13

KNOCKNASHEE, CO KERRY

December 1940

Dear Richard, Grace wrote, with tears in her eyes. *Thank you from the bottom of our hearts for taking time to find out about Alfie.*

She stopped and scribbled out all the letters in Alfie's name except for the A; there was no point in Richard being extra careful if she didn't follow suit.

His mother and sister wept with relief that he is alive and had escaped from danger without being harmed, and they're also so glad to hear he is engaged to C.

But also we all feel such terrible sadness for poor little Odile, who has lost her father.

Mary O'Hare asked the canon, who is back now and as awful as ever, to say a Mass for PD. He was a Jewish man, but a Mass couldn't do him any harm. I think we all pray to the same God in the end, and it is all we can do.

She told him he was A's brother-in-law, which is nearly true now, and had been murdered by the Germans while in custody. But the canon refused, saying he sounded like a man who died in mortal sin if he was breaking the law and that Mass for the repose of his soul was pointless.

Honestly you'd swear he wanted the Germans to win the way he goes on. When he mounted the pulpit last Sunday – it was for the first time since he came back – he said a lot of horrible things that were clearly directed at the likes of A and Maura O'Donoghue, who ran off to join the British Army last month, and then Sally O'Sullivan, who followed her last Friday...

Grace sighed and shook her head as she refilled her fountain pen from the bottle of lilac ink. Sally's midnight flit had been a big shock to her poor parents. No one expected the village beauty to run off to Belfast to sign up, even if she was very friendly with Maura O'Donoghue. Tilly said it was because Sally was disappointed about Declan and had gone off in a huff. If that was true, she hoped Bridie Keohane wouldn't follow suit, though she didn't think she would.

Nobody wants their sons and daughters in the war, of course they don't. Mary O'Hare longs to have her son and his bride safe at home, and the O'Donoghues and the O'Sullivans are shocked and embarrassed and worried sick about their daughters, so they certainly didn't need a sermon about it, but nonetheless that's what they got.

'This conflict is not of our making, and it is none of our business,' the canon decreed from the pulpit, his soft raspy voice every bit as forceful as a loud booming one. 'Any young man or woman of this parish with a notion to go off, defying their family and the direct orders of their Church, must accept then the fact that they are in a state of mortal sin. Thou shalt not kill. The Lord was very clear on that point, and anyone offering their services to the armed forces, directly or indirectly, is flying in the face of God.'

He scanned the church, his cold blue eyes seeming to bore into our souls. 'We are told to support Churchill, that the Germans are the enemy, but they are England's enemy, not ours. We have no gripe with Germany, and how they conduct their business of government is not our concern. They know best what is right for their country, I'm sure, and so if there is anyone in this church harbouring such foolish notions as going to join the British, then I warn you that doing so will place not just your life, but your immortal soul also, in very grave peril.'

So there you are, Richard. That's the sort of priest he is. So we lit candles and said our own prayers in silence for PD's soul. We are also praying every day that BD is safe and that A brings C home to us as soon as this is over.

What a terrible thing war is, Richard. Please, please keep yourself safe.

This is my third letter in a row, so again, I've kept it short.

Yours,

Grace

It struck her as she folded it into the envelope that once again she hadn't mentioned Declan – and they were off to Tralee this Saturday for a ring and they'd announce the engagement at Christmas.

There was no waiting any longer, though. The canon scowled at them suspiciously every time he passed them, and the buses were getting so infrequent that they risked missing the opportunity altogether.

So she really should tell Richard that she and Declan were now properly engaged, even if for some reason he still hadn't got her first letter, which she'd sent via the *Capital* – and it didn't look like he had, because surely he would have mentioned it? She loved Declan with all her heart and she was going to marry him, so to not even mention the engagement would be sort of strange and...well, disloyal.

She took the sheet of paper back out of the envelope.

PS I'm sure by now you've received the letter I sent to America in September, letting you know that myself and Declan are doing a line. We might have been content with that for a while, but the gossip was getting out of hand – nothing is ever secret in Knocknashee. There is a lot of pressure on teachers to be respectable in Ireland. I suppose it's the same everywhere, but I think here even more so – we're not allowed to be flighty at all. So we have decided to make it official and are now properly engaged. By the time you read this, I will have my ring!

PPS Any word from the amazing Mrs McHale? The canon's latest exploit is to sack Dymphna O'Connell for the crime of defending Father Iggy over blessing the grave of her late husband. It looks like Dymphna's own mother went running with tales to the canon, and he took it to the bishop, and that's how he's smarmed his way back here, on the back of Father Iggy's 'disgrace'. That man won't stop until he's made everyone's life as miserable as his own, because one thing I'm sure of, he can't be happy. Don't worry about Dymphna, by the way. She is now working for Tilly and Mary O'Hare up at the farmhouse, so she has enough for her weekly rent for Tom O'Donoghue's house and everything, and Tilly supplements her wages with plenty of fresh vegetables and eggs. It's worked out for the best for everyone. Dymphna is so much happier, and in just a few days, the farmhouse is already sparkling and Mary is delighted not to have to worry about running around after Odile with her bad knees.

CHAPTER 14

KNOCKNASHEE, CO. KERRY - DECEMBER 1940

It was a bitterly cold but bright, sunny Saturday when Declan helped Grace up into the bus for Tralee and down the aisle to the back, where there were only two seats left.

A few of the passengers already aboard looked a bit wet; apparently it had been lashing down in the previous village, Dún Chaoin. Grace prayed that was the end of the rain for today, especially as she had a new hairstyle. She wore her burgundy velvet dress, a lamb's wool cardigan over it, and she had her raincoat over her arm, an old one of Agnes's that she'd kept because it was long enough to cover her down to her blue shoes. But it was dark grey and not very stylish, so she hoped she wouldn't have to put it on.

Tilly, as one of the few people who knew what was afoot, had insisted on doing Grace's hair, using a picture and instructions out of a magazine that Eloise had given her. Tilly had stuck a paper roller on the top of Grace's head to create the victory roll that everyone was wearing these days and brushed the back out and curled it under, so for once it looked groomed and not a mop of wild copper curls. Even

Grace had to admit it was lovely, though she did get a bit tired of hearing, while they were waiting for it to dry by the range, how Eloise was so much more stylish, more cosmopolitan and generally all-round superior to anyone in Knocknashee. Apparently the Swiss woman also loved bright-red lipstick. She had yet to visit, but Grace was wondering how she was going to live up to the image Tilly had created of her.

The last time Grace was in Dingle, on a whim she'd bought herself a lovely lipstick, not bright red but a soft coral, though she still hadn't got around to wearing it – she hardly ever wore make-up. Now Tilly insisted she put it on – 'It looks wonderful on Eloise, I'm sure it will look great on you!' – and maybe it was a good idea, because Declan had whistled when he came to fetch her for the bus and said she looked beautiful with her copper hair and coral lips.

As the bus set off slowly down the hill, Dymphna appeared at the front door of Tom O'Donoghue's cottage. He'd inherited it from his grandmother and had lived there before he married Biddy, then moved in with her above the substantial grocer's shop. The shop had been in Biddy's family, not Tom's, not that you'd know it to see him swanning around like he was one of the Rockefellers. Dymphna waved happily at Grace and Declan, and then Charlie appeared beside her, also waving and mouthing 'good luck'.

Looking back with a smile out of the back window, she saw the widow handing Charlie a basket covered in a linen cloth. Eight-year-old Paudie had joined them, looking important with a sketchpad under his arm, and Kate was jigging around in excitement.

'Is Charlie taking Kate and Paudie somewhere?' she asked.

Declan nodded. 'He is. He's promised to take them to see the Bonaparte's gulls that nest on the cliffs out beyond Ceann Trá in winter. Paudie is fascinated by birds of all kinds, and he's like a sponge for information – he really is a very bright little lad. Dad thinks Kate will love them as well, so Dymphna has wrapped them up warm and packed a picnic for the three of them, and she's going to have a peaceful afternoon with her feet up.'

'That's so kind of your father!'

'It is, but it's no bother to him. He's fond of that little family, and he's especially good to Paudie. The poor little boy still misses his dad. He is old enough to remember him – he was six years old when he died. My father loves nature, as you know, and Paudie is fascinated, so it's nice for Da to have someone to share his knowledge with. He missed out on doing it with me.'

The by-now-familiar melancholy that would always and ever be part of this man she was going to marry passed over his face briefly, like a dark mist. Declan had been six years old when he lost his beloved mother. A few days later he was ripped from his loving father's arms, separated from his infant sister and sent to live in harsh, cruel conditions in the industrial school with no explanation or hope of release. Every time Grace thought about it, her eyes filled with tears.

Declan stayed quiet and pale for a moment but then smiled again. 'Did you see that sketchpad under Paudie's arm?'

'I did, and I was delighted. He's very good at drawing. But I didn't know Dymphna had managed to buy him one, they're so expensive.'

'It was Da who got it for him. He saved up and sent off for it, and he gave him a nice new 2B pencil as well. He showed him how to make a bird table in the yard of the cottage, and they put out nuts and berries from the hedgerows on the table and any crumbs left over from the bread so Paudie could sit quietly in the window sketching.'

Grace sat for a while thinking as the bus passed the turn to the ancient cemetery where her parents and Agnes were buried. It wasn't only Declan who had been devastated and changed forever by the canon's decision. Charlie mourned his wife, Maggie, and yearned for his baby girl, but he'd missed his son every day so much it had almost killed him. Grace was too young at the time to understand, but she knew now how he'd searched, and pleaded with the canon, written so many letters, did all he could.

Declan had finally come home twelve years later, mentally broken and crushed, and having to be minded and cared for until he became strong again.

Maybe Paudie was a sort of consolation for Charlie for having missed so many years of Declan's childhood, a boy he could take to see the puffins. She knew Declan didn't mind. Charlie wasn't attempting to replace those lost years; he'd probably not even thought about why he found Paudie's presence so comforting.

'I think it's nice for him how Paudie looks up to him,' said Declan, gazing out of the window as the bus took the bend at the strand. 'Dymphna says it makes her laugh how Paudie "preaches the gospel according to Charlie" to her every day. And it's good he'll have the company of the boy around the house after we, you know, after we get…'

He coloured slightly and gave a quick glance around the bus for flapping ears. Men from their part of the world were not comfortable talking about their relationships in public.

Grace stroked her fiancé's hand, laughing to herself when she thought about the things Richard had written to her about Sarah and Jacob, and Alfie and Constance. The scandals such goings-on would create in Knocknashee!

'After we start living together, Declan,' she whispered in his ear. 'And sharing the big room upstairs…'

He turned to her then, dark-blue eyes like the deepest part of the ocean, and she allowed her gaze to rest on his. He really was as handsome as any film star, dark wavy hair, pale skin with a smattering of cinnamon-coloured freckles, high cheekbones and hollowed cheeks leading to a sharp jaw. But the thing she liked best was his smile. He had a broad grin that crinkled his eyes, revealing straight white teeth.

She'd seen the way the girls admired him, not just Bridie and Sally, and they were right to – he was gorgeous. He could wink at one and she'd be a puddle; his smile made them sigh. Even the mothers of the schoolchildren seemed to always want to discuss something with Mr McKenna that they'd never needed to discuss with her, and she teased him mercilessly about it.

'I love you, Grace, so much,' he mouthed at her.

'And I love you too,' she mouthed back as the bus stopped at the foot of a track leading up to a remote farm. A woman carrying a cage of loudly objecting hens climbed on and pushed all the way to the back of the bus, squishing her large bottom into the seat beside them, with her indignant, smelly fowl on her lap.

Pushed into the corner, Declan took Grace's hand to squeeze it secretly. And even after the big woman got off in Dingle, he didn't withdraw his hand but kept hers in his strong grip all the way to Tralee.

* * *

THE BUS ARRIVED in the county town of County Kerry around lunchtime, and Declan offered her his arm as they strolled up the street to the hotel. They had always walked like this, long before they were together, because with her leg it made getting around easier if she had someone to lean on.

Christmas was going to be low-key this year on account of the shortages, not that anyone where they were from did anything extravagant anyway. A child might get a gift if the parents could afford it, and the family would roast a goose and boil a big ham and they'd probably have a pudding or a fruit cake, but even that was looking unlikely this year; dried fruit was close to impossible to come by.

She'd decorated her house, though, with holly and ivy and had made yule logs with the children, so she had a few of those to give the place a festive feeling.

For lunch in the hotel, they had chicken breast and potatoes, followed by apple crumble. Food rationing had hit the people in towns more than those in the country, where everyone grew their own vegetables and raised their own chickens, and Grace secretly thought there was better food to be had in Knocknashee. But it was a lovely setting in a bay window overlooking the rose garden, bare of blooms at this time of year, the chairs were upholstered in striped silk brocade, and the cutlery was solid silver, so it made it a special experience.

Afterwards they walked down Castle Street in the sunshine, and Declan opened the door into John Ross and Sons Watchmaker and Jeweller's Shop. As Grace stepped into the smart interior, she felt very conscious of being from the country, much more so than in the hotel. Maybe it was all Tilly's talk about Eloise being so cosmopolitan, but she half expected someone to tap them on the shoulder and demand to know what a pair like them were doing in such a swanky shop. Their feet sank into the plush carpet, and the subtle lighting bounced off the smudge-free glass surfaces. The man behind the counter, in his fifties, with a head of grey curls and dressed in a beautiful three-piece suit with a gold pocket watch and matching tie pin and cufflinks, greeted them warmly.

'Welcome, welcome! Aren't ye the sight for sore eyes now?' He chuckled. 'I was just about to take out my forms to fill in for the government, and ye've spared me that terrible duty, so immediately I'm inclined to give ye a five percent discount just for that reason alone. Now what can I do for ye?'

'We'd like to buy an engagement ring please,' Declan said, pride beaming from him.

'Well firstly, can I offer you my most sincere congratulations?'

'Thank you.' Grace smiled as she glanced at the diamond rings on cushions. She discreetly wandered to look at bracelets while the man and Declan had a quiet word about the budget, she assumed.

'Well, a beautiful young lady such as your fiancée must have a beautiful ring, so if the lovely lady would let me see her hand, I'll get an idea of size and we can start the process of elimination.' The man beckoned her back to him, and Grace, feeling very self-conscious of her limp, crossed the shop to offer him her left hand.

'Dainty like its owner.' He smiled gently. 'Now, tell me, Miss...?'

'Fitzgerald, Grace Fitzgerald.'

'And where might ye be from, tell me?'

'Knocknashee,' she and Declan answered together, and then laughed.

His eyes widened. 'Not Eddie and Kathy's daughter?'

'That's right!' Grace felt a warm glow that he knew her parents. It brought them close to this momentous occasion somehow.

'Well, let me tell you, my name is James Ross. My grandfather opened this shop a thousand years ago' – he winked to show he was joking – 'and your father bought your mother's ring in this very shop. I was the one that sold it to him, and I only a *garsun* of seventeen, so that wasn't today nor yesterday. It was my first sale of a diamond, and my father, John, who was not a man to lavish praise, I can tell you, said I did a good job. I'll never forget it.'

'I remember it, I think. In my mind it was beautiful, like a star...' She did remember a ring that scattered the light around the room, but she hadn't seen it since her mother's death. Neither of Kathleen Fitzgerald's rings could be removed when her swollen body was returned by the sea days after she'd drowned. That awful fact had been casually relayed to her by Agnes when Grace was twelve and had asked about their mother's rings, and the child within Grace had stored that horrific information away, only for it to emerge unbidden now. She took a deep breath, tears in her eyes.

'A white-gold filigree mounting holding a beautiful diamond. The stone's unique shape was an antique mine cut.' He gave her a look of pure sympathy. 'I was very sorry to hear about the accident. They bought their wedding rings from us too...a fine couple.'

'They were,' Grace managed, as Declan held her other hand.

'But today is a happy day, and I'm sure they're looking down on us now, God be good to them, urging us to choose wisely.'

The man had brought two cushions out onto the glass counter already, each with about twenty rings bedded in rows. 'These first are all beautiful, absolutely beautiful rings, and you won't go wrong with them, but these...' He went underneath the counter and extracted another tray. 'These are slightly more elaborate, a bit more exclusive.'

They were also clearly much more expensive, but Grace saw the almost imperceptible reassurance in the look this man gave Declan as he pointed to a stunning ring in the middle of the third tray. 'This one here, Miss Fitzgerald, is almost identical to your mother's, a little more modern maybe but very, very similar. But everything displayed here on the counter is all the same price more or less, so choose as you wish. Now I'll go and make myself a cup of tea and give ye some time to make a selection.'

The man withdrew, and Grace blinked back her tears as she

looked at the ring that was so like her mother's. 'Mammy's hands were so bloated from the seawater, Agnes told me they couldn't get her rings off.' Spoken aloud, the sentence shocked even her.

Declan put his arm around her. 'We can do this another day if it's too hard,' he said softly.

'Maybe we should.' But she couldn't take her eyes off that ring; it brought back so many happy memories: sitting on her mother's lap, listening to a story, watching the diamond catch the light as Kathleen's hands moved expressively to and fro; standing on a chair helping her mother stir the cake batter, the ring put carefully aside on the dresser to keep it safe.

'Or maybe your man is right and your parents are looking down on us and helping you choose?' said Declan softly.

She leant against him. 'I don't want to choose one that's too dear,' she said simply.

'The man said they were all the same price.'

'Do you think he really meant it?'

'It seems like a miracle, but that's what he said... So why not choose that one? He pointed it out to you specially.'

She gazed at it longingly. 'Are you sure? It's so beautiful, it must cost more than all the rest.'

'My lovely Grace, if that's the one you want, that's the one you'll have.'

'I don't want you going into debt or anything...'

He tightened his arm around her. 'I've the money saved, don't worry. If that's the one, I would love to buy it for you.'

It was no good, she couldn't refuse. The feeling of her mother was so strong – Kathleen's smiling eyes, the diamond reflecting their sparkle. 'Then yes, that's the one I'd like.'

The man materialised immediately, removed the ring from its cushion and held it up to the light, where it caught the shafts of sun coming through the shop window. Then he popped it back into its black velvet box and closed the lid. Declan put the box in his pocket, then got out his wallet, and the two men waited for Grace to leave them.

She went to look out of the door while they spoke in low voices behind her. Declan thanked the man very warmly, and then James Ross opened the door for them and he and Declan shook hands like old friends.

'What?' her smiling fiancé asked her as they walked further up Castle Street.

'Don't I get to put it on?'

'No, future Mrs McKenna, you don't, not yet at least. You'll have to wait.'

'Wait? Aren't you afraid I'll change my mind?' she teased, and he threw her a serious look.

'I'm terrified you will, if the truth be told,' he admitted. 'And if you want to, you should. Any man would love you, Grace. I don't want you settling for second best with me.'

'Ah, Declan, I was only joking. Of course I won't. You are so clever and kind and funny and handsome – any girl would be over the moon to marry you. I don't know if it's my parents or my guardian angel or who it is, but someone put us together and I can't believe my luck. And I can't wait to be your wife.'

Her little speech seemed to reassure him, and the anxiety left his face.

There was a lovely garden in the centre of the town, full of roses in summer, but this time of year they had planted purple heathers and a few evergreen shrubs. The trees were bare of their leaves, and she had to put on Agnes's raincoat as the breeze was cutting, it was so cold. He led her into the garden through a gate, then to a bench next to a small birch tree, its silver bark almost shimmering in the bright sunlight. Apart from a few children kicking a football and a pair of hardy young mothers pushing prams, their infants bundled up against the cold, they had the place to themselves.

He remained standing as she sat on the bench, then took the box out of his pocket and went down on one knee. For a few seconds he said nothing, just stayed there, as if summoning his courage. In the pause a robin landed cheekily on the branch of the tree beside her, and she smiled to see it. Mammy always said the robins were the souls of those loved ones who had moved on to the next life, so maybe her mother was watching over her now.

Looking up at her, Declan opened the box, and there was the beautiful ring, just like the one her father bought for her mother, in the same shop, from the same jeweller, all those years ago. Nothing ever felt so right.

'Grace Fitzgerald, would you do me the very great honour of becoming my wife?' he asked quietly.

Grace smiled, and years of pain and loneliness seemed to evaporate. She wasn't going to be alone; she wouldn't spend her days working but going home to an empty house at night, sleeping alone in her childhood bed until she was an old lady.

She would have a husband, a loyal, kind, decent man, and maybe even babies of her own, children who would call her Mammy, and Declan Daddy. Her house would ring with the sound of children's voices once more. It all seemed so incredible.

'Yes, please, I'd love it,' she managed, through a voice choked with emotion.

Declan took the ring and slipped it on her finger, and then he stood and drew her to her feet, into his embrace.

* * *

THE TRIP back to Knocknashee was blissful as they whispered about when they were going to be married.

Declan wanted it as soon as possible. 'A Christmas wedding?' he suggested.

'We don't have time to read the banns before Christmas – it's less than three weeks away...'

'I wish there was a way.'

She laughed softly at his impetuosity. 'Yeah, and everyone watching my belly like a hawk then, thinking it was a rush job. No, we're a respectable pair of teachers – we'll have no whiff of gossip, thank you very much. We're going to do this properly and wait a respectable amount of time, and besides, we need to study for our exams first and then see about the results. If we've passed, you will have a proper teacher's wage fit for a married man and I'll be on more money as well, and we'll be able to save up for a couple of years so if I need to take time off...'

'Time off for what?' He looked genuinely puzzled.

She leant over and whispered in his ear, *'Babies*, Declan...' and he went bright red and couldn't stop beaming from ear to ear. 'And I suppose another advantage of waiting is Canon Rafferty might be gone from the parish,' she added hopefully.

'Mm...' He looked extremely doubtful, and she realised she hadn't told him about Mrs McHale and her mission to dig up dirt on the canon and maybe liberate poor Father Dempsey. She opened her mouth to say it but then decided to leave it until later. Somehow she knew Richard Lewis's name would make Declan go quiet and thoughtful. She suspected Richard was why Declan had referred to himself as second best earlier, and she didn't want him feeling that way.

'I always wanted it to be Father Iggy who married me if it ever happened,' she said instead, smiling sadly.

'Well then, that's who will do it. We'll go to him in Cork and arrange for him to marry us,' said Declan, like that was settled.

Her heart lifted. 'Is it possible to get married outside the parish, if we're both from the same place?' She wasn't sure. She remembered what Tilly had said about the letter of freedom. Would that be necessary and who would grant it – the canon or the bishop? She would have to ask Nancy O'Flaherty, whose daughter had married a man from Annascaul before going off to live there. Had her husband needed to get a letter?

'Will you write to Hugh and Lizzie Warrington soon?' he asked as the bus passed a weathered milestone, carved with an arrow and the word CORK.

'Yes, I was thinking of going to Cork once we break up for the Christmas holidays. I haven't seen them for months, and I've promised them a visit anyway, and I know they'll be delighted for me.'

After all those long years in hospital, when the polio consultant and his wife acted as her guardians, she had grown to love them dearly and thought of them almost as surrogate parents. She'd never imagined she'd get married. 'I'm going to ask Hugh to give me away,' she said quietly. She paused, thinking. 'Why don't we go together? A little holiday in Cork? They'd be happy to put us up. And we can see Father Iggy as well, and ask what he thinks about marrying us, if it's possible.'

'I'd love it if you think they won't mind,' he replied. 'And I've a few places I'd like to visit. There's a fella out towards Douglas somewhere making a kind of voltage tester, a device to determine the strength of an electrical signal, so I'd love to go there and maybe get one if they aren't too dear.'

'And here I was, planning a romantic holiday.' Grace laughed, mock hurt.

'There's nothing more romantic than electricity, Grace. It's what makes sparks fly.' He winked at her and her heart fluttered.

The bus trundled into Dingle and stopped near the quay. The rain was threatening again now, and the ocean was whipped up white with the westerly winds, gulls wheeling on the boisterous air. Grace wondered if Charlie had found the Bonaparte's gulls and hoped he and the children hadn't ended up soaked by a rainy squall.

The big woman, still carrying the cage but without her hens, clambered onto the bus again and made her way to the same back seat, plonking herself down and shoving the two of them into the corner once more, making them giggle and blush as they were crushed against each other.

The bus engine started up, but then there was a wild shout and a tall figure came dashing up the road from the direction of the train station, carrying a small case, wearing a long, black, hooded raincoat. The new passenger sprung aboard and showed their ticket, and Bobby the Bus pointed them down the aisle to the one remaining seat, about halfway down the bus. It was next to Tomás Kinneally, who nobody else had wanted to sit beside, and who was now looking quite nervous.

As the figure stood in the aisle, stripping off the coat before sitting down, heads swivelled and mouths gaped, and Tomás himself went crimson as he emitted a sort of strangled gasp.

It was a woman, with hair so blond it was almost white. She wore bright-red lipstick, and her huge blue eyes were ringed with black pencil. She looked so like Jean Harlow that if Grace didn't know the famous actress had died three years ago, at the tragically young age of twenty-seven, she would have been tempted to think it was Harlow herself, come to the west of Ireland on a film shoot or something.

This woman was even dressed like a Hollywood star. Her cream jacket was wide on her shoulders and cinched around her waist, the blouse beneath was open-necked, and she wore loose stylish trousers, which somehow seemed perfectly feminine, unlike the men's overalls Tilly wore. Even more feminine, in fact, than the dresses and cardigans every other woman on the bus was wearing...including Grace, who suddenly felt very small and dowdy in her dress and lamb's wool cardigan. She touched her coppery hair dubiously with her free hand. It was fixed in the same victory roll as the strange woman's blond locks, but even though Tilly had done an amazing job, it just wasn't the same.

Declan slipped his arm around her waist and squeezed gently, almost as if he knew what she was feeling, while the tall woman sat down next to Tomás Kinneally, out of sight except for the top of her blond head with its perfect hairdo.

The next stage of the journey was made very entertaining by Tomás. All the passengers on the bus knew he was a poor farmer scratching a living off a rocky hillside, and they listened in delight as he boasted about his huge farm and enormous numbers of sheep and cattle, and what a great catch he was, how he had to beat desperate women off with a stick but that he might make an exception one day if he could find the perfect *colleen* to share his extensive wealth.

The woman didn't say much – she was obviously wondering what on earth she'd got herself into – but that didn't bother Tomás. He told her he liked a woman who didn't say much, that they were obviously made for each other, and that he had a fine big bed with three blankets that his grandmother had made by hand and any amount of crockery. A collective sigh of disappointment went up as the bus turned into the cobbled main street of Knocknashee and the fun was over.

Tilly was waiting at the bus stop outside the undertaker's, wearing her velvet fedora as usual. She'd told Grace she was going to welcome her and Declan off the bus so she could be first to see the ring.

Because her calliper always slowed her down so much, Grace waited until everyone who was for Knocknashee had got off the bus. The woman with the empty cage had dismounted at the turning before the strand, so she and Declan were alone on the back seat. Jean Harlow seemed to be getting off here as well; she stood in the aisle, putting on her black raincoat, while Tomás made his way to the door with many a flirtatious backward glance and gap-toothed grin. He clearly thought his luck was in and the woman had decided to stop here because of him.

Outside in the light misty rain, Tilly was getting quite hysterical, leaping up and down, waving. Tomás nodded at her in a superior fashion as he climbed down, like she was one of the many women he always had to 'beat off with a stick' and he was sorry for her but she'd missed her chance.

'Come on, Declan. We can't keep Tilly waiting any longer.' Grace smiled as she let him help her to her feet and down the aisle. 'She's desperate to see the ring.'

Except when she finally made it to the door of the bus, on the heels of Jean Harlow, it seemed the person Tilly was so excited to see wasn't Grace at all, but...

'Eloise! Eloise!' shrieked Tilly. 'I can't believe it's you!' And the next moment she and the blond stranger were in each other's arms.

CHAPTER 15

Grace tried very hard to like Eloise Meier. The woman was charming and funny. Her English – and even her Irish – were very good, and she had travelled to so many places and done so many things that she was a source of fascination. Everyone loved her.

She'd been in Knocknashee for a week now and acted like she was loving it. She made a point of reminding everyone she was from a farming background herself, raised in a remote corner of an alpine valley, that she was not some posh townie with her nose in the air. And she proved it as well by milking Tilly's solitary cow and helping to churn the butter, all somehow without getting a speck of dirt on her impeccable wardrobe.

She declared that Tilly's spare room at the farm was the prettiest room she'd ever slept in and Dymphna's blue quilt was lovely and warm and the whole place was gorgeous and quaint and just wonderful.

She loved the traditional music that was always around Knocknashee. She had heard of some old man further out on the peninsula who had a whole collection of songs from the Irish regiments in the Boer War and went to see him. He turned around and offered her his whole collection, but she told him no, that it should be in a museum and she'd help him with that.

She told Mary O'Hare she had never tasted apple tart like hers in her life, that her mother made strudel but it wasn't a patch on Mary's baking, and she said to Bríd Butler that there was no better ice cream in the world, not even in Italy, where she'd been many times. She told Charlie she could see how astute he was, how delivering post all of his life, good news, bad news, had given him an eye for understanding people and she found him fascinating.

She made all the right noises about the scenery and took endless photos of the coastline, as well as the various inhabitants of Knocknashee, standing at the doors of their thatched cottages. She was fascinated by the wildlife and made Paudie show her all his bird drawings, then let him use her very fancy equipment to photograph the feathered visitors to his bird table in the tiny back yard of his mother's cottage. Dymphna and Kate also fell for her charms when she insisted women could take photos just as well as men and encouraged them to do so.

She flirted with Declan, demanding to know why there were no dark, handsome strangers like him in Switzerland, and somehow he just found her funny and wasn't at all embarrassed. She promised to send Pádraig O Sé a pair of traditional Swiss dancing shoes with silver buckles, because he was amazed by the stitching on hers; she'd broken a heel clambering over rocks on the beach, and he'd repaired it for her, without saying one rude word to her. It was unheard of.

Grace grumbled privately to herself that it was all just flattery and *plámás*, but Eloise certainly knew exactly what to say and how to say it to have everyone charmed by her.

Even Odile was under her spell. After hearing Tilly's niece had a Parisian mother, Eloise chattered away to the baby in French, and Odile loved it. She cooed in delight whenever the Swiss woman picked her up, and Odile called Eloise 'Tante' in a high, sweet voice – her first word – which felt to Grace like a little stab of betrayal, even though she'd long ago thought it would be a wonderful idea if someone could speak to the child in French.

And of course it was obvious that Tilly 'hard as nails' O'Hare, the girl who prided herself on not suffering fools gladly, was totally besotted by this woman.

Grace had never felt jealous of anyone before, and she didn't like herself for it, but beside this stunning, accomplished, well-travelled woman, she felt small, insignificant, parochial and silly, especially after Eloise sat down at the piano in her house and played it better than Grace herself did.

Then one night Eloise insisted on cooking dinner for everyone up at the farm – Tilly and Mary, Grace and Declan, Charlie, Dymphna and her children.

She made a fondue, a sort of melted cheese dish. It should have had wine in it, she explained, but there was nowhere in Knocknashee that would have wine – the canon had red wine for the Mass, but that was about it – so they had to make do without. She'd brought out a fondue set, a pot to melt the cheese and nine long narrow forks on which they were to spear bread to dip in the cheese. It was an odd kind of meal, though everyone was polite and said it was lovely, and Grace felt very guilty for the satisfaction she felt when she saw Tilly quietly feed one of the cubes of cheesy bread to her sheepdog, Buachaill, under the table. Then when Buachaill spat it out, she couldn't help giggling and had to cover her mouth and pretend something had gone down the wrong way, which led to Eloise rushing to get her a glass of water and then going on at length about how wonderful it was to have water fresh and clear and bubbly from a mountain stream and not the awful stuff that came out of lead pipes in Dublin.

By the time school had finished for the holiday, Grace had begun to realise Eloise intended to stay around for Christmas. The Swiss woman tutored languages privately in Dublin and only did short terms, she said, which left her 'loads of time on her hands' to pursue her true love of photography and see her friends.

The only person who disliked her was the canon, which annoyingly made her even more likeable to everyone else.

Canon Rafferty had been behaving a bit better since Declan and Grace were engaged; he'd clearly decided to pull in his horns a bit, though Grace was sure he was just biding his time for the next opportunity. He had come in a second time to hear the children's catechism but got bored of it when even the youngest were word-perfect. He clicked his tongue disapprovingly when he looked around the classroom decked out in paper chains and paintings all over the walls of the Baby Jesus in the manger and the three Wise Men, but at least he didn't make Grace take it all down and replace it with some terrifying medieval painting of a tortured saint.

She'd blessed herself and said an act of contrition when she'd thrown a copy of a horrible painting of poor St Stephen being stoned to death on the fire. It had been one of Agnes's favourites, but the poor man looked so upset, Grace had hated to see it every day. There had also been one of poor old St Sebastian stuck with spears and blood dripping out of him, and that had gone into the range with St Stephen the same day. Luckily the canon hadn't asked about the pictures; she'd no idea what she'd say if he did.

There was a rocky moment when she had the children in the church – Father Lehane had said it was fine – singing carols around the crib in preparation for Christmas Eve. Canon Rafferty came storming out of the sacristy, demanding to know what that terrible noise was, even though the children had been practising all week and it sounded lovely.

'It's so pretty, Father, isn't it?' asked Eloise Meier in her husky accented English, appearing like an angel from the shadows in the back of the church. 'I was just standing here quietly listening, and it reminds me so much of home, where my reverend uncle holds beautiful carol services every Christmas…' She paused to wipe a tear from her huge blue eye, not smudging the mascara one bit, as all the children gazed at her in awe. 'The bishop comes every year. He says it's so beautiful to hear those innocent angelic voices singing their hearts out to worship our saviour Jesus when he was no more than a child himself.'

Grace didn't know whether to be grateful for her intervention or chew her own arm off.

The dour canon actually attempted a sickly smile. 'So your uncle is a Catholic priest, child?' he simpered, gliding towards her.

'Oh no, Father, he's a Protestant, but it's the same religion, isn't it? There's no difference really, not as far as I can see.'

The canon was so provoked, he ordered the Swiss woman out of the church, then stormed after her into the churchyard, ranting about the one true faith, while Grace and her pupils got on with the carol practice in peace.

That Sunday Canon Rafferty preached a long sermon about how Satan came in many forms, how the devil didn't always look like a monster, that sometimes he came with a pretty face and spoke in a soft, sweet voice, so to beware of taking him in as it would be like nurturing a serpent in one's bosom.

This was all clearly directed at Tilly, who sat there with a big grin and was seen in the street afterwards whispering gleefully to Eloise, who had come to meet her after Mass. The Swiss woman threw back her head and laughed, then waved and winked at the canon, who glared at them from the churchyard. Eloise then put her arm around Tilly and kissed her glossy hair, and the two of them ran off giggling together.

Grace found it hard to watch. It wasn't just jealousy this time; she was seriously worried that Eloise was going to get Tilly into desperate trouble one day. It was fine for Eloise, the canon had no say over her, but Tilly was from here, and like it or not, he could make her life very difficult if he chose to. If he decided she was an immoral influence on Odile, then he had considerable powers and the child could be taken away, and if he decided Mary O'Hare could no longer manage at home, he might even be able to have the little girl forcibly moved to the county home. Grace wished with all her heart that Tilly didn't antagonise him so; her friend was underestimating the spite of the man, Grace felt sure of it. She and Declan were going on their holidays to Cork tomorrow, and she hoped nothing too bad would happen before she came back.

* * *

CORK LOOKED wonderful in the snow, with all the big glass windows of the stores filled with bright, shiny gifts. It had been a surprise for them to see the flurries of powdery snow; it so rarely happened in Knocknashee on account of the ocean. There were windows made up like scenes from fairy tales and piled high with colourful boxes wrapped up in glittering string. Children stood with their noses pressed to the plate-glass front of Woolworths and Cashs, where all sorts of toys and games were on display.

Hugh and Lizzie Warrington greeted Grace and Declan with cries of congratulations as they got off the train from Tralee. Hugh drove them to their small terraced house, then helped Declan carry the bags up the stairs, and Lizzie fussed around Grace, admiring her engagement ring.

'Declan seems a lot more confident and happier in himself since last Easter,' Lizzie murmured to Grace as they put a tray of tea things together in the kitchen while Hugh showed Declan around the snowy garden and asked his advice about upgrading the water heating system for the hospital.

'Finding his little sister in New York, and seeing she was happy and safe, made a big difference to him.' Grace glanced out of the window at her two favourite men, deep in discussion. 'I think he'll always have a touch of melancholy about him, but that's just the way he is.'

'He's perfect for you, and I know he'll take good care of you,' asserted Lizzie, fetching a jug of milk from the pantry. 'And it's a good thing, I think, that he understands grief. Someone whose whole life has been nothing but sunny and easy might find it hard to understand what you've been through.'

'Oh, it's not been all hard.'

'Losing your parents so young? Then four years in hospital having operations and painful treatments for polio? And then being bullied by Agnes and having to mind her when she had the stroke? Grace, if anyone ever deserved a chance at happiness, it's you.'

'You make it sound worse than it was really,' she said, warming the teapot then adding two spoonfuls of tea. 'I had you and Hugh, and Tilly, and Richard...'

'How *is* your American friend?' asked Lizzie, looking closely at Grace.

'He's actually in England, reporting on the war, and writes very interesting letters and sends cuttings of his newspaper articles. I think I've learnt even more from him than you do from the foreign papers in the ladies' reading room because no one has got around to censoring people's letters yet,' she said cheerfully.

She had noticed and understood the meaning behind Lizzie's look, but the best way was to ignore it, she thought. She hadn't meant to mention Richard in the first place, his name had just sort of slipped out...but that was all right. She had nothing to hide when it came to Richard Lewis.

'Lizzie, do you think Hugh will be happy to give me away?'

The woman's face lit up and she clapped her hands. 'Oh, Grace, he'll be honoured.'

Hugh wasn't just honoured – he was moved to tears by being asked and had to leave the room for a moment before he recovered enough to come back in and give Grace a big hug. Later he came up with the perfect solution to them not wanting to get married by Canon Rafferty.

'Why don't you get married in the church in the hospital?' he suggested as he carved a huge chicken for dinner; Tilly had sent it down from the farm with Grace, wrapped up in newspaper and an old shirt, along with the usual jars of honey and trays of eggs. 'It's only a very small chapel, but it's also not the parish church of any priest, so you could ask Father Iggy to celebrate your wedding Mass without him having to worry about treading on the canon's – or anyone else's – toes.'

It seemed like a wonderful idea to Grace, but she was an engaged woman now so she turned to ask Declan what he thought. He just laughed and said he'd marry her in a coal shed so long as he was marrying her and that he was happy to do whatever she wanted.

After more discussion they decided the wedding should be in

August next year, before the children went back to school, and then Hugh and Lizzie announced their intention to pay for the wedding breakfast and then to treat the couple to a week's honeymoon in Cork's glamorous Imperial Hotel. When Grace and Declan protested that was far too generous, they said they considered themselves to be the parents of the bride and so were allowed to spend whatever they wanted.

The following day, while Hugh drove Declan to see the fellow in Douglas about the voltage tester, Grace took a bus to the Cathedral of St Mary and St Anne, known locally as the North Chapel, in time for Mass, to see her old friend.

Blackpool Parish was the sort of area where many of the parishioners were 'shawlies', the old women, wrapped in shawls, who sold their wares on the market lanes of the city. Father Iggy, looking thinner than when he'd left Knocknashee, mounted the pulpit and preached a sermon about the rich finding it a lot harder than the poor to get to heaven, and it seemed to go down well. The working men shook his hand afterwards, and the women murmured, 'God bless you, Father,' as they filed past him out of the church door. Grace hung back to the last; she had sat out of sight behind a pillar until the service was over.

The priest stood wiping his thick spectacles after everyone had gone, but he put them back on very quickly when she greeted him.

'Hello, Father Iggy.'

'I'd know that voice anywhere! How wonderful to see you, Grace!'

'It's wonderful to see you too, Father.' She held out her left hand to show him the ring, and he beamed with happiness, cupping her fingers in his palm, admiring the diamond as it sparkled.

'Ah, Grace. I'm so happy for you. Is it who I think it is?'

'It's Declan McKenna, Father.'

He nodded, satisfied. 'I hoped that was the case. You couldn't have chosen better. I've always thought he was a good match for you, ever since he made you that remarkable hot-water contraption. I can see a wonderful future for you together. I hope all is well in Knocknashee, and the school and everyone?'

'It is, Father. We're all grand but we miss you. The children talk about you all the time, remembering all the interesting and funny things you taught them. Johnny Keating was reminding us of the time his number was drawn in the village raffle last Christmas. The first prize was a bow and arrow and he was so excited, but his mother made him take second prize, which was a turkey. He was so upset – he badly wanted the bow and arrow – but times were tight and a turkey for the Christmas dinner was a treat they couldn't afford to reject. But then on Christmas morning, Santa brought him the bow and arrow. Though you were discreet, we all knew it was you who got it for him.'

Father Iggy smiled. 'The poor little fella was heartbroken to leave it after him and take the turkey instead. I had to get it for him.'

'I know you did, and plenty of others with it. Every child in the village got a toy last year, whether their parents had the money or not.'

He winked. 'Ah, that's just a Christmas miracle.'

Grace knew this Christmas morning would be different. Every year Father Iggy was in Knocknashee, he would say a joyful Mass, then he'd invite all the children up to the altar to look into the crib, see Mary and Joseph and the baby, the sheep and the shepherds and the Wise Men. They would all sing *lá breithe shona dhuit, a* Jesus.' And once they'd sung happy birthday to the new baby, he would give each child a sherbet lemon. He must have saved up his sweet ration for months to have enough for everyone.

'Things are' – she paused, remembering with a shudder the weekly catechism interrogations and the canon's malevolent presence – 'different now, but we're coping.'

Father Iggy knew exactly what she meant but didn't comment. 'Will you come up to the parochial house? I can surely manage to make you a cup of tea, and I think Margaret, that's our housekeeper, made a sponge cake.'

'I'd love to.' He offered her his arm and she took it, leaning on him a little as they strolled out of the cathedral grounds and up the hill to the priest's house. As she sat in the kitchen, spotless and smelling of baking, she chatted easily about everything. He told her about the adjustment to the new parish and how he was really enjoying working with the young people. It seemed that his opportunities in Knocknashee school had given him confidence and he was now doing several school visits a week.

'It's not like Knocknashee. People were poor there too, but not like this. If you have a bit of ground, you'll always be able to grow a few spuds, keep hens, and neighbours won't let you starve, but cities are different. People look out for each other, of course, but they have so little.'

'They're lucky to have you, and while we hated letting you go, maybe this parish's need is greater,' Grace conceded. 'But that brings me to something I wanted to ask. We want you to marry us, Father, and Hugh Warrington is suggesting we could use the hospital church if that makes it any easier for you? I don't want you to get into any trouble.'

The little priest chuckled. 'Grace Fitzgerald, I would marry you even if it brought a whole heap of trouble down on my head. But tell Dr Warrington that the hospital church is a splendid idea, and thank him for his offer. It will make everything much easier to arrange.'

'Thank you, Father Iggy.' She smiled. 'So you're happy here?'

'I am. Happier than I thought I'd be, to be truthful. My parishioners are good, honest people, but I hate to take money off them,' he confessed as he poured her another cup of tea. 'So I do get in a small bit of trouble with the bishop because the collections are so small, but people have to feed their families first and foremost. I do miss Knocknashee, though, and my friends there. I miss dropping into the school, or having tea in your house with yourself or Charlie or Tilly or whoever happened to be around.'

He sounded so wistful that she found herself asking him a very personal question. 'Do you ever regret it, Father? Becoming a priest?'

He looked at her then, weighing up whether to answer truthfully or to give the expected answer. They had a close, comfortable friendship but had never delved into the personal in any great way before this; she worried she'd crossed a line.

'Father, I'm sorry...'

'I do honestly, sometimes,' he said. 'I do sometimes wonder, if my life was different, maybe becoming a teacher, getting married, having a family of my own…if anyone would have me.' He laughed a bit as he sliced another piece of cake for himself as Grace refused a second helping with a wave of her hand.

'I'm sure they would,' Grace reassured him with a smile.

'It's lonely, being all by myself. That's why leaving Knocknashee was especially hard for me. I felt like I'd made friends there, with you, with Declan, and coming in and out of the school was a lovely part of my day. But that's the lot of a priest. Would I choose this life again? I don't know, Grace, is the honest truth. I was sent to the seminary at twelve, and it was decided then I'd be a priest. Nobody asked me. My brother got the farm, my sister is a nun in Enniscorthy, and my youngest sister stayed at home to mind my parents, and now she lives with my brother and his wife, who between you and me and the wall is not the easiest woman to be dealing with. Poor Abina, that's my little sister, is heart scalded from her, but by the time my mother died, she was too old to marry so…'

'She's stuck,' Grace finished for him.

'That's about the size of it. And to be honest, I fared fine in comparison. Even when I'm lonely, I like being a priest. I have a strong faith and I like helping people, like the poor of this parish, but sometimes I look at men my own age, walking up to receive with their wives and children, and I do feel a little pang…' He nodded slowly, his eyes fixed on the table.

Grace longed to hug him, but that wouldn't be appropriate. She laid her hand on his instead. 'You are a wonderful priest, and you make a big difference in people's lives. Nobody in Knocknashee forgets you, or all the little kindnesses you showed us all. Asking Mol O'Sullivan how Sally was getting on over in England, blessing the *cillín*, buying all those books for the school – the list of your kindnesses goes on and on. And just because you've moved parishes doesn't mean we are not your friends any more, because we are, always.'

CHAPTER 16

⁂

LONDON, ENGLAND

NEW YEAR'S EVE 1940

There were no Christmas or New Year's lights in London, no brightly lit shop windows or strings of lights. Everything had to be dark because of the German bombers that flew over every night. But people did their best to make the place look festive all the same.

There was cause for celebration – they were moving out of the boarding house today. Sarah had found them a charming little place in Marylebone that had a decent kitchen and four bedrooms all to themselves. So many people had left London, it hadn't been that hard to find, and their father had been happy to send the extra money needed.

Jacob complained of course – he loved his squalor, said it kept them closer to the ordinary people – but Sarah was utterly sick of their lodgings, which were freezing cold these nights, and the old leaky window frames and thin bedding did nothing to improve the situation. She was also fed up with sharing with people she didn't know. The coming and going of those in the boarding house was hard to keep up with. The man from Lubbock was still pining to go back there, but apart from him, the tenants kept changing.

When Jacob argued that it didn't feel right to live in the lap of luxury while the people of this city barely scraped by, she scoffed at him. She hadn't gone for a ridiculously upmarket place in Chelsea or Kensington, where a lot of the American newspapermen lived, or a suite at Claridge's or the Savoy, where they could take a long, luxurious bath with tons of hot water and sleep in a big comfortable bed. It was just a converted stable in a mews that backed onto a street of Georgian mansions. Fifty years ago, it would have been where the coachman lived, but now all the rich people had cars and nobody needed coachmen or horses any more.

What won Jacob over in the end was Sarah suggesting they set up one of the bedrooms as a darkroom so he could develop his own pictures instead of having to go to the United Press office for everything.

The office was where Richard was going now, in search of Cal South. Sarah had sent him to borrow Cal's car while she and Jacob stayed behind to pack.

Cal South from the *San Francisco Chronicle* was a West Coast playboy turned newspaperman, and he and Richard understood each other. Both came from money. The Souths had made it big in cotton after the Depression, and Cal was expected to go into the family business before he jumped ship for the life of a journalist. The similarity of their stories came out one night in a field in Kent, near Dover, when they were sitting in Cal's Ford Junior in that area known as Hell Corner, watching the Luftwaffe and the RAF slug it out, trying to find the words to capture the scene.

There was a concerted effort among all the American reporters to present Britain as a united nation, from the working class to the aristocracy, and therefore strong enough and valiant enough to hold out against Germany, contrary to the dire warnings of Ambassador Kennedy.

Ordinary Americans regarded British society as very divided and claimed to be offended by the infamous British class system. But Cal and Richard knew first-hand that rich Americans didn't really believe all men were created equal, any more than their counterparts in Britain did. United in their assessment, they'd become friends and often gave each other tips on scoops to be had. Together they'd written a series of articles about wealthy Americans in London. Jacob wouldn't have been welcome at the embassy in Grosvenor Square, but Cal and Richard had no problem getting into high society. Not that Richard openly flaunted his connections, but everything about him, he'd come to realise, told the story of old money. He blended seamlessly with the titled and the wealthy, in the same way that Jacob was their way in with the communists and the Jews.

Only last week Richard had introduced Cal to Virginia Cowles, a Vermont-born society figure who recognised Richard because she'd met his father. Connections like Virginia Cowles were invaluable. She was a columnist whose work appeared on both sides of the Atlantic, and she had become one of the most influential voices on the radio back home.

On June 29, 1940, she had broadcast to the United States on BBC Radio: *Reports current in America that England will be forced to negotiate a compromise – which means surrender – are unfounded and untrue. The Anglo-Saxon character is tough. Englishmen are proud of being Englishmen. They have been the most powerful race in Europe for over three hundred years, and they believe in themselves with passionate conviction. When an Englishman says 'It is better to be dead than live under Hitler', heed his words. He means it.*

She had been one of the first into the fray, but this was the tone all journalists worth their salt struck now, and it seemed to be working. The tide was turning back at home thanks to people like Virginia, and in a much smaller way due to newspapermen like himself and Cal.

Virginia Cowles had seemed to approve of Cal South and gave him a very interesting interview, so he owed Richard a favour.

Cal was in the United Press newsroom as Richard had anticipated, and willingly lent him his Ford Junior, tossing the keys to him as he typed furiously amidst a fog of cigarette smoke.

'It's goin' on the fumes, so you're gonna need a few stamps to get anywhere, but other than that, it's all yours,' Cal shouted over the din of men on the phone and the loud clacking of several typewriters.

'Thanks, Cal.'

Pocketing the keys, he went to get the car, which was parked outside the local café, the sort of place the British called aptly a 'greasy spoon'. The smell of bacon made his mouth water, so he decided to pop in for a sandwich. The bread was see-through thin, with a scrape of the horrible margarine, but the bacon was hot, fatty and salty and exactly what he needed. He had a mild hangover from the night before; Sarah had insisted on celebrating their last night in the boarding house with a bottle of champagne – another luxury that made Jacob grumble, though he still had to admit it was a damn sight nicer than English beer.

He ordered a cup of tea to go with the sandwich. At first seeing the English having big steaming mugs of milky tea with their meals made him shudder. He used to crave the iced tea Esme would make on the porch of the house on St Simons, filled with mint sprigs and orange slices. But he was getting used to it now. Just as well, given the recent rationing of coffee.

While he was still in the café, it began to rain outside. The weather here was so changeable, cool and wet one minute, dry and bright the next, but he liked it and didn't miss the Georgian hot sticky summers at all. But then the shower turned to persistent rain, and down the road, people scurried for shelter. It always made him smile at how the inhabitants of one of the rainiest places in the world were always taken by surprise by the rain.

He used a break in the downpour to run and jump into the car, and he found the needle was flat on the dial. He drove very slowly, worried he would run out altogether, when he spotted a gas station that mercifully still had gas and was serving. The government was very worried about running out of fuel, and so all of the major companies had been merged into one 'pool' to supply the meagre quantities of fuel allowed for civilian use. Richard used his allotted coupons. As press he was entitled to a decent gas ration, and his rations had built up as he'd not yet bought a car of his own. He got half a tank, which he felt should be enough for the day.

As he pulled up outside 17 Meadowfield Gardens, the old postman stopped by his car and rummaged in his sack.

'Here you go, sir, one for you, and a telegram for Jacob. I met the telegram boy in the neighbouring street and said I'd deliver it for him. Have you heard the one about the horse who went into the pub? The barman says, "Why the long face?"'

Richard laughed politely as he checked the envelope. *Grace*. Still smiling, he let himself into the house and ran up the stairs.

'Where were you? Did you get the car?' Jacob appeared at the door of his and Sarah's room, looking very stressed. He hated packing. He didn't own anything; he always travelled ridiculously light so he could leave wherever he was in an instant. But Sarah liked to buy things – books, make-up, clothes, a mirror, two candlesticks – enough to fill a large wooden trunk.

'I did – and here's a telegram for you, from Kirky, I think.'

'A telegram! Excellent! I hope to God it's something I have to do urgently...' Jacob seized it and ripped open the thin envelope. 'Ah! It is! Grab your notebook and follow me. We need to get some shots of St Paul's still standing majestic in the rubble. We'll take the car.'

Richard thought of begging for a few minutes to read his latest letter from Grace, but in the end, he left it on his bed in the little room. He didn't want to read it in a rush, with Jacob standing there hassling him; he wanted to enjoy it.

* * *

THE WHOLE AREA around the cathedral had been bombed last night, but somehow St Paul's itself was still standing. Kirky was right – it would make a great photograph, illustrating that battered but brave London had God on its side.

When Richard drew up as near to the cathedral as he dared – the heat from the burning houses was intense – he got out to talk to the ordinary civilians who were quenching the fires spread by the incendiary bombs. Lots of them were kids of only thirteen or fourteen, all busy emptying sandbags onto the flames to stop the spread and keep the fire away from the cathedral.

The bravery of the Londoners never ceased to amaze him. Women his mother's age driving ambulances through the smouldering, rubble-lined streets. Ladies even older supplying tea and sandwiches to those left homeless. Old guys working as firefighters or patrolling the bombed streets as ARP wardens, helping people to get to safety, and woe betide you if you didn't follow their instructions.

While Jacob snapped away, Richard gathered some rich expletive-laden quotes from several smutty-faced people and some cheerful chatter from the ladies serving food, who insisted on giving him a fish paste sandwich to go with his tea. If Richard never again in his entire life saw meat or fish paste, he would be a happy man. The things people dreamed up and considered as food in wartime was disconcerting at best and stomach-heaving at worst.

Hungry, though, he ate it, and afterwards, once he and Jacob felt they'd gotten enough, they drove further into the devastated East End, already flattened by the Blitz. The people of Wapping, Stepney and the docklands looked hungry and sick and badly dressed. They answered Richard's questions uncomplainingly about how they were surviving, but he felt ashamed of his American clothes, warm coat and hat, his strong shoes and the fact that he was obviously well fed.

'Don't worry about us, love, London can take it!' said one old woman in a headscarf, as Jacob balanced precariously on a cracked chimney pot to get a shot of a little girl lining her dollies up against a bombed-out wall. 'Keep calm and carry on!' He wasn't sure if the old dear was being ironic or not; sometimes British humour was very deadpan.

They ended up buying tea and cheese sandwiches for two land girls who had just joined up because their mothers refused to let them join the Wrens, which was what they wanted. Vi and Annie were funny and flirty and clearly saw the whole thing as a bit of a lark.

They had their uniforms in a paper bag – green jerseys, shirts and breeches – and were due to report for duty the following morning when they would be told where they were to go.

'Least we're going to the countryside. Everyone knows the food is better than in the cities, and we're fed up with rationing. We're hoping for a big juicy steak,' said Annie optimistically.

'Do you know anything about farming?' Richard asked with a smile as he took notes, thinking of Tilly in Knocknashee.

'I can't tell one end of a cow from another,' Vi announced triumphantly, 'but we'll soon figure it out. I suppose you feed one end and steer clear of the other, yeah, 'cause I ain't cleanin' it up, that's for sure!'

'You don't feed cows, you plonker.' Annie punched her friend on the arm. 'They eat grass, and I don't think they want us to clean up cow poo?' She looked horrified at the mere thought. 'Bad enough they want us to wear trousers…'

'Well, I ain't doing nothing like that, but I could look after lambs or something. Look, I dunno, but it's gotta be better than this, right, and no bloody bombs every night – I'm exhausted.'

'Me too. I'm looking forward to a long rest and a tummy full of lovely food.'

The girls went off after dropping several subtle-as-a-bag-of-hammers hints about going dancing at the Palais that night to ring in the New Year, and he and Jacob drove back by the houses of Parliament. He stopped the car to let Jacob photograph the statue of Richard the Lionheart outside the Palace of Westminster, still upright, though his sword was bent. The statue of Abraham Lincoln nearby and of George Washington in Trafalgar Square were both unscathed.

Jacob was delighted with their day's work. 'I think it will be a good angle, putting the English and American statues together, along with the image of St Paul's and that little girl's dolls in the East End. Kirky should be happy with that – it's what he's after, human interest. You type everything up and I'll develop the pictures of St Paul's and the statues, and we'll put a package together and get it sent tomorrow.'

'And then we'd better help Sarah get that trunk into the car,' said Richard, feeling slightly guilty.

'Yeah, hopefully she'll have finished packing by now,' agreed Jacob.

* * *

THE PROFOUND DARKNESS of the blackout had fallen by the time they got back to the boarding house in Elephant and Castle, and Sarah declared angrily that it was too late to move tonight – it was too hard and dangerous to drive around without lights – so they would have to do it in the morning.

She remained huffy about it until Jacob developed his pictures of St Paul's. He'd gone to the press office darkroom and then rejoined them after. She stared at them for a long time and then hugged him closely.

Richard banged his story out on the typewriter that he kept in Jacob and Sarah's room because his room only had space for the bed, then gave it to Jacob to send with the pictures. Declining Sarah's offer of some soup – he was still full after being plied with sandwiches at St Paul's and then drinking a bucket of tea with the land girls – he finally retired to his bedroom, sat on his bed leaning against the wall and opened Grace's letter.

It was, as he'd guessed, an answer to his short letter of condolence about Odile's father.

Dear Richard,

Thank you from the bottom of our hearts for taking time to find out about A. Mary and Tilly wept with relief that he is alive and had escaped from danger without being harmed, and they're also so glad to hear he is engaged to C.

He noted that she'd followed his lead, referring to the people involved in the French resistance by their initials only. He didn't know if it was necessary, but it did seem wise. Nobody in England was supposed to tell each other anything about ship sailing or troop movements, anything that could help the Germans. And he knew from Grace there were German sympathisers in Ireland.

The horrible Lord Haw-Haw, for instance, the aristocratic sounding propagandist who tried to terrify people by broadcasting chilling messages from the Nazis, was the American-born Irishman William Joyce, who grew up in Galway. Not that he was on the side of the Irish republican movement. As a teenager, during the Irish War of Independence, he had been an informant to the British forces about IRA members, and later he had turned to British fascism.

Mary O'Hare asked the canon, who is back now and as awful as ever, to say a Mass for PD. He was a Jewish man, but a Mass couldn't do him any harm. I think we all pray to the same God in the end, and it is all we can do. She told him he was A's brother-in-law, which is nearly true now, and had been murdered by the Germans while in custody. But the canon refused, claiming he sounded like a man who died in mortal sin if he was breaking the law and that Mass for the repose of his soul was pointless.

So Canon Rafferty was definitely back in Knocknashee. Poor Grace. Hopefully Mrs McHale would get back to him soon. He had written to his friend in the Bishop House in New York after receiving Grace's last letter and had received a short note in return saying she was still working on it, that she thought she had a lead and would let him know when she knew more herself.

He read on down the letter, shaking his head over how Canon Rafferty could think the war between England and Germany was no business of England's neighbour. He did understand why a lot of people in Ireland still stuck to the First World War belief that 'England's difficulty is Ireland's opportunity'. But the canon seemed almost fanatical in his opposition.

What a terrible thing war is, Richard. Please, please keep yourself safe.
This is my third letter in a row, so again, I've kept it short.
Yours,
Grace

A bit disappointed that it was another short letter – obviously the one she'd sent to America had been long and she didn't want to repeat herself – he turned over the sheet of paper to see if there were any postscripts on the back. There were two, and he smiled to himself. Her postscripts were often his favourite part, a funny story she'd suddenly remembered, or a flash of her everyday life. Stuff she thought was unimportant but which to him was a delight.

PS I'm sure by now you've received the letter I sent to America in September, letting you know that myself and Declan are doing a line.

Richard frowned to himself. Doing a line? What did that mean? He read on, curious.

We might have been content with that for a while, but the gossip was getting out of hand – nothing is ever secret in Knocknashee. There is a lot of pressure on teachers to be respectable in Ireland. I suppose it's the same everywhere, but I think here even more so – we're not allowed to be flighty at all. So we have decided to make it official, and are now properly engaged...

He could read no further. The words swam before his eyes, he couldn't focus, the blood roared in his ears, he felt as if ice water was sloshing around in his stomach. *Engaged. No. Impossible.* Grace was his girl, not Declan's. He loved her. He'd written to her that he loved her...in a letter that was probably at the bottom of the ocean.

'Richard?' It was Sarah.

He couldn't answer and just sat on his bed, trying to absorb this news.

'Richard, we're going out for some chips. Do you want some?'

'No thanks,' he managed, glad his voice sounded normal.

When he was sure they had gone, he picked up and read and reread her letter, forcing himself to do it, putting himself through the myriad emotions that threatened to drown him. She was the only girl he could imagine spending the rest of his life with. He should have said something when he was in Knocknashee. Why did he wait, then entrust his words to a letter that had to cross a war zone?

He should have gone back to Ireland once he realised the letter was lost. But he'd put off going, scared of rejection... And now he'd lost her. He was a coward. He deserved to lose her. For a wild moment, he thought of writing another desperate love note, or even sending a telegram.

No. Too late.

To tell her he loved her now would be like throwing a grenade into her life. And she would have to stop writing to him if he did; to continue would be a betrayal to that other man who loved her. Her fiancé. *Her fiancé. Oh God, what a mess...*

He couldn't even hate Declan McKenna. He was a good man. He adored Grace – that was as plain as the nose on his face. He was clearly perfect for her. He was her fellow teacher, he had known her all her life, they belonged to one another. Everything else had been a vain, silly dream.

He'd have to write back, wish her all the best, congratulate her. Carry on as normal.

Keep calm and carry on.

But first a shower. *Pull yourself together.* Making a gargantuan effort, he dragged himself upright and padded down the corridor to the bathroom.

In the freezing bathroom, the bath had a slightly mouldy rubber hose attached to the tap that somehow passed for a shower. Every time he used it, he yearned for their bathroom at home in Savannah, and in the beach house as well, powerful jets of piping-hot water, easing his muscles and soothing his mind. But this was not America.

He undressed and tried to get the water to mix, the cold and the hot to combine to some acceptable level of temperature, which was something that had eluded all three of them to date. Freezing with an occasional jet of scalding seemed to be the best the contraption could do.

He showered, shampooed his hair and shaved, then wrapped himself in a towel and went back to his room, where he pulled out the suitcase of clean clothes stored under his bed and got dressed. He glanced in the small flyblown mirror screwed to the wall and thought he looked a bit more human, even if under his smart clothes his heart ached painfully.

Sitting on his bed, he picked up his reporter's pad and uncapped his fountain pen.

Dear Grace,

Thank you for your letter.

This is just a quick note to offer both you and Declan my warmest congratulations on your engagement.

His hand shook as he wrote, but he tried to keep the words neat and even. He wasn't even sure why he was hurrying to write this now, but he told himself it was to give to Jacob before he went out first thing in the morning to mail today's article and pictures.

As you can imagine, life here is hectic, and while I find the work exhilarating and interesting, sleep and having any regular routine is close to impossible. Everyone is still on edge and afraid to relax.

I'm sorry to hear the canon has returned and is upsetting everyone again. I haven't yet heard anything definite back from Mrs. McHale but will let you know when I do.

I have to stop now as I need to catch the mail. Take care, Grace.

Yours,

Richard

He put it into an envelope, affixed a stamp and wrote out her name and address as he had done so many times before. Jacob and Sarah were back with chips wrapped in newspaper, and Richard gave him the letter to mail along with the photos and copy to Kirky.

Richard went back to lie on his bed, saying he had a headache, which was true, and he was going to sleep for a while. And even though he didn't think he would, he did drop off while still wearing his clothes, because when he opened his eyes and looked at his watch, it was midnight. The year 1941 was only minutes old.

He felt another wave of despair as he remembered that Grace Fitzgerald was engaged.

Then he lit a stump of candle rather than turn on the light; the blackout curtain was cheap and had a corner missing, and he didn't want to get in trouble with the ARP warden. By the faint flicker, he could see his breath in the freezing room, yet the atmosphere seemed oppressive. He felt hot…he could use some air. He went out to the kitchen to get a glass of water and saw the letter. Jacob must have decided there was no point in going out, that he would have been too late for the mail.

He decided to send it there and then, get rid of it, put an end to this chapter. He tiptoed down the creaky stairs and let himself out of the sleeping house.

It was a clear, cold night. The New Year had come in without any fireworks or fuss, though he supposed Vi and Annie were dancing away at the Palais. But he knew if he ran into an ARP warden, it would take more than his press pass to get him out of trouble. There had not been a raid yet tonight, but it was still early.

The mailbox was in the wall at the bottom of the long street. The building around it had had a direct hit, yet the wall remained standing and every day the letters and packages were collected by the elderly mailman who told all the jokes.

He popped the letter in just as the wailing of the siren rent the air. He groaned to himself. Yet another night sheltering in the London underground, packed with sweaty bodies.

He jogged back up the long road to 17 Meadowfield Gardens, thinking Sarah and Jacob would worry when he wasn't there and waste time looking for him. Then the scream of a bomb very close by sent him rushing to the wall. Stumbling on a kerb, he fell face forward, then crawled under the shelter of a doorway, feeling shards of glass cut his hands, his leg aching like someone had kicked him. A whistle, then the thudding crunch of another hit. Across the road a building crumpled, a water main burst and water sprayed everywhere, sirens, a klaxon, a cacophony of noise. As he wiped his eyes and coughed the dust from his throat, he looked up to see wave after wave of German bombers filling the night sky, dropping incendiaries like rain. The heavens lit up with anti-aircraft fire. Infernos erupted around him; plumes of smoke, flames, dust and flying debris made seeing more than a few feet impossible.

He managed to pull himself up against the door behind him. His leg throbbed, but he was unsure if he was injured. It was all so surreal, and his first time being caught outside during an attack; he had lost his bearings and had no idea which way was home or how to get to the underground.

"'Ere, mate, give us a 'and,' called an older man in khaki, with a tin helmet balancing precariously on his head.

The pain in his leg was subsiding, and Richard limped as fast as he could to where the man wielded a piece of iron railing. He was trying to force another door open, but the lintel had cracked and the door was wedged shut. Inside, he could hear a girl screaming.

The roof of the house was in flames. The upstairs windows had burst with the heat, and a curtain billowed through the aperture, ablaze. Whoever was in there didn't have long – the fire had engulfed the entire building.

Richard took off his jacket, wrapped it around his fist and smashed the downstairs window. The warden shouted through the mail slot, over the noise of the aircraft and bombs, 'Go to the window in your sitting room and we'll get you out!'

'I can't see, I can't see where I am! Auntie Irene is upstairs – you have to save her!' The girl sounded hysterical with fear and confusion, her voice hoarse from the smoke.

Picking up a brick, debris from the building adjacent, Richard broke the window's timber frame, cleared out the rest of the glass and managed to squeeze in. The room was filled with smoke, and a terrific crash came from upstairs, causing whoever it was nearby to scream once more.

'Auntie Irene! Oh my God!'

'Follow the sound of my voice!' he yelled. 'I'm over here! Follow my voice, I can get you out...' Through the smoke he could see a shape and reached out his hand. 'Come on, I'm here. Hurry...' He felt fingers touch his, fumbling and grasping, and he took the small hand and pulled its owner towards the window.

'You have to help Auntie Irene!' screamed the girl, a slip of a thing, barely out of her teens.

'I will, I promise. Let's just get you out first. Let me hold you up and you can climb out.' His eyes were streaming and his lungs burning, but eventually he got her up on the windowsill as a portion of the ceiling in the room collapsed. 'Quick, get out.'

He encouraged her out of the window, where she fell forward into the arms of the old man outside, then climbed out himself as the remainder of the burning ceiling came down behind him. The girl was being carried by two men on a stretcher towards an open ambulance. She was still screaming, 'Auntie Irene, Auntie Irene...'

'Well done, lad, good work.' The warden clapped him on the back as he stumbled forward into the open air, choking and wheezing, doubled over, hands on his knees. 'I reckon you need to get yourself to the shelter. Tube's that way. Off you go now, son.'

'But her aunt's still upstairs...' His coughing wouldn't stop, and his eyes were streaming so much he could barely see.

'Too late for her now, lad.'

'But I promised...' He twisted to look up at the blaze, the collapsing roof, the sparking timbers, the brick chimney on the roof staggering and sliding and falling...

CHAPTER 17

KNOCKNASHEE, CO KERRY

7TH JANUARY, 1941

Grace let herself into her classroom. School would start again tomorrow, and she wanted to check everything was clean and ready and that there were still no mice.

All was well. The place smelled of chalk and paint and glue, and she inhaled happily. She loved teaching, and even being here alone was nice, though she preferred it when the voices of the children filled the air.

As she went around taking down the Christmas decorations and pictures, she heard the postman coming up the corridor.

'Morning, Grace.' Charlie beamed as he popped his head into the junior classroom.

'Morning, Charlie. Lovely day, isn't it?' It was cold outside but crisp, with a silk-blue sky and glittering ocean.

"Tis surely, Grace, and the snowdrops are coming up in your

garden, I see. You're coming over later to Declan, going at the books again?'

'I am, no rest for the wicked.' She laughed. She and Declan still did their studying in Charlie's house. They didn't like him to be lonely, and anyway, it wouldn't be the done thing for them to be alone together in Grace's house. They didn't want to give the canon the slightest cause for complaint. Declan was worried what his father would do for company after he moved out and in with Grace. That wouldn't be until next August, of course. Though they were in the new year now, and soon it would be spring, then summer…

'I'll have a pan of mushroom soup on, and some soda bread to keep ye both going,' promised Charlie as he searched in his sack for letters. 'Will I give you the ones for the house as well as for the school?'

'Of course, Charlie, put them there on the desk.'

Agnes had always made Charlie go first to the house, then to the school, as if there was any point to making the time-strapped postman go that extra bit of distance.

'Here you are then, a big bundle today.' He handed her a sheaf of letters, several from the Department of Education about school matters; she always received these at the beginning of the term. There were five thick envelopes from Miss Harris at the teacher training college in Dublin; these would contain marked tests and the next stage of her correspondence teaching course. Five months to go, and then all being well, she would be qualified, something that had been her dream since she was sixteen. And Declan as well. Hopefully it would be Janie next. She'd already had a word with the girl about it, and Janie was keen to do the course.

Janie's family were too poor to pay for it, though, and with Canon Rafferty in charge of the school board, Grace doubted there would be any help coming from that direction. The only person the canon was interested in subsidising was Father Maurice. It had been mortifying for Grace at Christmas when the canon demanded his parishioners put an extra penny into the collection plate 'to support our brother and missionary, Father Maurice, in his holy work caring for the poor of the Philippines and saving their souls from hell.'

An unhappy ripple had gone around the church. Those pennies were children's toys, maybe a bottle of whiskey or a Christmas pudding. People had been saving up for these treats all year. Everyone paid up, though; they were too afraid not to do so.

Grace hoped the village knew this was nothing to do with her.

'And here's another letter, a personal one...'

This one had an English stamp, and like last time, it took her a moment to realise it was from Richard.

'It's your American friend,' said Charlie helpfully; he had obviously got over his fear of Richard Lewis now that she and Declan were properly engaged.

'Oh, so it is!' She stayed smiling, though her heart missed a beat. This was the first letter she'd had back since she'd told him she was engaged. Part of her had worried he wouldn't write back, that he would distance himself. Maybe he'd think it wasn't seemly to write to an almost married woman, or her to him.

She opened it at once, not wanting Charlie to think she wished to keep it private, and scanned the short note.

Dear Grace,

Thank you for your letter.

This is just a quick note to offer both you and Declan my warmest congratulations on your engagement.

As you can imagine, life here is hectic, and while I find the work here exhilarating and interesting, sleep and having any regular routine is close to impossible. Everyone is still on edge and afraid to relax.

I'm sorry to hear the canon has returned and is upsetting everyone again. I haven't yet heard anything definite back from Mrs. McHale but will let you know when I do.

I have to stop now as I need to catch the mail. Take care, Grace.

Yours,

Richard

She turned over the sheet in case there was any more, but there wasn't. She reread it. Never in the history of their correspondence had he ever written so formally. There was nothing wrong in anything he said, but it was so cold and detached, so short, as if they were bare acquaintances. She felt a tear sting her eye. Was this how it ended?

'Is everything all right, Grace?' Charlie sounded worried.

She'd forgotten he was there. 'Yes, it's all fine.' She smiled at him, blinking away the tiny tear. 'He's written to congratulate us on our engagement. It's disappointing, though – he was rushing and didn't have time to send any news. I was hoping to hear something about Alfie. Tilly is so gloomy at the moment.'

'You're right, it would have been nice to hear something more,' agreed Charlie as he shouldered his bag and headed out the door. 'The poor girl seems very down, especially since that Swiss woman left straight after Christmas. But as I said to her, she'll be back, especially if the Germans keep on bombing Dublin.'

'You're right, Charlie, I'm sure Eloise will be back in no time.'

It was hard to summon much enthusiasm at the prospect, though. She knew she shouldn't be childish about Tilly finding another friend, but now that Richard had abandoned her as well… At least that's what it felt like.

She tucked his short, cold letter into her basket of schoolbooks. *What should I write back to him? Anything?* There wasn't really anyone she could ask. Tilly didn't care about anyone except Eloise at the moment. And as for Declan, she knew he would never say it, but she suspected he would be relieved if her friendship with Richard fizzled out.

For the next two hours, she swept and dusted and cleaned, trying to get rid of her sadness by sheer hard work, until her leg ached even more than her heart.

* * *

As Grace limped into her front garden through the gate from the schoolyard, Tilly was tying her horse Rua to Grace's front fence; she'd come down in the cart. Rua, the Irish for red, was Ned's replacement, and he was a gelding with the most lovely sorrel coat and a long silky mane and tail. She still had Aonbharr the cob as well, he pulled the plough but his temperament wasn't suited to trips to town.

'I was bringing a load of winter cabbage down to Biddy's,' she explained as she followed Grace in through the house to the kitchen. 'And I thought I'd drop in to see ya.'

'You're very welcome. Will you have a cuppa? Where's Odile? Is she with Dymphna?'

'No, it's Dymphna's morning off. Odile is with Mam. She's grand and safe – I've built her a playpen, and she loves it. A cuppa would be good, and Mam's sent down a brown cake.' Tilly brought it out of a cloth bag she had slung over her shoulder and put it on the table. 'But what I'm here for is I want your help with something.'

'Of course, anything.' Grace felt a rush of pleasure. It was the first time in a while Tilly had come to her for help, and it was lovely to have her friend back.

'I think Eloise needs to get out of Dublin immediately and come and live here, where she'll be safe. And I think if you wrote to her, Grace, it might help make up her mind, you being a teacher and everything.'

Grace's heart sank, her silly jealousy flooding back. 'I'll do whatever you want me to, Tilly. I'll write if you want, but you know Eloise said she had to get back to her students in Dublin before she ran out of money.'

'I know, but I've been thinking I can look after her here. She won't need money, I have enough, and there's plenty of food up at the farm. And we have our own turf to burn, and everything anybody could need, and the place is as clean as a new pin now that Dymphna is there every day.' Tilly paced the kitchen, her hands behind her back, her boots leaving mud all over Grace's floor.

'Of course all that is true,' said Grace tiredly. 'But I still think she'd want her own money. She wouldn't want to be dependent.'

'Well, you could give her a job teaching languages in the school? Imagine if the children of Knocknashee knew Italian and French and German!'

'Mm. Imagine.' It would be amazing in a little country school, but

Grace doubted the canon would let her hire a specialist language teacher, especially not Eloise. 'The canon would never allow it, Til, you know he wouldn't, and I think she needs a good wage – she likes sophisticated things, like fashionable clothes. She wouldn't find that sort of thing here.'

'Era, don't mind him, the old *cábóg*. Sure you could do it like you did with Declan, kind of appoint her and let him be objecting away. And on the clothes thing, sure there's Peggy Donnelly's draper's and that's not too dear? No, Grace, I've made up my mind. Eloise has to get out of Dublin, and not just Dublin either. She has to leave the east coast altogether – they're bombing everything over there.'

Tilly wasn't wrong. The bombings of Dublin on the second and third of January had shaken Irish people to their foundations. They'd assumed neutrality would protect them, but clearly not. And it wasn't just Dublin. Bombs had fallen in Meath, Carlow, Kildare, Wicklow and Wexford. The whole world felt more terrifying every day, and who knew what would happen next? Maybe there would be a blitz like in London and Coventry and Belfast and all those places.

President Roosevelt had just made his Four Freedoms speech, reported on the radio yesterday, somehow getting past the censor, but while it was a lofty idea that people should live with the freedom of speech and worship and be free from want and fear, it didn't feel at all realistic as Hitler took country after country, seemingly unchecked by anyone.

'Dymphna, don't you agree with me?' asked Tilly. 'Doesn't Eloise need to come and live at the farm, at least until the war is over?'

'Oh, hello, Dymphna…' Grace turned in surprise to find Agnes's former carer standing in the door of the kitchen. A moment later she noticed what Tilly had overlooked in her single-minded fixation on Eloise. The widow's eyes were shining with unshed tears.

'Come in, Dymphna. Are you all right? Has something upset you?' Dymphna was usually so stoic. She hadn't looked this shaken since losing her job at the parochial house.

'Yerra, I'm all right, Grace.' The widow sighed and rubbed the back of her hand across her eyes, then absentmindedly took the sweeping brush from beside the door and began sweeping up the trail of dried mud left by Tilly's boots.

'Leave that, I can manage. Please sit down.' Grace pulled the sugán chair out from under the table and indicated that Dymphna should sit. 'Now, what is it?'

The widow hesitated, then said quietly, 'I...I had a visitor this morning while I was hanging out my laundry.'

'Who?' Tilly sat down as well, leaning her elbows on the kitchen table, finally paying attention. 'Not the canon?'

Dymphna shook her head with a shudder. 'No, nobody that bad, but...it was Miah Danny Gurteen...'

Grace's eyes widened. She brought over three mugs and the teapot to the table, as well as a knife and plates for the brown cake, then took her own seat. Miah Danny was the local matchmaker, the man people went to when they had their eye on someone they'd like to marry, and he 'did the deal' as it were. Dowries and land and entitlements and succession rights were important things and not to be taken lightly.

Miah Danny might not be as bad as the canon, but Grace didn't like him. There was something not altogether wholesome about the man. It was hard to put a finger on it, but he was what Charlie called a *sleeveen*, a kind of oily individual who would do or say anything to press his own advantage, which was to make matches in return for a payoff – a lump of money or a lamb or a load of turf.

'And what did Miah Danny want?'

'He said there was a man, and he had his eye on me, and he had a farm and no children, and he would be willing to take me and the children on. He knew we had no money, so he didn't expect anything like that, but he hoped I'd consider him, and he would be decent and had a fine house.'

'And who is this man?' Grace asked.

Dymphna looked miserable. 'Tomás Kinneally...'

Tilly hooted. 'No! That little *peist* was after me for years, and then he was hanging around after Eloise with his tongue out, and now he thinks he deserves a lovely capable woman like yourself? He has a puffed-up idea of himself, that's for sure. What do you think, Dymphna, would Tomás do the trick for you?'

'He would not that way at all,' said Dymphna with a grimace. 'But Miah Danny Gurteen said if I was only open to the idea, and had a think about it, I might find it was the best thing for me.'

'And are you? Open to it, I mean?' Grace was worried she was going to say the wrong thing. She didn't want to reveal what she really thought about Tomás in case Dymphna ended up married to him.

'No, well, not really... I don't know. Maybe. It would be some kind of protection, I suppose. I don't own the cottage, I'm only renting, and I'm scared of my life that Tom O'Donoghue is going to put me and the children out or...' She paused, her thin shoulders shaking.

'Or what?' Grace probed, with a bad feeling. Tom O'Donoghue was a good friend to Miah Danny, and he was another person Grace didn't like one bit. He was what people called 'a bit of a ladies' man' and was always the one for the suggestive remark or the wink as you came down from receiving at Mass. He even flirted at funerals.

'Dymphna, tell us,' begged Tilly.

'Tom O'Donoghue called and said he was putting the rent up, almost doubling it, and I can't afford that, but when I said that, he more or less suggested that I could pay off the extra another way...' The woman's cheeks burnt.

'That's a terrible thing to do! He's another *sleeveen*.' Grace was shocked. She knew Tom was a bit lecherous, but this was outrageous.

'So I thought maybe Tomás, maybe he wasn't so bad. At least it would mean a bit of security. The idea of being with any man ever again after Tommy...I just can't...but I've two children to rear...'

'You can always stay at the farm, Dymphna,' said Tilly, and Grace felt proud of her friend for saying that. It obviously cost her an effort, as it was only a three-roomed farmhouse, one of the rooms being the kitchen. Mary O'Hare slept in the settle bed by the range and Odile in a bassinet beside her. Tilly slept in the loft upstairs, and the only spare bed was in Alfie's little room.

'I won't do that, Tilly,' said Dymphna, squeezing Tilly's strong hand gratefully. 'I know you want that room for Eloise to come back to, and I won't want to get in the way of that.'

'But...' Tilly looked torn between Eloise and Odile's faithful minder.

'You don't need to worry, either of you,' said Grace, realising what the solution was and immediately wondering why she'd never thought of it before. 'You can come and live here, Dymphna, you and Paudie and Kate. I've plenty of room.'

Dymphna was even more touched. 'You're so good, Grace, but it wouldn't be right. This is your home, and the children would be in your way, and you and Declan are getting married soon and will have babies of your own...'

'I love Paudie and Kate and so does Declan, and our marriage and...well' – she blushed – 'that is all a ways off yet. I don't like living alone, that's the truth, so you'd be doing me a favour. It need not be forever, but it's for as long as you want it.' She put her hand on the other woman's thin shoulder.

The widow looked a lot happier. 'Are you sure, Grace? I can pay the same rent I was paying Tom O'Donoghue...'

'Dymphna, stop. I inherited this house, I don't pay anything for it, and I have three spare bedrooms. You and the children can have them for as long as you want, rent free.'

'I can't accept that, Grace!' Dymphna sounded horrified.

'You can and you should. People have shown me so much kindness in my life, with nothing in it for them at all, just to do a kind thing, and I'd love to be able to do this for you. Please accept it. And I hate the idea of Tom O'Donoghue sniffing around you, so I'm happy to thwart his nasty little game, and Miah Danny's as well. What a pair of weasels they are, disgusting.'

The older woman jumped up to give her a hug. 'Well, thank you, Grace, so much, and I'll take care of this place, cleaning and what have you, and cook and all of that too – let that be my rent.'

'There's no need for any of that, but if you've time, I'll never say no to your cooking.' Grace smiled, hugging her back. She knew Dymphna was a proud woman who didn't like to accept charity, so if it made her feel better to prepare the meals and do some baking, she wasn't going to say no, particularly as Dymphna was such a great cook.

'And it's not forever. I promise I'll find somewhere else before you're married.'

'Don't worry, Dymphna. It's been a hard few years for you, losing Tommy and everything. You take your time to find somewhere of your own, and that way at least if you did decide to make any great changes, or even marry again, it would be because you want it, not because you have to.'

Dymphna sighed heavily. 'Oh, I don't think I'll be marrying again, ever. Look at me. I'm a middle-aged widow without a shilling to my name, no house of my own and two small kids to raise. I'm hardly a catch now, am I? Unless for some old farmer on the side of a windy hill looking for a slave.'

'Go on out of that, you're a fine-looking woman, and you're nice and kind and a hard worker,' said Tilly, standing up and patting her on the shoulder. 'Anyone would be lucky to have you. Now, I'd better get back to Mam. I've left Odile with her long enough.'

'I'll be up to you in an hour, Tilly, just as soon as I've cleaned up here,' said Dymphna, standing herself to take the empty cups and plates from the table to the sink to wash them.

'Dymphna, leave all that. Go with Tilly now, that way you can get a lift up in the cart,' said Grace. 'And you can move in here tomorrow if you like. I just need a chance to get a few things moved around. I think I'll give Kate my room and move into my parents' room. I've been meaning to do it for a while but keep putting it off. And you can have Maurice's – there's really no point keeping it for him, he's never coming home, I'm sure – and Paudie can have the spare room.'

'This is just so kind of you, Grace.' Dymphna was close to tears again, but happy ones this time, as she moved to follow Tilly. 'Tilly, I'll just fetch the children. They ran up to Charlie's earlier – I told them to get out from under my feet while I was doing the washing. I expect he has Paudie drawing pictures out of books and Kate helping him in the garden – she loves that. The pair of them are mad about him. We're so lucky to have him in our lives.'

'I know, I'm so grateful he's going to be my father-in-law,' agreed Grace as she saw her two friends to the front door.

'And will you write that letter to Eloise?' asked Tilly, suddenly remembering what she'd come for.

'I will write to her and tell her how much I enjoyed meeting her, and if the situation gets any worse in the east, she's always welcome in Knocknashee,' said Grace, and Tilly nodded, satisfied, as she untied Rua from the fence, where he'd been eating all of Grace's snowdrops.

* * *

GRACE SPENT the afternoon moving her things from her small childhood room into the big front bedroom, which had belonged to her parents until they'd died and Agnes took it over. It was the largest and ran the full width of the house and had been empty since Agnes moved downstairs after her stroke.

Then she went to look in the other rooms. Maurice's was still as Agnes had kept it, immaculate and neat and ready for the elusive brother's return that would never come. She took the sheets off the bed; Dymphna would bring her own.

The spare room, which had held her parents' belongings and letters until Agnes burnt them in a fit of madness, along with Grace's beloved rag doll Nellie, was neat and clean and needed nothing doing. It still had a new bed and chair and desk from when the vile Francis Sheehan had lodged there. It would be perfect for Paudie. He could sit at the desk to do his drawings, and it looked over the garden behind so he could watch the birds.

As dinner time approached, she headed over to Charlie's to do her studies with Declan. She was looking forward to Charlie's fresh soda bread and his famous mushroom soup.

As they sat down to their books and the latest set of papers from Miss Harris in the teacher training college, she realised she should confess to her fiancé that she was moving Dymphna into her house.

She was so used to making all her own decisions, she'd forgotten that soon her home was going to be his as well.

He laughed at her shamefaced apology. 'It's your house, Grace,' he said, putting down his pen to smile at her. 'To do what you want with. And it's fine if she doesn't find anywhere else before we're married. She's a lovely woman, and Paudie and Kate are the best-behaved children in Knocknashee. But I thought she liked that little cottage of Tom O'Donoghue's?'

'Oh…well…' She hesitated, not sure whether it would be a breach of confidence to tell Declan and Charlie what had happened, but then she decided that's how men always got away with it, because women never told.

Declan was shocked, but Charlie got really upset and angry, both at the terrible behaviour of Tom O'Donoghue, about whom he expressed some very murderous thoughts, but also the idea that Dymphna would be so worried for her own safety, she would have to consider marrying Tomás Kinneally. 'Poor Paudie and Kate! Imagine having to put up with that eejit for a stepfather.'

After going on a long rant, he stood, grabbed his coat and said he had to walk around for a while to calm down.

'He really likes those children, doesn't he?' asked Grace, looking after Charlie as he closed the front door rather hard behind him.

'He does. I sometimes think he should make more of liking the mother.'

'What?' Grace stared at him. 'Your father…and Dymphna? Ah, sure…'

Declan looked amused and even slightly offended. 'Why not? He's only fifty, she's not yet forty, it's not a mad gap. Paudie and Kate already love him.'

'And your father is one of the nicest men for four parishes, I know that, and he'd make a wonderful husband, he would of course. I'm just… He never had interest in anyone since your mother died, and Dymphna always says there could never be anyone after Tommy.'

'But it would be nice for them, wouldn't it? Poor old Dymphna has had such a hard time trying to keep food on the table and a roof over the children's heads, and I think Da will find it lonely going back to living by himself after you and I are married. It would solve everything, wouldn't it?'

Grace thought about it and nodded. 'It would, but I don't know. They're both so sure no one would look sideways at them, I doubt they'd ever dare think of it, and it's not like we can make them.'

Declan slid his hand into hers, smiling into her eyes. 'I never dared think you'd look sideways at me, Grace, did I? But I risked it. And now look at us...'

'And now look at us.' She smiled back and lifted her mouth for a kiss.

* * *

IT WAS a cold night and her leg ached. The big bedroom was at the front of the house, and the winter Atlantic air blew through the window frame. She had the patchwork quilt she'd made when she was in the hospital, all the coloured squares sewn onto a woollen blanket on both sides, and an eiderdown. In her small childhood bedroom, this had always been enough, but tonight in the big front room, she needed more.

She got out of bed and opened the large oak chest of drawers against the wall between the two front windows. Dymphna had taken all of Agnes's clothes to the convent in Dingle for distribution to the poor and the needy, so there was not much left in the top and middle drawers, but she knew there was extra bedding in the bottom drawer of this chest.

Sure enough she found a lovely lilac coverlet she recalled once being on her parents' bed. It had a candlewick wave design and a fringed edge. She'd not seen it for years. She took it out, and when she did, something thumped onto the rug.

A fat bundle of papers bound with an elastic band and beside them, incredibly, a little rag doll.

Hardly able to believe her eyes, not daring to believe it, Grace picked up the doll. It was Nellie. The doll her mother had made for her when she was five.

No, it was impossible.

Agnes had burnt Nellie. Grace had found her blue glass eyes in the ashes in the front garden, where Agnes had also burnt Daddy's knitted jumpers, Mammy's easel and paintbrushes, all their love letters…

She unrolled the bundle, and to her delight she realised the letters had survived after all.

And this was definitely Nellie – all she was missing were her eyes.

Grace hurried to the room she'd slept in since she was a baby, taking Nellie with her. She found the matchbox in her bedside drawer and shook out the two glass eyes, and with her little sewing kit, she had them sewn back on in a moment, and then her childhood friend was back.

She sat on the little bed, hugging her doll, tears flowing unchecked down her cheeks. God alone knew what madness was going through Agnes's mind; she must have been half crazed. But the knowledge that her sister didn't really burn Nellie was such comfort. It was silly, she knew. A grown woman crying over a dolly was not something she'd like people to see, but Nellie meant the world to her. The doll had been made with such love and had slept beside her every night in the hospital, her one little bit of home, her one tangible link to her mother. The loss had been too profound to even put into words. But to have her back…

Later she returned to the big front bedroom and sat on the double bed with her parents' lilac coverlet wrapped around her, reading their letters. Her father had gone to Dublin to study to be a teacher, and while he was away, he and her mother wrote several times a week. Their love for each other shone through every page, and Grace had read them so many times, they were frayed on the edges and in the creases, but she didn't care.

It was like she had her parents back. She could hear their voices in these written words, the gentle teasing, the longing to be reunited. Over and over by candlelight she read them. There were forty-six letters in total, three postcards, two birthday cards, one memorial card for Grace's *mamó*, who died while her father was in Dublin. Those letters around the time of Mamó's death were heartbreaking to read, how Mammy had to grieve her mother without Daddy there to support her, and how much she missed him and longed to have his arms around her. She wrote of the robin who came to sit on her windowsill every morning, and how it gave her comfort, because a robin was the soul of a loved one passed on, of that she was certain.

It reminded Grace of the robin that had sat on the silver birch tree watching as Declan went down on one knee and proposed with the beautiful ring that was so like her mother's. If Mammy approved, then hopefully her marriage would be as happy as Mammy's had been, and she had a beautiful life to look forward to.

Strangely she didn't feel fury at her sister, instead just overwhelming gratitude, and she offered a prayer of thanks to Agnes in heaven for not destroying these precious memories after all.

The low winter sun woke her.

She must have fallen asleep reading the letters, with Nellie beside her. Aching and stiff, she got out of the big bed. The children would be gathering for their first day back at school very soon, so she would have to get organised and be there with Declan to greet them as all eighty-nine of them bounced happily through the door.

CHAPTER 18

LONDON, ENGLAND

JANUARY, 1941

*H*e was conscious of a girl's hand holding his.
Grace...
He tried to say her name, but his lips were so dry and blistered, they were stuck together, and he only managed a hoarse sound in his throat. The next moment the hand was withdrawn and a wet sponge placed to his mouth. A trickle of water squeezed between his lips, which he swallowed gratefully before darkness swept over him again.

She was walking away down the street, arm in arm with that schoolteacher. She hadn't seen him; she didn't know he was there. If he could make her turn... 'Grace! Grace!' But she didn't look back.

He woke again, drifting upwards into consciousness, and this time opened his eyes a fraction, but the daylight was so bright, he had to close them again. All around was noise, hustle, bustle, people talking, giving orders, children crying, someone sobbing in the distance. 'Hello?' he croaked weakly. 'Hello?'

The girl's hand seized his again. 'Nurse Simmons, come quick. I think 'e's awake properly this time!'

Footsteps tip-tapped briskly towards the bed and a deeper female voice said, 'Good morning, sir. Glad you've decided to join us at last. You took a nasty blow there when the chimney fell – the warden told the ambulance all about it. You've been in and out of consciousness for a few days – you were badly concussed – but you'll be fine. Can you tell me your name?'

'Richard... Richard Lewis...' he managed. His throat was so painful. 'More water...'

'Ooh, he's a Yank, ain't 'e?' asked the first woman excitedly. 'I ain't never met a Yank before, but I saw *Gone with the Wind* and 'e sounds just like that!'

'I'm going to lift you up a bit, Mr Lewis, so you can drink properly from a glass.' The nurse put her hand behind his head and brought a glass to his lips, before she lowered him gently back onto the pillow. 'There you are, Mr Lewis, well done. I'll leave you in Pippa's care now – she'll look after you. Lie there quietly for a while before you try to sit up by yourself.'

'I'll be 'ere soon as you need anything, Mr Lewis,' said the younger woman reassuringly.

'Thank you, ma'am...' His eyes still closed, he mentally checked himself over. His head ached and felt as if it was heavily bandaged, but he could move his fingers and toes; he seemed to be all in one piece. He made another effort to open his eyes. This time he succeeded.

A young woman of about twenty sat by the bed, knitting a sock. She had well-brushed strawberry-blond hair cut to her jawline, hazel eyes and that peaches-and-cream complexion common to so many English girls. On the nightstand behind her was a jug of water and a gas mask, a pile of socks of different colours and two folded scarves. That's what every woman seemed to do these days – whenever they had a moment with their hands free, they would immediately start knitting socks and scarves for the soldiers.

After lying there for a while looking at her, he decided he'd better find out where he was. 'Hello, ma'am...' His voice came out in a rusty croak. 'Can you please tell me where I am?'

She turned to him with a radiant smile, setting aside her wool and needles. ''Ello, Richard Lewis,' she said, holding out her hand to shake his. 'You're in Guy's 'Ospital, and I'm Pippa Wills, and you're the man what saved me from the burning 'ouse, thank you ever so much. I'm ever so grateful.'

Richard suddenly remembered that night, the fire, the ARP warden, the girl in the smoke-filled room. This must be her.

'You're welcome, miss.' She looked so different from the terrified girl he'd saved from the fire. Her face was bright and her hair shining. She was strangely attired, though, in a long old-fashioned dress several sizes too big, and plimsolls, which was what the English called a sort of sneaker without laces, usually worn by children. 'You look... very healthy.'

'I'm fine. A bit of smoke damage to my lungs, but I'll live.' She spoke in the Cockney way of the working class people of the East End of the city. 'They kicked me out of the bed after a couple of days, but you been here all week. How are you feeling now? Do you want some more water?' She stood and fussed around him, helping him up against the pillows, pouring him a glass. 'Can you hold the glass yourself, Mr Lewis? Oh, well done! The lunch trolley's due any moment. The nurses are busy, but they said to me as soon as you woke up again to feed you some chicken soup, just soup. You ain't had nothing but water for a week, and your stomach won't be up for more.'

'Thank you, ma'am.' Propped against the pillows, he was able to look around the busy, noisy, crammed ward. The last time he was in a hospital was in the Candler Hospital in Savannah to have his appendix out, when he was nine. The orderly, antiseptic-smelling place where people spoke in hushed tones and white-clad nurses walked silently from patient to patient who rested in perfectly made beds bore no resemblance to this. Here, everywhere was crowded, beds and gurneys shoved in any which way, the harassed-looking nurses doing their best to manoeuvre around them, exhausted and stressed, their white uniforms bloodstained.

A young nurse was taking the temperature of a person in the bed beside his; they were so bandaged up, it was hard to know if they were a man or a woman.

A trolley with a large tureen and plates of sandwiches trundled through the chaos, and Pippa hurried off and came back with a bowl of chicken soup. She perched on the bed beside him, holding the bowl for him while he spooned the weak brown liquid into his mouth. It was not very hot, and quite greasy, but he could feel the strength coming back into his body with every gulp.

'It's very kind of you to look after me, miss,' he said, putting the spoon down. His voice was still rough and weak, but it felt easier to speak after the warm soup. 'I hope I've not taken up too much of your precious time.'

She laughed and shrugged as she set the empty bowl aside on the locker. 'Maaah taahme,' she said, imitating his Southern accent, 'is all yours at the moment considering I ain't got nowhere to go since the fire, with the house burnt down and all. I'm living in the underground at night, but during the day, I'm welcome here. The nurses like it when there's a visitor who can take care of the patient – it takes the pressure off them – and I can get a cup of tea and a sandwich and dinner as well, so really it's you doing me the favour, Mr Lewis.'

'Richard, please…'

'All right, Richard. And I'm Pippa, not miss. I love your accent, Richard. Are you really a Yank?'

He laughed, which made him cough. 'My father wouldn't be best pleased to hear you call me a Yank. The Yankees are northerners, and we're from Georgia in the South, but I guess that's a difference that doesn't matter much over here. And I suppose I do work for what my father would call a "Yankee rag".'

'A Yankee rag?' She put her head to one side, bird-like.

'Yes, ma'am…Pippa. I'm a journalist for a newspaper in the United States. I'm here reporting on the war.'

'A reporter!' She clapped her hands, impressed. 'So, Mr Handsome

American, what do you think? Is it better or worse over here than you imagined?'

He thought about it as she handed him another glass of water. 'Worse in some ways, better in others, I guess.' He drank the whole glass straight down. 'I was in England in June, so I saw how it was before the Blitz, and boy, it's sure smashed up now. But I'm always amazed at how everything goes on anyway. You Brits are tough, I'll give you that.'

Pippa laughed, a lovely sound; it reminded him of a stream rushing over pebbles. 'Yeah, we're tough all right. It takes a lot of courage to eat powdered eggs. Do you know the last time I had an orange?'

Richard was amused. 'No, when?'

'Two years ago. And here you are, Mr American, when you could be at home eating oranges and bananas and having ice cream and sweets whenever you want. You're barmy, but I'm glad you came all the same.' She dropped her eyes and said more seriously, 'When the bomb hit and the door jammed, I thought I was going to burn to death. I was so frightened.'

Another memory came back to him of that night – this girl calling over and over for...what was the name? Auntie... *You have to help Auntie Irene!* He felt a rush of guilt. He'd promised her to go back for her aunt, but then the chimney... He hesitated, unsure whether to ask a question that could only have an unhappy answer.

'I know you tried to save my Auntie Irene, Richard,' she said softly, with a sideways glance from her large hazel eyes, 'but the warden came to see me, to see if I was all right, like, and he said it was a blessing in disguise you got hit by the flying bricks, because if you'd gone back in, you'd have died, like...like...'

She started knitting again, focussing on what she was doing, head bent, no longer making eye contact. Tears pooled on her lower lids.

'I'm so sorry,' he said softly.

'The warden says it was the smoke would 'ave killed 'er. She wouldn't 'ave suffered that bad,' she said, knitting furiously.

'Did you live with her, or were you visiting?'

'I lived with her. My older brother, Bill, died of TB when I was fifteen, and mum and then dad a year later, so my aunt – well, she was my great aunt really – she took me in. She was a nice woman, bit of a funny old fish but nice.'

'Have you any other family?' He felt a surge of protection for this brave, stoical girl.

'Not as I'm related to. I had a chap, but I haven't heard nothing from him for months. I think he was lost at Dunkirk, but I dunno. His mum and dad are still hopeful 'cause the telegram from the War Office just said he was missing...'

She shrugged and sighed, and he wasn't surprised she didn't hold out much hope. Over three hundred thousand were rescued last June, and that was what the government wanted the media to focus on, but what happened to the rest of the Allied servicemen, well, nobody knew. Dead, taken prisoner, it was hard to tell. But if her boyfriend didn't get home in those early days, then the chances of him ever showing up were not good.

'And my best mate, Ethel, she got married, moved to Liverpool, so I don't see her no more, and my other mate, Natalie, she copped it in a direct hit on the factory where she worked in the East End. She was only twenty, like me, and such a laugh.' She sounded very matter-of-fact, like it was all just a part of life, but he could sense behind the stoic surface a deep sadness for the past and anxiety about the future.

He wished he could make it a bit better for Pippa. She was such a courageous person despite her dire circumstances. He didn't know her at all, but something about saving someone's life... He felt closer to her than would be normal with a total stranger. 'So have you any plans about where to go next?'

She nodded with a small smile. 'I have, yeah. I signed up as a land girl soon as I got out of hospital. There's a farm just outside Oxford wanting girls to help out. The land office said to come back for my uniform soon as I was free from looking after you, and then I've to make my own way. I ain't never been outside of London before, but I'll find it somehow... Oh great, here comes the tea trolley! You must be gasping for a cuppa, not having had one for days!'

She went dashing off to get a couple of mugs and a few biscuits, the rule about just soup clearly forgotten, and to Richard's surprise, for the first time ever, he found he actually craved a cup of tea. He gulped it down with pleasure. Pippa showed him how to dunk his ginger biscuits into the hot milky liquid, and for some reason, the resulting soggy mess was delicious and he began to feel like he'd really arrived in England. This would make a great story for Kirky.

* * *

HE WAS DISCHARGED LATER that afternoon, after Nurse Simmons checked his head wound and pronounced it to be healing nicely. She was apologetic for not keeping him in longer, but these days as soon as a patient could walk, they had to be sent home, to make room for all the other victims of the Blitz with breaks and cuts and burns from last night's raids. As she replaced his bulky head bandage with a large sticky pad, she told him how they had to put all the radium used for cancer treatment below ground at night – boreholes had been drilled beneath the hospital for the storage – because a direct hit would result in a radium leak, which would be catastrophic. He wished he had his reporter's notebook on him, but he would just have to remember what she told him and write it down later.

Pippa helped him get dressed. He was grateful to find that she had washed and dried his clothes in one of the hospital bathrooms and stitched up all the rips and tears. 'Now, you look like a right dandy again,' she announced, standing back with her hands on her hips. 'Unlike yours truly.'

She spread out her arms and giggled as she did a twirl for him, and she did cut a comical figure in the big, long dress that utterly swamped her.

'Stuff I was wearing when I got here had to be binned, and some nice old dear gave me this frock and her grandson's plimsolls what he'd grown out of. It doesn't do much for me, does it?' She grinned. 'Just as well I'm off to the farm in Oxford tomorrow. I'd say it doesn't matter what I wear in the country – whatever it is will be covered in muck in no time, and anyway, they're going to give me overalls.'

From what he'd heard, though he didn't like to say so, the land girls were worked pretty hard, so she was probably right. There wouldn't be many nights off, and if you were stuck in the countryside, there wouldn't be much fun to be had. But the thought of her spending one more night down in the Tube, then off into the middle of nowhere for the duration of the war, with no friends or family to look after her...

'Look, come stay at my place for tonight,' he offered impulsively.

'Oh, I can't do that.' She looked very shocked.

'No, it's not just me,' he hastened to reassure her. 'I share a couple of rooms with my sister, Sarah, and a friend. You can bunk in with her.'

'Oh...' She looked relieved. 'But you know, your sister, she might not want to share her room with someone like me...' She blushed and looked a bit nervous, and he realised Pippa Wills wasn't as confident and devil-may-care as she liked to come across.

'Of course she will, she's a nice person. She'll love you,' he reassured her.

'I dunno...'

'And then the next day, I could drive you to pick up your uniform and then to this farm near Oxford, if you'd like?' he heard himself say.

'You got a car?' She was wide-eyed.

'No, but I know a guy who does, another reporter, and it would be interesting for me to see where you're going. I might write a piece about it.'

She hesitated a bit longer, but the temptation of being looked after for once was too great. 'Well then, if you're sure, thank you very much. It would be lovely to have somewhere to stay for the night, and to drive me would be really nice of you. I can chip in for food and petrol, give you my ration card.'

'Don't worry about that, I have plenty.'

She stuck out her chin with a touch of pride. 'I like to pay me own way, Mr Lewis,' she said firmly.

It was getting dark as they left the hospital, and the nurses were lowering the felt anti-splinter blinds to protect the patients from flying shrapnel. Pippa dropped off her completed knitting with a woman from the Red Cross, and then together they went out into the dusk. Outside the huge Victorian building, which was heavily sandbagged, a taxi dropped off an anxious-looking family, the woman with a baby in her arms. Richard hailed the driver. 'Elephant and Castle please,' he said, opening the door for Pippa.

'You live in Elephant and Castle?' She pealed with laughter. 'So that's why you were right nearby when the bomb dropped. I was sure by your fancy clothes we were going to Kensington or Sloane Square or somewhere, not Lambeth. You must be the only poor Yank in London.'

She seemed a lot less nervous of him now, and he smiled as he got in the back seat beside her. If only she knew… But he wasn't going to tell her if it made her more comfortable to think he was poor.

As the taxi drove carefully through the blackout, swerving around massive potholes in the road at the last moment, he remembered something else he'd forgotten. The night of the raid, he and Sarah and Jacob had been about to move to Marylebone. *Damn.* He hoped they'd waited for him in Number 17; he had no idea where the new house was.

As the taxi pulled up outside the boarding house, he told the driver to wait, just in case they needed to drive on.

'Stay here, Pippa, I'll be back in a second. I need to check something…'

As he got out of the cab, their Texan neighbour with broad shoulders and lamb-chop sideburns came out of the front door, in his well-cut suit and steer horns on his belt buckle.

'Howdy, Richard,' he called, lugging a massive leather suitcase down the steps, letting the light pour out of the house behind him. 'How are you doin'? You don't look so good, if you don't mind me saying so. Is everything alright son?'

Pippa stared out of the back window of the taxi, her eyes popping in amazement at this apparition.

The Texan spotted her and chuckled. 'Ya'll went on the missin' list. Your sister thought you were dead. She sure was mighty cut up, your photographer friend too – they were checkin' all the morgues. None of the hospitals had a patient named Richard Lewis. You really shoulda let her know.'

'I'm fine, I was hit by flying masonry and unconscious for a week,' explained Richard, trying to get past him. 'I had no identification on me since I was only going to mail a letter.'

'Got caught in a raid, huh? I dunno about you, but it's high time I high-tailed it outta here. Gettin' back Stateside. '

'Probably wise.' Richard agreed but he wasn't in the mood for small talk. He shut the door and ran up the stairs to the third floor. When he knocked at Sarah and Jacob's door, a small boy holding a little girl by the hand opened it slowly and told him Mummy wasn't in, that she'd gone back home to see if she could find Daddy, because their house had fallen down. Richard's heart sank. He peered into his old room. A nurse in her uniform was fast asleep, flat on her back on the bed, snoring softly, and his suitcase was gone from under the bed.

Downstairs the door to Mrs Price's apartment was locked. *Damn.* He'd have to come back later. Though if Sarah was sure he was dead, would she even have bothered to leave a forwarding address? He and Pippa would have to stay in a hotel. But he hadn't very much money left, only enough for the taxi, and the banks were closed. At this rate it was going to be the Tube station for both of them.

As he re-emerged into the dark street, closing the house door behind him, Pippa leant out of the cab, waving a piece of paper. 'That man in the suit gave me this to give to you.'

He took the paper from her with a sigh. By the faint light of the moon, it looked like some sort of address. 'Listen, Pippa, bit of a problem...' But then he had a thought and struck a match to read the address by. It was in Marylebone, written in Sarah's hand.

The taxi driver seemed to know exactly where to go. It was amazing how the London cabbies knew the city like the back of their hand; they called it the Knowledge – it was a test they had to pass to get their licence. He drove them carefully through the blackout, taking lots of side streets, and finally pulled up in a narrow cobbled lane lined with little white-plastered houses.

After paying the fare, Richard tapped on the door of Number 3, which had a brass knocker shaped like a horse's head. He heard feet come down the stairs, and the door opened.

'Where in the blazes were you?' screeched Sarah, sounding just like their father, beating at his chest with her fists, red-faced with fury, as Jacob came piling down the stairs behind her, whooping with delight.

'You scared us! What happened to your head?'

'I was in Guy's. Got a bit of a knock. They didn't know my name until today when I woke up, but I'm fine...' He drew his sister to him, enfolding her in a hug. She had stopped shrieking and hitting him and was weeping hysterically.

'Hello, I'm Pippa.' Pippa leant past Richard and Sarah and held her hand out to Jacob. 'Nice to meet you. It's my fault Richard was in the hospital. He saved my life when my house was on fire and I was trapped. If it wasn't for him, I would have been burnt to a crisp. And then he got hurt when he went back to save my aunt, God rest the poor old soul – she copped it. And I'm sorry you were both so worried, but he didn't come round until this morning.'

'Nice to meet you. I'm Jacob and this is Sarah. She's not usually like this, she's quite calm normally.'

'Pippa looked after me in the hospital all week,' explained Richard, still holding Sarah to his chest, where she was soaking his jacket with her tears. 'She has nowhere to go because her house burned down. She's off to be a land girl in Oxford tomorrow, so I'm going to borrow Cal South's car again and drive her, but for tonight I said we could put her up.'

'Oh God, yes, of course...' Sarah made a huge effort to pull herself together, wiping her face and hands on her sleeve and skirt, then turning to shake Pippa's hand. 'You're very welcome. We'll get you settled in one of the attic rooms.'

The house was small but charming, a little sitting room and kitchen downstairs, with a gas burner, then two bedrooms on the second floor and two more in the attic. Richard's suitcase was in one of the rooms on the second floor, which had a good-sized bed and a desk and an armchair as well. Sarah told him she'd left the address with Mrs Price and every lodger in Number 17. 'I knew you'd find us if you weren't…if you weren't…' With a huge effort she stopped herself from crying again. 'I was going to give it another week before I said anything to Daddy or Mother or Nathan. Oh, Richard, I love you so much…'

'Look, I'm starving,' Jacob interjected. He wasn't going to get into the emotional stuff; it was not his style. 'How about we go down to the Queen's Head? Reggie won't mind us bringing in fish and chips from the café next door.'

Sarah pulled herself together again. 'Good idea. Do you want fish and chips, Pippa?'

'No, no, I'm fine, not hungry at all, but you lot go on. I'll stay here and have a nap on my lovely bed.'

'Nonsense, you look like you need a good feed,' said Sarah kindly. 'Some fish and chips and a port and lemon inside you and then you really will be fine.'

'No, I don't think so. I can't go out in this elegant piece of haute couture.' She giggled to cover her nerves and indicated the shapeless navy tent in which she was dressed. 'I'm so overdressed, I'll put you all to shame.'

Sarah looked the Cockney girl up and down, her lips twitching. 'I see what you mean… Hmm. OK, boys, you two go ahead. We'll see you in the pub after we've sorted out the clothes situation. Come on up to my room, Pippa. I'll find you something to wear.'

* * *

'So, she's pretty.' Jacob nudged him as they walked down the street towards the Queen's Head.

'Is she?' Richard asked innocently.

'She is and you know she is, don't pretend you didn't notice. Should we order four portions of fish and chips in the café, then go for a beer while we're waiting?'

'Sure. Can't wait for a pint of good old English ale.' Richard groaned; his head was thumping now.

They settled into the corner of the dark pub off Baker Street and sipped the beer they would never get used to if they stayed here for a thousand years.

'Before Pippa gets here, I want to tell you who I saw two days ago,' Jacob said in a low voice, 'coming out of the *Daily Worker* office. I took some shots for them and went to drop them off –'

'The *Daily Worker*?' Richard was quite surprised Jacob was moonlighting for the Communist Party newspaper, which was either for or against the war depending on Moscow's latest position, at this point dictated by the nonaggression pact between Hitler and Stalin. Like the French communists they had met, Jacob had become disillusioned with his comrades, who he saw as blindly following the line of the Comintern without opening their eyes to the reality, and he had more or less abandoned his former political stance.

'Yeah, well, it was at a protest the Party arranged at one of Mosley's gatherings, so I thought, you know, as it was an anti-fascist thing…' He shrugged. 'Anyway, that's not the point. The guy I ran into was Didier Georges. I recognised him from your description, a wiry Frenchman with green eyes and a livid scar running all the way from his ear down under his shirt. So I took him for a pint and asked him about Alfie and the others.'

'Yes?' Richard sat forward eagerly.

'Alfie is fine. He's in the thick of it. There's a terrible conflict going on in Paris between the communists and the Jews and those who want to oppose Hitler without an affiliation to any political or religious group. Alfie being an outsider is proving invaluable in trying to unite them in the face of a common goal, the age-old theory of my enemy's enemy being my friend, and encouraging them to pull together for now and explaining they can argue their differences once Germany is beaten.'

Richard nodded. 'He's right. The infighting between the factions is playing right into the Germans' hands. This is exactly what they're after, the way it was in Spain. And de Gaulle in the mix as well…'

Jacob snorted. Like Didier, he hadn't much regard for the general, who he suspected of choosing to tell a nice story from the comfort of

London while those who were willing to get their hands dirty, and risk unmerciful retribution if they were caught, actually did the work.

'And Constance, is she OK as well?'

'Yes, working hard alongside Alfie, creating military disruption, hampering the Germans in every way they can, slashing tyres, filling petrol tanks with sugar, trying to throw spanners in the works on a daily basis.'

'It all sounds a bit juvenile until you consider the consequences they face if they're caught.' They'd all heard stories of the deportations, the interrogations and the retribution for the slightest acts of defiance, despite the German propaganda campaign to the French people that they came in peace. They'd seen a poster the Germans had plastered all over the place in France of a German officer, a small child in his arms, two more looking up at him with big grins, with the caption *Faites confiance au soldat Allamand!* It urged the population to trust the German soldiers as men of honour and kindness. It was total rubbish of course, and nobody was fooled.

He felt fear on their behalf, but also something like envy. To be a part of history, instead of just reporting on it... But what he was doing had to be done too. He and his colleagues from other American newspapers were here to tell what they saw – a small nation being battered daily but pulling together to defy Hitler. The lives of people like Alfie depended on America coming into the war, he could see that now, despite the awful human cost.

'Anything about Bernadette?' he asked.

'Still no word. Someone thought they might have seen her outside Lyon, but it was only a glimpse at a railway station and they couldn't be sure. It most likely wasn't.'

The two men sat in silence for a moment, absorbing this information.

Then Jacob took a pull of his disgusting beer. 'I was on the verge of writing to your friend Grace to tell her Alfie was still surviving, but I put it off because I'd have to explain why it was me writing the letter. You're back now, so I'll leave it to you.'

'Sure. I'll do it tonight.' He felt a cramp of pain at the sound of her name.

Jacob looked at him sharply. 'Problems in the Emerald Isle?' He'd put on a terrible Irish accent with a grin.

'Of course not. Everything's fine. Very good, in fact.'

'Come on.' Jacob had a sharp nose for when people were lying to him.

Richard really didn't want to talk about it, but at the same time, it would have to come out sooner or later. 'Do you remember that guy, Declan McKenna?'

'The good-looking teacher, a bit shy?' Jacob asked. 'Did something happen to him?'

'Yes. He got engaged to Grace.'

There was another long silence, almost as long as when they had contemplated Bernadette, and then Jacob, in an uncharacteristic display of sympathy, patted his hand. 'I'm sorry to hear that.'

'No need to be sorry,' Richard said almost fiercely. 'I'm happy for her.'

'Good. Good.' Jacob nodded approvingly. 'Good for you. That's the spirit. And if you don't mind me saying so, Richard, there are plenty more fish in the sea. Speaking of which…'

Pippa and Sarah had just come into the pub and sauntered over to their table, looking pleased with themselves. Pippa had donned the long-sleeved red dress Sarah had worn the night their father had come to see them, with a little red hat tipped sideways on her strawberry-blond hair, a black tight-waisted jacket and black heels. With a dash of lipstick and with mascara making her eyes even bigger, she looked not just pretty but beautiful.

For a stunned moment, Richard was so amazed at her transformation, he couldn't think of what to say. Then he cleared his throat, still rough from the smoke and fire. 'Pippa, you look…um…er…very elegant.'

The Cockney girl blushed and grinned. 'Thank you. It's all your sister's doing. She's so nice! I can't believe she's lent me something so beautiful. I'll be scared to get a speck on it.'

'I haven't lent it to you, I've given it to you,' said Sarah, amused.

'Oh no, you can't give it to me,' protested Pippa, eyes wide. 'I'll have my uniform tomorrow – they give you three shirts and a mackintosh and two pairs of boots and breeches and everything else. I'll be fine.'

Sarah brushed away her objections. 'Don't worry, I've loads of clothes. Jacob's always nagging at me to get rid of them.'

'Though there's no point. You'll only buy more.' Jacob grinned as he got to his feet. 'Richard, get these girls hot ports while I go get the fish and chips.'

'Just a glass of tap water for me, and no fish, just a pennyworth of chips. I have a penny in here somewhere.' Pippa started digging around in the bag in which she'd kept her knitting.

'Too late.' Jacob announced. 'Already ordered and paid for.'

She swallowed nervously. 'No, but I don't have enough money, y'see...'

'Don't worry, it's on me.'

She blushed again, more violently. 'I can't accept that. I don't want to be more of a burden than I already am, you've all been so good to me already.'

'Pippa, you are not a burden. You spent a whole week looking after my dumb baby brother in the hospital, so please let us do something for you,' said Sarah firmly, putting her hand on Pippa's shoulder and forcing her to sit down before taking a stool herself. 'Now, Richard, get those hot ports. And make them doubles.'

CHAPTER 19

KNOCKNASHEE, CO KERRY

FEBRUARY 1941

Grace popped into the post office to take a pound out of her savings account. She was going to visit Peggy Donnelly's draper's shop later that day, and the price of everything kept going up. She hoped that Peggy would have it, and she would be able to afford enough material for a long wedding dress that would cover her calliper and shoes. Luckily she was so small, she might be able to manage if it was cut on the bias.

And she had until August, so she could buy a piece at a time, enough for the bodice, then the skirt, then the train… She couldn't expect Peggy to magic up an extra couple of yards like she had done for the green dress; those days were gone.

'Grace, I'm glad to see you. Have yourself and Declan set a date yet?' The postmistress beamed as she handed over two ten-shilling notes.

'We haven't, Mrs O'Flaherty. We want to get our exams out of the way first before we sort it out.'

'Right enough you do, but be sure to give us plenty of notice because we'll want the altar looking beautiful that day. You know the way Eileen O'Flynn can grow hydrangeas like nobody else. Well, she'll do them for your wedding, but you'll need to give us time to arrange it all.'

Grace felt a twinge of guilt and hoped what she said next wasn't going to offend this kind-hearted woman. 'Thanks, Mrs O'Flaherty, I will, but I have to warn you – we haven't said anything to the canon yet, that's why we haven't told anyone a date – but we're intending to get Father Iggy to marry us in the hospital chapel in Cork sometime in August.'

'Well, isn't that a wonderful idea.' Nancy's smile grew even wider, and a gleam appeared in her squinty eye. 'I'll let Eileen know that then. She has a sister in Cork she visits regular, and I'm sure the hydrangeas will grow as well in the garden there as here. It will be a change for us to decorate a different church, and a lot more fun without' – she lowered her voice – '*himself* looking on with those awful eyes of his, God forgive me.'

'Well, we won't be doing anything too fancy, just a simple ceremony and a bit of a do after.' Grace was anxious this didn't grow legs and run away with itself.

'Oh, of course, nothing too fancy,' said Nancy O'Flaherty unconvincingly, patting the salt-and-pepper bun on the back of her head. 'Just a few nice arrangements, we won't go mad. And don't worry, when you decide on the day, nobody in Knocknashee will say a word to the canon.'

'Mm, well, thank you, Mrs O'Flaherty.' The idea of a small, plain wedding in the hospital chapel had appealed to Grace, but she was beginning to suspect that her friends and neighbours weren't going to let her get away with it that easily.

As she left the post office, ten-year-old Leonard O'Flynn and eight-year-old Mikey O'Shea came bumping down the slight hill on a home-made billy cart they'd made out of timber and old pram wheels. They swerved wildly to avoid her. 'Morning, Miss Fitz! Morning!' They waved as they sped past. It was midterm break, and the children were off school.

Neilus Collins waved his walking stick angrily as they nearly ran him off the footpath. He had a patch over one eye and his hand in plaster, no doubt yet another scrap with his brothers. There were five of them living on one farm, and the fighting that went on was nobody's business. Poor Dr Ryan had the unenviable job of patching them up each time, and he was sick to death of them. Last week it was over a fiddle bow – one accused the other of using it without rosin, and that had ended up with three of the brothers needing stitches and a fourth concussed. It was a ridiculous way to live, but not one of them had married – which was entirely understandable if you met them – so they were all living in the parents' small cottage.

'Mind where you're going with that thing!' Charlie McKenna called after the two boys, shaking his head. Her future father-in-law was pushing his bicycle out of the gate of his thatched cottage next door, his sack resting on the back of it. 'They really should put brakes on that. I'll ask Declan to see to it,' he said as he paused to hunt through his sack of mail. 'Hang on there, Gracie, I've something for ye… Here it is.' He handed her a letter with English stamps. 'Your American friend, with more news of the war, I suppose?'

Her heart lifted as she took it from him. After Richard's brief cold note in January, she'd almost thought she would never hear from him again. She hadn't been able to bring herself to write back. She'd tried several times, and each time a crumpled sheet of notepaper had ended up in the bin.

'I wonder if he has any more news of Alfie?' she said, feeling the envelope to see how thick it was. It seemed substantial; she thought it must contain some newspaper cuttings as well.

'Well, I'll let you at it. I'm running late. I've the whole round to do yet, but I was holding a bit of wire for your fiancé. He's trying to invent some new contraption, don't ask me what, and nothing would do him only I stand there for half an hour with the wire in my hand, and if I moved a quarter of an inch, he roared at me.'

Grace laughed. 'He's always tinkering with something. He went to see some man in Cork when we were there – Hugh drove him over to Douglas – and he's been thinking about electric current conducting ever since. I won't delay you so, Charlie. See you later on, when I come over to study.'

She was turning away when he coughed and spoke again. 'I... Um...Gracie...'

She stopped and smiled at him questioningly. He looked oddly uncomfortable. 'Is everything all right, Charlie?'

'Grand, grand entirely. I was just going to say...' He gazed at his feet, shifting his weight from one to the other, Grace was perplexed. Charlie McKenna was not a man to mince his words or not say what he meant. 'Well, I was going to say I won't see you later because I'm going to the pictures in Dingle this evening and won't be back till late.'

'That's great, Charlie. I hope you enjoy it. What are you going to see?' The new picture house that had opened in Dingle last summer had everyone excited; hardly anyone in Knocknashee had been to a film before then. 'Is it still the same feature they're showing?' She and Tilly had gone to see it on Saturday, *All This, and Heaven Too*, and Bette Davis was brilliant in it.

'Yeah, that's right.' He pursed his lips. Maybe he thought from the poster in Biddy's window that it was a bit romantic and, well, female.

'Well, Tilly and I thought it was very good,' she said, for the want of something more enlightening to say. 'Are you going on the bike?' The wind was biting today, and it would be worse tonight.

'Ah no, Dr Ryan is giving me a lend of his car...' He plunged his hands in his pockets and stared at a spot over Grace's head. Whatever was happening, this was not the usual Charlie.

'Ah, that's better. I wouldn't fancy cycling home against the wind tonight.'

'Indeed, grand so. Sure then...right. I'll be off so.' And before she could say anything else, he rode off on his bike.

Grace's brow furrowed as she gazed after him; she wondered what on earth that was all about. But then she remembered she was holding a letter from Richard in her hand, a nice thick one, and felt another surge of happiness as she headed back to the house to read it.

Dymphna was in the kitchen popping a loaf of soda bread into the oven, and the children were upstairs getting dressed in their warmest clothes. They loved going with their mother to the O'Hares' farm when they didn't have to go to school. Kate liked to play with Odile, while Paudie preferred to sit out on the rocky hillside, drawing the peregrine falcons that were always circling overhead, on the lookout for pygmy shrews and scurrying field mice.

'Oh, Dymphna, I'm glad I caught you.' Grace placed Richard's letter onto the shelf of the dresser, looking forward to reading it in private. 'I'm going to suggest Declan come here to dinner and for study tonight because Charlie won't be at home this evening – he just told me he's going to the pictures. I was a bit surprised. I didn't think that would be his thing at all, but he's going anyway, and you know how tongues will wag if Declan and myself spend any time together without anyone chaperoning us. It's ridiculous, I know, but... Is everything all right, Dymphna?'

The widow gazed at the floor, twisting her apron in her thin hands. She seemed very uncomfortable; it put Grace in mind of Charlie earlier. 'Ah, well, it's a wee bit awkward, you see. I'm going to Dingle myself tonight. The children will be staying up at the farm – Tilly said they can sleep in Alfie's room.'

'You're going to Dingle? Is everything OK? Is your mother ill?' As horrible as Dymphna's mother was, Grace knew her friend still worked hard to keep their relationship alive for the sake of the children.

'No, she's fine...everything's fine. It's just I'm going to the pictures too...' For some reason her cheeks were blazing.

'Oh, that's nice!' Grace was surprised but pleased to hear Dymphna had arranged a little outing for herself; usually she only thought about other people. 'Why don't you ask Charlie if you can travel in together? He's borrowing Dr Ryan's car to go – it's too cold to cycle.'

'Yes...mm...I know. I mean...mm...'

Grace, who'd been putting the kettle on, turned to look at her closely. Then it dawned on her. 'Dymphna, are you and Charlie going to the pictures tonight together?'

'Mm, yes, mm, if you don't mind...'

'Of course I don't mind, why would I mind?' She was delighted. Both of her friends had endured such hardship and loss, and if they found a bit of comfort in each other's company for an evening, then there was no harm in that – it was something to be celebrated.

'Well, only if it's not a problem for you and Declan...'

'Ah, don't worry. We can stand being apart for one evening without dying of misery. Go on off to the pictures, the pair of you, and don't be worrying.' Grace gave an airy wave of her hand as she went back to making herself some tea.

'Ah...mm... I mean, if it's not a problem if we... I mean...'

Grace put down the tea caddy and stared at her. 'Is this about more than one cinema trip, Dymphna?' She wondered what else could happen today. It was not yet ten in the morning and already her world had been turned upside down. 'Are you and Charlie... I mean...' She hardly liked to ask if they were 'doing a line', as it seemed a bit intrusive, but that's what it was beginning to look like.

'Yes, well, Charlie seems to think... He...mm...he seems to think I'm all right. So if you and Declan don't mind...'

'Oh, Dymphna, of course we don't mind.' With tears in her eyes, Grace went to hug the woman who had been such a rock of support to her when Agnes was alive. She was touched by how much her approval meant to her friend. 'If you two are happy together, I'm more than happy for you, and I know I speak for Declan as well.'

'But Declan might...you know...he might think I want to replace his mother, but I promise I don't...'

'I know you don't. No one can replace Maggie, but you're not Maggie, you're Dymphna, and Declan will be delighted. Sure he only said to me the other day, he said he'd love it if you and Charlie got together, because when he and I are married, he didn't like the idea of his father being alone.'

'He really said that?' The widow beamed, twisting her apron again, her cheeks bright pink. 'Are ye sure?'

'Of course I'm sure. The only thing we were worried about is if Charlie didn't get up the courage to ask you. He's such a pillar of strength to everyone else, but he's always saying how he is neither use nor ornament.'

'He's both use and ornament,' Dymphna said in a show of spirit. 'Sure he was apologising to me for being an auld lad, but there's only twelve years in it.'

'And better be an old man's darling than a young man's slave.' Grace laughed. 'Mammy used to always say that, because she was three years younger than Daddy and loved to tease him about it.'

'And I told him as well, the older the fiddle, the sweeter the tune.' Dymphna laughed with her, then went bright red, as if she thought maybe she'd been too daring.

'Charlie McKenna is one of the best men on this earth, and you are a wonderful, kind, loving woman.' Grace grinned and shooed the blushing woman towards the kitchen door. 'Now your children are waiting. Let you go on up to the farm and come back in plenty of time – I'm going to help you get ready. It's well past time that coral lipstick of mine had another outing, and a victory roll will look wonderful on you. I still have Eloise's magazine with the instructions how to do it.'

As soon as Dymphna had her coat on and was gone, holding a child by each hand and with such a spring in her step she looked girlish herself, Grace settled down with a mug of tea to read Richard's letter.

3 Coachman's Mews, Marylebone, London NW1.

Dear Grace,

First things first, I have news of A and C. They are definitely engaged and doing great work. I won't go into what, but you can tell A's mother and sister that they can be very proud. A slim chance of a sighting of B in another part of the country, but most likely not her. So no real news but nothing to suggest the worst either, so we have to keep on hoping. Please tell your friends I am thinking of them.

Secondly, Grace, congratulations again on your engagement. I'm sorry I sent such a short note earlier. I was in a rush...

Her heart swelled with pleasure. His tone was so much warmer than in those few cold lines. Maybe it was just as he said, that he was tired and on edge from living in London with the nightly raids.

...and then I got hit by falling masonry, which landed me in the hospital. Like a fool, I got caught outside in an air raid.

Grace's stomach turned over. This was exactly what she'd feared might happen to him in England.

Don't worry, it was just a concussion and I'm fine.

She breathed a shaky sigh of relief.

And anyway, it was for the best, because while the raid was going on, I managed to save a very brave girl from a burning house, though sadly I got knocked out before I could help her aunt. Pippa Wills is the girl's name, and she looked after me while I was in the hospital.

Grace felt a little tremor in her heart. She wondered what this 'very brave girl' looked like, then instantly berated herself for feeling jealous, like she felt jealous of Eloise. Silly, childish, selfish emotions.

It's so sad for Pippa. Her aunt was her only relative, and her boyfriend went missing at Dunkirk, and her closest friend in London got married and moved north and her other friend was killed when her factory was bombed, and yet she carries on regardless. She's got guts, that girl. The first thing she did after losing everything in the raid was sign up to be a land girl. I drove her to Oxford yesterday, to the farm where she's going to work, and it didn't look like much fun. There are about a million pigs to be looked after, and she was going to have to bed down in a barn with eight or nine other girls who all looked half starved and overworked. The farmer's wife was not the most welcoming. She looked Pippa up and down like she was an animal she was considering buying at the market. She seemed to think, probably correctly, that Pippa didn't know much about farming. I felt bad leaving her there, to be honest, and I said if she wanted me to take her back to London, she could stay with us. But she said she had to do her bit for England and that if this was the only way to do it, then so be it. All said in her cheery Cockney accent.

Girls like Pippa put me to shame. They seem able to cope with everything that gets thrown at them. It makes me realize how Sarah and I were raised like greenhouse flowers that can only survive in a very specific set of circumstances. I'm so glad I broke out of the greenhouse, at least to some extent. Everything I can do here in England to encourage America to join the fight against Hitler is vital for the good of people like Pippa and our friends in Paris and the whole world really, and I'm glad I am doing my bit to make it happen.

Sarah says the same, that she is in awe of all the bravery she sees. She and Jacob are members of the Jewish Refugees Committee now, and she helps new arrivals every spare chance she gets.

We know we're the lucky ones. We have money, we're living in a nice little house in Marylebone that costs us £2 a week (see new address at the top of the letter), we can buy our fish and chips and go to the pub and even have dinner in the Savoy if we want to. There is no problem getting fine food if you have money, though Jacob grumbles if we do.

The ministry of food here has said they won't ration fish and chips, which is a stroke of compassion in otherwise gruelling rationing. It's to keep morale up and it works. People here love it. I do too now. Though it's nothing like what we eat, I've gotten accustomed to it. Did I tell you I like tea now? Inconceivable to me last year, but now I do and find myself craving it.

Good news is, my and Jacob's articles have been syndicated in the Boston Globe and the Washington Post among others, and Kirky is ecstatic (meaning he sent us a telegram saying "it seems you three are not a total waste of money") and has given us a pay raise. He trusts our judgment now, which is a complete turnaround from the dire warnings of behaving ourselves and the strong sense that we were on probation.

I've enclosed a few of our pieces if you would care to read them and let me know what you think.

There's a long feature I wrote at Kirky's request on diet and rationing. Our editor says the Americans love to eat, and the idea of provisions being in short supply brings back terrible memories of the Depression. People back home have an almost macabre fascination for it, much more than for what Churchill says in the Commons. It is more relatable to their lives.

The other pieces are shorter, but I hope you enjoy them.

So I'm off now. Don't forget to send me news of Knocknashee, and give my regards to Declan.

Yours,

Richard

She didn't know why she felt slightly bereft as she set his letter aside. It was long, it was friendly, he still valued her opinion. And of course she was dying to read anything he'd written. It was just... No, she was being stupid.

The feature on rationing was fascinating. Richard explained how meat was rationed by money, not weight, considering the different varieties. So a person was allowed around thirty cents worth of meat per person per week, which meant about two pounds of beef. Fowl wasn't rationed, but liver and other sweetmeats were. There was some confusion over rabbits, because the government had set a maximum price for retailers but not wholesalers, so grocery store owners had to pay seventeen cents a pound for rabbits but could only charge fifteen cents, which meant warehouses full of rabbits were going off.

He wrote that just because something was rationed, it didn't mean it was in short supply; it just meant they didn't want rich people eating up all the stores and the poor having no access to good nutrition. It was a fair way of doing it, he thought. Tea, butter and bacon were hard to get, but what pained people the most was the dearth of chocolate, sweets and biscuits. Sweets, he explained to his American readers, were what the English called candy, and biscuits were not biscuits like at home but a thing more like a sweet cracker. Grace wondered what Americans called biscuits; she thought she must remember to ask him.

Apparently the lack of sugar was hard for the British to bear, though a doctor Richard interviewed about it said it would do people no harm whatsoever to cut back; they were eating far more than was good for them.

The article was accompanied by a great shot by Jacob of a single chocolate bar left on a general store shelf and all of the people waiting in line, young and old, eyeing it greedily.

The other articles covered things like spending nights in the Tube station when the bombing was at its worst.

Grace's head filled with images kept from her by her own

government as she read Richard's stories about lice and fleas down on the platforms, and how people abandoned the government-issued pallet beds because they were too narrow and short, opting for the floor or deckchairs they carried down. He described the horrors of shelter throat and spotted fever, a form of meningitis that was rampant due to malnourished people being confined in such close quarters. But through all of it, he peppered his articles with admiration. The songs sung as the bombs pounded above, the delight at a cup of tea at a Lyons' Corner House, or a slice of cake if you were lucky. Sometimes a band would play, or a man on a piano, and it cheered everyone. He wrote of people going to the movie theatres to see *The Great Dictator* or *The Thief of Bagdad* or *Strike Up the Band*. These days the movies had to be over by five. It was too dangerous to have people out at night, especially now that they'd started ignoring the sirens to get to the end of the film. But like all the other deprivations, the Londoners accepted this restriction with stoic good cheer.

When she had finished reading, Grace gathered the articles and his letter and brought them slowly upstairs to her new bedroom at the front of the house, where she placed them in the biscuit tin Charlie had given her when that first letter arrived from Richard. That felt like a lifetime ago.

She used the tin to store all her letters now, and there were many in there: the ones Tilly had written when she was in hospital, letters from the Warringtons as well as birthday cards from them, all of Richard's and now her parents' letters as well, miraculously restored. This box was surely her most treasured possession.

Sometimes Grace thought the written word was even more important than the spoken word. Talking to someone in person was nicest probably, but there was a magic in the written word, the way you could return to it over and over again.

On impulse she took out Richard's first-ever letter and read the opening lines.

Dear Miss Fitzgerald,

My name is Richard Lewis, and while walking my dog, I found your bottle on the beach here on St. Simons Island, Georgia. The bottle turned out to contain your letter...

What a lovely young man he was. How kind it had been of him to reply, just to make her feel better.

The same sort of kindness that led him to drive that wonderfully brave Cockney girl, Pippa Wills, all the way to Oxford.

CHAPTER 20

LONDON, ENGLAND

21ST JUNE, 1941

There were four letters on the entry table as he let himself in, all for him. Quite a haul. He made himself a cup of tea and a sandwich, then brought the letters and his dinner on a tray up to his bedroom. He kicked off his shoes, sat down on the bed with his feet up, leant against the pillows and shuffled through the envelopes as he ate his sandwich.

The first letter was from his father, and the second letter was also from America; it looked like Mrs McHale's handwriting. The third was from Grace, the lilac ink unmistakeable. It was now June, and since February they had gone back to writing each other cheerful, newsy letters; this one felt long. The fourth letter was posted in England and had loopy writing that looked childlike.

He opened his father's letter first as he sipped his tea.

Nathan and Rebecca were expecting another baby, and his mother needed a small operation on her knee. They had been to dinner at the yacht club with Algy Smythe's parents, and Arthur had made a lucrative business trip to Raleigh. It was strange, reading about his parents' lives in America. While it was nice to hear from his father, Savannah might as well be the moon for all the relevance it had for Richard now.

He put his empty mug and plate on the desk beside the bed and opened the one from Mrs McHale.

Dear Mr Lewis,

I thought you might be interested to know I tracked down the man who complained to the bishop in New York about having to pay three thousand dollars to adopt an Irish baby, and he told me something you might consider useful.

Richard sat up straight with excitement as he read on.

The gentleman didn't want to talk to me at first. He'd never heard back from the bishop, and naturally he and his wife didn't want his daughter to find out she's adopted, but when I promised it would go no further, he agreed to meet me in a coffee shop in Manhattan.

Well, I don't drink coffee and they don't do proper tea in these places – it's desperate – but at least we had a nice slice of lemon cake. I asked the waitress for the recipe, but she didn't know. Apparently it's made somewhere else altogether...

He skipped down the letter, looking for the main point.

...I asked him did he remember the woman who brought the baby, and he did and said she was called Kit Gallagher, and there had been an Irish priest with her. Was it Father Noel Dempsey, says I, and he said he didn't know the name, he wasn't introduced to him, but he had an Irish accent, not American, and you said Father Dempsey was born here, didn't you? So it couldn't have been him. He described a tall, scrawny-looking man, sparse white hair, with long eyebrows and a very whispery voice, and he said he would never forget the gleam in his eyes as he counted out the money in hundred-dollar bills.

Now I don't know if this is enough to get Father Dempsey off the hook, Mr Lewis, but I still thought you might be interested on behalf of your Irish friend.

She finished off by telling him she still wore her sheepskin slippers every day and how good they were for the arthritis in her toes.

Richard kissed her letter before he dropped it beside him on the bed. What an amazing woman. He couldn't wait to write to Grace about this.

It was Grace's letter that he picked up to open next, but then he put it down again. Not that he was afraid to open it. He was over the pain of her engagement now. Every so often she appeared in his dreams, tormenting him by walking hand in hand with Declan McKenna, and it would put him in a foul mood for the whole day. But then he would go back to being glad he hadn't lost her as a friend.

Still, he left hers aside while he opened the letter with English postage and the childlike handwriting and extracted a single sheet covered on both sides.

The address was Wilmington Farm, Oxfordshire, and it was from Pippa.

Dear Richard,

I hope you don't mind me writing to you like this, but I'm losing my marbles here with boredom and loneliness. All the other girls have their family and friends visiting and get letters from their blokes, and I get so jealous because I have nobody, so I've decided to write to you in the hope you will write back. Just if you do, the farmer's wife is right nosy – the girls all suspect her of reading their letters. And Hayseed (her name is Mrs Hayworth but we call her Hayseed), if you are reading this, you should be ashamed of yourself. People are entitled to a bit of privacy, you know!

Richard felt the corner of his mouth twitch. Pippa was such a Cockney, and he could hear the letter being read in her voice. Not 'hope' but ''ope', and not 'Hayseed' but ''Ayseed'.

Anyway, Richard, I swear I'm gonna go barmy if I have to stay here with nobody to visit me or get a letter from.

So I'll fill you in on what I do here all day, because that's all I've got. It's not going to set your world on fire, but here it is.

We wake at dawn to feed the pigs a load of disgusting swill.

Then we have breakfast, which is fried potatoes and tinned tomatoes.

You'd think there'd be a bit of bacon given it's a pig farm, but no. Maybe it would be a bit insensitive haha!

Morning is planting potatoes under the suspicious gaze of the elderly Farmer Hayseed, who thinks we are useless and flighty, but he's stuck with us because his five big strapping sons have gone off to war. No telegrams yet, and I hope they all come back in one piece, though God knows why they would want to, to this hellhole.

At midday we have lunch. Bread and marg and a bowl of soup, and on Fridays we have tinned pears with this white stuff they call cream but it ain't like no cream I've ever had. It's all right, though, and anyway, there's a war on.

Afternoon we scrape the pig muck out of the pig sheds and mix it up with the human muck from the toilets, which are just holes in the ground, to spread on the potato fields. It smells disgusting, and some of the girls get sick as parrots, throwing up and everything, but I've got used to it.

After dinner – you guessed it, all cabbage and no pork – we do some sewing or something, we knit socks and sweaters for the boys in the forces, and then we go to bed.

Bed is the only good part. It's nice to be away from the blooming bombs, I can tell you. I sleep like a baby here.

Please write back and tell me about your life, or don't if you don't want to. But I am really lonely and could use a mate.

Yours, Pippa XOXO

She'd sent him kisses and hugs. How sweet. The image of the girl he pulled from her burning house formed in his mind. Her strawberry-blond hair cut neatly to her jaw, her hazel eyes, her creamy skin…and wearing that ridiculously huge dress and the child's plimsolls.

Feeling in a very good mood now, he picked up Grace's letter.

Dear Richard,

Myself and Declan have just taken our exams, and they seemed to go well enough. If we get the right results, we will be fully qualified teachers by the autumn term, and much harder for the canon to dislodge if he takes a notion in that regard.

He's been giving us some funny looks recently. He knows we're engaged, but we haven't yet been to him about the wedding. Normally a couple would go to the priest to have the banns read and then set a date, but we've not gone near him.

Richard's good mood faded; he wished she wouldn't talk to him about Declan and her marriage. But that was stupid. He and Grace were friends. They'd always talked openly to each other from the beginning; he couldn't expect her not to write to him about something so important to her.

Meanwhile the wedding preparations continue behind the scenes, and everyone has kept our secret. Most people of this place know the truth – that to have the canon marry us would leave a bitter taste on what should be the happiest day. So Peggy Donnelly, who is making my dress, comes in and out of the house through the field behind, and Nancy O'Flaherty and Eileen O'Flynn are growing the flowers in Eileen's sister's garden in Cork, while Eileen's garden here is unnaturally bare. Biddy O'Donoghue is stockpiling sugar, and Bríd Butler is making batches of toffee on the quiet – you can tell by the smell if you pass there at night.

Tilly has agreed to be my bridesmaid, though she wanted to wear trousers, and it took Eloise, who came back for Easter, to convince her to wear a dress. Then Tilly asked if she could invite Eloise, that Eloise could take the wedding photos, and of course I had to say yes, though God knows this wedding is going to be much too fancy and big as it is – half of Knocknashee has invited themselves. Where on earth the canon is going to think everyone has gone for the day, I don't know.

Which brings me to my other big wedding news. It's not just me and Declan who will be getting married on the day, it will be...

Charlie and Dymphna!

As I think I told you in my letter in May, they are engaged now, and so I thought with all this fuss and people travelling, why not make it a double wedding? They don't want to be married by the canon any more than we do, so I wrote to Father Iggy asking what he thought, and he said he'd be delighted, so he'll do the two weddings on the one day!

Dymphna was worried she'd be getting in the way of my big day, but I said I didn't mind that if she didn't mind me getting in the way of hers, and then she worried Declan might not like the idea, but of course he was delighted. It means when we come home, Dymphna and the children will be able to move straight in with Charlie, and Declan and I will have the house to ourselves. Which makes everything so much easier and nicer.

I'm praying we can keep all this from the canon until it's done. I think he has his suspicions, though. He has an unnatural ability to sniff out other people's secrets, and he preached a sermon last Sunday that was a bit close to the bone.

'There are some among us who think they are too good for Knocknashee,' he said in his whispery voice. 'Who have deemed themselves to be above the rest of you, who clearly by their actions are saying we are better than you. But let me warn them now, pride goeth before a fall, and a fall from the grace of God is inevitable for those filled with foolish pride. This sacred church here in this town has served the people of this parish faithfully, and to reject it is to reject this place and indeed its clergy.'

Half the town didn't know what he was on about, and the other half stared innocently back at him, knowing well what he was on about but not caring one bit. It's a long time since Canon Rafferty could frighten us with hellfire. We all know about his having his hand in the collection plate, and then how he got rid of Father Iggy over blessing Tommy O'Connell's grave. People still have to be polite to him because he has the Church behind him and it would be dangerous not to, but mostly they just do their own thing and keep out of his way.

Now before I finish this letter, I want you to know that I won't be at all offended if you can't make it, but it would be very strange of me not to invite such a dear friend to my wedding, so I've enclosed an invitation. Sarah and Jacob are welcome to come as well. But I know you've all got far more important things to do, so as I say, please don't feel you have to come – I'll be happy with a letter!

His good mood entirely evaporated now, Richard tipped up the envelope. A modest square of thin card came sliding out, handwritten, nothing like the very fancy card emblazoned in gold printed lettering that he had received inviting him to Miranda's wedding.

Grace Fitzgerald and Declan McKenna would like to invite Richard

Lewis to their wedding on 15 August 1941 at 11 a.m. in Our Lady's Chapel in Dr Kathleen Lynn Hospital, Cork. Reception afterwards at the Imperial Hotel.

All in her neat handwriting – and written in lilac ink, which somehow he'd always imagined was a special ink she used just for him.

With a groan he flung himself back on the bed. Was she really so unaware of his affection? Clearly she was. They were not finely tuned to each other, and he'd thought they were. His irritation and misery were tempered with a profound sense of feeling very stupid indeed.

There was a knock on his door, but he ignored it. The door opened anyway.

'Hey, little brother.' It was Sarah, her dark curls tucked neatly under a fashionable little velvet hat. She nudged his feet over and sat on the end of his bed, nodding at the letters strewn across it. 'I got one from Daddy too. We're to have another member of the family, it seems?'

'Yeah, I'm sure Nathan and Rebecca are pleased,' he said, trying to summon up some enthusiasm.

'And Algernon was made yacht club captain, which will delight him, I'm sure, and make everyone else consider jumping off their own yachts into the ocean rather than endure him.'

He rewarded her with a shrug.

She sighed. 'Richard, what's the matter? Bad news?'

He picked up the wedding invitation and handed it to her, closing his eyes as she read it.

She took a breath in through her teeth. 'I see. Are you planning to go?'

He shrugged. 'I don't know.'

'Well, I definitely wouldn't if you're going to mooch around being miserable like you are now.'

'I'm not.'

'You are. Take some advice from your big sister for once. Just send them a lovely wedding gift and stay away. Who's this one from?'

'Pippa. Remember her?' Her letter had put him in such a good mood, but now he just felt deflated.

'Of course I do, she's great.' Sarah read it from end to end, laughing a few times, then said, 'Why don't you borrow Cal South's car again and go and visit her?'

'What?' The idea hadn't occurred to him.

'She's a sweet girl, and she could use a friend right now, plus she's hilarious and really, really gorgeous.'

'But I don't –'

'Think she's attractive? OK, well, I'll let you in on a secret. You don't have to be into a girl before you can be bothered to help them. She is still a real person who could use a friend and she asked you, so what are you going to do about it?'

'I don't know…I guess you're right. I should. OK.'

'Good. And now I'll tell you a funny story to cheer you up.'

He groaned. 'Not a shaggy dog story, please. I got enough of those from the old mailman.'

She laughed. 'No, a real one. A huge container came to the Jewish refugee centre today from the States, full of packages, and Miss Alderton – you know her, with the white hair in a bun and the long fingernails?'

Richard nodded; he'd met her. She was a haughty spinster and spoke so quietly you had to strain to hear, but she did trojan work.

'Well, she was gazing at the labels on the parcels, and she beckoned me over and asked me, "Could you please translate, dear? We are baffled."' Sarah's upper-class British accent was impeccable; she was a brilliant mimic.

'Oh, you mean because they didn't understand the words?' It was a frequent source of amusement to them both how English on this side of the Atlantic and American English were so different.

'Not just that, American things altogether, really. There were union suits, which I had to take out and show her. She actually shuddered at the idea of an all-in-one head-to-foot undergarment. So she put that aside, then she said, "And what might a mackinaw be?"

'I explained it was a blanket, warm and felted, and sure enough she opened a huge box of plaid blankets, which delighted her a lot more than the union suits. On we went – gum boots are wellingtons apparently, and slickers are mackintoshes. I pointed out that a slicker made more sense, it slicked the rain off, but she gave me that pitying look, you know the one she has, as if we were naked savages gnawing on raw meat. "That's as may be, dear, but here in Great Britain, this will always be a mackintosh. Thank you for your assistance."'

Richard guffawed at her impression and could just picture the scene. People like Miss Alderton were kind, but they did look down on anyone they saw as 'Johnny Foreigner', and that included Americans. As far as Miss Alderton was concerned, if everyone behaved as the British did, then the world would not be in this mess, but it was now, and once again it was left to the English to sort it all out.

'Anyway, Richard, what I came to tell you was that Lord Beaverbrook is dining in the Savoy tonight and Jacob wants to swing by, and I'm going as well because it's a great excuse to buy us a decent meal without him grumbling about the injustice of it.'

Richard was intrigued. 'Is Beaverbrook going to speak?' Max Beaverbrook was the publisher of the largest circulation newspaper in the world, the *Daily Express*, and was held in high esteem by everyone in their world.

'Nothing official, he's just there for dinner. But Jacob says he'll have something to say if he thinks he has an audience. Once a newspaperman, always a newspaperman.'

As Minister of Aircraft Production and a friend of Churchill's, the Canadian was a firm favourite with the aristocracy and the working classes alike. He had an energizing way of speaking, plain talking that people liked, but with that never-say-die attitude that people had come to rely on so much from Churchill.

'Maybe I will join you then.' His bad mood hadn't entirely lifted, but Sarah had managed to take his mind off the wedding invitation.

'Good.' She pointed at him, schoolmistress like. 'And I bet Cal will be there, so remember to borrow his car. And by the way, I want to ask Father for some money to buy a car of our own. We could really use one. It looks like this war is going to drag on a lot longer than we thought it would.'

'I don't know…you could be right. It's a tough one for Britain, standing alone, but she'll hold out forever, I'm sure of it. If Hitler invades the Soviet Union as everyone thinks he will, that's their cosy relationship over and he's facing a two-front war, historically unwinnable.'

'Here's hoping.' Sarah crossed her fingers and left.

CHAPTER 21

WILMINGTON FARM, OXFORDSHIRE

JULY 1941

Richard pulled the Ford Junior into the yard of an ancient two-storey Elizabethan farmhouse in the Oxford countryside, with fields and pig sheds stretching in every direction around it. The stench hung on the air, and he wondered how Pippa dealt with it all the time. He rolled up the window, but it was too late. It had been almost six months since he'd dropped her here at the gate, wearing her land girl's uniform and with the old blue dress and plimsolls in her bag. She'd insisted on leaving Sarah's expensive clothes behind, because as she'd said to Richard, 'They'll get ruined in the country, and I won't have anywhere to wear them anyway, and the other girls will think I'm all la-di-da, and you've all been good enough to me already.'

She was such a brave, independent girl, and he knew now he should have visited her before and not left it until she'd had to swallow her pride enough to write to him. The thing was, Grace had occupied his mind too much, he'd taken a long time to get over the shock of her engagement, and it had made him a bad friend to the girl who'd looked after him in the hospital.

He was here now, though, and would have been here three weeks ago except for Hitler attacking the Soviet Union. He'd had to stay in London to report on all the resulting political upheaval, including the *Daily Worker* overnight becoming as fiercely pro-war now as it had been against it last month. Finally, bored stiff by parliamentary politics, he'd managed to persuade Kirky to let him take a month-long trip out of London to see how other cities had been hit by the Blitz. It wasn't just London that had been devastated, it was Birmingham, Manchester, Coventry, Portsmouth, Southampton, Brighton, Plymouth, Glasgow, Belfast… The list went on and on.

It was a lot easier to tour the country now that he had the car.

When he'd gone to see Cal South in the Savoy on the night of Beaverbrook's speech and asked to borrow his car again, Cal said he was going home to San Francisco and that Richard could hang on to the Ford Junior for good, if he 'just made a decent donation to that refugee charity Jacob Nunez and your sister work with, helping these poor wretches on the run from Hitler.'

Richard had been impressed and surprised. Cal was one of the newspapermen who lived the high life in London, champagne flowing in the Ritz and the Savoy, eating the finest food while the population struggled. He wasn't a bad man, he was just used to always having the best of everything, so it was good to see he had a soft side.

'Are you really sure, Cal?'

'Sure, I'm sure.' He'd dismissed it as if it was nothing, giving him a car, but to Cal it probably wasn't much. Changing the subject Cal said, 'Say, did you hear about the green ticket roundup?'

'Something, but just rumours.'

'Ran into a French guy called Georges yesterday…'

'Didier Georges?'

'You know him?' Cal raised his eyebrows in surprise.

'Met him a couple of times.'

'Well, OK. He's a bit of a thorn in the side of the Gestapo by all accounts, communist to his marrow, but he seemed honest enough. Wherever he's getting his intel, it's right, and he told me 3500 Jews were asked to register in Paris, foreigners mainly – well, what they call foreigners, families of people who came after the last war to replace the workforce in France because so many of their own men are dead. People from Eastern Europe mainly, I think. Anyway, they were sent green postcards and told to bring someone with them, presumably so people wouldn't worry. They thought it was just a simple registration, a status check or something like that.' He called a waiter for a second glass and poured champagne for Richard.

'No, I'm fine. I'm with my sister and her boyfriend.'

'Drink it. You'll need it for this story.'

'OK.' Richard dreaded hearing what Cal would say next.

'They told the Jews to stay and anyone non-Jewish who came with them to go home and gather food and clothing and money for a long trip. They were told they were being sent to work in Germany. But then the Jews that were left were taken away in four long trains.'

'Taken where?'

'Who knows? But I doubt it was to a garden party,' Cal said darkly.

'No, I don't suppose it was.' Richard immediately thought of Paul Dreyfus and his friends. Paul was dead, but he had hopes for his wife and the others they'd met during the various nights in the Dreyfuses' apartment, eating *boeuf bourguignon* and drinking red wine, outspoken, idealistic young Jewish communists who believed they could make the world better.

'Exactly. So take the car and donate.' He chucked the keys at Richard.

'Thanks, Cal.' He thought briefly of asking his fellow American if Didi had said anything about an Irishman named Alfie O'Hare but decided against it. Loose lips sink ships, as Didi had said, and even here you never knew who was listening.

Sarah was delighted by Cal's generosity and did as she'd originally planned; she telegrammed their father for money in the amount of a car, which he wired across the next day, and she then donated it to the Jewish Refugees Committee. And now she and Richard were the proud joint owners of Cal's comfortable red Ford Junior. Richard had given her a few driving lessons, and she was improving, not like when she was at home, grinding gears and dinging the car off mailboxes. This was a different Sarah, one who knew the value of a buck and was more cautious and more conscientious.

He parked near the farmhouse porch, purple with wisteria, and got out. He'd not written ahead to say he was visiting Pippa, so he hoped he would be allowed to see her without an appointment, though he didn't see why not.

The yellow-brick farmhouse had a date carved into the stone lintel: 1582, only ninety years after Columbus discovered America. The ancient brickwork had become gently lopsided with age. It was a constant source of amazement to Richard how old some buildings were in England. He pulled the thick rope that hung beside the double-width door and heard a faint ringing inside.

Nobody came to the door, but eventually a very thin girl appeared across the farmyard, carrying a basket of potatoes, freshly dug. She looked young, no more than sixteen or seventeen, and was wearing the farm-girl uniform of a green jersey, breeches, long boots and a cowboy-style hat covering her light-brown hair.

'Oh, hi,' he said with a smile. He'd come to realise his American accent was an asset with the opposite sex. 'I was hoping to visit with someone staying here?'

She dimpled and batted her eyelashes at him. 'Everyone's busy in the fields, digging up potatoes, sorry. You'll have to come back when we break for dinner. You one of the girls' boyfriends or something? The farmer's wife won't like that. She don't like us to 'ave boyfriends, distracts us from the work, she says. Family and girlfriends only.'

He thought of saying he was Pippa Wills's brother…but his accent was unavoidably not Cockney. He decided not to mention her at all. 'No, I'm an American journalist. I wonder if I could look around the farm?'

The girl still looked unsure but then made a decision. 'Wait here,

I'll check.' She went off around the side of the house, down a little path lined with neglected box hedging.

Richard thrust his hands in his pockets and waited, until eventually the door opened and a tough-looking woman in her fifties stood before him. She was dressed in a grey skirt past her knee, heavy boots, woollen stockings and a rather tattered jumper. She had her thin hair badly done in the very popular victory roll, though Richard suspected she was a little too old for the style. On her chin was a mole with several long dark hairs sprouting from it. She reminded him of a book he'd had as a child, *Cinderella*, and one of the ugly sisters looked just like this woman. She glared at him suspiciously.

He stuck out his hand. 'Mrs Haysee...' He stopped himself. Pippa had only called the farmer's wife Hayseed as a joke. If he opened with an insult, he could be ordered off the premises immediately. 'Mrs Hayworth.' He gave her his most charming smile.

'Yes?' She continued to glare at him.

He relaxed. 'My name is Richard Lewis. I write for the *Capital* newspaper in New York, and I was hoping to feature your farm in a piece about the land girls.'

She looked him up and down suspiciously, and he smiled widely back at her, doing his best to ooze charm. He normally just wore trousers and a shirt with a sleeveless pullover to blend in with the crowd, but today he was wearing his suit, a navy double-breasted one he'd brought from home. Double-breasted suits and pleated designs had been banned in Britain to save cloth, so it always drew people's attention. Though this woman looked more disapproving than impressed.

'How do I know you're telling the truth and you're not after one of my girls? I'm like a mother to them, you see. I have to take care of them. I don't allow no hanky-panky, can't have them getting up the duff...'

Richard winced. Mrs Hayseed was forthright, he'd give her that; maybe it was to do with working with pigs. He extracted his press pass with his photograph from his wallet and showed it to her.

'It's a beautiful farm, and my editor is very interested in the valuable work being done in the British countryside,' he said as she examined it.

'You want to write about my pigs?' She looked a bit more pleased.

'Well, the girls…and the pigs, of course.'

Her thin mouth tightened. 'What, that bunch of useless ninnies? I'd rather have my five sons back – you can write that in your article. Go on. The lazy things are idling around in the two-acre field.' She pointed a skinny finger in the direction of a muddy track that straggled away between briar hedges, then grinned for the first time as she glanced at his smart American city shoes and trousers, showing crooked yellow teeth. 'Pity you Yanks don't know how to dress right for a farm. Don't you have none over there?'

'One or two, ma'am,' he said, thinking of the vast farms of Georgia alone, not to mention the whole rest of the country, farms the size of whole counties in this country. 'But you're right, I've gotten too used to city living.'

By the time he'd made it to the end of the lane, the mud was splattered up his good trousers and had ruined his shoes and socks. In the two-acre field through the gate at the far end were ten girls, all working hard, harvesting potatoes and dumping them into big wicker baskets, all dressed like the teenager he'd seen earlier.

And there she was, Pippa, in the same uniform as the rest but unmistakeable with her strawberry-blond hair, though it was cut more raggedly now; her peaches-and-cream complexion had turned a golden shade of brown. She was waif thin when he'd dragged her from the burning house, and she looked even thinner now, swamped by her clothes.

One of the girls looked up, shading her eyes against the sun, and said something to the rest, then they all straightened and stared.

The next minute Pippa was racing across the furrowed field towards him. 'Richard, I don't believe it, you came!'

Her beam was like a searchlight, and he doubted anyone in his life had ever looked so happy to see him. She rushed into his arms and hugged him. He hugged her back, then held her at arm's length. 'Hi, Pippa, how are you doing?'

'All the better for seeing you, Mr American! Have you come to carry me away from this hellhole on your white horse?'

He laughed. She really was a bright spark. 'I've a car with me, not a horse, but yes, maybe we could go out somewhere.' He wasn't keen on stepping even deeper into the mud, and he'd left his notebook in the glove compartment. Anyway, he could get all he needed to write about this place from Pippa, and it would be easier if they were sitting down somewhere comfortable. 'Will they allow that, do you think?'

'Easier to ask for forgiveness than permission.' She glanced quickly up and down the field; the other girls were all staring, and she gestured at them to get back to work like they hadn't noticed anything. 'Right, quick, let's get out of here while Farmer Hayseed is taking a dump behind the cart. Ooph, the stink of it on the breeze, it's like something crawled up his bum and died. Come on.'

She clambered through a narrow gap in the briar hedge, beckoning him to follow her.

'Better take you this way. The old witch watches that front door like a hawk, or is it an owl? I can never remember that saying. Owl seems more likely with their big round eyes, but I think it might be hawks...'

'Hawks definitely,' he said as he followed her, pausing only to unhook his jacket from a long thorn before it tore.

On the far side of the hedge was a field of pens and pigsties, and huge saddle-backed sows glared at them malevolently as they made their way across the field towards the road; they reminded him of Mrs Hayseed.

'Right then, where's this car of yours?' she asked as they ploughed through more mud.

'In the yard out in front of the farm.'

'Right, you better go that way and get it – there's another gate over there. I'll slip out, and when you drive out of the farm, turn left. I'll be down the road there about fifty yards.' And she was gone like a rabbit across the field.

He did as she said and managed to collect the Ford Junior without being interrupted. He drove out of the farm, turned left as she told him to, and sure enough, there she was on the side of the road. He slowed down, then stopped, and she jumped into the passenger seat.

'You got your mate Cal's car again,' she said as she settled in.

'Sure do, except it's mine and Sarah's now. He was going home to San Francisco and gave it to us for free. We just needed to donate some money to a war charity,' he said as he put it in gear and drove off again.

'How about donating to me? I'm a blooming war charity.' She laughed.

He glanced at her as he navigated the narrow country road. 'Do you need money?'

She looked alarmed and embarrassed. 'Nah, don't be daft, that was a joke. I pay me own way, me. Ain't got nothing to spend it on in the Hayseed hellhole anyway.' She rolled down the window and leant her elbow on the door, enjoying the sun on her face and the breeze in her hair. 'Ooh, it's nice here. I like the countryside when there's no pigs.'

'You want to drive around for a while?'

'Whatever you want, Sir Gadabout.' She winked at him. 'Take me on a magical mystery tour.'

Later that day he was going to head to Coventry to see the destruction. But for now he was content to drive this pretty girl around the gently rolling Oxfordshire countryside. If it weren't for the barrage balloons and the trenches dug in the fields, one could be forgiven for thinking it was peacetime. They kept passing through little villages of thatched stone houses, people popping in and out of quaint little shops, kids and old men playing cricket on the green.

He spotted a small pub overlooking a tumbling brook, with a blackboard outside, 'soup, pies and puddings' written on it in chalk.

'Want to stop for some lunch? I'm starving,' he said as he pulled over next to a wall covered in climbing roses.

Pippa's big hazel eyes widened. 'Oh no, I'm not hungry. I'll just sit here in the car, if you don't mind – I'm ever so warm and comfortable. You go in.'

'Pippa, don't be ridiculous. You're as thin as a rake and you have to be hungry after working all morning. If this is about money, relax, it's my treat of course.'

'No, that's not right.' She looked even more panicked. 'Your friend bought the fish and chips the last time – it should be my twist now...'

'OK. Fine. I'm not leaving you in the car by yourself while I eat, so I'll have to starve.'

'That's blackmail...'

'And then I'm gonna drive around, weak with hunger, and it'll be all your fault when we get in a wreck.'

'Oh, cor blimey. All right, don't get your knickers in a twist,' she conceded with a roll of her eyes. 'But this is the last time you do this to me, I swear.'

'And don't make me feel bad by asking for water and a slice of bread with no butter on it.'

'All right, all right, lobster and champagne it is.' She went to open the car door and then stopped, turning back to him with a sweet smile. 'Last night I was awake – my bunk is by a gap in the boards of the barn – and I saw something like a silver penny dropping from the sky. Well, I thought at first it was bloody Gerry, but no, it was a shooting star, and I made a wish for someone to care, even a little bit. I think you're my wish come true today, Mr Lewis.'

'Happy to be of service, ma'am,' he said as he walked around and opened her door for her, offering her his hand to get out, which she accepted graciously. The next moment they realised their clothes and footwear were still caked with dried mud.

'Oh God, I look like a pig myself.' Pippa sighed as she rubbed at her breeches with her hands. 'Me boots are disgusting. I can't go in like this.'

'Hold on...' Richard had spotted an old hand-operated pump on the village green, with a metal cup on a chain. He pointed. 'You can wash your boots there. I'll see if I've got something we can use to brush ourselves down.' He poked around in the back of the car and found some copies of the *Boston Herald* and *Washington Post* that Cal South had left.

While Pippa washed her boots in the freezing water and scrubbed herself with the *Boston Herald*, he stood in the sun glancing through the *Washington Post*.

Hitler had said Russia was as good as beat, and that the Germans could take on anyone, including the Americans. Usual bluster from him, but it was true the Germans were making advances in Russia. Roosevelt promised American hardware to help Stalin, a man he didn't trust an inch, and hopefully that would turn things around. He had an uphill job now. Getting Americans to back a war with Britain as an ally was one thing, but becoming buddies with Joseph Stalin was a whole other ballgame.

The more Hitler baited the Americans, the better. Roosevelt was arming American merchant ships too and adding his own fighting talk, how nobody would tell the United States where they could and couldn't sail their ships. Much as the thought distressed everyone, it was time to escalate this war before Hitler got even stronger. If he managed to win in Russia and captured their resources, well, it didn't bear thinking about.

There was another article about how things were looking worse for the Jews. The forced wearing of a yellow star in occupied countries must be terrifying for them, Richard thought. And now the Germans had banned them from leaving as well, so it would be like shooting fish in a barrel.

With a shudder, he turned to the sports pages. The Yankees were shaping up well for the World Series in October, with Joe DiMaggio in top form. How he longed for the days when the sports results were the only thing to get worked up about.

Pippa, looking a lot cleaner, made room for him at the pump, and he used the newspaper to clean his shoes and trousers as best he could. *Scrubbing away the dirt with history's pages*, he thought. And a memory came to him as he balled the dirty pages up and dropped them into a nearby bin, of Kirky scoffing, 'Yesterday's paper, today's garbage.'

* * *

THEY HAD A WONDERFUL LUNCH. For all the pomp and ceremony in fancy hotels like the Savoy, the food was so much better in the countryside. They had creamy vegetable soup with farmhouse bread, and then Pippa persuaded him to try the bizarrely named 'toad in the hole'.

Richard had seen it on menus before and thought it sounded horrific, so he'd avoided it. He'd been duped into eating tripe and onions once in Stepney a few months ago, and the disgusting feathery texture of the cow's stomach nearly made him vomit, so he only ordered what he could recognise now.

He poked suspiciously at the sheet of batter with mysterious lumps buried in it and covered in thick brown gravy.

'It's nice, trust me.' She grinned at him, then tucked in with gusto, moaning in pleasure.

He decided to be brave and picked up his knife and fork. To his astonishment it was delicious. The golden batter was salty and buttery, the hidden ingredient was juicy pork sausages, and the gravy was rich. They both polished off their entire portions, washing them down with huge mugs of hot, milky tea.

The owner, a tall rotund man with a broken nose – the result of many altercations, Richard imagined – and an apron tied around his waist came to clear the plates.

'Didn't think much of that then, eh?' he said with a chuckle.

'You're lucky me plate's still got a pattern,' Pippa replied, sighing contentedly.

'Well, if you've room, I've some fresh spotted dick...' The man grinned and raised an inquiring eyebrow at her, and Richard frowned suspiciously, ready to defend Pippa's honour if this man was trying to embarrass her. It was a problem for farm girls, getting respect. He knew from others he'd spoken to that because they wore breeches like a boy, they often got treated coarsely when they were out and about.

Pippa didn't seem to mind, though. 'Ooh, lovely, that would be smashing... Can we?' Suddenly remembering Richard was paying, she turned to him pleadingly. 'I haven't had a spotted dick since the start of the war, what d'ya say?' Her face showed no sign of teasing.

'Ah sure, you go right ahead, have whatever you want,' he said uncertainly.

'One or two bowls?' asked the man. 'My missus is slicing it up right now.'

'Go on, Richard, I bet you ain't never had it neither, being a Yank.'

'Ah…no…I can't say that I ever did…' Maybe this was a prank, two English people mocking an American?

'Well, you're in for a treat then. Two bowls it is.' The man walked away whistling.

'Is this a joke?' he whispered, leaning forward, as the man disappeared into the kitchen.

'Is what a joke?' She looked confused.

'He's going to serve us sliced spotted dick?'

She nodded, beaming. 'Auntie Irene loved spotted dick. We used to have it all the time before the rationing and…' Remembering her loss, her eyes brimmed for a moment with tears, but then she brushed them away and said bravely, 'It's lovely, so it is, a steamed pudding with raisins and lemon, all covered in custard.'

As it turned out, despite the peculiar name, the dessert was delicious, as was all the food. He hadn't eaten so well since arriving in England. He paid the bill, and together, stuffed to the gills, they walked out arm in arm and full of goodwill into the warm sunshine.

The church clock struck two as they emerged, and Pippa got alarmed and said she really should get back to the farm. The girls would cover for her, she thought, maybe say she was ill, but she couldn't be away too long without getting found out and into trouble.

They made their way back through the winding green lanes – slowly, with a lot of wrong turns because of the infuriating lack of road signage or maps. Everything had been removed in case the Germans invaded, so the Boche wouldn't know where to go. They asked directions of a farmer herding sheep, and a woman on a bike, who had a child balanced on the luggage rack behind, and two boys fishing in a river, and finally they got there, pulling up on the road outside the field of pigs so Pippa could slip in again unnoticed.

'I'm ever so grateful you visited me, Richard. Where are you off to now?'

'Touring England for a month, if I can only find my way around, writing a series of articles about all the different cities that have been flattened by German bombs in the last year.'

'Your mate Jacob not going?'

'No, this was my idea. He and my sister are too busy with the refugee committee right now. There are more than enough stories in London for them to write. Sarah can do the copy while I'm gone, but I was just a bit fed up, so I asked to go on a research trip. I bought myself a Kodak Brownie – I'll take a few snaps.'

'A Kodak Brownie!' Her eyes lit up. 'My brother, Bill, he had one of those, and he showed me how to use it. I love taking pictures.'

'You should come along with me and fill in for Jacob,' he teased.

'But what would the pigs do without me?' She rolled her eyes.

'And looking after pigs is your dream job?'

'Well, I don't got much choice, do I? I ain't got no money, Richard, or family, or place to go, or friends.' In a split second, she had gone from humorous to serious, and he kicked himself for making a joke out of her situation.

'Well, that might all be true, except for one thing,' he said, wanting to make her feel better again. 'You do have a friend. You have me.'

'Yeah, but you're going away again and…' A fat tear rolled down her cheek.

'I'll be back, I promise.' His heart broke for this cheeky, funny girl.

'Will you, though?' And now the tears flowed in earnest as she crouched over in the passenger seat, the sobs convulsing her whole body. For a while he sat staring ahead of him, the engine running, his hands on the wheel. Until slowly he reached out and put his arm around her and held her.

There was a rap on the window.

It was the farmer's wife, in her grey skirt and boots and wispy victory roll, glaring in at them. 'Get out of there at once, you slut, sneaking off with a man! Your wages are docked for the week. And you' – she pointed at Richard – 'I know your sort. Journalist indeed. I know what you want, and it looks like you got it too. Don't know why I let you take me in, I must be going soft in the head. Off with you before I call the police!'

'I am a reporter, ma'am. My name is Richard Lewis, and I'm a friend of Pippa's, and I simply brought her out to lunch.'

She banged on Pippa's window again. 'Get out of the car, Miss Wills. There's no dinner for you tonight. You'll be out in the field spreading muck until sunset. And I'll be reporting you to the War Office, you see if I don't...'

He didn't exactly intend to do it, but Pippa was crying even harder and this place was the reason. He took his foot off the brake and pressed it to the accelerator, edging slowly past the woman as she banged on the window, her face contorted. 'Stop! Come back!'

'What are you doing, Richard? You have to let me out!' Pippa was tear-stained and frightened. 'If the Hayseeds chuck me out, I'll have nowhere to go...'

'Is there anything you own here, Pippa?'

'I...I... Well, my blue dress...'

'I mean, anything you actually want to bring with you?' He was driving a bit faster now, towards Oxford – he hoped.

'I... No... Where are we going? What are you doing?' she asked breathlessly as the apoplectic Mrs Hayseed dwindled into the distance.

'I'm carrying you away from this hellhole on my white horse,' he said, with a sideways glance at her to see how she'd take it.

'Oh my God.' She sounded both exhilarated and terrified as she pressed her hands to her cheeks. 'What do you mean?'

'Do you want to travel with me around England for a month? I'm on my way to Coventry now. Come with me.'

Fear flooded her face, and she put her hand on the handle of the door, like she was getting ready to jump and run even while he was driving. 'No thank you. Can you let me out please...'

He was startled and slowed the car. 'You really want to go back to the farm?' He pulled into a gateway and turned to her, resting his forearm on the wheel.

She shrank from him. 'No, I don't, but I don't want to be some man's cheap floozy neither.' Her voice had gone from gleeful to angry. 'That's why I always pay me own way, so no man can get ideas about me. I shouldn't have let you buy me lunch.'

He realised then how it looked from her point of view, driving her away from the farm without asking her, stopping the car in the middle of nowhere. 'Oh God, Pippa, I'm sorry. I didn't mean to frighten you. Of course you don't want to come with me. Look, let me find you a nice hotel in Oxford where you can stay, and I'll pick you up on my way back to London.'

'No. Thank you but that ain't fair. You know I can't stay in a hotel. I've nothing, no clothes, no money…'

'I'll pay for the hotel. I'll buy you clothes.'

'I don't want you to!' She shrank from him again.

'Listen, Pippa, I don't want anything from you.'

'I never met no man who didn't want nothing for his hard-earned money!'

'Please, listen to me.' He sighed and took a moment, then made up his mind. 'I don't tell many people this, or anyone really, but my money isn't hard earned. My family is, well, very wealthy, and while I earn money as a journalist, I have access to…' He found he was a little embarrassed. 'Look, my father is a millionaire, and I don't want for anything. So please believe me when I say I just want to help. I'm not wanting you to do anything. My family owns a bank in Savannah, Georgia. I can spend whatever I like on you or anyone else without it impinging on me in the least.'

'An actual millionaire?' Her eyes widened in amazement. 'Like he has a million pounds?'

'Dollars, and yes, several millions actually. So you see? I'm just trying to help.'

Slowly she relaxed a little. 'But why?' she asked shakily. 'I mean, it ain't like there's anything in it for you?'

'I'm grateful to you for looking after me. And I like you.'

'You already saved my life. You don't owe me nothing.'

He sighed and thought of a different way to put it. 'Well, the

Chinese have a saying, if you save someone's life, you kind of become responsible for that life. I feel responsible for you.'

'Well, you ain't –' She was getting belligerent again.

He cut across her, not wanting to start the fight again. 'Pippa, please, I want to help you. Is that so hard to believe?'

There was a long pause. 'I'm just not used to men being nice to me, I suppose.' Something about the lack of self-pity in her voice made his heart melt even more.

'Well, you better start getting used to it. Now...any idea how to get to Oxford?'

She managed a weak smile and shrugged. 'Not a clue, I'm afraid.'

It took a lot of stopping and asking, but they made it at last.

After booking her into a small, ivy-covered hotel in the town centre, they took a walk down the main street, gazing up at magnificent gold-stone colleges. Next to a pub called the White Horse was a clothing store, with ladies' garments in the window, and he pulled her in there by the hand. He still had his full sixty-six clothing ration points that had been allocated to him when he arrived because Sarah had insisted on shipping a trunkful of his clothes as well as her own, and besides, he could send back home for anything he needed.

'Ask for what you want,' he whispered to her, but she stood there tongue-tied, overwhelmed by the stylishness of the place; there were mahogany shelves right up to the high ceiling, and it smelled of wool and silk and leather. The lady behind the counter had a sharp face and eyebrows drawn on with a pencil in a perfect arch. She was dressed to perfection and exuded superiority.

Richard went up to talk to Madam Snooty himself. 'We're here to buy some dresses and shoes, a couple of coats...' He tried to remember all the items in Sarah's wardrobe. 'Some gloves, I suppose...'

The lady sniffed disparagingly and looked past him at Pippa, taking in the farm-girl breeches and her ringless wedding-ring finger. 'I don't know if this is the right shop. There's a –'

'Yeah, it might not be, darling,' Pippa said, in her broadest Cockney, recovering her usual courage in the face of the woman's snobbery and linking Richard's arm. She faced the shop owner then. 'I'm very particular, me, and me husband only ever buys me the best.'

The pencilled eyebrows shot up even further at the accent. 'Now, look here, young lady –'

'Honey, I think this place will do until we can make it to Harrods,' Richard said smoothly. 'And madam, I'm happy for my wife to use all my coupons.' He opened his wallet to show her not just the coupons but also a wad of notes. 'She's been doing her bit for England, but while I was away in the States, our house was bombed and everything was lost in the fire, so she needs a whole new wardrobe. Please spare no expense.'

At the sight of his wallet full of money, the woman's attitude changed completely, as he'd known it would – ring or no ring. Though he could see a ring would have made it easier on Pippa.

'Now then' – she came out from behind the counter with a tape measure – 'your wife will need evening dresses, day dresses, long jackets, a fur stole, shoes with heels – we have some lovely styles...'

'That sounds ideal, and whatever else my wife might need. Nightwear and that sort of thing, and, you know, um...stockings and, er... undergarments...' Richard was hazy on what this last might entail and thought it might be best if he made himself scarce. 'Honey, I'm just going to stretch my legs after that big lunch. You stay here with this nice lady, um, Mrs...?'

'Hitchins, sir, Mrs Hitchins.'

'I'm Richard Lewis. Now Mrs Hitchins, you are to give my wife everything she needs, a full wardrobe, even if she thinks she doesn't need it, and I'll be back in an hour to settle the bill. I'll leave the coupons with you.'

'Well, now, Mrs Lewis, you *are* a lucky girl,' purred Mrs Hitchins, pound signs in her eyes. 'No doubt about it.'

'That's me, all right. Lucky Lucy they call me,' said Pippa cheekily. 'Lucky Lucy Lewis.'

'Lucy Lewis, what a charming name...'

Richard had to get out of there before he burst out laughing.

Across the main street was a very expensive-looking antique shop, and he browsed the window and then went in and bought two things: a simple antique gold band, which he took out of its velvet box and put in his pocket – it was a considerable price, explained the dealer, because it was an eighteen-karat-gold Cartier ring, engraved with their stamp – and then a very expensive set of Victorian silver cake forks and a cake server nestled in a leather box on royal-blue velvet.

He also took Mrs McHale's letter out of his inside jacket pocket; he'd been keeping it to send to Grace when he recovered his good temper enough to reply to her last letter. It would make an ideal wedding present. *Just in case the canon gets cantankerous about your marrying in a different parish*, he wrote on the back of the American envelope. *This should put a stop to his gallop, as you might say.* And he gave it to the jeweller's obsequious assistant to wrap with the cake set, in lilac tissue and silver paper, with a silver string around it.

He had passed a post office on the way here, and before he left for Coventry, he would send it to Grace Fitzgerald and Declan McKenna, Knocknashee, Co Kerry, Ireland, with a message on a greeting card wishing them all the best on their upcoming nuptials, from their devoted friend Richard Lewis. He had considered going – he had been invited after all – but Sarah had pointed out that even thinking about it was a form of masochism he should reject immediately. She was right, he knew. This gift would have to be his only connection to their wedding.

Back over the road, in the boutique, Mrs Hitchins was just wrapping up a huge brown parcel of clothes for Pippa, who was already wearing one of her purchases, a silk georgette navy dress with white polka dots, matched with navy shoes and a little navy handbag.

She blushed and looked guilty as he gazed at her. 'I'm awful sorry if I went a bit mad, Richard. Mrs Hitchins made me get way too much – we can put it all back...'

'Nonsense, darling, you know I always encourage you to look your best. And I have something else for you as well.'

'You mustn't spend any more money on me!' she protested, glancing in fright at the package under his arm.

'Not this, honey, just a little something I found in my pocket. It must have slipped in there when I was holding your hand last night. So now you can stop apologising for losing it.'

'What is it?' she looked up at him, her face a mask of confusion.

He handed her the antique gold band. 'I found your ring.'

'Oh, Richard.' Her huge hazel eyes flooded with tears, part panic, part gratitude. 'Oh...'

'I found it when I was buying this,' he said, tapping the silver-wrapped parcel under his arm. 'A wedding present for Grace and Declan.'

'You two are off to a wedding?' asked Mrs Hitchins, no longer the snooty lady who had looked Pippa up and down so disapprovingly; she was eating out of his hand now.

'No, I'm afraid not, it's in the west of Ireland, too far to travel. But now I think of it...' He'd just remembered it wasn't only Grace and Declan's wedding, but Dymphna and Charlie's as well. He should send them something too. Not as fancy as the cake set, more practical. He glanced around the shop. 'There's another couple as well. They're both widowed, so it's their second marriage. Have you anything suitable as a gift?'

'A length of silk cloth?' suggested Mrs Hitchins instantly. 'The rationing in Ireland is as bad as it is here now – I'm sure the bride would be grateful. She won't be wearing white if she's been married before, so any shade would be suitable. Could you describe her colouring and size?'

He had met Dymphna very briefly in Knocknashee, when she brought over the pram her late husband had made for their children and given it to Tilly for Odile. He remembered a thin, careworn woman, her mousy hair already greying at the temples, but with soft, expressive eyes. 'Light-brown hair, dark-brown eyes, a similar build to yourself, Mrs Hitchins.'

She disappeared into the back and returned with a roll of mauve silk with gold thread shot through it. 'I think you'll find seven yards of this will make the perfect present,' she said, and smiled happily as he took out his wallet to pay for everything. 'And have a very pleasant stay in Oxford, Mr and Mrs Lewis.'

* * *

After going to the post office to mail the wedding presents, he took Pippa to the Randolph for tea, then drove her back to the ivy-covered hotel, where he told her he'd collect her in three or four weeks and settle the bill then.

'And I'll be here all that time by meself?' She looked crestfallen. 'What will I do?'

'I don't know…' He didn't want to repeat his offer to take her with him and make her scared of him again. 'Look around the colleges? I'm sure there are museums and churches and things. Go to tea shops?' He reached into his wallet and took out twenty pounds in five-pound notes, folded them and handed them to her. That's to keep you in food and drink and whatever until I get back.'

She stared at the folded notes but didn't take them. He stuck the money in the pocket of her jacket.

Doubt came back into her eyes. 'And there's no catch, you aren't going to make me do nothing for this money?'

'No, Pippa, I'm not.'

'It's just…'

'I know. But I'm not.' He got into the Ford Junior, which was parked by the kerb, while she stood on the pavement with the big parcel of clothes in her arms, looking bereft.

'Do you really have to leave me here, Richard?' she asked in a small voice. 'I'll be awful lonely.'

CHAPTER 22

KNOCKNASHEE, CO KERRY

15TH AUGUST, 1941

Grace stood on a chair in the Warringtons' little sitting room as Peggy Donnelly knelt beside her, her mouth full of pins, making a last-minute adjustment to the length before allowing anyone else in to see it.

In the kitchen, waiting for the big reveal with Hugh Warrington, were Tilly and Eloise, who was going to be taking Grace's photo, and Dymphna's as well. Grace had tried hard to stop being jealous of Eloise; the Swiss woman clearly made Tilly very happy and that's what mattered, though she still refused to leave Dublin for life on the farm.

Dymphna was upstairs with Lizzie, getting dressed in her own outfit, a skirt and jacket she'd made herself with Richard's thoughtful gift, seven yards of mauve silk with a hint of gold, neither too flashy nor too plain for a second wedding. Up until his package had arrived,

Dymphna had been going to wear a plain yellow dress she already owned, and she'd flatly refused when Grace tried to buy her something nicer from Peggy's. Charlie had been no help; when Grace appealed to him, he said he wouldn't care if Dymphna was wearing one of his old postbags with holes cut out for her arms and legs as long as she married him. Typical man. Thank goodness Richard had more sense and had saved the day.

His present to her and Declan was also beautiful but not so practical. A silver set of cake forks and a cake server, which she had left in its box because it made the rest of her kitchenware look very plain. The letter from Mrs McHale had been a much better present; it made her feel less anxious about what would happen when the canon found out they'd all got married by Father Iggy in Cork. She couldn't imagine using it against him, but if she had to, maybe... Either way it was good to have it. It gave her confidence.

He was bound to find out because half the town was here, including Nancy O'Flaherty and Eileen O'Flynn, who were busy putting the last touches to the flowers in the chapel.

'Right, let me see you now,' Peggy muttered through pursed lips as she got off her knees and stood with a groan at the ache in her back. 'What do you think?'

Grace stepped down off the stool and gazed at herself in the long mirror on the wall. The skirt was made of crêpe white silk, and the length was perfect. The trick was to have it lightly skim the floor, hiding her lightweight calliper and blue shoes, without it being so long she would stand on the hem and tear it.

Peggy had managed it to perfection, and the whole dress was beautiful.

It was actually a two-piece, but no one would know that; the bodice tucked into the skirt, and a belt covered over the join. The top had a square neck and capped sleeves, and Peggy had sewn in shoulder pads, giving it a stiff, almost military look, which Eloise told them was all the style in Dublin.

Lizzie had wanted to buy enough silk to make the whole dress, but there had been only three yards, so she'd bought some ivory brocade from an upholstery shop for the bodice. Peggy had done marvels with it, though it was heavy to work with, and she'd painstakingly sewed seed pearls all over it that caught the light; they'd begun life on a hat of Lizzie's, but the doctor's wife had snipped off every single tiny one and sent them down in the post to Knocknashee along with the rest of the material.

In silence, Grace gazed at herself in wonder. Eloise had done her hair earlier in a soft style, taming her natural curls and pinning them back from her face. She then gave her some mascara for her eyelashes and a bit of bronze powder for her eyelids, then the faintest hint of rouge for her cheeks. She'd added her coral lipstick, and she was done. And now in the dress, she couldn't take her eyes off her reflection – her slim waist, her neat bust, the way the fabric enhanced the creaminess of her skin. She hoped Declan would think she looked beautiful; the thought gave her a tingle of anticipation.

'Do you like it, Grace?' Peggy asked, standing behind her.

'Like it?' Grace echoed. 'I... Peggy, I've never in my life seen myself as pretty or anything. My mad hair that springs into curls no matter what I do, the limp, the twisted leg... But in this dress, I feel like a princess, honest to God, I do. When I was small, Daddy used to tell me stories about Oisín going to Tír na nÓg, and how it was the land of eternal youth. The fairy princess he followed there was called Niamh, and he always said she had red hair like me and green eyes and white skin, and how every man that ever saw her fell instantly in love with her. I believed that was the case for me until I went to school and realised that I was just ordinary looking, not like a princess at all, just a normal girl.'

'You're not ordinary looking at all, *a chroí*.' The plump little dressmaker winked at her in the mirror.

'Well, then I got the polio and my leg and all of that, and I knew then that no man was ever going to fall in love with me, let alone every single one.' She laughed at the memory of her father's story, but Peggy said nothing, just let her talk. 'But standing here now, in this dress, I feel like that princess Daddy told me I was.' She turned to admire herself from the side. 'If Lizzie hadn't found the material and the buttons and everything, I know it would never have come together, but you making this, without a pattern, and putting such care into it – I'll never forget it, Peggy.'

The dressmaker smiled. 'Well, you deserve the best, Grace, after all you've been through and all you've done for the children in Knocknashee, and I'm glad you like it.' She opened the door to call the others in from the kitchen. 'Now, here she is,' she announced, ushering in Tilly, Eloise and Hugh.

'Oh, Grace, you... Oh my... You look so very beautiful...' The fatherly doctor was almost in tears.

Eloise was getting her camera out of her bag, but Tilly stood dumbfounded, a very rare occurrence. She had Odile in her arms. The sixteen-month-old toddler was going to be a flower girl and walk hand in hand with 'Aintín Tilly' up the aisle, carrying Nellie the rag doll, though Teresa O'Flaherty was going to be on standby as backup if Odile got too lively. She'd been walking for two months now and there was no stopping her.

'You look like a film star,' said Grace's best friend eventually. 'Truly, that dress, your figure, your hair, your eyes, everything. I always knew you were pretty, but...' She turned to hug Peggy. 'You are wasted in Knocknashee, Mrs Donnelly. You could have your own business up in Cork or Dublin. They'd be queueing out the door looking at the latest' – she put on a French accent – 'Kerry couture.' She laughed. 'Don't you think, Eloise?'

'I do. Mrs Donnelly's fashions would be a great success,' agreed the Swiss woman as she made Grace pose for pictures, first by herself, then with a beaming Peggy, then with Tilly, in a dress for once, an elegant yellow silk outfit that Eloise had lent to her and which showed off her muscular curves because it was a bit tight. She'd paired it with the black velvet jacket she'd bought in Dublin but had been persuaded to leave off the wine-coloured fedora for once.

Then Eloise took Grace's picture with Hugh, who was looking very smart in his 'father of the bride' morning suit, borrowed from a colleague at work. Dr Davies was an ear, nose and throat consultant who drove a Bentley, because unlike Hugh Warrington, he didn't plough most of his salary back into the hospital.

'We should bring down the other bride,' said Grace, awkward at being the centre of all attention. She stuck her head out the door of the sitting room and called up the stairs, 'Are you ready for a showing of your outfit too, Dymphna?'

'Just finished now,' Lizzie called back down the stairs, and a minute later, Dymphna descended slowly, a pleased flush on her cheeks. She looked stunning.

Eloise had pinned her hair in a way that hid the grey at her temples and had given her a full face of make-up, with powder and lipstick and mascara, when she'd never worn make-up before in her life, and she was wearing a pair of Lizzie's shoes with a slight heel, which Lizzie had got dyed to match.

'Oh, Dymphna, you're beautiful,' Grace exclaimed, as everyone applauded. 'You look so elegant. Come over by the window, and Eloise will take your picture.'

Dymphna beamed shyly as she posed for the camera, by herself and then with Grace.

'I'm so happy for you, and don't let Charlie take you away from us up at the farm,' said Tilly as she sat watching from the sofa, cuddling Odile on her lap, half in affection and half to restrain her. 'We couldn't manage without you.'

'Oh, don't you worry, you won't get rid of me in a hurry.' Dymphna laughed happily. 'I love that little girl too much to stay away.'

'And you love me too, I hope.' Tilly grinned.

'I do, and I'll never forget how you gave me a job when I needed it. And Grace, you put a roof over my and my children's heads, and I won't ever forget that either. You're the two best friends a woman could ever have.'

She held out her arms to them both. Tilly stood, still holding Odile, and the three women embraced for a long minute, until Odile grabbed Dymphna's nose and pulled, making her squeal, and had to be whisked away again by Tilly as they all laughed.

And then it was time. Hugh led the brides out to the Bentley, which Dr Davies had insisted on lending to him as well, and Eloise drove the rest of them in Hugh's own car, because – and why was Grace not amazed by this? – she was an excellent driver.

* * *

'Do you, Grace Margaret Fitzgerald, take this man, Edward Declan McKenna, to be your lawfully wedded husband? Do you promise to honour, love and obey him...' Father Iggy said 'obey' with a slight chuckle in his voice. He'd come to see them last night, and Grace had joked that if she had to vow to obey Declan, then he'd sure as anything better agree to obey her too, especially at work.

'For richer, for poorer, in sickness and in health, forsaking all others, as long as you both shall live?'

'I do.' Grace gazed into Declan's indigo eyes and felt the powerful warmth of his love.

'And do you, Edward Declan McKenna, take this woman, Grace Margaret Fitzgerald, to be your lawfully wedded wife? Do you promise to love and honour her, for richer, for poorer, in sickness and in health, forsaking all others as long as you both shall live?'

'I do. And I'll obey her as well,' Declan said, to a ripple of laughter from the packed gathering.

It was ridiculous how many people had managed to cram into the small hospital chapel, which was already made a lot smaller by the extravagant displays of hydrangeas and roses that Nancy O'Flaherty and Eileen O'Flynn had arranged on the altar and along the walls. Everyone had come down on the bus that morning, having booked their seats with Bobby the Bus in advance, jammed in like sardines.

There were lots of parents from her school, farmers and fishermen, all the shopkeepers, including Pádraig O Sé, and even Dymphna's mother had got on in Dingle; she looked like she was sucking a lemon but at least minded Paudie and Kate during the ceremony. Nurses from the hospital who remembered Grace from her time there kept looking in the door, trying to get a peek.

Then Dymphna and Charlie's ceremony followed straight afterwards, with Declan standing as his father's best man, returning the favour that Charlie had done for him. Grace could not have been happier, except for wishing her parents were still alive to see this day.

The Warringtons hosted the wedding breakfast in the Imperial Hotel in Cork, though Grace had begged them to move somewhere more low-key when she realised how many of her neighbours were set on coming and thinking of the bill, but they refused and insisted that the more, the merrier. They never spent much but the Warringtons were not poor, and eventually she gave up objecting, seeing how happy they were to do it for her.

It was a happy, noisy affair, the main joke of the day being how puzzled the canon would be when all the shops were closed. 'He'll worry it's a Sunday and he's forgotten to say Mass,' Biddy O'Donoghue giggled. She had left her husband, Tom, behind to give the storeroom a good clean while the shop was shut. Just as well. Dymphna still went bright red whenever she saw Biddy's husband, thanks to the way he'd tried to get her to 'pay the rent', and Grace wondered if his wife had some idea and that was the reason she'd not brought him along.

Grace and Declan, and Charlie and Dymphna, sat at the two ends of the long table, and the waitresses served the chattering company with tea, coffee, chicken and ham sandwiches and trifle and cake.

The older couple were beaming, delighted with each other and the day. They were going back to Knocknashee afterwards on the bus because of Paudie and Kate. Dymphna's mother had refused to have the youngsters overnight, and Dymphna didn't want her to anyway, so they'd have their honeymoon when Grace and Declan were back to mind the children.

Odile was loving every minute. The toddler had been so well behaved at the wedding, trotting up the aisle in her flower girl dress, which Mary O'Hare had made out of her own wedding dress, most of which had been eaten by moths, and cuddling Nellie, who was wearing a tiny version of the same.

Grace and Declan's honeymoon, which would begin as soon as the breakfast was over, was going to be a whole week in this sumptuous hotel.

'This is a delicious meal, but I wish everyone would go now,' Declan whispered in her ear, and Grace giggled and squeezed his hand under the table in agreement. She was having a wonderful day, and she loved everyone there, but at the same time...

Dymphna had always been so lovely if Declan called over in the evening during the summer. They had no more exams to study for now – both of them had passed with high marks – but the widow made sure they got some time alone; she would find something she needed to do upstairs after putting Kate and Paudie to bed, and then she would say she was exhausted and needed an early night.

Those nights they would sit on the sofa in the sitting room, Declan's arm around Grace as she leant against him. They made plans, imagined having a family, talked about the future. Then he would kiss her, and it surprised and delighted her how her body reacted to his, and his to hers, and sometimes he groaned with the frustration of it all, having to stop, and she felt the same way. She could hardly believe that this very night, in the honeymoon suite upstairs, she would be able to sleep in a huge double bed with him, his naked body beside hers, and nobody could stop them. The thought thrilled her.

At last all the speeches were made and the food eaten and tea drunk and everyone was ready to leave. Bobby the Bus helped to wind it all up – he was getting bored because there was no whiskey and was chivvying people to get their coats on.

Father Iggy and the Warringtons were the last to go, but they didn't linger a moment longer than necessary for a last hug, and after they'd been waved off, Grace and Declan turned to each other, smiling, before walking slowly up the stairs to the honeymoon suite, where Declan lifted her and carried her over the threshold. She felt tiny in his arms.

The suite was beautifully furnished and overlooked the wide street, brilliant in the summer sun, and the fine houses of Cork. Someone had sprinkled rose petals on the bed, and there was a bottle of wine on the table at the window.

'Oh, Grace, I can't believe it actually… Am I dreaming?' Declan asked her softly as he set her on her feet and stood facing her, his hands by his sides. Then he opened his arms, and without either saying another word, she walked into them, feeling them wrap around her.

Her face rested against his chest; she could hear his heart beating as he embraced her tightly. She allowed her own arms to go around his back, holding him close to her. On and on they stood there, in each other's arms, until eventually he stood back from her, placed his hands on her shoulders and gazed into her face.

'I've never in my whole life been as close to anyone as I am to you, Grace. You know everything there is to know about me, and I think I know everything there is to know about you, for now at least. And I… I love you, Grace McKenna.' He took her hand in his and led her towards the bed, and there he slowly and carefully undressed her, first taking off the brocade belt, then unhooking her bodice, and then…

Suddenly afraid of his reaction, she stopped him from unbuttoning her skirt. 'No, it's light still, let's wait until dark…'

He looked at her, an eyebrow raised quizzically. 'Why would we wait until dark?' he asked.

'My leg…' she said quietly, her voice low and ashamed. She'd never forgot the way Agnes said it turned her stomach to see it, so twisted and deformed.

Declan didn't reply but dropped to his knees and gently took her bad leg in his hands, removing the blue leather shoe and unbuckling her calliper. When he'd freed it from the steel, he kissed her twisted knee and gently traced his lips along the length of her shin to the top of her stocking. Then he looked up.

'I love your leg, Grace,' he said simply. 'The same way I love your hands, your hair, your eyes, your lips. I love you. All of you. Exactly as you are or ever will be. Forever.'

CHAPTER 23

PLYMOUTH, ENGLAND

20ᵀᴴ AUGUST, 1941

Richard sat on the sofa facing the bay window overlooking the grey, white-tipped waves as Pippa slept in the other single bed. The morning had dawned blustery, despite it being midsummer, and the gulls were wheeling and crying on the wind.

Not much of Plymouth had escaped the German bombing raids, which had gone on until three months ago. It was sad when you saw what was left of it, the fine Queen Anne houses in a ring around the edge of the town centre, reduced to a heap of rubble. So much was gone, so many people dead, injured, homeless, needing shelter.

He and Pippa had arrived here from Bristol yesterday morning, and it had been impossible to get two hotel rooms. For the first time in the month they'd been travelling, they'd had to bunk in together as Mr and Mrs Lewis, with Pippa wearing her ring.

Their trip around the country had proved fruitful, and he knew

Kirky would be pleased. Their first stop, Coventry, had been absolutely flattened by a raid last November, killing or wounding over a thousand people. King George VI had paid an impromptu visit the day after the bombing, and he'd walked around and said he felt what the people felt. The people of that city were still talking about the royal visit as they carried on clearing up the rubble when he and Pippa passed through in July; it was like it gave them strength, that they believed their king suffered alongside them.

As an American he failed to understand the British obsession with the royal family, but Pippa was a huge fan. She especially admired the young princesses, Elizabeth and Margaret, who had an allotment as part of the national 'Dig for Victory' campaign. The local councils gave people small patches of land on which to grow vegetables and they were proving very popular. She told him in awe how the fifteen-year-old Princess Elizabeth had broadcast a message on the radio programme *Children's Hour*, urging child evacuees to have courage, because she and her younger sister had also been sent away from home – from Buckingham Palace to Windsor Castle.

Richard tried to keep a straight face when Pippa earnestly compared the plight of the princesses moving from palace to castle to the plight of working-class children being pulled away from their parents in the East End to unknown homes in the countryside.

It was a mystery, but for her sake, he made an effort to explain it all to his readers. He wrote about how as commander of all branches of the armed forces, the king inspected the troops regularly, and how, when they had the opportunity to escape to the relative safety of any number of castles around the country, he and the queen had chosen to stay in London. He wrote about how the queen had been heard to remark she was glad Buckingham Palace had been bombed, because she 'could now look the East End in the face'.

To his amusement his articles about the royals went down very well with the readership of the *Capital*, and Kirky, that champion of the ordinary man, gave him carte blanche to write about them as much as he liked.

So he was grateful to Pippa for climbing into his car that day, saying with a martyred sigh that she might as well risk going with him as die of boredom in Oxford.

And she wasn't just good at explaining the English psyche. She proved very capable with the Kodak Brownie. She didn't have Jacob's artistic talent, but the powerful subject matter – destroyed streets and tough, cheerful people carrying on – didn't take much artistry to capture. They stopped at various local newspaper offices to use the darkrooms, and no one batted an eye at a girl knowing how to develop pictures. Now that all the men were off to war, women did plenty of things they never used to do.

They'd gone north first, stopping in Birmingham and then Manchester, then all the way up to Glasgow.

Two miles either side of the Clyde was probably the largest shipbuilding operation anywhere in the world. The hard-working and hard-drinking men of Glasgow suffered no fools, but Richard found them welcoming and decent men, determined to do their bit to beat Hitler despite the devastating bombing raids in March, where whole apartment blocks had come down on top of the people sheltering under them.

They may not get the glory, he'd written in a piece, *they may not be the subject of parliamentary speeches, but if, and I hope when, Britain wins this war, the debt of gratitude will not just be to the brave service personnel of the land, air and sea, but also the men who shovelled coal, who fed furnaces, who made steel, and, by their own sweat and strength, built the mighty British war machine.*

He and Pippa had made their way through the darkened rubble-strewn streets, carrying their flashlights; he'd learnt to call them torches. Everyone had one now, with extra batteries in their pockets, and used them to light their way. They came upon an impressive stone town hall, where several elderly members of the Home Guard were emerging into the night.

On a whim Richard had entered, Pippa dutifully following him with the camera, and he explained to the retired sea captain who he was and what he was doing and spent a pleasant half an hour talking to him and his septuagenarian sergeant, mainly about their lack of equipment.

These men had memories of the Somme, the Dardanelles and the Messines Ridge, and he wrote their words furiously while never losing eye contact. He felt a surge of affection for them. To have endured so much, only to face the same enemy again a short generation later, was so hard. Since Dunkirk, re-arming the army, navy and air force was the priority; the Home Guard was the last line of defence. It was made up of the old men who couldn't fight, men from protected professions who gave their time in the evenings and weekends and those deemed medically unfit to serve in the regular forces. They were also last in line to get weapons. These old war veterans were having to make do with what they had at home.

He mentioned the hit Noël Coward parody 'Could You Please Oblige Us with a Bren Gun?' And without missing a beat, the two men struck up and sang remarkably tunefully. It was a very funny song about how the members of the Home Guard were reduced to using whatever was to hand instead of actual weapons.

Pippa and the two men sang together with gusto.

'Could you please oblige us with a Bren gun? Or failing that, a hand grenade will do. We've got some ammunition, in a rather damp condition, and Major Huss has an arquebus that was used at Waterloo.

'With the vicar's stirrup pump, a pitchfork and a stave, it's rather hard to guard an aerodrome. So if you can't oblige us with a Bren gun, the Home Guard might as well go home.'

After the rousing rendition, sung word-perfect, they bade them farewell, leaving a few packets of cigarettes as they left. They proved to be a very welcome parting gift wherever he and Pippa went. That and the candy bars that Sarah asked their father to ship over. Lynette, his secretary, sent a box every week, and Richard had filled the trunk of the car with them before leaving London. They were a good way to sweeten any deal, as it were, and made Pippa very happy as well.

They stayed in small lodging houses and big hotels. There were no decent showers anywhere, the baths had a paint mark five inches up the side to show the mark beyond which you were not allowed to fill the tub, and there was never enough toilet paper.

It wasn't just in the hotels of course; the daily deprivations applied to everyone – one roll of toilet paper per family per week, only one gas ring to be used to cook a dinner.

The food in the cities was mostly dreadful and in short supply now. He and Pippa counted themselves lucky if they got one boiled egg between them for breakfast, and there was only margarine for the bread, no butter. The chicory-root coffee was beyond disgusting, though he'd learnt to swallow it without grimacing when there was no tea. At one stop, in a pub outside Chester, the publican's wife had given them a big dollop of home-made blackberry jam with their toast, and the memory of it had sustained him and Pippa all day.

He liked having her along. She was so funny, and there was a kind of tender fierceness to her that made him admire and want to protect her at the same time. He enjoyed listening to her stories about her life in the East End, before her brother and parents died, tales from a madcap childhood spent running free in a community where everyone shared everything and the children ate their dinner in whatever house they ended up. It was as different from his childhood as night from day. She asked him so many questions about their house, what they had, his school, his hobbies, and she'd actually hooted when he told her that their 'cottage' on St Simons had eleven bedrooms and a swimming pool.

The month was up now, but he planned to take a little longer, stop in Portsmouth and Southampton on the way home. He didn't want to get back to London too soon. Grace's wedding had been five days ago, and he dreaded finding another letter from her waiting for him. A letter in lilac ink, thanking him for his present, describing her perfect wedding day. Maybe her honeymoon as well. He needed to give it a week or two before he risked having to think about it.

He'd given himself a good talking to yesterday evening as he walked the seafront, watching the sun going down over the Plymouth harbour, giving Pippa some privacy while she got ready for bed.

Grace was a friend of his, nothing more, and she never could be more. She was another man's wife now, and a decent man at that. She'd made her choice. Declan McKenna was it, and Richard would have to just accept it and move on. He would meet someone – arguably anybody would be more suitable than a girl rooted in the west of Ireland – he would fall in love and marry, as Grace had done, and he and Grace would hopefully maintain their friendship through the years.

Back in the hotel room, Pippa had already been asleep. He'd gotten into his own bed and closed his eyes, and not long afterwards, he was dreaming of Grace and Declan McKenna, walking hand in hand…

He woke early. And now he was sitting here on a lumpy sofa in the bay window, in his dressing gown, as the yellow dawn came up over the grey sea.

He heard the bed creak and glanced across the room to see Pippa sit up, clutching the bedclothes to her. She was wearing the elegant blue silk pyjamas that Mrs Hitchins had insisted were perfect for her. She'd done her best to buy a cotton-sprigged nightie, she said, but the astonished Mrs Hitchins had declared it more suitable for a grandmother than the wife of a wealthy American.

'Is it very late? Have we missed breakfast?' she asked, yawning. She was wearing the antique gold ring, which she'd let slip a few days ago she thought was brass. He'd left her to believe that in case she accused him of trying to buy her again.

'No, breakfast is not for about an hour or so. You can go back to sleep.'

She yawned once more and got out of bed, took some clothes out of the wardrobe and padded across the hall to the bathroom. She shut the door, and he heard the bath run.

He remained sitting there, watching the sky and the sea brighten.

Twenty minutes later she plopped down on the sofa beside him, drawing her legs up under her. She smelled fresh and clean, of coal tar soap. She was wearing a pretty summer dress, yellow with a white collar and cuffs, and her golden hair was piled on her head. He continued to sit in silence, not sorry to have her company but too low in spirit to have anything to say.

After a while she said, 'Do you mind if I ask you something, Richard?'

'If it's do I think we will have bacon and eggs and buttered toast and tea with sugar and milk for breakfast, I doubt it,' he said, with a slight smile. 'But feel free to dream.'

'It was dreaming I was going to ask you about. Who's Grace?'

He shot her a startled look, his stomach clenching slightly at the sound of that name spoken aloud. 'What do you mean?'

'You were saying her name last night, like you were really upset. You woke me up, took me ages to get back to sleep.'

'I'm sorry.'

'I'm not complaining, I'm just saying. Who is she?'

He sighed. 'Just someone.'

'Look, that week in Guy's Hospital in London, you were the same, always saying her name, and in the post office in Oxford, you addressed that box to Grace Fitzgerald and Declan McKenna in Ireland. I wondered if it was 'er and what that meant. Was it her, Richard?'

Richard let his head loll to one side, observing her.

She gazed back at him with her large hazel eyes. 'Tell me. I've told you all my stories, tell me yours.'

It was true, she had told him all about her past, with an honesty that was uncommon in people of such short acquaintance. Their lives had collided at a particular juncture, and it had somehow united them. And he'd been open with her. He'd told her all about his background, his parents, his brother, Sarah, Jacob...

'Please, Richard. I know there's something else, something deep, and it's been eating you up this whole month. I wish you would tell me.'

She was right; he'd held back on the most important thing.

He took a deep breath, like he was diving into the cold dawn sea. 'She was someone I thought I loved, and I thought she had feelings for me, but she married someone else last week.' It felt good to say the words aloud, like he'd eased the pain in his chest a little.

She blinked and looked away, out the window, across the sea. 'And she lives in Ireland?'

'Yeah. It's complicated.'

'And is she why you don't have a girl of your own? A bloke like you could have anyone in London.'

'Like I said, it's complicated.'

'I wish you'd explain it to me how it came about.'

'It's a very long story,' he said reluctantly.

She looked back at him with a slow smile. 'I ain't going nowhere.'

There was something in the way she said it that shifted something inside him. He felt his heart melt slightly. Something about this girl, the funny, determined face, the way she was so buoyant – that was the word – nothing kept her down for long. She epitomised the British spirit, he thought. Like the personification of the whole country right here in one brave girl, standing with her chin up against the fates.

I ain't going nowhere.

'I guess in that case,' he said, 'neither am I.'

The End.

I REALLY HOPE that you enjoyed the latest story in the Knocknashee story. The next part of the story, *Sincerely, Grace* is in the works and will be with you in the summer of 2025. You can pre-order it HERE for delivery on launch day.

HERE IS a sneak preview of the first two chapters in case you can't wait!

SINCERELY, GRACE

. . .

Knocknashee, Co Kerry - November 1941

Chapter 1

The wind and rain off the ocean buffeted the house, causing the windows to rattle and the front door to creak. It was a feature of life on the Dingle Peninsula, and nobody ever truly won against the wind. Draught excluders and heavy curtains could only do so much. The storm had been raging since early afternoon, but the old fishermen said it would blow itself out before midnight, and they knew far more than the Dublin weatherman who used to be on the wireless.

That man was silent now. The government had put a stop to his forecast once the Emergency began two years ago, just in case the Germans were listening in to Irish radio. Not that it would have done Hitler any good if they were; the man's predictions were always wildly wrong. The only way to properly tell the weather on the Dingle Peninsula was to listen to what the old fishermen had to say as they sat mending their nets of an evening.

The weather was the reason two German spies had come ashore in Dingle last year with all sorts of meteorological equipment. They didn't get away with it. The local publican saw sand on the shoes of the first man, and something about his accent was off, so he got him drunk on whiskey until the guards turned up. The second German kept his transmitter buried on the beach and did get a few messages sent off, but he was picked up after two days. Strangers stood out in the rural west of Ireland; nobody could do anything without getting noticed straight away.

For instance, there wasn't a soul in Knocknashee who didn't know Charlie McKenna's new wife, Dymphna, was expecting, even though she had told nobody, only made the mistake of looking at baby clothes in Peggy Donnelly's drapery shop and mentioning she'd asked Mary O'Hare for a remedy for a sick stomach.

Grace was so happy for her friend, but she'd also felt a twinge of envy at first. Her new 'mother-in-law', as she laughingly called Dymphna these days, would be forty next year, while Grace was still only twenty-one, and they'd been married the same length of time, three months, Dymphna to Charlie and Grace to Charlie's son, Declan.

But her jealousy had subsided because, if her calculations were correct, she was ten days late, so it looked like having polio as a child hadn't ruined her chances of having a baby after all, despite that horrible comment from Canon Rafferty about her 'ill health' precluding her from her duty to God.

She hoped with all her heart that she was about to prove that horrible priest wrong. She was in such a hurry to fill this home with the happy voices of children. For a long time after her parents died and her sister, Agnes, ruled the roost, this house was cold and austere. But now it was back as she remembered it as a little girl, warm and cosy and welcoming to all.

Smiling at the thought, Grace put aside the letter she was writing and reached across from her armchair to turn the wireless up; there was a lovely programme of songs on, and she enjoyed having it playing in the background as the weather raged outside. The fire crackled merrily in the sitting room grate, and her young husband sat in the armchair on the opposite side of the hearth, reading a Dickens novel, his long legs stretched out towards the warmth. The light of the flames played across his fine-boned face, lending his high cheekbones a faint flush, and he looked so well and healthy.

His tall frame had filled out, and even without the help of the firelight, he was so much less pale than when he'd returned from the reformatory four years ago. Twelve years of his life he had spent in Letterfrack – his mother dead, his baby sister sent to be adopted – taken from his father as a six-year-old boy because the canon deemed Charlie McKenna, then a humble labourer, unfit to cope as a single father. At last, after everything the priests did to him in the reformatory, the cold and fear and endless beatings, Declan had come home. His father, now the village postman, had minded him until he was strong, physically and mentally, and then Declan had fallen in love with Grace, and she with him of course, and at long last, he was safe and happy.

Grace watched him as he read, slowly turning the pages of Great Expectations. She loved the serious face he made when concentrating, whether on a novel, or on one of his construction projects, or as a teacher gently explaining something to the senior children in her school, giving them the impression that there was all the time in the world.

He would make a wonderful father. She hadn't said anything to him about her missing period yet. She would leave it another two weeks maybe, to be safe…

Sensing her gaze, Declan glanced up with a smile of his own, using his finger to keep his place in the book. 'Am I in trouble?' His indigo-blue eyes twinkled at her as he raised his dark eyebrows under the mop of his dark-brown silky hair.

Grace smiled. 'No, why?'

'Because you were staring at me the way you do when one of the children is doing something they shouldn't.'

'No, you're on your best behaviour, Mr McKenna. Just keep it up and I'll give you a gold star.' Her heart swelled with love for him.

'I'd prefer a different reward.' He winked.

She chuckled. 'Well, we'll see…'

'Seriously, though, is there something on your mind?'

How well he knew her. 'Oh, nothing,' she said airily, and cast around for something interesting to say to stop herself blurting out about the possibility of her being pregnant. 'Tilly was here this morning while you were out with Paudie and Kate at the beach.'

Paudie and Kate were Dymphna's children from her tragic first marriage to Tommy O'Connell, and Declan and his father had taken them down to the strand to see the barnacle geese, newly arrived from Greenland for the winter. Though the real reason was to give Dymphna time to rest. Paudie and Kate weren't difficult children, but Kate was only seven, and nine-year-old Paudie could be exhausting. He was an exceptionally bright little boy, and when he got interested in a topic, he needed to know every single thing about it. At the moment it was migratory birds, and everyone in Knocknashee, from Bríd Butler in the sweetshop to Nancy O'Flaherty in the post office, had become much more knowledgeable about the flight patterns and laying habits of all of the different types on the peninsula.

Paudie was such a sweet little lad, nobody thought him a know-it-all; they just accepted his cleverness and loved him for it. Hilariously his best friend was Teddy Lonergan, who couldn't give two hoots about school and only wanted to be farming all day, every day. As was often the way of friendships, it couldn't be explained but worked perfectly.

'And the damp makes Tilly's mam's rheumatism so much worse,' Grace added. 'Poor Mary is really struggling now Dymphna has the morning sickness and can't go up to mind baby Odile while Tilly is out in the fields. And the farmhouse is up in a heap again – they've even lost that lovely photo of Alfie and Constance. Tilly's been searching everywhere, but the clutter has got really bad. Everything disappears, especially now Odile is nearly two and toddling around. Tilly's getting panicky about it all because Eloise is coming for Christmas and she wants to have the place nice.'

'Ah, Eloise is easy-going enough, and I'm sure she'll muck in and help clean,' said Declan lightly, going back to his book. 'And Odile loves her.'

'I know she does.' Grace sighed. Sometimes she wished she hadn't encouraged Eloise Meier to speak French to Tilly's Parisian niece; the two of them chatted away now in baby-French, and it made Grace feel left out even though she knew that was silly.

Grace had done her best to like Tilly's new friend, but it was tough. Tilly and Grace had been best friends since junior infants, so it hurt to feel she was now playing second fiddle to a Jean Harlow lookalike from the Swiss Alps, a language teacher who spoke fluent Irish as well as English, French, German and Italian, who was an amazing amateur photographer and brilliant at the piano and who could climb the local cliffs like a mountain goat.

Eloise had won over everyone in the village – even the bad-tempered cobbler Padraig O Sé, to whom she'd presented a pair of traditional Swiss dancing shoes with silver buckles because he was so fascinated by the stitching on hers. The only person who didn't think Eloise was marvellous was the canon, and that only made everyone like her even more. Grace wished the Swiss woman could have just one fault, but it seemed she couldn't put a foot wrong.

Of course Grace knew she shouldn't be a dog in the manger. She spent so much time with Declan now, and she didn't begrudge Tilly the companionship of Eloise. It was just…

She went back to her letter, resting the sheet of thick cream paper on the encyclopaedia of Irish seabirds she'd been reading earlier in an attempt to keep up with Paudie's endless questions. The letter was to Richard, who had written to her a week ago, sending news of the war from London. Everything about the Emergency was censored in the Irish press, so it had been fascinating to hear his eye-witness account.

The British have done so well, amazingly so, he had written, standing up to Hitler alone, but that little weasel with his stupid moustache and his horrible voice had better be shaking in his boots now. If he's not, I think he will be soon. He has poked the wrong bear, and if he thinks the valiant RAF were a lot to contend with, he won't know what hit him when the might of the US military bears down upon him. I really hope so anyway. Something has to happen soon to change things…

She was glad they were corresponding properly again, as friends. He'd written her such a cold, short letter after she'd told him about her engagement to Declan. And then for a wedding present, he'd sent that very expensive set of Victorian silver cake forks and a cake server nestled in a leather box on royal-blue velvet. As if she was someone snooty like his ex-girlfriend, Miranda, and not a girl from a simple village in the west of Ireland, with no use for fancy cake servers – if indeed there was any cake, which there hardly was these days thanks to the rationing. Dymphna, when she felt well enough to bake, was doing her best with lard instead of butter, but it wasn't the same.

Anyway, it must have been the stress of the Blitz that made Richard act so out of character, because now in the aftermath, he'd gone back to being his warm, chatty, good-natured self, thank God, though no less busy in his job as the Capital's London war correspondent. He and his friend, the photographer Jacob Nunez, worked around the clock, and their New York editor was so voracious for copy and pictures that Richard's sister, Sarah, also sent stories for the women's column. She was working with a female photographer called Pippa Wells, the girl Richard had pulled from a burning house and who now seemed to have moved in with the three Americans.

'She sounds like a nice girl. I hope that turns into something,' Declan had commented when she'd told him about Pippa. Her husband never asked to see her letters, but she always read them to him anyway; she felt it was important for Declan to know she kept no secrets. And besides, Richard's letters were very entertaining.

In this last one, for instance, he had given several examples of how England and America were 'two countries separated by a common language', as the Irish playwright George Bernard Shaw said. He'd written a whole column to prepare Americans for coming over. He'd explained how a drug store was a chemist's shop, a subway was the Tube, stout was black beer, a faucet was a tap, the trunk of a car was the boot and Friday week meant the Friday after next Friday. She'd already made a lesson out of it in school, and the children had had great fun speaking American and confusing their parents by referring to footpaths as sidewalks and bins as trash cans.

Most of the children spoke English, if a little haltingly and very reluctantly, and they didn't enjoy learning it, preferring their own native language, so anything to make it seem a bit more fun was a good thing. Associating the language with America instead of England was in its favour too. Memories were long here, and the English language, the accent, everything about it, caused a visceral reaction in a population brutalised by their nearest neighbour for so long.

Picking up her fountain pen, a gift from the Warringtons, Grace scanned what she'd written to Richard so far, using her usual lilac ink. She'd talked about the school, and how the canon had got bored trying to catch the children out on their catechism; they were too quick and clever for him, so he barely bothered coming into the class any more. There was a new housekeeper at the priest's house, a meek older lady called Mrs Coughlan, and the curate was gone.

Now she added that Tilly had still heard nothing from her brother, Alfie, and his fiancée, Constance; Grace called them 'A' and 'C' because they were fighting for the French resistance and no one knew who was reading these letters. Then she wrote a bit about the awful weather, though when she stopped to listen, she realised the wind had died down and the rain was only tapping lightly on the window now. The old fishermen were right – the storm was fading.

What else should she say? Something about Pippa perhaps. Richard had not said as much but, like Declan, Grace suspected it might 'turn into something'. And she hoped it would, of course. She sucked the end of the pen, then wrote, I'm delighted your editor is paying Sarah and your friend Pippa to write and take photos for the Capital. I wish it hadn't taken a war for people to realise what women can do given half a chance.

She sucked her pen again, thinking she should cross out the last sentence, because it seemed very callous, like she thought the war was a good thing…

A loud knock on the door interrupted her thoughts.

'Who can be calling at this time of night?' Declan said as he laid his book down and went out into the hall.

Grace heard muffled voices, and then Declan reappeared with his father, Charlie, damp and windswept, looking stern. Immediately she feared for the baby. Charlie was so excited to be a father again. It would be a terrible tragedy if Dymphna lost the child.

'What's wrong?' she asked anxiously, looking from one to the other of them.

'A lifeboat is after being pulled ashore,' Declan told her. 'English merchant seamen, two dead, three alive just about. Their ship was hit by a U-boat about half a mile out.'

'Oh God...' Though she was relieved it wasn't bad news about the baby, her heart sank. There had been several attacks on cargo ships in Irish waters since the war started. Technically the U-boats were not meant to violate Irish neutrality, and that included territorial waters, but Hitler cared nothing for those kinds of laws.

'Dr Ryan has taken the three survivors to hospital in his car,' added Charlie, unbuttoning the collar of his coat in the warmth of the sitting room. 'They said there's five bodies in the water, all dead they think, but two other lifeboats too. Those men are still alive, but their own boat was drifting without oars and they lost visual contact a few hours ago as the sun set.'

'Oh God, that's awful.' She knew now what was coming next, and her stomach tightened.

'So we're getting a crew of local men together to take out their naomhógs.' Naomhóg, or 'little saint', was the Kerry name for a currach, the traditional west-of-Ireland fishing boat, ideal for the shallow coves and choppy waters. 'The more eyes we can have out there, the better the chance of finding them. The chances are slim, but you never know.'

'Will you come out with me, Da?' Declan was dragging his oilskin jacket on over his shirt and sweater, ready to go.

Charlie didn't have his own currach, but Declan had one he had built himself with the help of Seán O'Connor. The local undertaker had made the sturdy frame, his coffin-making skills coming in handy, and Declan had covered the hull in cow hides, then slathered them inside and out with tar. And he'd fitted an outboard motor, something few fishermen had ever seen. He'd got it from a shipyard in Cork, and it had worked for a bit but then gave up. Declan stripped it down and repaired it and then decided he could build a better one himself, which of course he did. His was the only currach with a motor; all the others were still propelled by oars.

'No, you've only room for Seán and John O'Shea. John can't row since he hurt his shoulder, but he knows the coves better than anyone. I'll go in with Oliver Daly's grandsons – there's two of them in it so they have room for one more.' Charlie buttoned up his collar again and headed off down the hall to the front door. 'I'm just going to let Dymphna know we're both going.'

'I'll join you outside in a minute, Da.'

'Right, I'll make some sandwiches and a flask of tea, and I'll bring it to the pier.' Now that she was alone with Declan, Grace hitched up her skirt and put her calliper back on; she'd removed it earlier to be more comfortable. She loved that she didn't have to be shy about her crippled leg in front of her husband; he seemed to genuinely worship every part of her. Only that evening he had helped her with her exercises after she'd had her hot bath. She blushed now to think what that had nearly turned into...

Declan gently helped her with the straps and fitting the steel into her shoe. 'I can wait and take the sandwiches with me, save you going out in the rain.'

'Not at all, I'm grand. The rain is easing off now. You go down and get organised. I'll see you below.' She hugged him and sent him on his way. Alone in the kitchen, she cut bread and some leftover bacon from their dinner and made up some sandwiches. She wrapped them, along with some currant bread, in waxed paper, made a big flask of tea to go with it and put it all in a wicker basket.

In the hall she dragged on her mackintosh and tied it tightly at her waist, then pulled her hat right down over her curly copper hair, nearly covering her round green eyes and turned-up nose. She couldn't wear wellington boots because of her calliper, so she'd just have to stuff her blue leather shoes with newspaper when she got back and set them by the fire, where hopefully they'd dry out by morning.

Within five minutes she was making her way with the basket to the harbour where the fishermen pulled their naomhógs up onto the shore. The wind was still quite strong and she was tiny, less than five foot tall and as light as a feather – that's what Declan said every time he lifted her up into his arms – and a sudden gust hurried her along the street and around the corner down to the sea, where the waves were splashing high against the narrow slip.

At the pier everyone was pitching in, hauling rope and loading first-aid boxes and flasks of hot tea and baskets of sandwiches the women had prepared into the boats; every available vessel in the town was employed. An emergency at sea was something the town was used to, and everyone seemed determined to help, glad now the wind was dying down, though the waves were still high.

Declan and Charlie stood on the pier, discussing with Oliver Daly – who at eighty-four was far too old to join the search but still the best head for the currents out there – which boat should go in which direction. Grace knew that Declan would be intending to go the furthest. His own naomhóg was rocking by the slip, tied to a bollard; John O'Shea, who was Janie's uncle as well as Mikey's father, was already aboard and eager to go, and Seán O'Connor was climbing in.

'Declan,' Grace called. He looked around, said something to his father and Oliver, then came towards her. 'Be careful, won't you?' she begged him softly as she handed him his sandwiches. 'I'm worried. When Mammy and Daddy...' She remembered with a shudder the day her parents were lost. The local men searched so long for them. And that had been in daylight, in perfect weather. It had been just one of those terrible unexpected squalls that sometimes struck the coast off the west of Ireland.

He wrapped his arms around her, not caring that it wasn't done in rural Ireland to show public affection to your wife, and cradled her head to his chest, her face against the wet oilskin. 'I'll be fine. Sure we all know this coast like the back of our hands. We probably haven't much hope of finding them, but we'll try anyway.' He pulled back slightly so he could look into her face. 'Please God we'll find the other poor men, but either way, I'll see you in a few hours.'

'I'll be awake and waiting for you.' She smiled and reached up to kiss him. 'I love you.'

'And that fact, Mrs Grace McKenna, is a source of constant astonishment and delight to me.' He winked at her in that way that made her heart melt. 'I love you too. You mean more to me than anything.'

She felt a sudden urge to tell him about being ten days late. That there might be another person now for him to love more than anything. But just then Charlie came striding over. 'Gracie, will you go up to Dymphna and keep her company and make sure she doesn't worry too much, and reassure Paudie and Kate if they wake up, and don't let them wear my poor wife out with questions.'

'Of course I will, Charlie.' It always touched Grace how affectionate and gentle Charlie was towards Dymphna and her children. They'd all had a very hard time in their lives, so it was lovely to see them so happy together.

'Declan, we're ready, come on let you!' Seán O'Connor and John O'Shea were shouting for her husband, and Declan dropped a last quick kiss on Grace's head and ran.

All around, farmers and fishermen readied their oars. Dotted on the pier, holding lanterns, were the wives of the men going out, and as the men rowed away, there was nothing left for the women to do but stand along the shore and watch. As the boats disappeared into the dark, the splash of oars faded and only Declan's motor could be heard, chug-chugging softly until that too was gone. The rain was softer now and the breeze light as the women stood, watching and waiting.

Grace heard Nancy O'Flaherty begin the hymn, and soon all the voices of the women of Knocknashee joined in unison in the hymn of the ocean, begging the Virgin Mary to look over their men this night.

Hail, Queen of Heaven, the Ocean Star,
guide of the wanderer here below.
Thrown on life's surge, we claim thy care,
save us from peril and from woe.
Mother of Christ, Star of the Sea,
pray for the wanderer, pray for me.
O gentle chaste and spotless maid,
we sinners make our prayers through thee.
Remind thy Son, that He has paid
the price of our iniquity.
Virgin most pure, Star of the Sea,
pray for the sinner, pray for me.
And while to Him, who reigns above,
in Godhead one, in persons three,
the source of life, of grace, of love,

homage we pay on bended knee.
Do, thou, bright Queen, Star of the Sea,
pray for thy children, pray for me.

Grace felt a sudden longing for Father Iggy. If he was still in Knocknashee, he would have been down here with them at the pier, offering them comfort and friendship. He would have blessed the boats and the men. He'd have opened the church to let people light a candle or say a special prayer to beg for their safe return. But of Canon Rafferty, there was no sign. Not that anyone wanted him, but still. He wouldn't dream of coming out in the rain.

Chapter 2

The hours dragged on, each feeling as long as a day.

Grace and Dymphna drank tea – weak because of the rationing – as the fire burnt in the range. Conversations began but fell away on their lips. Mostly they just sat as the wind died to a whisper, though the persistent rain still pattered on the window.

An hour before dawn, Tilly O'Hare appeared, letting herself in the back door of the postman's kitchen. She had ridden her horse, Rua, a sorrel gelding with a silky mane and tail, down from the farm on the hill, leaving her mother to mind Odile if the little girl woke up.

'I knew you'd be here when I didn't find you home,' she said to Grace, hugging her and then Dymphna, who was pale with morning sickness, not made better by being awake all night worrying. 'Tomás Kinneally from the farm next door came to tell me about the men going out. Do you want me to go down to the pier and see what's going on?'

'No, let you stay here with Dymphna and I'll go. The sun will be coming up soon, and the tide has turned, so it should be bringing the men home.' Grace tried to sound cheerful and confident, for Dymphna's sake as much as her own. And why wouldn't she be confident? All the fishermen knew this coast well. It was only because of what happened to her parents that she felt so nervous, and there was no logic in that. Dymphna's first husband had also died in the sea, but that was his own decision; unlike Declan, he had never recovered from his brutal treatment in the orphanage.

Dymphna was on her feet, shaky but determined. 'I'll come with you.'

'But I promised Charlie to mind you?'

'I'll tell him you couldn't stop me! I am your mother-in-law after all.' She grinned as Grace and Tilly laughed. 'And it will feel good to have something to do, not just be sitting here staring at the wall. Let's make a few more sandwiches and a flask of tea to bring down – they'll be starving and freezing when they get home.'

'Oh, but the children…' Grace glanced towards the stairs of the little one-up, one-down postman's cottage. Declan had built a sleeping loft above Charlie's bedroom for himself when he came home from the reformatory, but now that he and Grace were married and lived in her parents' house beside the school, it was perfect for Paudie and Kate.

'Tilly, will you stay behind to feed the children when they get up?' asked Dymphna. 'There's porridge in the press. Tell them I'm going down to meet Da.'

Charlie had never tried to take the place of the children's father, but Paudie and Kate had asked if they could call Charlie 'Da', the same as their new baby brother or sister was going to do. And they already looked on Declan as their big brother, Grace knew, because she'd heard Kate boasting to her friends in the junior class about being related to Mr McKenna who taught the seniors.

Tilly was pleased to be useful. 'I will, of course, and I have some of Daisy's nice creamy milk to go with it – it's outside the back door keeping cool.' Daisy was Tilly's Jersey cow, who ate thick, rich grass on a corner of the land that Tilly had reclaimed from the stony bog.

'Thanks, Tilly. They can walk over to school themselves,' said Grace, beginning to butter bread.

'School?' Dymphna sounded surprised. 'Surely you won't open the school today? Declan will be too exhausted to teach?'

'But the canon will have something to say about me closing up without permission from the patron, so Janie will have to mind the juniors while I take the older class.'

Tilly frowned. 'You haven't slept a wink either, Grace.'

'That's true, but I don't suppose telling Canon Rafferty that will make any difference to...' Grace bit back a nasty word for the priest. She was reluctant to speak badly of a man of the cloth; it was a dangerous thing to do, especially when you were the headmistress of the village school. Nobody would be spying on her, at least she hoped not, but in Knocknashee neighbours wandered in and out of each other's houses all the time.

'The auld divil,' finished Tilly under her breath.

Dymphna crossed herself. She also hated the canon, who'd had Father Iggy banished to the poorest, roughest area in Cork for blessing poor Tommy's grave, but like Grace, she knew it was safer not to say it. 'I suppose you're right, Grace. We all have to keep on going despite the emergency. And now you've said it, I'll ask Nancy to get Fiachra to do Charlie's post round as well as his own. Charlie will probably grumble I'm making an old man of him, but he's not got his full strength back since he had the shingles last year, so he'll need his rest when the tide brings them home.'

Pale light crept over the horizon as the two women trudged slowly down to the harbour, each carrying a small basket of supplies and leaning a little on each other. Grace's leg was aching with tiredness, and Dymphna was frail with the morning sickness, even though she pretended not to be.

John O'Shea's wife, Catherine, was there already, standing on the edge of the pier, wrapped up in her threadbare shawl, looking out across the grey sea. Seán O'Connor's snobby wife, Margaret, was beside her, a thin, wiry woman with a slight dowager's hump, a headscarf tied under her chin and wearing a good woollen coat. As the wife of the village publican and undertaker, she would normally consider herself a cut above Catherine O'Shea, a poor farmer's wife with fourteen children and barely two pennies to rub together, but this morning she seemed to have made an exception.

'Hello, Mrs O'Shea, Mrs O'Connor.' Grace greeted them with a friendly smile. They were all in this together.

Catherine glanced at Grace unhappily but said nothing as Margaret whispered in her ear. Declan had warned Grace that Margaret O'Connor thought the outboard motor very dangerous and was always trying to persuade her husband against going out in the boat, even though he'd helped build it himself, because she was convinced it would go on fire or something. It looked like she was frightening Catherine with the same story.

The other wives were arriving in a steady trickle now, and a ripple of excitement flowed through the younger ones, who were holding their babies in their arms. 'They're coming, they're coming…' But it was only a pod of dolphins leaping and dancing far off in the early light.

Then another dark shape came over the horizon. At least ten boats had gone out, so the wait to have them all back could be a long one. As the boats drew near, Grace could make out lacy wings of water, a shower of silver drops in the rising sun, as the men rowed for shore on the incoming tide, their oars rising and dipping in the dawn.

Oliver Daly's boat was the first to the slip, rowed by Oliver's two strapping grandsons and Charlie, and Dymphna rushed with a cry of joy to embrace her husband as he climbed stiffly ashore while the younger bucks bounded out. But Grace's heart dropped, because although Charlie looked glad to see his wife, he was also clearly distressed. She hung back, afraid to ask, while Margaret O'Connor and Catherine O'Shea rushed forwards.

'Where are Seán and John and Declan?' snapped Margaret O'Connor, who looked more ready to be angry than upset. Catherine was a gentle little woman shrivelled by years of poverty and childbirth, but Margaret had a hard look; it was she who counted the money in the O'Connor household and made sure that her husband never buried anyone for nothing, not even the families that didn't have it, nor slipped a penniless farmer a free pint, unless half a dozen eggs were placed on the counter in return.

Charlie shuddered and looked ill. 'They're behind, I'm sure. We found the other two lifeboats, capsized, God rest them, and no sign of the other men. The empty boats were found drifting off An Fear Marbh.'

'Oh, the lifeboats…' Grace swallowed, guilty to feel relieved. So it was the English sailors that had her father-in-law so upset; they were clearly lost forever. An Fear Marbh, translated as 'the dead man', was a nickname for Inis Tuaisceart, the most northerly of the six Blasket Islands. An Fear Marbh resembled a man lying on his back, his hands on his chest. Her parents had been returning home from the school on Great Blasket when they drowned all those years ago, and so the islands off the coast, though beautiful, always filled her with dread. 'So you have given up the search?'

Some other boats were arriving now, pulling up alongside the pier. Wet, tired, cold men clambered out and were hugged by smiling wives and ushered away for a breakfast of fresh baked soda bread and boiled eggs and pints of tea. There were five or six boats still unaccounted for, and one or two black silhouettes against the rising sun. Grace strained her eyes to see the only boat without oars and to hear the soft chugging of its engine. The rain was getting heavy again.

Charlie put his strong, sinewy arm around her shivering shoulders and addressed all four of the women around him with a reassuring smile. 'Declan, John and Seán had another canister of petrol, so we decided they could do one more circle of the island, for fear there were any survivors in one of the caves or something.'

The undertaker's wife looked furious. 'Charlie, how could you let my Seán and Catherine's John risk their lives like that? Sure everyone knows the waters around those islands are treacherous even on a calm day, and the sea is still high after the storm. If anything happens to our husbands, while you were safely looking after yourself in Oliver Daly's boat, I'll be holding someone responsible.'

Charlie looked astonished. 'Mrs O'Connor, isn't my son out there as well? 'Twas the men's own decision.'

'To go in a boat with an engine that could go on fire any moment?' sobbed Catherine O'Shea, clinging to Margaret.

'Mrs O'Shea, please don't worry yourself about that. Declan knows exactly what he's at, and he wouldn't take such a risk with anyone's life. I wouldn't allow him to risk his own either, he's my only son –'

'That's not true, Charlie,' snapped Margaret O'Connor. 'You have another baby on the way now. And as for Declan, he can afford to be reckless because he has no children of his own to care for, and probably never will.'

'Mrs O'Connor!' Grace felt sick with shock. Dymphna grabbed her hand and pressed it.

'Well, I'm sorry, but it's true.' Though the undertaker's wife didn't look or sound sorry at all. 'Everyone knows you will never have any children, Grace. Didn't the canon say it was impossible with the polio? But Catherine here has fourteen mouths to feed, and I have six, all boys. And a young man like Declan, brought up in a reformatory, he shouldn't have been fiddling with things he knows nothing about. No good will come of him taking a notion that the way the men rowed boats for as long as anyone can remember wasn't good enough for him. Sure he's probably as careless with his own life as your own husband was, Dymphna, when he walked out into the sea.'

Poor gentle Catherine gasped, scared and ashamed, as Dymphna stood stoically. 'Margaret, you shouldn't say such things.'

Charlie was only half listening, his gaze trained on the horizon.

Grace tried to tell herself it was only fear that made Margaret O'Connor speak so cruelly. She longed to shout back at her how wrong she was, that at that very moment a tiny baby was growing in her and as soon as her husband got home from the sea, she would tell him, even if it was too soon. For years she'd dreaded that she would grow up to be a spinster with no family of her own in a cold and lonely house – that's what her sister, Agnes, had always told her would happen – but it was no longer true. She was a wife, a much loved wife, and this baby in her womb was going to be the first of many.

But before she could open her mouth, a deafening roll of thunder crashed across the sea from the direction of the islands, and the next moment, a terrible scream went up among the women further down the pier as a pillar of fire rose from the horizon towards the sky.

'Oh, good God.' Charlie spun around and limped stiffly back down the slip towards the naomhóg, where young Ambrose Cotter was already pushing Oliver's boat to the water's edge, along with the Daly boys. 'Ambrose, get away and let me in there.'

'Charlie, for the love of God, would you have a bit of sense! You don't know what you're going to find, and besides, you're exhausted and will only slow Liam and Dathai down. We need to get out there before the strong currents wash everything away as far as America.' Ambrose was short and stocky and, like most men around Knocknashee, both a fisherman and a farmer.

'I'm as fit as you are, and it might be my son out there!' roared Charlie. 'Let me in!'

'It might be nothing to do with them at all.' Dymphna tried to soothe him. 'If the English ship was carrying explosives, it might have been –'

'Let the strong young men go, Charlie McKenna!' screeched Margaret O'Connor, beating her fist on Charlie's back as Catherine clung to the undertaker's wife with terror in her eyes. 'Encouraging that delinquent son of yours in his prideful ideas of motors and the like, and now look what's happened?'

'Please don't say that, Margaret,' sobbed Catherine O'Shea. 'We don't know what –'

'Don't go without me, Liam, Dathai!' Charlie shrugged off the bitter woman and tried to grab the rope, but Oliver Daly approached then, placing his hand on Charlie's shoulder and leading him back up the pier away from the water.

'Ambrose is right, Charlie. Leave them to it. This is for the garsúns to do. 'Twill be some very hard rowing now the tide has turned, and with this southwesterly blowing, they'll have their work cut out. My son's boys and young Cotter are fine, strong men. They have it in them, and you'll only be in the way.' He led Charlie back. 'And as Dymphna says, it could be anything. It doesn't mean anyone is hurt. But let the lads get out there as fast as they can to put everyone's mind at rest. The swell is strong out there, Charlie. I'm sure the other men not back yet are grand, probably sheltering in one of the coves on the islands. Be patient, there's a good man. We'll just have to pray they'll be safe.'

Dymphna joined Oliver and her husband then. Grace couldn't hear what Dymphna said to Charlie, but she could guess. After a few minutes, the postman's shoulders slumped in defeat. Dymphna placed her basket of sandwiches in the hull of Oliver Daly's naomhóg, then took the other basket from Grace's numb hand and added that to the supplies.

Several other men from the gathered crowd ran forward to push the boat out on the water, then stood in silence as the strong young fishermen rowed out into the frothing, foaming surf. The increasing rain meant there was very poor visibility, so within a few short minutes, they were swallowed up in the fog and the spray.

'Come on, Charlie, let's go home and wait.' Dymphna took one of her husband's arms and Grace the other, and together they walked him away from the treacherous sea. 'I'm sure Ambrose and the lads will find out what's happened, but Declan and all of the others will be safe. They'll be sheltering in a cove somewhere.'

'I pray so.' Charlie's voice sounded mechanical. Grace squeezed his arm, unable to say anything at all, her heart full of unnamed fears. What on earth was that explosion? Of course it wasn't the outboard motor – Declan had explained to her why Margaret O'Connor was completely wrong about the chance of that blowing up. But then what was it? Surely the Germans hadn't fired a torpedo at a little rowboat?

Nancy O'Flaherty was at the school gate. 'I hope I'm doing the right thing, but I'll be sending back home any child who comes, Grace. Most people will know not to come anyway, but some of the ones from further out won't have heard yet. But you can't be in the classroom today. There are five boats not back yet, and everyone is too worried to concentrate on anything else. And Charlie, we won't bother with the post at all today. The whole village will understand.'

Nancy didn't need to explain why things had changed, why it was no longer necessary to deliver the post and why not even the canon would expect the school to be opened. Everyone was fearful that before the day was out, there would be more new widows in the town.

In Charlie's house Tilly had Kate and Paudie up and dressed, each finishing a bowl of porridge. Without asking she put out three more bowls and served them out, brown sugar and the top of the milk on each. 'Let the children see you eating,' she whispered as Grace pushed the bowl away.

It was strange, but once she took a mouthful of the warm, soothing, sweet porridge, Grace found she was hungry after all. And of course what Dymphna had said was true. The explosion was probably nothing to do with any of the naomhógs. It was all the talk about outboard motors and Margaret O'Connor's foolish hysteria that had got under her skin… Obviously it wasn't true. God wouldn't let that happen to her, to have the sea take her parents and then to take Declan. It wasn't possible. That would be too cruel.

TO PREORDER this next instalment - click here. Sincerely, Grace.

I promise I'm working hard to get it to you as soon as possible.

In the meantime, if you would like to join my readers club please pop over to www.jeangrainger.com and sign up. It's free and always will be and I'll give you a full novel to download as a welcome gift.

ABOUT THE AUTHOR

Jean Grainger is a USA Today bestselling Irish author. She writes historical and contemporary Irish fiction and her work has very flatteringly been compared to the late great Maeve Binchy.

She lives in a stone cottage in Cork with her lovely husband Diarmuid and the youngest two of her four children. The older two come home for a break when adulting gets too exhausting. There are a variety of animals there too, all led by two cute but clueless microdogs called Scrappy and Scoobi.

ALSO BY JEAN GRAINGER

The Tour Series

The Tour
Safe at the Edge of the World
The Story of Grenville King
The Homecoming of Bubbles O'Leary
Finding Billie Romano
Kayla's Trick

The Carmel Sheehan Story

Letters of Freedom
The Future's Not Ours To See
What Will Be

The Robinswood Story

What Once Was True
Return To Robinswood
Trials and Tribulations

The Star and the Shamrock Series

The Star and the Shamrock
The Emerald Horizon
The Hard Way Home
The World Starts Anew

The Queenstown Series

Last Port of Call

The West's Awake

The Harp and the Rose

Roaring Liberty

Standalone Books

So Much Owed

Shadow of a Century

Under Heaven's Shining Stars

Catriona's War

Sisters of the Southern Cross

The Kilteegan Bridge Series

The Trouble with Secrets

What Divides Us

More Harm Than Good

When Irish Eyes Are Lying

A Silent Understanding

The Mags Munroe Story

The Existential Worries of Mags Munroe

Growing Wild in the Shade

Each to their Own

Closer Than You Think

Chance your Arm

The Aisling Series

For All The World

A Beautiful Ferocity

Rivers of Wrath

The Gem of Ireland's Crown

The Knocknashee Series

Lilac Ink

Yesterday's Paper

History's Pages

Printed in Great Britain
by Amazon